MARY'S LAMENT

JOSEPH C. NYCE

WESTBOW
P R E S S®
A DIVISION OF THOMAS NELSON
& ZONDERVAN

Scripture quotations taken from the New English Bible, copyright © Cambridge
University Press and Oxford University Press 1961, 1970. All rights reserved.

Interior Image Credit: Joseph C. Nyce

WestBow Press books may be ordered through booksellers or by contacting:

WestBow Press
A Division of Thomas Nelson & Zondervan
1663 Liberty Drive
Bloomington, IN 47403
www.westbowpress.com
1 (866) 928-1240

Because of the dynamic nature of the Internet, any web addresses or
links contained in this book may have changed since publication and
may no longer be valid. The views expressed in this work are solely those
of the author and do not necessarily reflect the views of the publisher,
and the publisher hereby disclaims any responsibility for them.

Any people depicted in stock imagery provided by Getty Images are
models, and such images are being used for illustrative purposes only.
Certain stock imagery © Getty Images.

ISBN: 978-1-9736-2699-2 (sc)
ISBN: 978-1-9736-2698-5 (hc)
ISBN: 978-1-9736-2700-5 (e)

Library of Congress Control Number: 2018905077

Print information available on the last page.

WestBow Press rev. date: 07/12/2018

CONTENTS

Dedicated to:

My wife Kathryn
Son David
Daughter Shari
For willingly disrupting their lives for me to go to seminary
And to
Doris and Leroy Alderfer
For listening hours to me read a rough draft
of this novel without complaining.

FOREWORD

Mother in Israel
By John L. Ruith

You have known much, Mother in Israel:
You have come far, borne much, hoped long.
You have waited till you have seen the salvation of our God.
You have been planted in the house of the Lord,
Have flourished in the courts of our God –
You shall bring forth fruit in old age.
What you have seen stands on your face;
Your voice brings to us thoughts of God's works of old.
Before we breathed, you had tasted his grace.
Now, Mother in Israel, as you move slowly in our company
Your words are precious in our fellowship.
For you can look far back into the valleys of our days,
What beauty you have seen, what laughter you have heard!
What tears, what heavy suffering, what delight!
What weddings and weepings!
What meetings, what partings!
What songs, what poems, what stories you have heard!
What absent faces you can call to mind!
What letters you have sent, what prayers you have sown!
What changes you have suffered! or rejoiced in!
What leanness, what abundance!

What slogans and campaigns!
What wars and rumors of wars!
What waiting, what working!
What bitterness of soul, what fullness of spirit!
What resignation, what consecration!
What quarrels, what reconciliations!
What landscapes of remembrance!
How much those eyes have seen, Mother in Israel!
Your voice is precious in our fellowship.

Readers appreciating "Mary's Lament" for its astonishingly re-imagined plot and cast of historic characters will be powerfully drawn into their surprising conversation. The narrative method of pursuing truth, as old as Plato's dialogues, is just as urgent in this story, and addresses themes – Hebrew, Roman and Christian, sacred and secular – that are just as foundational. Every page invites serious reflection. Decades after his crucifixion, his aging mother shares with her children and a range of characters from soldiers to officials to a Christian missionary a profoundly disturbing, yet ecstatically re-orienting take on life's mysteries. Author Nyce wrestles with the conundrum of how religion, whether Hebrew or Christian, has seemed to promote rather than heal humanity's existential violence. We listen to extended, pungent conversations that challenge and comfort even those who will be shocked by the sensation of heresy. It is in humility and the rhythms of the heart (the language of Creation rather than ideation, Jesus rather than Paul) that faith finds hope and recognizes Jesus' truth. Mary's poignant, counter-intuitive lament gives all this color, body and personality that will glow long in the thoughts of a serious reader.

John L. Ruth

Introduction

Earliest records of human existence reveal an ongoing endeavor on the part of mankind to understand the cause and meaning of living. Eventually, this activity came to be known as religion. While the articulations of these conjectures are extremely varied, they all rely on a common premise: the beliefs undergirding all explanations are made on faith, faith in statements about something beyond our empirical knowing. Indeed, religions often use the words *faith* and *belief* interchangeably.

A common trend, particularly with monotheistic religions, is that passionate religious practice often translates beliefs into truths, converting into dogma an activity that started out as conjecture. When this occurs, our faith, necessitated by the nagging realization that we can never really know God, gets transformed into definitive statements about God, and God's purpose for our living. Religion becomes the mouthpiece for God, and an ageless human activity of natural obeisance—indeed reverence and awe—regresses into battles over beliefs.

It takes little effort, when surveying human history, to realize that many, if not most, of the violent struggles between various groups are religious disputes motivated by religious beliefs. Religion has been no stranger to violence, often being the instigator. I can't be alone in wondering if this is the surest way to realize the meaning of life and pay homage to our Creator. Each continuing beat of my heart cries for a gentler journey in understanding why I am here, and how I should respond to the gift of life.

I grew up in an Anabaptist nonresistant tradition, so it comes naturally for me to question establishment authority and abhor violence. My experience and background, encouraged by New Testament studies and contemporary Jewish and early Christian research, suggests another look at a particular period in the history of the development of religions, to a time when one religion literally emerged from the womb of another. This story, entitled *Mary's Lament*, is set in 62 CE, a transformative time for the Jewish religion, and the incubation period of Christianity. There are no writings from this period focusing on the nature and progress of this birth. Everything that can be known has to be surmised from writings of the period focusing on other issues, or gleaned from later writings favoring one of many differing responses to this less-than-pacific disunion. Why did a group of people all worshipping the same God, and agreeing that righteousness was the way to honor God, disassociate so dramatically that violence often has described their interactions? These vivid scars, extant even today, call for another look at this birth process. *Mary's Lament* is an attempt to discover a deeper meaning of faith through imagining real persons caught up in this division. Do those who knew Jesus best, his own family members, have something to say to us about the God of love, and the kingdom Jesus proclaimed as already among us? Maybe it is not the differences among us that are our true religious expressions, but, rather what unites us.

Joseph C. Nyce
April 29, 2017

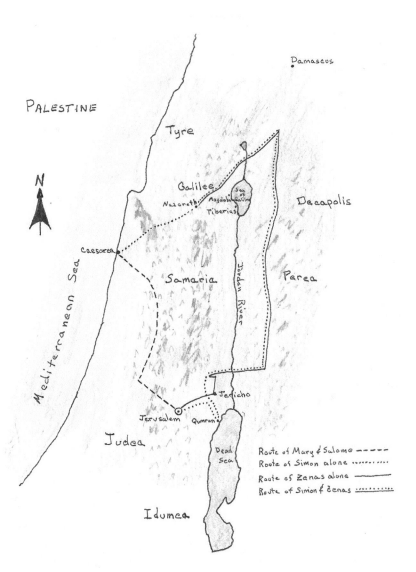

PALESTINE

N

Damascus

Tyre

Galilee

Nazareth Magdala Sea of Galilee
            Tiberias

Decapolis

Caesarea

Samaria

Jordan River

Perea

Mediterranean Sea

Jericho

Jerusalem   Qumran

Judea

Dead Sea

Idumea

Route of Mary & Salome ------
Route of Simon alone ....
Route of Zanas alone ————
Route of Simon & Zenas ············

CHAPTER 1

JAMES IN THE TEMPLE

Jerusalem, the morning of Yom Kippur, 62 CE

"James, please don't! For God's sake, don't do it!"

Mary's agonized pleas sprang from the scorching fire in her lungs, brought there from each breath she drew, and from her belly, a seething pit of vipers. She knew that James's plan to speak to the people from the temple pinnacle was a direct affront to the high priest, Ananus. Neither her pleading nor her tears could stop him.

"Mother, you know full well that I do it *for* the sake of God."

Mary turned away in misery. The fire in her lungs vividly brought back the thirty-year-old memory of the time when she first experienced the same sensation. It came back now, as if it had happened just yesterday. She grimaced, recalling the awful smell of the donkey they had brought to him. It must have slept on a dung heap. Sobbing, she had begged Jesus to stay away from the crowd, the memory of which still frightened her so many years later. She recalled it now. They were wild and uncontrollable and wanted to make him king. Some of them even seemed crazed, screaming wildly and dancing through the narrow streets, knocking over vendors' tables and pushing aside anyone in their way, even children and beggars. Others acted like soldiers on a march to put the temple under siege. Then, too, she had failed to persuade her son. This vivid recollection only heightened her anxiety. Mary never liked crowds, even those who poured adulation on her sons; but particularly that Jerusalem crowd, which had seemed so volatile then—and promised to be so again now. She struggled to suppress feelings of fear and rage.

Every moment since Jesus's crucifixion, she had struggled to fight off feelings of anger. First, the Romans had killed Jesus; then, the Herodians had beheaded Judas Thomas—two of her precious sons. Was James going to be the third one killed? She breathed a prayer for James's safety, and another for the strength to ward off feelings of enmity.

James was going in front of a nervous crowd. This would not be a festive crowd, as it was Yom Kippur, the Day of Atonement, the most solemn of Jewish holy days. Jerusalem was bursting at the seams with pilgrims from all over. Swelled to what seemed nearly twice its size, no one knew the true character of the masses James would address. Mary's anxiety was just as severe as when Jesus rode into this same city those many years ago. Scattered throughout this crowd would be the native inhabitants of this city and from the cities throughout Judea, Idumea, Samaria, and Galilee—all areas seething with resentment toward the Roman occupiers and boiling with dreams of revolution. Jerusalem was anything but a city at peace.

The mother in her wished to deny the truth that her sons were at the center of all the turmoil, just close it off like shutting a door. Sadly, she knew it was the truth, and she could not deny it or shut it away. Jesus had proclaimed a simple message of hope for humanity, gladdening the hearts of the common folk—a message that severely threatened all efforts of power to control human activity. The authorities hoped that his crucifixion would erase his message from the hearts of the people. Along with the remaining members of his family and his closest disciples in Jerusalem, she struggled daily against forces that wished to wipe his memory from the pages of history, or contort his message into new avenues for power. How often must she be visited by this most demonic curse to any mother: the violent death of her child?

James, his brother Simon and sister Salome, stood with their mother, Mary, in the sparsely furnished front room of their small house well down the eastern slope of the city, not far above the Dung Gate. The furniture in the room revealed the touch of a master carpenter. If the four were not so preoccupied with the issue of the moment, one of Mary's children could have pointed out the delicate carvings on the drawers of the head-high chest as those of Joseph their father. The spindles on the two chairs on either side of the chest matched perfectly, indicating extreme care and artistry. The four persons stood as silent as the furniture. They were done talking. James would not be dissuaded from his task.

Mary, swallowing her sobs, looked on her oldest living child, now a man of better than sixty years. Such a lovely man! She adored him, especially for his efforts to keep the truth of Jesus's message alive. James wore nothing on his feet, and a plain white robe covered his body. A white linen scarf partially concealed his uncut hair and wrapped around his neck, covering much of his unshaven beard. Above his broad nose and high cheekbones, his eyes drew your attention. Clear and penetrating, they sparkled, as if holding back a smile. Oh, how she adored him!

James, vividly aware of the pain he inflicted on his mother, moved in front of her and took both of her hands in his. "Forgive me, Mother, for causing you such pain. I can't turn my back on God; and you know all too well that these hands I hold have molded that into the very fabric of my being. My prayer is that God will smile on my actions today. I only wish that you could smile along with God." He then planted a kiss on her forehead.

Mary collapsed onto his chest. The two embraced.

Sobbing, Mary said, "You have been a blessing beyond

imagination. Your dedication to God has never been in question; however, nothing will ever deter a mother's love from seeking safety for her child. I pray that nothing I ever desire is contrary to God's will. Go, with my prayer for your safety. You walk so well in your brother's footsteps. I am proud that you show to all the love that is the presence of the kingdom of God."

Salome and Simon stood in silence, holding hands, tears running down their cheeks. James came over and put his arm around Salome, and Simon went to Mary, kissing her on the cheek. The two men then turned and walked from the house, both stooping to clear the doorway. The two women moved to the doorway. Shielding their eyes from the sun just rising over Mount Olivet, they watched as James and Simon, also barefoot and in a plain white linen robe, began walking up the hill toward the Temple Mount. They saw the men get jostled and swallowed up by the throng of pilgrims moving toward the temple.

Salome turned to Mary. "Look how eager those people are to get to the temple. They had to pass through Poor Town on their way into the city. Do you think the poverty and suffering there even registered with persons so eager to please God with their sacrifice?"

Mary smiled at Salome's observation. "How easy it is to look for the presence of God in all the wrong places!"

Salome continued to look, after the men had disappeared into the crowd. After a long moment, she said, "Watching James and Simon walk up the hill, if you didn't know better, you would think they were twins."

"I know I sound like a proud mother, but those two, more than anyone else, have kept the truth of Jesus's gospel of love before the people."

Mary shuddered as the fire in her lungs blotted out her pride. Would hubris, greed, and lust for power forever work to destroy the gospel of love? The lines on the faces of both women revealed the deep pain inflicted by such forces.

It was a morning like every other. The sun followed its charted pathway through the sky. Birds sang the song of every day. Animals fell into familiar routines. Even the unwelcome Romans woke to another business-as-usual day. Only for the Jew was this a most special day. On this day, a Jew would not be surprised if the sun stood still. Today, on Yom Kippur, every Jewish woman and man must stop dead in their tracks, clear their minds of everything else, and stand before God, exposing all their transgressions and seeking atonement. The gravity of this day weighed heavily on every Jew's heart. Yet it was not merely a day of individual circumspection. The minds and hearts of every Jew went to Jerusalem, where one man, the high priest, symbolizing the holiest of mankind, would approach the presence of God and plead for the people's redemption. The Holy of Holies, a special room in the temple of Jerusalem, symbolized the presence of God among the people of God. So sacred was this space that no man was allowed into it except on this day, and even then, only one man, the high priest, could enter its portal. This singular act of the high priest symbolized for all of Judaism the behavior of every individual Jew on this day: standing before God, pleading for redemption.

However, Judaism was in a period of severe crisis. Even before the popular kingships of David and Solomon, the lines of sacred authority had been an issue for Judaism. Popular or not, the insertion of a king complicated the question of religious authority. Never had this problem been more severe than presently. As usual, the issue was the purity or righteousness of those the Torah established to protect, preserve, and propagate the sacred relationship between God and God's people: the priests. Separated out for this godly task, the priests were not counted with the others to perform ordinary duties. The priests were the bellwether of purity and righteousness, the lining on the conduit that connected God with the people of God.

Occupation by foreign forces compounded the problem.

Authority now resided in many separate and competing hands. Everyday behaviors were impacted by these competing forces. Every Jew felt the pressures to accommodate and compromise sacred traditions. Weak and nefarious agreements at the highest levels of authority eroded trust, and the people searched desperately for beacons of righteousness and signs that the face of God had not turned away from them.

On this morning of Yom Kippur, two priests prepared for this holiest of days. James, known as James the Just, the brother of Jesus, was recognized as the leader of an opposition priesthood that had grown in reaction to corruption and malfeasance among the establishment priests. The followers of Jesus in Jerusalem remembered James as "the disciple Jesus loved." His righteousness, purity, and reputation among the common folk elevated him to his present status. He had already left his humble abode, headed for the Temple Mount.

The other priest was Ananus, the official high priest, credentialed by the Roman emperor through a very substantial gratuity that sealed the deal. Poorly concealed collaboration between Ananus—along with the religious ruling classes— and the Romans created a great chasm between the rulers and the common Jews. Their standards of living rapidly moved in opposite directions. The people saw this as a betrayal of the priestly function, and looked with scorn on the high priest and his prosperous priesthood.

Ananus's preparation contrasted sharply with that of James. He stood in the opulent great hall of his palace in the southwest part of the city, up against its western wall. Surrounded on three sides by stately mansions, this section of the city represented the core of Jerusalem's wealth and power. The great hall in which Ananus stood could hold at least three houses the size of Mary's. Twenty-four priests, all in white robes, waited in the outer courtyard to escort the high priest to the temple. He, too, wore no sandals, but soft silk stockings covered his feet, to protect them from the dirt of Jerusalem's streets. The bottom of his white linen robe was adorned with many tassels, each containing a bell that announced to all his coming. Aides made last-minute touches to his neatly trimmed beard and hair, which showed beneath the mantle and turban on his head. A careful observer would immediately recognize that the style of his headpiece was not distinctly Jewish. A conscientious Jew would surely wonder if this was not a deliberate affront to the faithful, just more evidence that this man's loyalty was to power, not piety. Two young women waved long-handled ostrich fans to keep him as cool as possible. His entire pathway to the temple had been cleared by the Roman soldiers, who now stood at every intersection along the way. Herodian guards lined the streets, standing between the Roman soldiers. Ananus moved into the outer courtyard, and the priests formed a circle around him. From the pinnacle of David's tomb across the street, the high priest's cortege looked like a white cocoon moving out into the street and down toward the temple.

James and Simon arrived at the temple, well before Ananus. By the beginning of the tenth hour, they were situated on a pillar where, looking north, one could see the Women's Court to the right and the Court of the Israelites to the left. On the far left, the steps leading to the porch of the temple were visible. (James knelt on these steps for countless hours, pleading to God for forgiveness for the transgressions of the people. Many told the story that his knees were callused like those of a camel because of the number of hours he spent interceding on the people's behalf.) South of this pillar, the vast southern half of the courtyard of the Temple Mount was already packed with pilgrims. From this prominent position, James intended to address the crowd.

Word spread like a wildfire that James was going to stand before the people. The common people considered him the true high priest. His righteousness and benevolence won their hearts. They trusted his judgment and respected his wisdom. His popularity had not brought pomposity; he always conducted himself with great humility, never seeking publicity or popular acclaim. A public utterance on his part was unusual, and so it raised great curiosity. The fact that he was the leader of the opposition priesthood, and Yom Kippur a special day for the high priest, suggested a very special event. Excitement and eager expectation grew along with the size of the crowd.

Nevertheless, the crowd was apprehensive. The solemnity of the event infused the crowd with a heightened awareness of the gravity of standing before the God above all gods, seeking forgiveness for human failure and pleading for mercy. Nothing makes hypocrisy more evident than to admit one's own. In less than an hour, the high priest, who, in the minds of many in the crowd, represented the height of hypocrisy, would once again enter the Holy of Holies and plead for the people. Was James going to speak truth to power?

James raised his arms, indicating that he wished to speak. Almost immediately, the din of the crowd ceased. Even those in the eastern courtyard, who could not see James, quieted down as the word spread that James was about to speak. Ananus's cortege was still outside the temple.

In a resonant baritone voice that carried well out into the crowd, James began to speak.

"I beg your forgiveness for my intrusion into this holy occasion, and pray that my words be pleasing to God the Most High. More than thirty years ago, my brother Jesus entered this temple and condemned the activities being carried out in the name of God on these premises. He said that God's house of prayer had become a cave of robbers. On this Day of Atonement, I ask you to look around. What do we see? We see this city overflowing with people who have come to this temple to express their faith in a God who forgives transgressions and promises health and happiness to those who live in righteousness. That is the essence of this Day of Atonement. Many of these poor pilgrims have sacrificed much to make this journey of faith.

"What else do we see? A Roman soldier stands on every corner of this city, paid for by a tax taken off the top of every hard-earned coin. What health and happiness have the Romans brought us?

"We see a king who shares a bedroom with his sister, throwing lavish, licentious parties in the basilica, parties whose boisterous depravity showers down on Poor Town, which has grown fourfold in these last thirty years, right up to the very walls of this Temple Mount. Indeed, Poor Town has grown almost as rapidly as the wealth of those who wield religious and political power.

"We see a high priest who is apparently untroubled by the king's debauchery. Instead, he orders his priests to fleece the poor pilgrims, requiring them to buy sacrificial offerings only from an approved agent directly connected to the temple priesthood. The poor are asked to pay extra to the rich. Is this the way of God?

"The activities Jesus condemned years ago have not brought health and happiness, but, rather, suffering and more poverty; and they continue to multiply to this very day. Jesus preached the presence of the kingdom of God, the God above all gods: the God of love. This temple is God's house, where we offer prayers to the God of love, prayers decrying our shortcomings and failures and affirming our desire to live by the laws of God's love. Love does not take from another; love gives. God's love is turning upside down this corrupt world based on power. That is the good news of God's gospel. My brother Jesus began that message and will return again and again to fulfill it as all creation moves to live according to the precepts of God's love."

Many in the crowd erupted in wild applause and shouts of Hosanna. Those who were beyond the sound of James's voice knew that something had greatly excited those inside the temple. Ananus was still not close enough to hear what James had said.

James moved quickly down from the pillar and over to the stairs leading through Nicanor's Gate. The crowd moved aside for him as he progressed. He quickly moved on through the Court of the Priests and knelt down before the steps to the temple porch.

He bent over and placed his forehead on the next step. Repeating this on all three steps, he finally stood at the entrance to the porch. There, he stopped momentarily and then prostrated himself in silent prayer. A great hush fell over the part of the crowd able to see what was happening, a hush that contagiously radiated out among the larger crowd. After a long silence, James rose again to his knees and proceeded forward, stopping just short of the entrance to the Holy of Holies. Again, he prostrated himself for what seemed an eternity. A reverent silence filled the temple. Finally, he raised himself up on his knees.

With his head bowed and arms raised high above his head, he spoke in a loud voice. "I, though unworthy and in utter humility, bring to you the supplications of your children Israel and all who seek to live by your love. Wipe clean our slates of all our sins, and receive our pledge to walk in the ways of your love. Come quickly, Lord, to complete the work of consummation of the kingdom of love."

Still on his knees, James backed out the way he had entered, until he was once again at the foot of the stairs. Here, he stood up but immediately began to faint. Simon, who had followed James to this point, rushed up and gathered James in his arms, keeping him from falling.

The crowd couldn't believe what they had seen and heard. Word describing what happened spread quickly. Extremely disparate reactions emanated from the crowd. Most faces showed shock, and many were dismayed. Some went away rejoicing; others were incensed. But, as realization of what had really happened began to sink in, a good portion of the people began to reveal their jubilation.

Simon, with the help of a few friendly priests, managed to get James through the crowd of pilgrims, who reverently separated, allowing them to get back to Mary's house.

When Mary heard what had happened, she struggled to keep her face from displaying the utter agony that boiled in the pit of her stomach. She immediately set about to make James comfortable. He was no longer faint, but he said nothing at first.

Finally, James began reciting Psalm 121. Before long, all four were reciting psalms of assurance and comfort.

Ananus's cortege entered the Temple Mount through the southernmost gate on the western wall. They had heard the roar of the crowd. As they slowly moved through the packed courtyard, a Herodian guard rushed up and shouted to Ananus, "James just entered the Holy of Holies. He denounced you and the king, and profaned the name of God."

Hearing this, Ananus flew into a rage. "What blasphemy, a disastrous outrage! Arrest that man immediately. He must be stoned for blasphemy. We will hold court right here and pronounce his sentence."

Cooler heads suggested that Ananus should continue on and perform his duties in the Holy of Holies. Ananus flatly refused, claiming that the Holy of Holies had been defiled and he would not set foot in it until it had gone through a serious cleansing procedure. No one had any idea what that was about, as there was no protocol for such a transgression. Ananus finally agreed to go back to his palace, and then convene the Sanhedrin after sundown. Once he was back at his palace, in secret he called the head of his house guard and ordered him to take some men he could trust to keep their actions quiet, and seize James and hold him secretly until further notice.

Less than two hours after James had made his proclamation from the pinnacle of the temple, a group of eight of Ananus's strongmen stormed into Mary's house. They moved quickly to grab James, who stood quiet, offering no resistance. Simon, attempting to move between James and one of the strongmen, was slapped hard across the face. He stopped in his tracks.

Mary jumped up, crying, "This man has done nothing to merit such an affront. What right do you have to take him from his home?"

"Orders from the high priest, lady, if you must know!" said the leader of the group, with a hostile sneer.

Two of the men roughly grabbed James's arms and twisted them around his back. Another pushed James toward the door.

Mary grabbed with both hands for one of the men holding James's arm. She grasped his arm tightly, and as he roughly pulled away, her fingernails cut into his arms. He let out a yell. "You swine! Keep your filthy hands off me!"

The strongmen rushed James out the door, knocking his head against the lintel. They quickly surrounded him and dragged him up toward the temple. Soon he was locked in a secret place deep in the bowels of the temple.

The remaining members of Jesus's family huddled, dejected, in the back room of their house.

Salome finally rose and began storming back and forth across the room. "Men! Men! Men! Animals! Animals! Animals! Why do they think the only way to get through life is to muscle their way through? I hate men!" As these last words passed her lips, her eyes fell on Simon, and on the large red mark on the side of his face where he had been struck. "Forgive me, Simon, not all men. Sometimes my anger makes me say things I do not really believe. It's just that there has to be a better way."

"I know what you mean, my lovely sister. Men have more muscles than brains, and I, too, hate the fact that we so often give our muscles full rein."

Mary remained silent, sitting with her hands spread out on her lap. She stared at her cracked fingernails and the blood and skin beneath them. She mused, "He was so rough with James, hitting and pushing him even though James made no effort to resist arrest. I was just trying to stop him from really hurting James." Regretfully, she realized that violence has roots in all of us. She knew she couldn't take much more violence meted out on her loved ones.

A numbing cold swept over her body. She hugged herself,

trying to keep from shivering. She tried to make sense of her thoughts and feelings. Jesus, James, and Simon all opposed violence; yet, in the face of evil, her very soul reacted. Are there not times when love must resist evil? Mary closed her eyes, begging God and Jesus to walk with her through this dark and troubling valley of uncertainty.

As the people of the city reacted to what they saw and heard, anger grew at the affront of this opposition priest defiling the very heart of Judaism. But, just down the street and around the corner, elation blossomed because someone had finally openly addressed the rot infecting the very core of Jewish leadership, eroding God's long-ago promise to Abraham. A sharp division was exposed among the people; within hours, this distinction could be read on the faces of the people. The angry and dour began to collect together, clearly distinct from the joyful, emphasizing yet another dissension within an already-troubled Jerusalem. It was a hornet's nest: a tempestuous buzzing of contending arguments, conflicting factions, and divergent allegiances, all restrained by a ruthless, violent foreign occupier.

Chapter 2

The Hornet's Nest

Sleep refused to come to Mary as she lay awake, flooded with visions of James in chains. She prayed to the God of love: "How long will this evil menace overshadow Jesus's beautiful gospel of love? Everything and everybody fights against it. The transforming power of God's love is right at our fingertips, yet everyone builds walls to protect themselves from it. Please, God, open the eyes of our hearts to see the presence of your kingdom."

Addressing God always brought a warming calm to Mary, now turning her thoughts to the moment that changed her life forever. She said aloud, "Nothing fit, yet everything did. He was right there in front of me. His strong arms embraced me and drew the breath from my lungs, filling my whole being with a blessed peace. His breath moved the hair around my ear, but his words made my whole body tremble. He whispered, 'God is love, Mama; come, follow me.' That very moment all he taught and did became so clear to me. God is love. Love just is; it is not something you do. … What a freeing feeling! Love is out there, waiting for our participation."

Mary could tell that story over and over. The gospel of love—so simple, so unitary, so natural—went to the heart of Torah, making sense of what she had always been taught: that Torah is to love God and one's neighbor. Jesus had taught Mary that Torah was the doorway to love—love as God intended it to be—which must be shared with one's neighbor.

Coming out of her reverie, Mary realized she was standing beside her bed, trembling. She wanted to wake Salome or Simon, just to hold the fruit of her womb. She sat back on the bed to stop the trembling, which she realized was rooted in her anxiety, her anger, at what was happening again to one of her children. Jesus coming to her from the grave had changed forever the way she saw life; but it also changed the way life impacted her, and that had been anything but gentle. More than half of her offspring had visited death before she did: one in a construction accident, one during childbirth, both tragic events; but then, two did so at the hands of authority, something well beyond tragedy.

The turmoil gripping Jerusalem compounded Mary's anxiety. She knew James was in grave danger. He was a central figure in much of the agitation disrupting the city. She would never deny her pride that the common Jews, desperate for a voice decrying the accommodations the establishment priesthood made with the Roman invaders, claimed him as their leader. They saw his righteousness as the true image of the priestly class, which stood in sharp contrast to the behaviors of the establishment priesthood, actions designed solely to increase power and wealth at the expense of the common Jews. She didn't deny for a moment that the religious authorities wanted him gone. It was no secret that the high priest, Ananus, wanted him out of the picture. Mary had no doubt that he would take the first opportunity to be rid of James.

She also greatly feared the attention James received from a group of radicals known as the Zealots. They embraced his message of the presence of the kingdom of God as a call to arms, to violently remove the unfaithful priests and begin the war to throw out the Romans. In spite of his message of love and opposition to violence, the rebels looked to James as their spiritual leader. In the eyes of the authorities, James was a member of the Zealots, just one of the radicals threatening the fragile so-called peace with

Rome. Not a moment went by that Mary did not fear for his safety. Now, with him in the hands of Ananus's strongmen, fear almost overwhelmed her. How long could she continue to fight the forces distorting the gospel of love?

James's bold act on Yom Kippur flew like a banner over the city announcing the seething tumult just below the surface of Jerusalem life. It was unprecedented, but its seeds had been sown in the days directly before.

Just two days before Yom Kippur, the sullen faces of more than sixty men in the great hall of the high priest's palace stood in sharp contrast to the room's opulence. The massive chandelier hanging in the center of the room burned more oil in an hour than was consumed in Poor Town in a week. The large tapestry hanging on the only solid wall of the room was taller than five men standing atop one another and wider than seven arm spans. The weaving was a beautiful work of art that had certainly occupied months of a poor Bedouin family's total attention, yet yielded them only a fraction of the gain the high priest now claimed as its worth. The faces on the head-high Grecian urns that stood at each side of the portal to the indoor garden portrayed a love eons away from the dour men of the Sanhedrin who now shifted uncomfortably in the room. If only some of the beauty in the mosaic floor could make its way up the legs and into the hearts of these men, perhaps the scene would not be so ominous.

The men stood in groups of twos and threes around the edge of the room, whispering in an almost conspiratorial manner. A larger group, known as the insiders, stood in the center of the room. They waited impatiently for the high priest, Ananus ben Ananus, to appear. All stood; no one reclined on the many cushions placed strategically around on the floor. No one was happy for this emergency meeting right in the middle of preparations for the most sacred day of the year.

Suddenly, the high priest strode into the room with a pace unnatural to him. His face exuding anger, he said, "This is going to stop. Not one more priest is going to be lost to this vermin. If we have to travel in pairs, or even teams of three or more, we have to do something to protect our loyal priests." He went on to explain that it now appeared one of his nephews had been a victim of the Sicarii blade. This threat that was just a nuisance yesterday had now become a crisis. (Sicarii, derived from a small Arab-style knife called the *sicae*, was a name that for the past twelve years had aroused great fear, especially among the priesthood. Less than ten years earlier, a Jewish rebel under Menahem had succeeded in killing the high priest, Jonathan, by slitting his throat and then melting into the crowd. Those who violently opposed the establishment priesthood began using this means of murdering priests in the temple area. They and this practice became known as Sicarii.)

Shlomo, usually the one to speak first, said, "Do we have enough priests to travel in pairs or larger groups? We can barely provide the services required now. There was a time when every priest in the temple was under our control; now the opposition priests outnumber us at least two to one. They have already moved in and are performing some of the duties we can no longer handle."

"That's another thing," Ananus said, his anger seeming only to elevate. "We have to find a way to choke off James's influence over the young priests. His phony righteousness recruits more than all our economic incentives."

"That exposes another problem." The speaker, Amos, oversaw the financial books for the high priest. "Our donations are down substantially. We certainly cannot impose another temple tax right on the heels of the last one. Excess donations are falling dramatically. Quite a few who always over-tithed are now giving only the required minimum." He paused and looked specifically at a number of men in the room. "We are experiencing reductions all across the board. I suspect that many are now dividing their giving between us and the opposition priests."

A number of men in the room knew he was referring to them. Most of them were Pharisees, but even a few Sadducees had begun to shift loyalties. King Herod Agrippa II, living with his sister as if they were husband and wife, was more than even some Sadducees could endure. Some of the Pharisees, particularly those who were merchants, had always made sure to give faithfully to both groups of priests. However, the emphasis on righteousness, purity, and Torah observance on the part of the Essenes and Jesus's followers was appealing, and this began to show in a shift in excess contributions to the opposition priests. This amounted to sizable sums from some of the wealthier contributors.

Amos's complaint about the finances opened the floodgate. The meeting quickly degenerated into numerous gripes of the dramatic drop in influence they sensed and the amount of disrespect their priests encountered from persons they met on the street. Others sat silent, not revealing a hint of their inner thoughts.

Ananus soon had enough of this pitiful grumbling. Like a moth to a flame, he went back to James. "I want you to organize a group to watch every move James makes and document every word he utters. We must catch him saying or doing something that will discredit and disgrace him. He is the leader of all the opposition priests. If we can eliminate his influence, the others will wander off in many directions."

Ananus then abruptly ended the meeting and walked out of the hall.

Many closely associated with the high priest felt his growing obsession with James was beginning to influence his judgment, and not for the better.

Outside the walls of the city, deep within the ruins of the old City of David, another meeting was going on simultaneous to the one in the high priest's palace. Here, the setting was completely reversed. In contrast to the deathly stillness of the broken columns and crumbled arches of a once-magnificent city, the faces of the men were animated. Regardless of whether a man was standing, sitting cross-legged, or squatting on his haunches, eagerness and intensity described his demeanor. The man standing in the middle of the group, James, was obviously the leader. His brother Simon stood by his side. This was a gathering of some of the leaders of the opposition priests.

The Zealots were once again pressuring James to be more aggressive. The speaker was a young firebrand from Galilee. "There has to be some movement. How long are we to tolerate the desecration of the temple by the high priest and his cronies? Yom Kippur is upon us. We are supposed to atone for our sins, but in two days that swine will once again step into the Holy of Holies and defecate on our sacred heritage. Jesus will never return as long as such abomination goes on." Malachi's face was very red, and the veins of his neck stood out like earthworms.

Jesse, an older man, stood and put his hand on Malachi's arm. "Anger and name-calling will not bring Jesus back either. We are citizens of the kingdom of God. Our actions must reflect the nature of God."

"These very stones once felt the soles of a great man of God: David, who established a kingdom that demonstrated God's power and might." Malachi was almost shouting. "His blood and the blood of his brave soldiers soaked into this very soil, and can rise once again through our feet into our legs and arms, giving us the power to throw off the barbaric Romans."

"I love your zeal and share your vision, but we are not yet at the point of dispatching the Romans." Jesse looked to James for help.

James looked at Malachi, then Jesse, then to each man one by one. His dark eyes sparkled with blessing, but his lips suggested indisposition. "It takes great patience and humility to wait on the Lord. We know for certain that violence always brings on more violence. Perhaps we should look to Joshua as well as David. Or, do we think Jericho was small enough for God, but the whole Roman Empire ... ?"

"Forgive me, James, but Joshua did not stand around and do nothing." Jesse was cautious in challenging a man he respected as highly as James. "You have such respect among so many of the

Jews in Jerusalem. Isn't there something you could do that would expose the hypocrisy of the high priest and show the people that we are serious about purifying the temple for Jesus's return?"

James looked like he wanted to say something, but reluctance was winning the battle. Finally, with his eyes fixed on a truncated ruptured column hanging like a stalactite above the heads of the men, he spoke. "I have often dreamed that I was standing in the Holy of Holies. Each time I would ask, 'God, are you really here, or is this place just your insurance that we will never fully know who you are?' God never answered me in any of my dreams, but every time I awoke from one of those dreams, my heart burned within my chest, as if I were closer to God in my bed than I could ever be in the Holy of Holies. Now, I believe I realize what is being asked of me. The Lord wants me, a humble example of the vigorous pursuit of righteousness, to stand before the Holy of Holies to demonstrate that we already know all we are going to know about God. We must learn that our connection to God is not through the temple, the priesthood, and on down that hierarchical chain, but through the heart. Love is our connection to God. The temple, the Holy of Holies, the priesthood, and all other monuments to God are only expressions of our humility. The message of my brother Jesus has never been clearer to me. I will stand tomorrow before the Holy of Holies and proclaim the good news Jesus taught and demonstrate our true connection to God."

The men, more silent than the ruins surrounding them in the cave where they clustered, made it appear as if the deformed columns and broken arches were more likely to utter an amen than the men themselves were. Simon couldn't believe what he just heard. Did James realize what he had just said? Ananus wouldn't stand for such an affront. He might even call for James to be stoned. Or would he? Would he risk the ire of Rome and the chaos that would be unleashed? There was no Roman governor at present to approve of his execution of James. The responsibility would be totally on his shoulders. Simon judged Ananus too weak a man to take such a risk. James's suggestion made Simon uncomfortable, yet he could not find the will to speak in opposition to it.

Even though no words were spoken, thoughts ran rampant. Every man in the cave clearly understood the danger James had just committed himself to. Such a defiant act gave Malachi goose bumps. Finally, someone would stand up and speak truth to power. Jesse knew that the people were eager for a sign that would hasten the glorious day of Jesus's return. What could be a more glorious witness?

Finally, James spoke. "Your silence reveals how uncomfortable you are with what I just said. I suggest we go back to our homes and prayerfully prepare for Yom Kippur. We must seek the will of our Father in heaven. God be with you all."

The men left, one by one, in silence. No one spoke or looked at either James or Simon, who were the last to leave the cave. The smoldering heat and fetid squalor of Poor Town shocked the pair as they moved out from the damp coolness of the cave and into the bright sun.

Sensing Simon's discomfort, James suggested, "We have time before sundown. Let's cross over to Mount Olivet and sit in the shade for a time."

"Nothing pleases me more than to spend time with a brother I adore and revere." Simon knew his silence in the meeting puzzled James. Seldom was Simon reluctant to add his opinion to any issue.

Jerusalem overflowed with pilgrims for the upcoming holy day. Many tents and campsites covered the hillside. The two men weaved their way across the upper edge of the Kidron Valley and halfway up the mountain, to a shady spot not far from where Jesus had been arrested many years ago. As they walked, they talked.

James spoke first. "Your silence at the meeting was unusual. I'm sure what I said shocked you, but it's unusual that something silences you."

"I had so many thoughts, I couldn't find a place to start. Besides, what you are planning to do frightens me more than the fires of hell. Ananus will not tolerate such an act of insult, especially on Yom Kippur. Besides, your speech could incite the crowd. There could be riots. It may get ugly."

James stood and walked over to a low-hanging branch to pick a ripe olive. "Do you want one?"

"Yes, thank you. Bring a few."

James picked a number of olives and gave some to Simon. He ate one before responding to Simon's concern. "We have worked together for years, trying to spread the good news of the presence of the kingdom of God. We have witnessed the miracles of the power of love. Yet men of ambition and power have fought us at every turn. Love is a poison to power. We cannot let that deter us. Only righteous humility understands love, and until righteousness reigns, Jesus will not return to fulfill God's kingdom."

"But maybe Jesus is already among us, with God's judgment already happening in ways we are unaware." Simon felt awkward wading into these strange waters.

James pondered what Simon was saying. "The will of God is beyond our comprehension, and the course of history is in God's hands. Yet, if God is not love, all is vanity, and our lives are of no worth. We must live love, and speak against all that resist it."

Simon knew James spoke the truth, but he could not bear the thought of the danger facing James if he spoke before the Holy of Holies. "I fear for your safety. You know Jesus felt the same urges you now feel. We were just a small movement then. Caiaphas was not under nearly as much pressure Ananus is today, and look what happened to Jesus. You are much more valuable to us alive than dead. Shouldn't we just continue what we have been doing rather than throw burning coals into the face of the high priest?"

"Hypocrisy and evil must be named whenever encountered. The good news is being denied and distorted on many fronts. Integrity demands truth, and love is consumed by power when truth and integrity are avoided. I must speak truth, especially on Yom Kippur. One thing I have realized over the years is that what is important is not what God has done in the past or going to do in the future, but what God is doing in the present. Always remember that while seeking love, and you will not be far from truth."

These words of wisdom from his brother smothered Simon's will to dissuade James. He stood up. "We should be getting back. The women will wonder what happened to us."

The two men retraced their steps back across the Kidron, through Poor Town, through the Dung Gate, and up the hill to their house, reminiscing the whole way about their lives bound so closely together for as long as they could remember.

Now, just two days later, the same threat to James's life that Simon had feared stared Mary square in the face. Would this struggle with the demonic forces of power and control never end? Where was the protective hand of God for the righteous? She knew that James's proclamation from the pinnacle of the temple and petition before the portal to the Holy of Holies would inflame the ongoing battle for the hearts of the people, and anger the Romans. She grimaced as she pictured a Roman patrol on every corner, and felt the intimidation of the jingle of Roman armor. Even though James spoke only of love, and made no allusions to revolution or violence, his bold act would surely incite new talk of insurgence. She had no doubt that activity to remove the polluted priests from the temple would increase, and the radicals would escalate their resistance to the Romans. No market stall would escape the debate; no casual exchange would lack the suspicion of loyalty. A new crescendo surely would infuse the buzzing within the hornet's nest.

Mary's agony consumed her. It brought to mind all the history that had funneled her precious family into this horrendous situation. This buzzing was nothing new. A number of wars waged just below the surface of Jerusalem life. The Jews lived under a religious/ political structure. Religious considerations dominated all social, economic, and political activities. God's will for human behavior, expressed through the ancient Torah, infused every decision.

The Jews loathed the Romans. The Romans were invaders,

a brutal race whose violent power exposed their barbarian nature. They arrogantly elevated their murderous and adulteress leaders into gods. Their licentious culture mocked goodness and righteousness, and their hypocritical laws served only the privileged. Nothing they brought to God's Holy Land was of value. The Jews abhorred the Roman presence, which constricted every chest and caused every heart to beat faster. Roman occupation agitated the very air the Jews breathed. The stones of the streets and walkways seemed to cringe at the pressure of Roman sandals. Mary, and every Jew in Jerusalem, groaned along with the walls and streets of Jerusalem at the Roman presence.

To the Romans, the Jews were a strange people trapped within a religion that defied reason. Suffering under oppressive customs that repressed freedom, they lived a life of senseless behaviors; plus, thanks to the Greeks, the Romans had the teachings of philosophy, which offered a way of separating religion into a distinct category, blinding the Romans to the essence of Jewish life.

This category of religion could never fully explain the Jew. Rooted in a history of faith, the Jew lives a constant effort to recognize, worship, and please the Creator of all. A life of righteousness is the goal of the Jew, and every breath, thought, and action is to express that quest. Mary, along with all Jews, carried this special connection with God the Creator in her heart, sealed off from the understanding of the Romans, who effectively denied the existence of God by elevating themselves to be one with God.

Mary continued to ponder. Clearly, the truth of Jesus's life and message had once again brought her to a terrifying position. For the third time, she faced the radical dichotomy of being blessed as the mother of the one proclaiming God's love, yet afflicted by the pain of having that beloved one victimized by power's reaction to that good news. Why was the truth of his message so misunderstood? *Lament* was the only word she could think of to describe her agony.

This embattled mother could not deny or negate her history.

She, along with every other Jew in Palestine, looked back with pride at the successful efforts of the Maccabees to establish a nation free to respond to God's commands. Since that time, the embers of a free Jewish nation smoldered in every Jewish hearth. Almost a hundred years of Romans occupation assured that any act suggesting resistance to the Romans was enough to light a torch for liberty. In the last forty years, a number of fires had been lit, but they were quickly extinguished by the Romans.

The Jewish society consisted of two main parties, the Sadducees and the Pharisees, governed by a weak royal class known as the Herodians. Less definitive groups, such as the Essenes, Zealots, and Ebionites, consistently railed against the accommodations the ruling parties made to the Romans. The presence of the Romans always raised the question, Do we obey the Romans or Torah? The quest for power provided the only meaningful connection between the Jews and the Romans; it was the only link between the Jewish ruling elite and the despised foreigners. A central part of the unrest within the hornet's nest was the constant tension between accommodation to Rome and faithfulness to Torah.

Mary's heart beat along with every Jewish heart to the cadence of God's promise to Abraham that they would be a great kingdom, a light of righteousness to all the nations. Now, along with fighting the allure of Greek secularism, the Jews had to endure an occupying army that mocked the very essence of who they were.

Almost forty years earlier, in the wilderness east of Jerusalem, a man had begun preaching a message that quickened the hearts of many Jews. Mary remembered the excitement caused by this strange wild man who exhorted the people to repent of their unrighteousness and prepare for the arrival of the kingdom of God by being baptized. The people flocked to the banks of the Jordan to hear his message and be baptized. The embers in the Jewish hearths began to glow with messianic expectations. God had not forgotten. Against much pressure to claim him the Messiah, John said he was not the one, but only the man who had been sent to announce the Messiah.

She remembered how she worried when Jesus left to follow and learn from this man who seemed to have no connections to the recognized priesthood. When he returned and began preaching a message not heard from the rabbis, she swallowed many apprehensions. He announced the presence of the kingdom of God and proclaimed love as the true face of God. Love was the way to see God, and the way to interact with each other. As a Jew, she easily recognized this as the essence of Torah. She was not alone; large crowds followed him, not only because of his message but also because he seemed to have the ability to unleash powers to heal many from their afflictions.

Anxiously she followed his climb up the hill of popularity. The size of the crowds increased, not only with the sick and afflicted but also with those oppressed by the heavy hand of Roman occupation. Jesus's rants against the hypocritical Torah-defiling actions of the Herodians, Sadducees, and Pharisees, and their accommodations to the Romans, fanned glowing messianic coals into open flames in the hearths of common Jews. Mary's fears increased as this cauldron moved toward Jerusalem.

Once the popularity of the baptizer John, and Jesus, reached Jerusalem, the revolutionary aspirations they incited in the masses threatened all the ruling bodies, both religious and political. Mary watched in horror as these rulers—the Sanhedrin, the Herodians, and the Romans—combined forces to eliminate the men so popular with the people. John and Jesus's message of the presence of the kingdom of the God of love was simply more than the authorities of organized power could tolerate. John was beheaded by Herod Antipas, and Jesus was crucified by the Roman governor, Pontius Pilate, with the encouragement of the Jewish leaders. For Mary, hell could not have served a more horrible offering. Jesus never uttered a word of violent overthrow, just the peaceful alternative of humility, yet he was eliminated by the cruel hand of organized society. In her grief she questioned, *God, are you not watching? Where is love, or even justice?*

Thankfully, history did not stop with that awful day she saw her son hung on a cross. As soon as Mary heard his voice call her name, she knew that his life and message would live forever. When she felt his embrace, she knew God's will for mankind was captured in the truth he taught. In an instant, her grief turned to joy, and she knew the kingdom of the God of love was truly here.

Mary harbored neither scorn nor contempt for the disbelief of her friends and neighbors. How could they know? Only humility could open the doorway to God, and only love had the key to that doorway. Her pathway was clear. Love must rule, and all selfishness must be swept aside.

Almost simultaneously, Jesus's closest friends began to repeat the claim of the members of Jesus's family, insisting that he rose from the dead, appeared to them, and promised to return shortly to fully institute the kingdom of God. Now, an apocalyptic wind fanned the messianic flames into a bonfire. The God of love, the author of Torah, was about to intervene in the course of history and establish the reign of righteousness. God's promise to Abraham was about to be fulfilled. God would establish the realm of righteousness, and the wicked and evil would be cast aside.

Mary's fear rose again as she saw many radical revolutionary groups latch onto the news of Jesus's return and the fulfillment of God's promise to Abraham. The buzzing in the hornet's nest increased yet again. Roman oppression, a massive burden on the Jews, skimmed the cream, and most of the milk, off life. The sound of a marching soldier was always present. Tax collectors had their hands in every transaction. Precious customs were mocked and ridiculed. One's very life seemed to matter not at all to these intruders; they could cut your throat as easily as look at you. To the common Jew, the longer the Romans remained, the worse life got. Continued Roman domination would only bring longer nights and shortened days, until, one day, the sun would no longer shine.

The messages of John the Baptist and Jesus had brought hope to the masses. The bold assertion of Jesus's followers found fertile ground in this hope. Quite rapidly, the good news of the presence of the kingdom of God and its imminent fulfillment spread among the synagogues, radiating out from Jerusalem in all directions. As in all of life, practical questions began to emerge, affecting how one understood the meaning of this good news, and also how one ought to respond. What was Torah's word for this new situation? Some pooled their resources and formed commune-like fellowships as the best way to prepare for God's final act. Others moved away in isolation, so as to be unencumbered by the diversions of secular culture. Still others felt that working within the local synagogue to establish righteousness among the faithful was the best way to live out the wait. Regardless of the paths chosen, the existing order was on its way out. The hated Romans and their scandalous sympathizers would be destroyed. Furthermore, the priesthood had been compromised by accommodation to the Romans, and a new priesthood was needed.

As days became months and months became years, many diverse predictions about Jesus's return emerged. Mary saw group after group latch onto the promise of a new world and claim her son Jesus as the power behind their cause. Each group sought to legitimize itself by identifying a priesthood to replace the tarnished one. Many sought to associate themselves with Jesus and his family. The arguments and battles for authentication sickened Mary, who saw them as selfish efforts for power, a grave distortion of the gospel of love. Nevertheless, since James was the leader of the Jesus followers, these groups all sought James's approval.

These messianic movements severely eroded the power of the ruling classes. A high-ranking Pharisee in Jerusalem, named Saul, zealously persecuted these radical followers of Jesus as heretics. In the midst of his suppression campaign, he encountered a vision of Jesus that challenged his violent opposition to Jesus's message. This experience radically transformed his life, evidenced by his name change from Saul to Paul. He reacted by passionately proclaiming the good news of Jesus's imminent return and the establishment of the kingdom of God. As a Pharisee, he had rigorously pursued righteousness. His transformation convinced him that such efforts were useless. Righteousness could not be earned; it had to be a gift of grace from God. Paul claimed that God revealed to him that Jesus was God's son sent to redeem humanity from its sinfulness. For Paul, this was the true expression of God's love. Drawing on the Greek division of soul and body, he articulated a spiritual salvation that allied the spirit with life and the body with death.

Many Jews far from Palestine struggled daily with the pressures secular culture placed on those who were Torah observant. Paul's message of justification by faith alone lifted a tremendous burden from the shoulders of those seeking righteousness. Righteousness was not, according to Paul, obtained by observing Torah. Salvation for the soul was a gift from God, a loving sacrifice of his son for our sins. Torah, with its demanding practices, was not a road to salvation. It wasn't long before Paul and many of his followers saw Torah as an icon of the world that was passing away, no longer relevant for the new kingdom of God.

Paul's gospel of Jesus as the Christ drew a distinct line between the followers of Jesus, who followed him, and all Torah-observant Jews who believed that Jesus was the Messiah or had proclaimed the message of messiah. Paul's gospel created a serious and obvious distinction between Christian and Jew.

Mary, her family, and the followers of Jesus in Jerusalem were aware of Paul and the growing movement known as Christians. The radical differences between these two groups became evident during both times Paul visited Jerusalem, where most followers of Jesus were still Torah observant. In fact, just a few years earlier much of the buzzing in the Jerusalem hornet's nest centered precisely on this issue. Paul came to Jerusalem, preaching his gospel of salvation through justification by faith alone. On the steps of the great temple, the implications of his message for Torah reverberated through the temple like a call to arms. Here in Jerusalem, Paul's message of salvation from sin was seen as a message of liberation from Torah, an anathema to those faithful Jews. Severe riots ensued, escalating to the point where the Romans had to intervene for fear of the city going up in flames. Paul's connections with the Herodians, and possibly even the Romans, resulted in him being taken into protective custody and quickly removed to Caesarea, where he was kept under house arrest for nearly two years. However, the distinction between Christian and Jew was now exposed in Jerusalem for all to see, adding greatly to the buzzing chaotic atmosphere.

Mary's recollection of Paul, however, was rooted in her motherhood. Many years earlier, during Paul's first visit to Jerusalem, she remembered that his actions had resulted in an incident where James was severely injured when Paul shoved him and he fell down the temple steps. She always wondered what had motivated Paul.

For the Jews of Jerusalem, however, other crises ranked higher than the distinction between Christian and Jew. One in particular reached right down to the eternal human struggle between the haves and the have-nots. Foreign rule and influence had greatly upset the social balance Torah sought to maintain. All facets of Torah point toward concern for the less fortunate, the year of Jubilee being a perfect example. Laws imposed by the Greek, Syrian, and Roman invaders brought many challenges to Torah practices. Secular laws always protect those who write them. During the period of foreign control, laws and, particularly, taxes forced a great shift of wealth. Where once the countryside was dotted with small independent farmers and artisans, excessive taxation forced many landowners and business people into debt and, eventually, servitude. In 62 CE, Jerusalem, and many towns and cities of Palestine, were full of poor day workers who once were, or whose fathers had been, landowners and businessmen. Wealth gravitated into the hands of the ruling elite, protected by a priesthood that appeared to do whatever was necessary to keep peace with the pagan occupiers. Torah, and its concern for the less fortunate, became more and more malleable in the hands of the leaders.

This societal shift raised its ugly head in every market exchange.

Mary's friend Jethro set up a stand to sell handmade cooking pots twice a week, on a corner just outside the Dung Gate. Mary often stopped to talk with him on her trips to or from Poor Town.

Jethro watched as an obviously wealthy man picked up one of his pots. He thought, *Perhaps I will make a sale today. Our temple tax is overdue, and I don't have money to buy copper for new pots.* He walked up to the man. "Would you care to share a cup of tea?"

"Thank you, but no. I have to be at a meeting in the upper city in a few minutes." The man held out the pot, asking, "Did you make this pot, or do you buy your pots from someone else?"

"I only sell what I make with my own hands. You will not find a better pot in all Jerusalem."

The shopper snapped the back of his middle finger near the top of the rim of the pot, making it ring like a bell. "It appears you do fine work. How much for this pot?"

Jethro stroked his beard, ruminating. He knew what the material cost to make the pot. He knew how much time he had put into its creation. He also knew that this person in front of him would never pay the price he offered, even if he was honest with his costs and markup. He had played this game as long as he could remember. He knew he would always lose, that this man could buy every pot in his stand and not feel the loss, yet he would not buy unless he felt that he had made a bargain. *He is buying out of excess; I am selling out of necessity.* He thought, but then he thought of the overdue taxes. *I must sell this pot.* Knowing there were pots for sale in the other markets of the city, he had to offer a price just a little above what he needed to keep his business growing, for once it started to regress, it could not be stopped. "Sixty shekels; as God is my witness, a fair price."

The man shook his head from side to side. He thought, *That is what he would like to get; what he really needs is probably half that.* "I'll give you thirty-five shekels for your fine work. I can buy one like it for that price at the Sheep Market."

"I can't make another one for that amount. I want to stay in business." Jethro did not want to insult this man, or lose a sale he so desperately needed. "I assure you, if you see a pot like this for thirty-five shekels, it will not ring like that one just did," he said, pointing to the pot in the man's hand.

The man put the pot down and turned to leave.

Jethro moved alongside the man so that he would have to walk around him to leave. "I'll take fifty-one shekels. It certainly is worth more than that."

The man looked surprised. "Forty shekels is all I will pay. I must be going."

Jethro's face showed his great disappointment. With lowered eyes, he said, "The pot will be more useful in your hands than in mine. It will serve you well." He picked it up and handed it to the man.

Coins changed hands and the rich man walked away with the pot under his arm, pleased to have obtained a good bargain, completely oblivious of the damage this commercial exchange inflicted on Jethro's spirit. Failure to understand or to care for the real situation of the other is at the heart of the divide between the rich and poor, a monumental divide manifesting itself in anger and mistrust, underlying most social unrest. The freedom of the buyer blinded him to the bondage of the seller. Healthy commercial intercourse relies on freedom, honesty, and integrity of both parties, with the quest for righteousness the only source for these. Once mistrust invades the exchange, the two parties begin to move in opposite directions. The great divide only widens: the seller quoting prices designed to hedge against bickering instead of reflecting true value, and buyers seeking to discover the extent of the hedge. Only concern for the situation of the other, coupled with honesty and integrity, can bridge this gap.

Mary's family knew well of this social deterioration. She experienced it in the vocation of Joseph, who, as a young man, had started out a skilled furniture maker. She witnessed how honesty and integrity got lost when taken from the hands of the individual and placed at the mercy of the collective. As the Romans moved in and began raping the local economies for their international needs, local commerce took a terrible hit. Alongside the ravaging Romans, King Herod, primarily to impress the Romans, instituted massive building projects that robbed the local economies of funds and manpower. Economics forced Joseph to abandon his business and go with his sons as day laborers to Sepphoris. Alongside other poor Jews, Mary experienced the economic pressures of secularization and the strain it brought to their efforts to live Torah. It was as if someone or something was trying to tear them apart or physically turn them inside out, a brutal affront to their personhood.

Mary recalled the anger that welled up in her at this nameless, faceless force challenging Torah at every turn, mocking her efforts to live righteously. She looked with horror as, time and again, the Jewish political and religious rulers shunned Torah in favor of Roman largesse. It brought tears to her eyes to remember how the worth of the rural life was robbed and taken to the metropolises of wealth and power. Over the course of her life, she witnessed the growth of the great divide between the rich and the poor. It was very clear to her that it paralleled the rise of selfishness and the fall of the quest for righteousness. She knew full well the source of the great anger and resentment in the bellies of the poor and downtrodden. She also saw how self-indulgence blinded the rich and powerful to the conditions of the poor, and, more importantly, how power protected that impairment.

Mary thanked God daily that Jesus's gospel of love offered real hope to the poor. Yet she grieved that so many contorted his message into other avenues for power. She agonized over how the quest for salvation threatened to overshadow his message of the

JOSEPH C. NYCE

presence of the kingdom of God's love and distort its blessing for humanity. Why did it get caught up in so many arguments and battles? Now it threatened to take another of her precious sons. James's name was always prominent in these battles and arguments. His message of the presence of the kingdom of the God of love and the return of Jesus kept the messianic and apocalyptic fires alive. From every perspective, he was at the heart of the chaos.

Every trip to the market placed one squarely in the middle of this buzzing frenzy, which seemed to have as many versions as there were columns on the basilica of the temple. No conversation could avoid for long the impact these messianic and apocalyptic movements had on everyday life. An exchange the day before Yom Kippur, just behind Micah's meat stall in the Upper Market, was no exception.

Micah was surprised to see Samuel, who had not been to his stall for months. "What brings you in from the compound? I haven't seen you in months."

"I'm here recruiting youth for the movement. Time is growing short. There is no question that something big is about to happen."

"You really think that Jesus is just going to sweep back in here and throw out the Romans like a woman shakes out a dust rag?" Nathaniel, was a Pharisee impressed with the teachings of James, because they promised a way of transforming the world through openness and love and resisted the closed circle of violence; but, to him, a Maccabean-like revolt just seemed delusional.

"Have you forgotten our history? How Joshua captured a city without lifting a weapon; and David defeated a whole Philistine army with a sling and a stone?" Samuel did not have much time for those of little faith. "With God, anything is possible. The priest James is as expectant of Jesus's return as I am, and rumor has it that he is going to speak in the temple tomorrow. This could be the beginning of the revolution."

Daniel, a Pharisee who wondered why Nathaniel was taken

34

with this dream of Jesus coming back, poked his finger at Samuel. "You will get us all killed. Rome controls the world, and no little group of hotheads relying on some avenging spirit is going to change that. You will just destroy us along with everything else. Have you already forgotten what it was like under Festus? The quicker we make peace with Rome, the sooner we will be able to worship God the way we have been called to do."

Samuel was not to be subdued. "The people will rise up in great numbers. Real power resides in the people."

Nathaniel shook his head. "Violence through power is not the answer. Rome is proof of that. Nothing they bring leads to goodness, only suffering and death. They live by violence and spread it like seeds of wheat. Daniel is right; Festus has shown us all we need to see of Rome. A concerted effort toward righteousness and holiness among the priesthood and the people will hasten the return of Jesus and the nonviolent establishment of an earthly kingdom exemplary of the love of God: a beacon that will draw all nations unto its righteousness and goodness."

"You can't fight tyrannical power with kisses on the cheek. Violence only knows violence, and it must be crushed." Samuel had enough of this conversation. He walked away, regretting the time he'd wasted when he should have been recruiting.

Samuel was a member of the Zealots, and this radical group believed the current messianic movement was the initial phase of the revolution to restore a Jewish kingdom. He gave these weak men a look of disgust, turned abruptly, and walked away. He headed for Poor Town, where he knew he would find a more favorable response. He walked down the Kidron Valley to the bottom of Poor Town, where he found Jesse and Malachi in a makeshift hovel. "It's good to find some kindred spirits. I just left a group of spineless old codgers who think the revolution is going to happen through love and kisses. I couldn't get away from there fast enough."

"Whoa, there, Samuel, I'm an old codger. You're not pushing

us old guys out of the movement, are you?" Jesse saw that Samuel was agitated and wanted to calm him down.

"You know better than that." Samuel respected Jesse. "It's just that there is so much foot-dragging, and such a fear of the Romans that it feels like the movement is bogging down. Is the rumor I heard real? Is James going to speak in the temple tomorrow?"

"Yes, finally!" Malachi's excitement was noticeable. "Someone is finally going to expose those hypocrites."

"Do you think he is actually going to confront the Romans?" Samuel surely hated the Romans.

"I hope so." Malachi looked to Jesse for confirmation.

Jesse paused before speaking. "James has never shied away from condemning the actions of the Romans. However, he has always focused primarily on the behaviors of us Jews. My guess is, since it is Yom Kippur, he will seek God's forgiveness for the people's transgressions and ask God to look favorably on the plight of the poor and oppressed. He will, as always, proclaim the Day of the Lord, and the presence of the kingdom of the God of love."

"Yes, but will he get more specific? The people are tiring of expectations. It's going to take more than promises to move us ahead. Will he say anything about the Romans, the disgraceful king's offenses, or the profanity of the priesthood? That has to stop before Jesus will return." Samuel yearned for an action, an event that would spark the revolution he knew was coming.

"James did not tell us what he would say tomorrow. He only said he would stand before the Holy of Holies, and proclaim the good news Jesus taught and demonstrate our true connection to God. He said something about the temple, the Holy of Holies, and the priesthood being only monuments to God and expressions of our humility. It was not quite clear what he meant by that. We were all so shocked that he said he would stand before the Holy of Holies on Yom Kippur that no one knew what to say. The meeting broke up in silence."

"Blessed be King David! Something big is going to happen

tomorrow! I have to spread the news." Samuel hurried away, his recruiting task forgotten in the excitement of his expectations.

He hurried back into the city, up to the northern section, beyond the fortress, to a small house near the Sheep Market, where a number of the opposition priests lived. The house was quiet, and in the back room he found his three closest friends, in a gloomy mood. "Haven't you heard the news? James is going to get in the face of the high priest tomorrow. Ananus," he spat out the name like it was poison, "that soiled rag, is going to explode in rage."

"What?" the three men said at once.

Johan asked, "What are you talking about?"

"You haven't heard? James is going to speak in front of the Holy of Holies tomorrow, on Yom Kippur. Just picture this: that putrid example of religious contamination being confronted by James, the most righteous man in all Israel, on the most sacred day of the year. Tomorrow, the final battle begins."

Johan spoke for the other two. "Where did you get your information? We heard rumors that something was going to happen, but nothing like that."

"I just came from talking to Jesse and Malachi. They heard it from James himself."

"Well, that's pretty much from the horse's mouth. Did they say what James is going to do or say?"

"They didn't know much, except that James is going to proclaim Jesus's good news in front of the Holy of Holies, and claim that the temple, the Holy of Holies, and the priesthood are only monuments to God and expressions of our humility."

"Wow! Throwing it right in the face of the high priest. You are right; the fight comes out in the open tomorrow. We'd better get ready."

These four men were members of a secret group within the Zealot movement not opposed to violence. Many referred to them as the Sicarii.

James always vigorously opposed such violence; however, some of the messianic Zealot groups did not. So, any group inclined toward violence was potentially the Sicarii. Samuel and his three companions were part of a group committed to the purification of the priesthood and the temple. Believing the Messiah would not return until this purification was accomplished, they understood their task as a necessary step in bringing about the complete establishment of the kingdom of God.

All of these messianic groups, from the violent Zealots to the pacific Ebionites, looked to James as the authentic high priest. He was the most respected and influential priest in Jerusalem. His righteousness and wisdom were broadly recognized, and his service to the poor and downtrodden earned him the love of the masses. His gentleness and kindness reflected his abhorrence of violence, and all this was widely recognized. Indeed, few denied it was the influence of James on the most-violent Zealots that helped keep their dreaded Sicarii activity in check.

Even with James's positive influence, the buzzing for open insurgence in the hornet's nest continued to grow. It had been germinating over thirty years. None of the many versions of messiah had a coherent theology or an organized structure. Within each was a myriad of interpretations of scripture, prophecy, and beliefs, all trying to explain something more dependent on the unreality of the future than on the reality of the present, or the traditions of the past. These beliefs grew out of efforts to actualize faith into the daily process of living. Over time, an opposition priesthood, authenticating these actions and integrating them into the quest for righteousness, developed. In actuality, many subcultures emerged, all believing their adjustments to the norm essential for the future to become reality. A war of ideas and beliefs fueled the unrest in the nest. Naturally these beliefs created divisions. Boundary lines formed along the differences and became the basis of disputes, which challenged Torah, the arbiter of these disputes for more than a thousand years. Interpretations of Torah grew with each new question, some even claiming it no longer necessary. The future held the answers, but there were many conflicting roads to that future. Perhaps only fear kept the nest together; fear that the Romans would react to unrest and the threat of anarchy in the only way they knew: brutal devastation.

So the hornet's nest buzzed, with apparently nothing to subdue the chaotic unrest. Lawlessness began to rule the streets of Jerusalem, particularly the temple area, threatening order. The Jewish rulers' ability to control the situation eroded, and chaos increased daily. Time was running short. If they could not calm down the situation quickly, the Romans were sure to move in with force.

Now, James, as his older brother had done thirty years before, boldly and conspicuously condemned the apostasy of the religious leaders and called the people to remember the Lordship of God and live according to the precepts of the kingdom of God. No one knew if the nest could contain such a challenge.

All this past and present history Mary wore like clothing on her back: some of it so old and familiar, she hardly realized it was there; some so new and ill-fitting, she wasn't sure how to wear it. No amount of wishing or prayer could free her of its implications and fate. She, along with her abused family, was caught squarely in the center of the hornet's nest. They struggled to preserve the essence of Jesus's message: the glorious truth of the presence of the kingdom of the God of love. They warded off forces from all sides who wished to ride Jesus's popularity to positions of power. They argued daily with those who wanted to use Jesus as the banner for violent revolt against Rome. They stood as a bulwark against modernizing movements that claimed to know God and God's distinct plan for humankind. As an old woman, she desperately yearned for the peace the kingdom of the God of love promised. Could love resist the thirst for power and the lure of all forms of selfishness?

Chapter 3

Killing James

The grief-contorted faces of Mary, Simon, and Salome reflected the tomb-like atmosphere of the room. Yom Kippur, a sacred day that should have brought a sense of peace and hope, had instead left this family fully dejected. Their broken hearts asked, *Where is this kingdom of God?* Anguish wanted to challenge the very idea of love and encourage the cursing of all who wielded power over other men. The basest human instincts sought control of their emotions. Only their concern for each other kept them from falling over the precipice of hatred. Love, even in the ugliest conditions, can weave its way through forests of nightmarish agony.

Throughout the city, the solemnity of Yom Kippur suppressed the reaction to James's defiant act. Its gravity, however, was sure to soon have a public face. By the time James was in chains, many knew what he had said and done. Deep-rooted reactions traversed the spectrum of opinion. James exposed the nerves of the city. His words and deeds went straight to the heart, regardless of each person's own beliefs. By nightfall, reactions began to take real form.

Shortly after sundown, the Sanhedrin was once again gathered in the great hall of the high priest's palace. No grand entry this time, as Ananus was the first one there, waiting with angry impatience for the others to arrive. Standing by the entrance to the great hall, he looked each man in the face, trying to discern his inclination while making evident his own. He anticipated a battle. The past months had revealed a growing admiration on the part of some of these religious leaders for the integrity and righteousness of James, whose popularity was not limited solely to the lower classes. But James had made a colossal mistake; no one could ignore it or defend it. In Ananus's mind, James had sealed his doom.

Ananus began speaking before all the men had arrived. "An evil, blasphemous act was performed today that will certainly bring the wrath of God down upon us if not addressed immediately. James, the rebel priest, transgressed into the Holy of Holies and uttered the name of God. According to our law, this act is punishable by death. We must move immediately. I have the man in secret custody, and we must carry out his execution as quickly as possible. His brashness will most certainly incite the radicals, so we should proceed with caution and in secrecy. Our task here tonight is to try the victim, find him guilty, and pronounce the sentence. Judging from the exposure of the crime, this should be routine. Obadiah, you shall act as presiding judge and conduct the trial."

Obadiah slowly, almost reluctantly, moved to the center of the room and asked that someone state the charges.

"I have already done that." Ananus's impatience was clear to all. "Must I relay them again, or can they stand as previously stated?"

Joseph, whose loyalty had been questioned recently, spoke. "It would be ideal if we could have an eyewitness present the charges. I understand you did not witness the event. Is there anyone here who witnessed the transgression?"

Ebenezer, moving forward from against the wall under the massive tapestry, spoke slowly and carefully. "After addressing the people, James, the opposition priest, moved on his knees up the stairs to the portal of the Holy of Holies and cried out in a voice loud enough for many to hear. He first expressed his unworthiness and humility, and then offered supplications for all the people. He asked that the slates of the people be wiped clean of all sins

41

and that their pledge to walk in the way of God's love be received. He then appealed to the Lord to return quickly and complete the establishment of the kingdom of love. That is the extent of the words he uttered."

"I was told he uttered the name of God in the Holy of Holies." Ananus was livid. "Was somebody else there to confirm that? Ebenezer, you said he was at the portal of the Holy of Holies and said 'Lord'; was he inside the Holy of Holies, and did he utter the name of God?"

"He just said 'Lord' and was at the portal of the Holy of Holies. Was anybody else there to hear what James said?"

No one else spoke up. The men began whispering in the room. Obadiah asked for silence. "If what Ebenezer just related to us is all that James said and did, it appears we do not have enough to continue with this trial."

Ananus interrupted, saying, "We must find someone who will confirm what I was told. We cannot go on just one man's word. Perhaps Ebenezer did not hear and see everything. This trial is recessed until the eleventh hour tomorrow. We will reconvene then."

Ananus turned and stomped out of the room. He went immediately to his private quarters and called for the captain of the men who were holding James.

When the captain arrived, Ananus gave him clear instructions. "Summon all the priests to immediately start spreading the word that James not only desecrated the Holy of Holies but also blasphemed God and, therefore, must be stoned to death. I want this profane crime broadcast all over the city by tomorrow morning. I want the markets to be full of people brisling with anger at this profanation. God will not tolerate such blasphemy and will bring vengeance upon us if it goes unpunished. Report back to me at the eighth hour tomorrow morning."

Soon, wherever there was activity anywhere in the city, well into the late hours of the night, people were talking about this act of desecration.

The next morning, the markets were abuzz with the news of James's act. Daniel and Nathaniel were back at Micah's stall in the Upper Market.

Daniel was wringing his hands. "What was he thinking? Blasphemy is bad enough, but to bring the city to the brink of war is unconscionable. He condemned everyone, even the Romans. Was this his death wish?"

Nathaniel put his hand on Daniel's arm. "Just calm down! This was not a political speech but a religious one. Remember, yesterday was Yom Kippur. James spoke directly to the polluted religious authorities."

"You got that right. You can tell by the sour faces on all the priests this morning." The location of Micah's stall meant that much of his clientele were the establishment priests and those associated with the religious leaders. Micah could read these people like a book. He knew what they wanted and how to satisfy their needs. "I have never seen such a reaction. I'm not quite sure how to read it. You can see the anger on their faces; yet their posture portrays children who have just been slapped. The priests I've seen this morning look pathetic. Well, not all of them. A few look like soldiers ready for battle. I believe we are in for quite a row."

"That's what I'm afraid of." Daniel was shaking his head. "We keep testing the Romans with our squabbles."

"You have to remember it was James who spoke, not some firebrand revolutionary," said Nathaniel. "He is the last person to advocate violence. He only preaches love."

"The Sicarii also claim to be followers of James. Can his love control them?"

A bit of uncertainty crossed Nathaniel's eyes. Fear was not far from anyone at this time. Indeed, fear was like a cockroach, appearing whenever the light of certainty dimmed.

The atmosphere was different at the Sheep Market, at least on the surface. Here, many of the priests walked with a purpose, as if they had just received a call to arms.

Samuel felt invigorated. "Someone has finally spoken openly against the corruption in high places. James gave the masses a glimpse of the presence of the kingdom of God, a stark contrast to the dung of the religious establishment." Samuel was speaking to his friends, but broadcasting it as if preaching to the crowds.

Many in the crowded market shied away from this boisterous young man. A mother grabbed her young boy and hurried him away, not wanting her son to be influenced by him. She bristled at the constant agitation among the people and wondered where peace could be found.

Peter asked, "What do you think is going to happen next? Is James in danger? Do you think we should set up some protection for him?"

Samuel looked surprised. "I hadn't thought about that. Perhaps we should go back to the house and come up with a plan. I know he would not approve, but someone has to protect him. He has been a friend to all of us."

As they were leaving the market they stopped to listen to a rather loud exchange. A woman, with a baby at her breast and holding two young children with one hand to prevent them from running into the crowds of the market, was talking. "What kind of a priest is it that doesn't even respect sacred traditions? There's a good reason why death is the punishment for such a transgression."

An older woman standing by answered, "So, you're comfortable with someone as soiled as the high priest punishing someone as righteous as James?"

The mother with the children replied, "That's the law. Besides, the whole Sanhedrin will convict him. That's a collection of the holiest men in Judaism."

An old man sitting against the wall of a stall said, "God help us if that group of money-grubbers are the holiest we have. Doesn't anyone want to stop and consider what James said? We aren't on the road to righteousness; we need a radical reformation. What's wrong with living within the kingdom of God? What we have certainly isn't working."

The young mother's face showed fear. "Have you forgotten about the Romans? Their blood boils when they hear the phrase 'the kingdom of God.'"

Samuel and his friends moved on, chuckling at the futility of verbal arguments.

In Poor Town, there was little argument and much jubilation.

Ada, a widow before reaching her thirtieth year, said with a smile rarely seen on her face, "James has shone a light on our horrible conditions and told the whole world that the privileges of the kingdom of God are for the poor too."

Noah, a foot missing and one shrunken arm strapped to his chest, agreed. "He has poured out his life for our needs, and he has lived the truth of God's love."

Hope rose out of the squalor of Poor Town on this morning, warming many dejected hearts.

The slaves and servants of the high priest noticed that Ananus did not sleep that night. Numerous visitors came at different times throughout the night, usually singly or in groups of two or three, all men completely loyal to the high priest. A few of the visitors could only be described as unsavory. Watching this activity, no one would deny that the high priest was putting plans in place to control the proceedings in the morning. Ananus was taking no chances that James would escape condemnation and death.

The fact that the new governor had not yet arrived emboldened Ananus's actions. The only authority above him was King Herod Agrippa II. The king shared the high priest's hatred of James, who had outwardly condemned the king for living with his sister. These two men salivated over the idea of getting rid of James.

Ananus's sinister plans began to emerge through the instructions he gave to the head of his house guard, whom he summoned soon after sunrise. "I want James delivered to the great hall no later than the eleventh hour. Bring him out the

Huldah Gate, and then proceed up through the upper city, past the market, and on to the great hall." (If truth be told, he was uncertain if he would be able to wrest a guilty verdict from a group he had diminishing influence over. Perhaps an angry mob would do the job the soft Sanhedrin had no stomach for.)

The city, still crowded with pilgrims, exuded an air of urgency. Small clusters of highly animated people gathered and whispered among themselves. Something sinister seemed to be hiding among some of the people. An especially large and boisterous crowd formed on the massive steps at the south end of the Temple Mount. Near the Huldah Gate, a great number of priests were agitating the crowd. One priest remarked, "The blasphemer is not even a Levite. He's from the tribe of Judah. What a mockery!" Others joined in condemning James, whipping the crowd into a frenzy.

Standing by the edge of the crowd was a large man carrying a laundryman's club. He had stopped on his way to his shop to see what the commotion was about. As he listened to the rants of the priests, his face showed growing agitation. As he moved toward the front of the crowd, his tense jaw and fiery eyes displayed rage.

Shortly after the tenth hour, the Huldah Gate opened, and eight temple guards emerged, leading a prisoner shackled hand and foot. The guards formed a loose circle around the prisoner and began to walk slowly along the southern wall, in the direction of the upper city. The prisoner was James, still in his pure white robe, now with nothing covering his head. His knotted, uncombed hair spread out like a lion's mane around his face and head. His hair and beard badly needed some oil. He still had nothing on his feet.

Someone in the crowd yelled, "It's the blasphemer! The law says he must be stoned." Others taunted, hurling verbal insults, but no one moved to attack James. As they reached the end of the south wall of the Temple Mount, the large laundryman raced out of a group of priests, standing close to the circle of guards. Easily pushing through the guards surrounding James, he swung his club, hitting the side of James's head, knocking him down. A large gash opened up behind

James's ear. The guards, seeming rather slow to react, grabbed the man with the club and moved him away. James was slow getting to his feet when someone in the crowd said, "He has been condemned and must be stoned." Two of the guards made a weak effort to protect James. The group of priests out of which the attacker had come now began throwing stones at James. Others started to follow. When the first stones flew, the guards abandoned James. A large stone hit James in the face, and he fell to the ground. Within minutes, stones were raining down on him, and he was motionless. The assault raged on until James was covered with stones, some larger than a man's head. When it was obvious James was dead, some of the men stalked around as if they had just delivered a great gift. It was obvious this was not simply a spontaneous crowd reaction. Some had performed an ordered duty. The crowd moved away from James, and the guards uncovered him and carried him back through the Huldah Gate, closing it with a clang behind them.

The news reached the great hall of the high priest's palace even before all the Sanhedrin members had arrived. Ananus quickly retreated to his private quarters. Exactly on the eleventh hour, he strode into the great hall. "A terrible incident has just occurred. An unruly mob assaulted James as he was being brought here for the trial. He was stoned to death. The guards of the king, and my guards, are doing everything they can to keep the situation from getting out of hand. I have informed the Roman garrison of the situation, and soldiers are mobilizing. We must find the culprits who are responsible and punish them immediately. Our purpose for meeting has been taken away by this act; you are excused to go." Ananus was proud of his performance, but even more elated by the prospects of what James's death would mean for the stability of Jerusalem.

Word spread quickly throughout the city, mostly by the high priest's sympathizers running through the streets and shouting, "The blasphemer is dead." Many in the city heard this news even before the men of the Sanhedrin.

Samuel and his friends heard well before the eleventh hour. "The trial hasn't even begun, and James is dead! He was not executed; he was murdered. Ananus, the scoundrel, will pay for this! The path is now clear: first the high priest and his cronies, and then the Romans."

As the news spread and sank in, a great sadness spread over the city. Nothing could better describe the reverence and respect felt for James than the pall that fell on Jerusalem. As the men of the Sanhedrin left the high priest's palace, they encountered looks of scorn and revulsion from many who believed them responsible for James's death. A moan of agony rose up from Poor Town, spreading over the city.

It didn't take long, however, for the truth to come out that James was not tried and executed, but murdered. The members of the Sanhedrin were not about to cover for the high priest. Less than an hour after news of the covert murder hit the streets, Ananus's palace was surrounded by an angry mob. Roman soldiers, including recruits from Jericho, were summoned to disperse the mob. By nightfall, the city was in complete chaos. During the night, Ananus and some of his closest aides were spirited out of the city to Herod's palace on the Dead Sea.

By sunrise, grief had been replaced by outrage. The messianic groups grew restless, and real anger overshadowed the love James had preached. Repressed fear vanished on the wings of hostility, sharpening the lines of division. Disputes quickly flared into physical violence, with stones and rocks thrown. Incidents were scattered all over the city. No one was sure of the battle lines or just who was involved. Pandemonium reigned, and fear rose to a new level. Whereas the Sicarii murders had only threatened the priests, now all were threatened. As the riots increased, more and more Roman soldiers were brought into the city to quell the fighting. The Jews' greatest fear was building right before their eyes, the very opposite of what the disputants wanted.

Ananus had greatly miscalculated. Instead of removing an

irritant from the city, he had broken open the hornet's nest, unleashing chaos. The immediate increase in violence since the murder made it apparent that James had exerted an immense amount of positive influence over many of these messianic groups, keeping their radical and violent impulses in check. Now the nest was broken, and the hornets were swarming!

Word quickly reached Rome, and Nero ordered Albinus, the newly appointed governor, to go immediately to Jerusalem. The dreaded Roman eagle had awoken, now focusing its suspicious eye on this city of Jews. The turf wars in Jerusalem were launched on their way to an epic battle. The fetters restraining this union of deep-seated hatred of Roman occupation with an apocalyptic promise of a new Israel were gone, inciting the most radical to action. Now the Romans saw clearly the threat of this messianic fervor. These squabbling Jews, and probably a subgroup called Christians, looked beyond the power and authority of Rome—an intolerable insurrection!

Mary, Simon, and Salome heard the news of James's death—as did most of Jerusalem—from the lips of jubilant heralds. It was as if the roof had fallen in on them, crushing their chests so that they couldn't breathe. Their anguished cries led the grieving chorus of Jerusalem and Poor Town beneath it. Mary, Simon, and Salome huddled together, holding each other up. No words could describe the depth of their agony.

As is sometimes the case when agony is unbearable, Mary had to do something. "We must find his body and give him a proper burial."

Calling on a reservoir of strength deep within themselves, the three left the house to get James's body.

It's hard to tell what moved the three up the steep slope toward the Temple Mount. Huddled together, their heads covered by their shawls, they inched their way along, moving as one. Words were swallowed before reaching the lips, and breathing came in painful gasps.

Chapter 4

The Family of Jesus

Mary looked much younger than her eighty-one years. Everywhere she went, eyes seemed to gravitate toward her. This was not because of her stature, as she was slightly shorter than the average woman; rather, it was because her whole persona seemed to say "I am here for you." Erect for her years, her face radiated warmth and acceptance. Her mouth appeared always on the verge of a smile, which came very easily. Her eyes sparkled like those of an excited child. She made you feel glad to be in her presence. Her strong alto voice welcomed response, and her hands revealed many years of giving and caring. The mother of seven children—Jesus, James, Joseph, twins Marta and Judas Thomas, Simon, and Salome—everyone who knew Mary loved and respected her.

Simon, Mary's only living son now that James was dead, served under James as one of the opposition priests. Taller than all his other brothers except James, Simon, with his large graying beard, was a striking figure. He was beginning to show his age, possibly on account of the great deal of traveling he had done to many of the groups of followers of Jesus in the East. Unlike the other children, who mostly resembled their father, Joseph, killed along with his son Joseph in a construction accident thirty-five years ago, Simon definitely had his mother's facial features. Like his mother, Simon was a favorite of the people because of his openness and gentle disposition.

Salome was the baby of the family, born more than nineteen years after Jesus and twelve years after Simon. She grew up idolizing her older siblings, whom she remembered only as adults. Soft-spoken and reserved, she never married like her older sister, Marta, had. Taller than her mother, Salome stood just as erect. She had her father's eyes, which drew you in like magnets. Her smile, often slow in coming, sparkled like morning sunlight on dew-laden roses. Although not gregarious or quick to speak—probably the result of growing up in the shadow of her popular older brothers—when she did speak, she revealed a quick and perceptive mind. She was loved by the people in Poor Town for her kind and gentle caring. Some referred to her as their angel. She seemed always content to accompany her mother as they served the poor, and her being a spinster never was spoken of. However, Mary often pondered whether something she had done kept Salome from experiencing the joys of marriage and motherhood.

The task of preparing and burying James's body diverted for a time their incapacitating sense of agony. Their home in the lower city felt so very empty! It was a small house with three small rooms on the lower level and two above, a space that now felt massive without James. Its emptiness weighed on all three like chains pulling their spirits into a black pit.

This home, located on the steep slope facing east, three streets back from the western wall of the Temple Mount, was convenient to the Dung Gate and Poor Town, just beyond. James had chosen this location—rather than the upper northern sector, where most of the opposition priests resided—because of its proximity to Poor Town, a sprawling complex of tents, hand-dug caves, and temporary hovels littered over the steep slopes just outside the city walls, cascading into the Tyropean and Kidron Valleys. Over the last many years, Mary, James, Simon, and Salome had spent much of their time serving the insatiable needs of the residents of

Poor Town, the poorest of the poor. The suffering of these hapless citizens pulled the four of them toward Poor Town.

Poor Town hung on the side of the hills just outside the city walls. It covered a vast area, going well down and across the Kidron Valley and up to the grave sites on the south western side of Mount Olivet. Buried under its dirty walkways were the ruins of the centuries-old City of David, the majestic homes and palaces of Israel's glory days under kings David and Solomon. The contrast with the current Poor Town couldn't be greater.

Poor Town started right at the city walls. It had no streets. The footpaths, created by the flow of water that happened occasionally, were littered with filth. Every level or protected spot had been converted into a bed for a beggar or cripple. Most of the structures were temporary, tent-like hovels. A few structures appeared a bit more permanent, constructed by stacking some stones on one another, with sticks for a roof. Sadly, most of these did not withstand the heavy rains that occasionally soaked these valleys. Just outside Dung Gate, clinging to the steep slopes of the upper Tyropean Valley, was a leper's colony.

The whole area was really a city unto itself, with its own economy and power structure. The center of Poor Town was its market. Unlike the two big markets within the walls of Jerusalem, the dominant currency here was not coins but bartering. The rowdy exchanges often included many more than two people, each trying to outbid the other. Market day was every day, and many who set up their makeshift stands were not residents but people who came in from the hills around Jerusalem. The powerful were those physically strongest, who could bully their way into the best locations and situations. The residents were the very poor; mostly those who could not work. Most of the beggars (the authentic ones) encountered on the streets of Jerusalem spent their nights in Poor Town. Sadly, the robbers and thieves also found safe haven here. It was not the destination of those Jews who flocked to Jerusalem on the Holy Days. No, many of them went out of their way to enter

Jerusalem by another gate. Most of the benevolence bestowed on Poor Town came from the hands of the Jesus followers under the leadership of the murdered James, and also from his family members.

The suffering of Poor Town offered a respite for the disabling grief of this broken family. Here, they could confirm their faith in love, and live the presence of God in vivid reality.

It was more than two weeks since James's murder, and so late that in one hour's time, it would be the next day. Mary felt great relief when she and Simon finally arrived home. She did not like walking the streets of Jerusalem after dark; they were rough, and her balance was not what it used to be. They had walked all the way from Mathias's house near the Sheep Market on the other side of the temple. Their fellowship met in secret since James's murder, only going to the synagogue for Sabbath. The purpose of this meeting was to install Simon as the head of the followers of Jesus in Jerusalem. James had established himself, in the eyes of the common people, as truly righteous: a man honoring the greatest commandment by defending the sacred space of the temple, and dedicating his life to serving the poor, thereby honoring the second commandment to love one's neighbor. James owned the hearts of the people. Simon knew he had big shoes to fill.

Mary was extremely uncomfortable. The meeting had been boisterous and at times downright scary. Some of the more militant were outwardly goading Simon to demonstrate that he was not going to continue James's position on nonviolence. They were tired of waiting, convinced that Jesus would not return as long as the Jews cowered at the sight of the Romans. It saddened Mary that the younger members of the fellowship had not had the benefit of walking with Jesus and hearing his teachings. Would Simon be as successful as James in conveying the essence of Jesus's message of God's love?

Simon sensed his mother's discomfort. It was her eyes! Eyes told him everything about a person. Were they orbs of iron, not letting anything in or out? Were they deep dark wells, perceptive, but always alert to danger, never revealing anything? Or, were they clear as air, through which love could flow? Yes, hers were always clear; but, now they revealed a pain so deep it broke his heart. Ever since James's murder Simon recognized a pain that went straight to the core of his mother's being. He was concerned for her. He knew this pain could kill her more rapidly than any disease. James's murder, the third execution of one of her sons by the authorities, had broken open her heart, and her lifeblood was gushing away.

"What can I do for you, Mother?"

"You can run away!" Her grief and distress, even anger, showed in her voice. "Run away and hide from all this insanity that has already killed three of my sons. You are my last son; for God's sake, get away before they kill you too."

"It's not that easy, Mother. Your grief is making you say things you don't really believe."

"What do I believe? What is one to believe? I had five sons all dedicated to the righteous pursuit of Torah; now four are dead. You tell me what to believe!"

"God's promise to Abraham will never die. We must keep Torah and protect the holiness of the temple, especially now. You know messiah will come! You heard what Jesus and James taught. You can't lose faith now!" Simon didn't need to hear any disbelief just now. He was still reeling from the venom cast at him during the meeting.

"Maybe it's all a bad dream; no, a miserable nightmare!" Mary continued.

"Mother, don't say that!"

"Say what? Three sons dead, killed by the authorities. Sons who were loved by so many, sons who gave common people hope, sons who healed the sick and faithfully sought to do God's will. What for—to be crucified, beheaded, and stoned to death? What is that if not a nightmare? They will kill you too; and my three grandsons. Then what will you say about God's promise to Abraham? Where are my seed? Run away, Simon. Start up a carpenter shop, get a wife, and have some children, so I can believe in the promise again."

"At my age? Don't be silly! Mama, you're upset! You're not thinking clearly right now. Lie down and get some rest; we will talk more tomorrow."

It shook Simon to hear his mother say such things; it troubled him deeply. Her faith had always been the rock the whole family depended on. Her faith produced four priestly sons, rabbis everyone looked up to and respected. Was she losing her faith, or maybe even her mind?

Simon shared his concern for his mother with Salome, and then left the house. He needed to be alone. He needed time to think and pray. He disappeared into Poor Town.

Salome could not sleep. Simon had told her about their mother's disturbing remarks. This was not like their mother. Simon had even said that he thought their mother might be losing her mind. Could this woman Salome knew as a tower of strength be crumbling? Was it possible that this woman, who had raised seven successful children on a carpenter's meager earnings, who had rejoiced in their successes and grieved their tragedies, always with an unshakable faith in the goodness of God, was actually going crazy? Worse yet, if not that, was she losing the faith she had worked so hard to instill in all her children?

Salome knew she was not the one to talk to her mother about this. She knew her brothers were exceptional persons, but some of the things said about them, and some of the things people believed about them, were just too much for her to take in. She wondered why everything always had to have an explanation. If we determined a reason and purpose for everything, where was the openness to newness or the urge to be creative? She couldn't imagine God creating this miraculous universe using such a mind-set. Religion seemed to throw a blanket over God. It was so confining to claim to know so much about God. She often pictured God shaking his head at some of the strange religious beliefs and practices.

Salome had never been able to talk to her mother about these things because her mother would get so upset by her skepticism. Salome knew that all this talk about her brother being the Messiah who would return to establish God's kingdom on earth would eventually destroy the whole family. It had already taken three of her brothers and might now be taking her mother.

Why is religion so destructive? What is God up to anyway? Why can't God just be God and people just be people? Why do men think they have to know who God is, what God demands, and then force others to believe what they pretend to know? Why can't people just be kind and helpful to one another, and just worship God? I thought that is what the covenant with Abraham was all about. If we worshipped God and took care of each other, we would prosper. We have the Torah to help us do that. In fact, I thought that was really what my brother Jesus taught. On this last thought, her mother and she agreed.

On second thought, Salome realized, maybe she *could* talk to her mother. She also considered that, perhaps, Simon had exaggerated.

Yes, she would talk about this with her mother. She knew they would spend the first three or four minutes in a crushing embrace, with tears flowing like torrential rain. It had been like this ever since James was murdered by the high priest's thugs. That was almost three weeks ago! When would the pain be bearable? Her precious brother was slaughtered because he was too righteous, because he dedicated his life to the poor and to keeping the temple pure for God's presence. What beasts! They walked around in their long robes, ordering servants to satisfy their every need. They took alms from the poor to feed their lavish lifestyles, then acted like they were preserving the temple when they were actually using it as a way to gain favor with the ruthless Romans. Torah, for them, was not a gracious response to the one true God for having a special eye for Israel, but, rather, an avenue to power and lavish displays of hypocrisy. They would even bow down to Rome if they were left alone to follow their distortions of Torah. They saw no problem in serving both God and the murderous Caesar. What hypocrites! They themselves were murderers.

The next morning, after prayers, Mary and Salome went to the roof to enjoy the beautiful morning. As they sat on the roof, the smell of baking bread mingled with the aroma of sage in the tea they were sipping, offering a fitting backdrop to the plaintive song of a sparrow performing from the bougainvillea. A yellow-and-white cat was lounging in the sun, hoping its bath would soothe all the scratches from last night's encounter, caring nothing about the tension gripping the city. What did the cat know that the frantic Jews of Jerusalem were missing? The cat's serenity was rudely shattered by a bossy crow on the parapet wall of a neighbor's house, seemingly unwilling to take no for an answer.

Salome looked at her mother and saw the tears were still there, lurking on her lower eyelids, threatening to once more cascade down her cheeks and onto her breasts. She moved to her mother, the sobs beginning before they embraced.

After the tears, Salome stepped back to look her mother in the eyes. As she had suspected, Simon had exaggerated. The solid resolve was still there, the determination to not let selfish minds and ambitious wills drag her away from faith in God, who had sustained her through life. Even in her deepest agony, she remained the fortress of faith Salome always relied on and desperately needed right now.

"Simon was worried about you. He thought you might have lost your mind."

"Why? Because I told him to get away before they kill him too?"

"Is that what you said to him?"

"That and a little bit more. I told him I wondered if all we were hoping for was just a bad nightmare."

Salome was afraid Mary was going to go over all that old ground again. "Mama, please don't let us get into a fuss again. That's the last thing either of us needs right now."

"Oh, Salome, you are such a comfort to me. You, my last born, are truly the anchor of my life. You have been at my side through all my sorrows; our pain and grief as if from one heart. I cannot imagine a greater blessing than what you have been to me. Nothing could come between us, because love holds us together."

"Yes, but when you started talking about 'all we were hoping for' … well, you know how uncomfortable that makes me feel."

"Yes, dear, I do." Mary stepped closer to Salome and rubbed her finger gently over her cheek. "Your reluctance to be swept off your feet with grandiose schemes has been very helpful to me. With each passing day, I feel you are more grounded in God's plan than most of those going around preaching and sounding the alarm of the end of days. You live love every day. You bring a smile to the face of those who have very little to smile about. You are an active citizen of the kingdom of God. The more I watch you, and Simon—and James," Mary said, swallowing a sob, "the more I'm sure messiah is not a person, but an event or an awakening."

Just then, a disturbance down on the street attracted both women's attention. It sounded like soldiers approaching.

Salome grabbed Mary in a hug. "I hate the sound of soldiers … but what you just said sounds so good to me. Say more."

"I'm not sure what more there is to say. Perhaps messiah is simply an awakening, the awareness of the opportunity to love. As I say that, it feels like Jesus is right here."

A strange, stern voice came from the front of the house, shouting, "Simon, come out! You're under arrest!"

Salome hurried down to the front entryway. She froze in horror at the sight of a massive Roman centurion just outside the opening, completely filling it. To her, he looked like a giant bear ready to snatch her up. She was so frightened that her scream caught in her throat, choking her. She turned to run into the back room and bumped into Mary, who was right behind her. The women clutched each other and cowered in fear at the sight of this huge man. It appeared that there were a number of soldiers behind him.

The man in the doorway, Zenas, was at least four cubits high. He stood with his legs spread apart, and his one hand on the hilt of a sword at his side and the other across his chest. His face was expressionless, but the repeated opening and closing of his hand revealed agitation or discomfort.

Mary noticed his hand, and, immediately, her fear began to subside.

Salome felt the change in Mary, opened her eyes, and for the first time was able to see the man standing in front of them. Mountainous waves of fear swept over her. Yet, like sunlight bouncing off the tips of these waves, she couldn't help but think, *What a beautiful man.* His cropped hair showed off perfect ears and a powerful neck. His eyes were alive and engaging. His mouth suggested confidence and concern. His muscular arms and legs were things of beauty. She turned away, embarrassed by her fascination with this loathsome creature.

Zenas turned, and in a language the women could not understand, said to the five soldiers standing behind him, "This is where he lives; search the house."

Seeing that the soldiers moved to enter the house, Mary moved to the doorway, right in front of Zenas. Salome tried to hold her back.

Mary spoke in anguish, "Please, I beg you, don't profane our home. He is not here. He was here, but he left last night. We haven't seen him since." Her fearful eyes were brimming with tears, but she stood tall, giving no hint that she was about to step aside.

Salome feared that Zenas would just brush her mother aside and was surprised that he did not.

Almost overcome with fear, Salome moved to pull her mother

aside. "Please, Mama, don't resist them." This man was big enough to crush both of them if he was angered.

Zenas put out his arms to stop the men from entering the house. This was the first time he really looked at Salome. His gaze lingered; there was something about her eyes. He turned to Mary and said, "If he is not here, tell us where he is."

A strange look came over Mary's face as she realized this Roman was speaking Aramaic to them. "I have no idea where he is, but if I did, do you think a mother would throw her son to the wolves?"

"Woman, hold your tongue. I have orders to arrest anyone who gives us trouble."

Mary was about to say something when Salome interrupted her. "Mama, please don't say anything else."

Mary looked at Salome in gentle rebuke. She felt the same fear Salome was experiencing, but something deep inside pushed her to go on. "I know you are just following orders, and I do not mean to be disrespectful, but Simon is a priest, a very holy man. He would do nothing deserving arrest."

"Every mother in the world thinks that of her son." Zenas's discomfort was increasing, and the men behind him showed impatience. "Two more priests were killed overnight. Our information is that this is the work of the Sicarii, who follow orders of the opposition priesthood. Your son is one of their leaders. He is a prime suspect in these murders."

"You Romans don't have a clue about what is going on, but you come in here and start throwing your weight around. The only thing you will accomplish is that more innocents will be killed." Mary was surprised at her rashness. "The Sicarii tactics are as deeply entrenched in the establishment priesthood as anywhere else. Power and violence will not solve the problem; they are at the root of it." Anger, deeply repressed by her grief, surfaced in a boldness that startled her.

It petrified Salome, who walked over to a bench and sat down.

Mary's words aroused Zenas's curiosity, but his eyes followed Salome. "I hope your impudent comments are not meant as insults." Zenas used the word *impudent,* but he really thought the old woman was brave. Perhaps, if he got her to say a bit more, he could learn something useful. The governor certainly had little or no knowledge of what was going on.

Zenas turned to his men and dispatched three to find a way to the back of the house, to make sure no one had escaped that way, and the other two to stand guard at each corner of the street in front.

After they had left, Zenas turned to Mary and said, "I admire your bravery. If you are being untruthful or condescending, you will pay dearly for that. Frankly, I do not suspect you are either one. You didn't have to speak at all, and the fact that you did makes me curious."

Mary noticed that Zenas's hands were now relaxed. Her fear abated further.

Salome's fear decreased not one bit. She wanted to run away but wouldn't think of leaving Mary alone. She listened with great anticipation, certain that something awful was going to happen to them.

Zenas put his hands on his hips, a gesture Salome took as mocking, and said to Mary, "So, you think power and violence are the root of the problem, and Rome will only increase it. You said that with a lot of conviction." He paused, and didn't say more.

Mary hesitated, and looked him in the eyes. She remained silent.

Zenas was obviously uncomfortable. He took his hands off his hips and leaned forward, trying not to look frightening. "Look, I am just following orders. I was ordered to come here and arrest Simon and everyone with him. You said he isn't here, and you begged me not to search your house. Then, you hurled an angry slur at us Romans and went on to say something I thought might be helpful. You said something about both groups of priests killing

61

each other. I would like to hear more. Or, I can just take the two of you in, as instructed."

Mary detected a note of sincerity in this soldier's voice. There appeared to be some humanity behind that armor. She looked up into his face. "The two groups of priests have been killing each other for a number of years. That is nothing new; only the frequency has increased recently. As for my comment on power and violence, I should not have to explain that to you." Mary's expression softened, and her tone changed to one of sympathy. "Do you go anywhere where you are welcomed with open arms? Does the fact that people fear you make you think you are helping solve the world's problems? Peace coerced by the edge of a sword and the tip of a spear mocks the very meaning of the word."

Zenas was thankful the other soldiers were not present. He hoped he did not reveal how sharp a blow those words were to him. He stood up very erect and said, "Thank you for clarifying. I respect your honesty and bravery. I'll take your word that Simon is not here, and we will leave you here. Please do not try to hide Simon from us; it will put you in grave danger if you do." He turned and walked into the street.

Salome rushed up to Mary and embraced her. Mary could feel her trembling. They heard Zenas call the men from the back of the house. They could hear the men shouting at each other as they walked up the street, toward the fortress.

Salome slowly calmed down. "Whew ... that was frightening! How could you stand up to that monster like that? I really thought you were going to make him so angry that he might hurt us."

Mary just shook her head. She realized that she, too, had been extremely frightened, and just now was beginning to breathe normally. "Something about him made me do what I did and say what I said. I'm not sure I can explain it. Sometimes your heart just takes over, and you do what needs to be done. Weren't you surprised that he spoke in our native tongue?"

Salome looked at her mother in wonderment. "Yes, but you amaze me, Mama."

Mary was now almost fully herself. "We really ought to get to Poor Town. Without James—" She had to stop, for fear of bursting into tears. "There is so much more for us to do now. Besides, Simon will probably not be there either. Are the Romans going to imprison him? They really don't have a clue, do they?"

For many years, Mary, James, Simon, and Salome had walked daily the short distance from their house, out the Dung Gate and into Poor Town. There, they fanned out, addressing the various needs of the poorest residences. One of them always went into the leper colony to treat those suffering most. Many of the other Jesus followers did the same. To the residents of Poor Town, these loving folks were the only bright light in their lives.

This day was no different. Immediately beyond the gate, they stopped at the leper colony to see what was needed, so they could bring it back on their way home.

Nebor, the self-appointed guard of the colony, greeted the women as the best of friends. "Salome and Mary, you are a sight for sore eyes. Of all God's children, you deserve his greatest blessings. Where is Simon?"

Salome responded, "In hiding! Would you believe, the Romans want to arrest him for the priestly killings in the temple!"

"Those fools! Obviously, the swine Ananus, or some of the patronizing Pharisees, have already filled the Romans' heads with lies. Simon abhors violence." Nebor spat on the ground. "At least the two of you are here. God has not forgotten us."

Salome rubbed Nebor on the arm. "We will see you this afternoon."

Mary went from tent to tent, washing festering sores. At one point, she was completely unaware that she was barely a stone's throw away from a meeting going on in the cave—the very place that had prompted James to speak in the temple. This time, only Simon and Jesse were present.

Jesse was pleading with Simon. "You have to go to the Zealot strongholds, both in Galilee and beyond Jericho. They have to bring some pressure on the hotheads here. Now that James is gone, the militant Zealots could take over and really make a mess of things. I don't think we have a clue as to just how effective James's nonviolent teachings have been."

"Jesus didn't say how often we are to turn the other cheek." Simon just shook his head. "Jesus, even more than James, was so confident that love would win out over violence. At a time like this, it's so easy to understand the appeal of violence. Doesn't righteousness call for justice?" He paused. "I'm not losing faith in love. I just need some encouragement right now."

"Don't we all? The presence of the new Roman legions certainly doesn't help. They only increase the level of fear and agitate radical impulses. Of course, they also show the downside of violence. What an ugly lesson!" Jesse paused. He then looked to Simon. "You can't do much here in hiding. Let's find a way for you to get out of the city, and put your persuasive skills to work."

"I want to see Mother and Salome before I leave. They are so strong, but their grief is dragging them down. Please watch out for them. I'll leave tonight."

The two men left the cave separately, knowing that someone could be watching, and anyone could be a spy.

Salome went to a fruit stand, got a small bag of figs and a few wheat cakes, and took them to Ruth, a crippled woman who always sat under an old knurled olive tree near Zechariah's tomb at the bottom edge of the cemetery. Some said she was more than one hundred years old. Nothing seemed to happen in Poor Town that she didn't see or know about. Salome wanted to know if she heard anything about Simon.

As Salome approached, Ruth said, "Ah, my angel of the morning. God bless you for never forgetting me."

"Ruth, you are always on my mind; but, this morning, I am worried sick over Simon. The Romans came to the house this morning to arrest him. Have you heard anything about his whereabouts?"

"No, I haven't." Ruth motioned for Salome to sit by her side. "I know some of the priests are thinking of leaving Jerusalem. Apparently, the new governor who just arrived is focused on Poor Town. Do you think he is going to build us a lovely new city like the high priest has?" she said with a chuckle. "If he is, I guess he is going to build it with swords and spears."

"Ruth, I have no time to sit and talk today. Mama and I have more to do than we can handle. If you hear from Simon, please tell him to get in touch with us." A frightened look came over her face. "No ... tell him to run away from this horrible place." She burst into tears as she hurried away.

Mary and Salome hurried through their work that day, feeling they were shortchanging everyone they touched. Nothing they did felt rewarding, just burdensome. After spending the last two hours in the leper colony, they arrived home, exhausted and dejected. There was no joy as they prepared for Sabbath. The Sabbath meal was minimal, and the prayers almost perfunctory. They were asleep well before their normal hour. Sleep, however, was fitful, with worry over Simon the cause.

Well past the midnight hour, Mary and Salome were awaken by a loud pounding on the front of their house.

When Mary reached the front room, there were three soldiers already in the room. Mary slumped in dejection at the affront.

Salome, hurrying up behind Mary, let out a wail. "Don't you beasts ever sleep?"

One of the soldiers held up his hand and yelled, "Silence! We are going to search this house and then take you in. Stay where you are, and don't say a word." With one hand on the hilt of his sword and the other holding a lance, he ordered the other two to search the house. The two soldiers returned in a few minutes and said the house was empty. "Grab those two, and let's get back."

One soldier roughly grabbed the arm of each woman and

marched them out of the house. Two other soldiers, holding torches and standing in the street, led the way up the hill to the fortress.

Mary and Salome were released from the fortress late in the afternoon on the Sabbath. They arrived home exhausted, but glad to be free.

As they were getting ready to go to sleep, Salome noticed someone leaning against the wall of the house in back. "Mama, there's a man out there. I think it's a beggar."

"What!" said Mary, straining to get a better view. Immediately, she knew it was Simon! "Come in, you fresh beggar, and we will give you a crust of bread." Mary knew the Romans might be watching the front of the house; they had spies everywhere.

Simon hurried in and took Mary in his arms. "Mother, I'm so worried for you. Are you all right?"

"Yes, we are fine, but you should not have come here. They are looking all over for you. I'm sure they will keep a sharp eye on our house. Where are you hiding?"

"I am staying in Poor Town, next to the leper colony. Whenever we hear that the soldiers are making a sweep of the area, I hide in the colony. They won't set foot in that place."

"But you can't stay there long. Sooner or later, they will find out." Mary's fear was palpable.

"I know, but I am so worried about what is going to happen. Every day now, another one or two priests are murdered. Everyone is so afraid, and no one knows what to do. Violence is becoming contagious.

"But the militant Zealots worry me the most. They are getting too bold. As long as James was alive, Jesus's messiah of love was able to keep them in check. They respected him so much. They would not pursue their radical ideas because they knew James would not stand for violence. But now he is gone, and there is no one to hold them back. I'm afraid this could explode into something disastrous."

"They respect you too. Why don't you try to get them to pull back?" asked Mary.

"No! The Zealots here in Jerusalem have turned their backs on nonviolence. They are convinced the time has come to throw off the Romans. They have cast aside the mantle of peace. I am no longer their ally.

"One of the reasons I came here tonight is to tell you that I am leaving in a few hours to go beyond Jericho and into Galilee, to the Zealot strongholds, to try one last time to convince them of the folly of these radical plans. Ever since James's murder, the violent position is gaining strength. The Sicarii murders are increasing. Most of the leaders here believe the Messiah is ready to return and sweep away the Romans and the corrupt Herodians. They believe the first step is to punish the high priests. They think they are an integral part, and their job is to take the temple away from the high priests and purify it for the Messiah's arrival. They believe the Romans will not stop them because they are so mad at Ananus."

Mary's face showed her anxiety at what Simon was telling her. "Certainly, messiah will not reign until the temple is purified, but it must not be done through violence. That's what Jesus, James, and you have always taught—it is the bedrock of Jesus's teaching that God is the God of love. Why does everything always seem to gravitate to violence? Judas the Galilean and his sons should have finally taught us that lesson. Violence only brings on more violence."

Just then, there was a sound out in the street. "Quick, Simon, you must leave; someone is coming."

Simon slipped out the back just as there was a knock at the front door. Salome went to the doorway and found a soldier standing there. These brutes were everywhere!

"Did a man sneak in here a while back?" he inquired. "A neighbor thought she saw someone sneak in."

"Yes," Salome said reassuringly, "a desperate beggar asked for a scrap of bread. We gave him some and sent him on his way."

"It is not very safe opening up your house at night to strangers," cautioned the soldier, "especially when there are only two women in the house."

Salome blanched at the thought that this soldier knew that it was just she and her mother in this house. How much else did the authorities know about them? She shuddered at the thought that there were spies and informants everywhere.

Mary's daughter-in law, Sarah, the widow of Judas Thomas, had returned to Jerusalem a number of years back, after her husband's beheading, with a clear mission of Jesus's message of love. She expressed shock at the horrible conditions of Poor Town, and the apparent apathy of the religious establishment to even try to address it. Using her exceptional organizational skills, she, with the help of Mary, and her family, went to work. Working through the many fellowships of the followers of Jesus, she established a whole network of services and aid that directly addressed the most serious needs of the poor and destitute. Members of these fellowships delivered food to the hungry of Poor Town and administered aid to the infirm and maimed. She organized teams of workers who rebuilt collapsed tents and cleaned away the putrid filth that never seemed to subside. She devised a way for excess food from the markets to be collected and taken to those who desperately needed it. In effect, she created a kind of pipeline through which the excess of the wealthy could be delivered to the poor. Part of her vision was to see love turn the leper colony from a pit of avoidance into a grove of care. She and her small army of saints befriended the outcast and discarded of Jerusalem and brought some relief to their abject suffering. The people of Poor Town called her the Miracle Woman. A woman of great compassion, she constantly struggled for the means for this critical aid. Once, she expressed a recurring thought to Mary. "I'm struck by the irony of our friends going down the streets of

Jerusalem to meet the needs of the poor as the wealthy pass them going up these same streets, hoping to buy favor with the leaders and religious authorities at the upper end of the city." Mary was so proud of her only daughter-in law.

This day, Sarah came to Mary as others often did. "My son Jacob's friend is here and wants to talk to you."

Behind her was a strapping young man who looked to be barely beyond his teen years. He stood awkwardly, his hands clasp in front of him.

Mary held out her hand to give his hands something to do. "So, you are a friend of my grandson. Who is it my pleasure to meet?"

The young man looked to Sarah, as if to ask if it was all right to shake Mary's hand. He then reached out rather cautiously and shook Mary's hand briefly, letting go very quickly. "My name is Amos, son of Joseph from Magdala."

"Ah! Magdala is such a beautiful little town. How long have you known Jacob?"

"We met in James's classroom. It's been almost a year now."

"Sarah said you wanted to talk to me. What's on your mind?"

"I'm really troubled, and Jacob said I should talk to you. I hate to bother you, especially now in your time of grieving. Please forgive my intrusion."

"You are not intruding or being a bother. Sarah, please get us all some tea. Come, Amos, let's sit in the garden."

The two walked to the garden and sat across a narrow walkway from each other on the low walls separating a number of garden plots, the smell of coriander strong in the air.

"Now, tell me what is bothering you," Mary said.

Amos appeared unsure of where to begin. "Well, it's really just come up since Rabbi James was killed, which has really shaken up all of us." He paused. "I'm sorry ... certainly not in comparison to what you must be going through."

Mary nodded in gratitude as she swallowed a sob that

prevented her from responding. Concerned that he had started off wrong, Amos looked down at his hands.

Mary, realizing his discomfort, said, "Forgive me. Please go on."

Amos decided to get right to the point. "It's all about violence. Violence took my rabbi, and, since then, all anyone can talk about is violence. James taught the kingdom of God abhors violence. Now it seems everyone is calling for us to take up arms to hasten the return of Jesus. Do we need to take up arms in order for God's kingdom to prevail?"

"Amos, you ask a most profound question."

At this point, Sarah brought out the tea. Mary was glad for the interruption. She understood Amos's dilemma and wanted a few moments to collect her thoughts. She was impressed with the depth of his concern. She looked at the leaves floating in her teacup, as if they were enlightening her.

After a prolonged silence, Mary continued. "I have to start with the messiah my son Jesus taught us about. I like to think of it as the dream of life. The dream is not a goal or an end, but a journey. It is not a big house, great wealth, position, or eternal life. The dream is the purpose in living. The only positive contribution we can make to the dream is to help perpetuate it. It is part of the purpose of creation. Our perspective is much too narrow to understand this purpose. The most we can do is direct our actions and behaviors to affirm the dream, not negate it.

"You have listened to James teach you the message of the messiah Jesus brought to all of us. I often heard Jesus teach that message. He never once spoke of taking up the sword for anything. In fact, he spoke of turning the other cheek when struck. Even during his arrest and trial at the hands of the high priests and the Romans, he never raised his hand to protect himself."

Amos felt uncomfortable interrupting, but he said, "But power and violence always seem to win."

Mary reached over and put her hand on Amos's forearm.

"Don't be so sure about that. Love can be very powerful as well." Mary had to pause. Amos's question was so close to her feelings the past number of days. "Believe me, I have been pondering the same problem. Violence has never been an option for me. The more I consider, the more I think we are looking for the wrong thing. I'm pretty sure our expectations are the root of the problem."

Now Amos was confused. "What do expectations have to do with violence?" He was surprised by his forwardness with this renowned woman.

Mary warmed to this young man's bravery and seriousness. "I can see how that is confusing. I believe we have come to expect that the change we hope for can only come about by force. We Jews remember, even yearn for, the glory days of David and Solomon. Those kingdoms were obtained through power and violence. We tend to believe that is how the kingdom of God will have to be established. But is God's kingdom a kingdom of power or of love?"

Mary could see in Amos's eyes that wheels were going around in his head.

"Don't you believe that sin and evil have to be punished?" he asked.

"God cannot abide sin or evil, but does the God of love punish? Maybe sin and evil bring on their own punishment."

Amos was amazed. This woman spoke with such passion and assuredness. He was hanging on her every word. "Please say more!"

"If you think back, the Holy Scriptures teach that it was not God's idea to have a king. Samuel said that God looked on this demand by the people as a rejection of God. God's idea of a kingdom is obviously different from ours. Has God changed? Are we now to expect God to give us what was once considered a rejection? Do power and kingship have anything to do with the messiah?

"My son Jesus never seemed to have this understanding of the messiah. I believe Jesus's understanding of how the kingdom of

God is realized is radically different from what many Jews long for today."

Amos could hardly contain his excitement. "That's what James taught. The Jews were selected, not because we are to be separated out from the rest of humanity, but because we are to be examples of true humanity. We were given Torah to help us be righteous, by following laws not to demonstrate obedience but to foster a humble life that will generate righteousness. He said Jesus's simple message was that righteousness is nothing more than discovering that God is love and passing that along to our neighbor."

Mary praised him, saying, "You obviously were listening very well, Amos. James would be proud of you. James responded to Jesus by humbly dedicating himself to teaching Torah as the route toward righteousness. He believed the messiah would only fully mature when righteousness completely permeated the people, and the temple once again became God's house of prayer, not a center of human power. That's what he taught. He never considered violence as an option."

Amos had his answer. "You have answered my questions. I will never use the Sicarii blade. Martial activity pulls heavily on my manly urges, yet I cannot entertain violence."

Amos knew he just had a brush with truth. Mary's eyes drove her words directly to his heart.

Salome, too, was impressed. While most of the messiah talk frightened her, to hear her mother so clearly and concisely talk about Jesus's message of messiah made her want to hear more.

After Sarah and Amos were gone, they talked in depth about Mary's expectations and Salome's fears. In the course of the discussion, Mary pointed out that Salome's brother Judas Thomas's death, too, had been the result of him being seen as aligned with the radical Zealots. The Herodians and the high priests had convinced the Romans that Judas Thomas was what they called a Sicarios, when all he ever taught was zealous adherence to Torah.

Salome's head was spinning. *Why are there so many different groups all seeming to be at one another's throats? Is it all about power? Are even the Zealots guilty of simply pursuing power? There is even fighting among those who do not openly advocate violence.*

Salome remembered a few years ago, and once many years before that, the furious disputes that erupted when the self-proclaimed apostle Paul came to Jerusalem. Ironically, religion seemed to bring out the worst in men.

CHAPTER 5

ZENAS

Albinus was furious! "His Holiness, Caesar Nero, sends me here to subdue some crazy Jews disrupting the peace of Rome, and you let an old Jewess sweet-talk you into disobeying my orders? You are to take no one's word as truth but mine!" Albinus's anger only increased as he realized that Zenas was the only Roman soldier here with him in Jerusalem who could speak the common street language. In a rage, he turned to his aide and ordered, "Throw him and his hapless assistants in chains!"

The centurion, Zenas, and his five soldiers were dragged away to the basement of the guardhouse and locked in chains. The clammy cell under the fortress did nothing to dampen the fury among the six.

"Albinus did not see that woman's eyes," Zenas explained to his companions. "If ever there were symbols of truth, they were it."

"If I weren't in these chains, I'd choke the life out of you," said Lucius. "Symbols of truth! You fool! Your weakness for that woman has destroyed all of us. Are you a soldier, or is there something missing between your legs?"

Zenas burned red with anger. "I've beaten you in the gymnasium every time we battled, and my manhood can't be challenged by the likes of you. You'll never be more than a dog following a master and barking only when told to bark."

Zenas was distraught over the fact that he had brought disgrace upon his men. However, he couldn't let his guilt show, or these men would never respect him again. But those eyes! Not even a legion of soldiers was going to defile that woman's house. He never realized truth could be so obvious or so powerful.

The other soldiers would not let up. The shouting among the six became so loud that the guards finally moved Zenas to another part of the compound, into a solitary cell. There he sat, alone with his guilt and his questions, wondering if Albinus would kill him, or whether he would just pull oars the rest of his life.

Zenas was a real thoroughbred: the son of an influential senator and a Julian mother, and the nephew of a highly respected Stoic senator. Many considered him emperor material. Upon reaching manhood, he had the psychic of Tiberius and the integrity of Germanicus. The sky was the limit for this young man. His decision to reject nepotism and instead earn his promotions only enhanced his image among those who knew him. All these expectations now flowed like the sweat down his back, into the damp earth of this lonely cell in Jerusalem.

Sleep would not come to Zenas that night. His thoughts went back to Rome, to his father, and especially his uncle, Thrasea Paetus, both senators whom he loved and deeply respected. He remembered his father's great disappointment when he refused the position with the Praetorian Guard, a position Zenas felt he hadn't earned. He also recalled his uncle's look of gratification that he chose instead to earn his way through the military ranks.

Zenas wiped the sweat from his forehead. "What have I done to you, my beloved father and uncle?" he whispered. "I have ruined all you worked so hard to give me." He held his head in his hands, his face distorted in agony. He groaned from deep within his loins. He wanted to kick down these four stone walls, indeed bring down this whole fortress. He sat in a state of deep disillusionment.

Zenas had happily left Rome. He remembered his uncle's continuous rants about deifying men who committed regicide and fratricide, forced suicides of honorable citizens, all the while living lavish licentious lives. (Zenas could picture his uncle spitting out the words *regicide* and *fratricide*.) In his mind, Rome no longer stood as the center of all good and right. It had become a pit of vipers. No one dared turn a back on friend or foe. Righteousness, honor, and integrity were detriments to success. The closer he got to the seats of power, the uglier it became.

His skin began to crawl as he recalled the incident outside Alexandria a little over a month ago. More than twenty young Egyptian men slaughtered simply because they turned their backs to the Roman standard! He understood his superior's frustration, not being able to identify the persons who threw eggs at their column of soldiers—and the laughter and mocking from the crowd was demeaning—yet, to respond with such violence, just because he could, struck him as simply inhuman. That feeling of not wanting to be a part of such behavior came back so clearly here in this dark cell, which felt like the bottom of the dungeon of despair.

The questions of that brave Jewish woman earlier in the day now hit him like arrows to the heart. He thrashed his arms in utter frustration. He rattled his chains, which pulled hard on the ring anchors in the wall. He noticed some particles fall to the floor of the cell from where the ring was anchored into the wall. Those falling particles told him the ring was loose. He looked closer in the dim light, and, sure enough, some of the mortar around the stones next to the ring was cracked and crumbling. This ring was loose! He might be able to free himself of these chains.

Immediately, his attitude changed. *I'm going to get out of here,* he told himself. *I'm going to start all over, and I know where to begin.*

The image of the woman he could not dishonor, the stranger whose questions struck at the very core of his being, stood large and clear with him in the cell. Her whole being exhibited truth and righteousness, not through power but through openness. Her face radiated compassion, and her voice lacked fear. This image said *life* to Zenas.

He thought of Leah, the teenage daughter of the Palestinian slave in his parents' home, the one he had hounded as a very young boy, begging her to teach him the language of her mother's homeland. It was Leah's mother who Mary reminded him of. She had the same fearlessness and sense that something more important than her condition of slavery mattered most. Hatred of her condition had not overshadowed her compassion.

Well past midnight, Zenas heard someone being locked into the next cell.

Presently, he heard soft sobs coming from that cell. He also heard someone talking softly, consoling the one sobbing. He heard a woman's voice he knew he had heard before. He strained to hear what they said.

"We must be brave," she was saying. "And we can't let them think that we know where Simon is. He's in real danger now."

Just then, Zenas heard the voice of Gaius, the second in command, approaching the next cell. He spoke in Greek. Our law does not allow us to retain you once we have determined that you are not hiding a criminal. However, we are not convinced that you don't know where Simon is hiding. He is wanted for inciting the violence that has overtaken this city. Your cooperation will hasten your release."

Mary's voice was firm. "First of all, he is the last person to incite violence. We have no idea where my son Simon is. He was with us yesterday, but he went away very upset. ."

As Mary was talking, Gaius would not look her in the eyes. His eyes darted all around the cell, as if he were tracing the flight of a fly. As soon as she stopped talking, he turned and left the cell. He stepped around the corner to Zenas's cell and motioned for him to come close.

He whispered to Zenas, "We can't hold them much longer. If you hear anything from them concerning the whereabouts of this

Simon, it will help your situation to pass that information along to us." He turned and left.

Zenas recognized these two as the women he had visited yesterday. Strange sensations came over him as he remembered the eyes of the younger woman.

Once the sound of Gaius's footsteps faded away, Zenas said softly, "I am Zenas the—"

The women both gasped. They had thought they were alone. The sound of a man's voice startled them.

"Please forgive me. I didn't mean to scare you. I guess you had no idea I was here. I'm the centurion who came to your house yesterday. My name is Zenas. You don't know how I regret the horror I forced on you yesterday. I am truly sorry."

Mary recognized his voice immediately. Salome couldn't associate the soft deep voice with the terror she remembered from yesterday. His voice, here in this damp cell, actually felt comforting.

"I am Mary, and my daughter Salome is here with me. We do not hold your actions against you. You were most respectful of us, and we are thankful for that. The bruises on our arms show that the soldiers who came in the middle of the night were not as respectful as you. Are you being punished for your kindness?"

"Yes. Apparently, being a soldier in an occupied country does not call for respect." Zenas could not help but notice how her voice soothed him and made him feel at ease.

They were interrupted by someone coming. A woman approached the women's cell. Zenas continued to listen.

"Rachael, what are you doing here?" exclaimed Mary.

"I had this dream that something awful happened to you. I couldn't get back to sleep and walked over to your house. The neighbors, who were all up and agitated by what happened to you, told me you were arrested. I begged to come and see you. I was so worried. Are you all right? What have you done? Why are they retaining you? What is going on?" Rachael's questions tumbled out like water overflowing a fountain.

"They are holding us because they think we have information about where Simon is," Salome explained. "They want to arrest Simon because they think he is behind all the killings and violence in the temple."

"Simon? That's ridiculous!"

"You know that, we know that, but the Romans don't know that," said Mary. "He's in trouble, and we don't even know if he knows it."

"Oh, he knows it; he wanted to come here to make sure you were all right. The others wouldn't let him and sent me instead."

"Goodness, they will follow you! You will lead them right to him!" moaned Salome.

Rachael assured them that they had thought about that. She told them she would not be going back to Simon. "In fact," she whispered, "Simon is leaving town tonight. Many of the opposition leaders are fleeing the city for a while."

"Where will they go?" asked Mary.

"I'm not sure. Pella, Galilee, and beyond Jericho were the places mentioned," replied Rachael.

"At least he'll be away from here," said Mary.

Zenas tried not to listen, but his curiosity would not let him close his ears.

As soon as Rachael left, Gaius returned to Zenas's cell. "What did you find out?"

Zenas saw right through the game Gaius was playing: speaking loud enough so those in the next cell could hear him betray what he had learned. He wasn't going to play along. "You're wasting your time holding those two. They have no idea where Simon is. Possibly, the Roman army could do better than harassing some defenseless women." Zenas knew he had said too much, but he also realized he had withheld some vital information.

Gaius raised his hand, as if to strike Zenas. "You are begging to pull oars for a galley!" He turned and left.

"What bravery to speak to a superior so truthfully!" Mary said, after Gaius departed. "I hope the Lord will protect such bravery and bless you."

"Sadly, dear woman, the Roman gods are less powerful than the emperor and his governors."

Salome realized she was actually wishing she could get another look at this man who had appeared yesterday to be a monster.

"Perhaps, you are looking to the wrong gods," said Mary. "There is only one God, the God who created all, before whom everyone, governors and emperors included, will stand in judgment. This God of Israel respects such bravery and blesses righteousness."

For the rest of that day and into the night, Zenas worked on the loose ring anchor. During the time Mary and Salome were being released, he was careful not to make any sounds. He brushed the crumbled mortar into a dark corner, and stood blocking the ring when the guard was present. Before the guard made his early morning rounds, Zenas had freed the ring anchor, looped the chain around his neck, and replaced the anchor so that it looked undisturbed. He then assumed a position looking like he had hung himself with his chains. The poor light from the guard's torch conveyed the image Zenas hoped for. The guard opened the cell door and entered. As he moved close to Zenas, he realized too late that he had been fooled. He was no match for Zenas, who knocked him unconscious. With the guard's keys, he freed himself from the chains and placed them on the guard. Taking the keys with him, he escaped, unnoticed, from the fortress.

Still shaking from their prison experience, Mary and Salome sat in the rear room of their house, thinking of Zenas.

Mary said, "I feel sad for Zenas, but it's comforting to see that real compassion can exist under Roman armor."

"I feel so awful for him," said Salome. "He will probably

be killed by those butchers, or shipped off to a galley to slowly die. Why are men so cruel? It doesn't seem manly to me at all. Sometimes I think men should have one male eye and one female eye. That way, they might see things a little differently."

The next afternoon, after returning from Poor Town, Mary and Salome were met in front of their home by a troubled neighbor. "I'm sure there is a stranger in your house. About one hour ago, a large man just walked in your front door. He has not come out."

"What are we going to do, Mama?" asked Salome.

"He probably left when you weren't looking, or maybe went out the back," explained Mary. "We certainly don't have anything of value for him to take. Let's go in and see what damage he did."

"What if he is still in there?" Salome was truly frightened. "Maybe we should get Joshua to go in with us."

"I'm going in," said Mary.

There was no one in the front room, and nothing was disturbed. As Mary entered the back room she saw a man in a toga standing in the corner. His face was in the shadows. He said, "Don't be afraid, Mary."

As soon as she heard him say her name, Mary knew it was Zenas. "What are you doing here?" she asked.

"I'm sorry to bring you trouble. I've been in this city only a few days and don't know where to go. Albinus will not think to look for me here. I overpowered my guard and escaped. The anchor for my chains was loose, and I was able to free myself. I need help to escape this city. I didn't know where else to go."

Just then, Salome entered the room and swallowed a scream. Who was this strange man? His size was intimidating. She turned and ran out of the room. Something made her stop before she ran out of the house. *Mama! She's in there alone with that strange man. But she wasn't afraid. She was standing there with him.* Salome turned and slowly moved back toward the room. She heard them talking. She knew that voice; it wasn't a stranger. Then, it dawned on her. Could it be? This was the voice of the man in the cell next to them yesterday. She went to the doorway and looked in.

"Zenas, is that really you?"

"Yes, I'm sorry to have frightened you. I'm on the run, and I need help." Zenas tried to make it sound matter-of-fact. Once again, he noticed her eyes. They were so alive, yet there was real fear in them.

"They will come right here for you," explained Salome.

"Why? Why would they assume there was any connection between us? Besides, they believe I have escaped with a caravan going to Damascus. I traded my soldier's uniform for this toga with a merchant only too glad to put one over on the Romans. The last thing I want to do is make any trouble for you; I just didn't know where else to go. Please just help me get out of Jerusalem."

"Salome, first go and assure Miriam that everything is all right. She must not suspect that Zenas is still here," Mary instructed. "Then we have to figure out what to do."

"What shall I tell her? You know how nosy she is!"

"Tell her that it was probably someone intending to rob us and, finding nothing, apparently left out the back way." Mary tried not to betray the truth.

Salome knew that such an answer would not go far in assaying Miriam's curiosity, so she embellished the story just a little. Miriam seemed to be satisfied.

Mary, fully conscious of Zenas's plight, knew the difficulty they faced in finding him a means of escape. "We will need some time to figure this out. Zenas may have to stay here for a few days until I can make connections for his escape."

"Mama, do you know what you are saying?" asked Salome incredulously. "Zenas, eating and sleeping in our house!"

"The Lord brought him to us! Are we to turn our backs or slap the Lord in the face?" Mary asked sternly. "I'm not sure why the Lord brought him to us, but this man was kind to us and even protected us when we were in the prison. The least we can do is repay his kindness. Sometimes, it appears, God has strange ways of teaching Torah. Do you forget the lesson Jesus taught concerning the Samaritan who helped the injured man, while the priest and Levi ignored him to protect their purity?"

Salome was flustered. Fear that some Roman official would knock on the door any minute consumed her. Zenas would be killed on the spot, and they would be taken away—this time, to rot in prison. Other more mundane questions filled her mind. What dishes should she use? Should she follow the standard cooking and table practices? Or, should they be suspended as long as there was a Gentile in the house? She couldn't understand why her mother seemed so comfortable with the situation. She also knew that below all this agitation, a strange strong force drew her to this young man.

Later, they were sitting in the middle room, lit by a single candle. Zenas was full of questions. His interest focused on this extraordinary woman who sat with him. Why was it so easy for her to accept her situation, regardless how precarious, and immediately take hold of it to make the best of it? She seemed to have no fear. Yet she also seemed to have a resolve that almost implied that someone else, who guided and protected her, was telling her what to do. Yet she displayed none of the arrogance that usually accompanied such assuredness. She seemed to trust the future more than the present. She truly amazed him, and baffled him.

He tried to make some sense of these questions. "You amaze me! You seem to not get rattled, regardless of your situation. I don't know if I have ever met a soldier who is as fearless as you. What is your secret?"

Mary, a bit flustered by the flattery, replied, "There is no secret. My *life* is a gift, a blessing from God. To react to what befalls me in any other way than to accept it graciously and with responsibility, is an insult to God. I'm here, so I already have my blessing. My response must be to glorify the giver of that blessing by living righteously. Most people try to fit God into their own selves. Selfishness causes them see things as if they are the center, so everything is happening *to* them. God, the Creator of all, is the center, a presence everywhere and in everything. All creation is God's kingdom, readily available to all. Life's task is to honor our connection to God. If I see God in terms of what is happening to me, I will be angry with God much of the time. Selfishness imprisons me in my own ignorance and shortcomings, blinding me to the true presence of God."

There was a pause, and Zenas was almost ashamed to break the silence. "But in the few days since I met you, your life has been anything but blessed. And your eyes reveal a pain you are struggling desperately to keep from overwhelming you. What pain are you repressing?"

Mary could barely hold back the tears. To be with someone so perceptive and sensitive generated tears of joy, which could now so easily overflow on the wave of tears for her murdered son that she was stoically resisting. "I certainly did not mean to imply that there has been no sadness in my life. Indeed, I am just this close (she held up her hand with the thumb and first finger almost touching) to being overcome with grief over the recent death of my son James, who was killed by Ananus; killed for no other reason than because he displayed all the goodness and righteousness that Ananus, as high priest, should have demonstrated. James was the true protector of the temple's holiness, while Ananus only perverted it."

Zenas knew nothing about the Jewish temple or what it meant to protect its holiness, but he was well aware of James's murder and the role Ananus had played in it. Indeed, it had been the total focus of his leader, Albinus, ever since their arrival in Jerusalem. "So, James was your son? Does that mean he was the brother of Simon?"

"Yes, they are two of my five boys. Only Simon remains; three of the other four were murdered by the authorities." Mary's voice was now so low, Zenas could barely hear her.

Zenas felt a pang of guilt. He knew his visit to her house the other night had shocked her already broken heart. "Please forgive my brutality the other night. I had no idea of the pain I was imposing on you."

"You are kind to recognize that, but I must say that your behavior was not offensive. You conducted yourself with great integrity, to your own detriment." Mary had regained her composure and was able to affect her words with the gratitude and respect she truly felt.

Zenas was confused. What was this woman not telling him? Her assuredness and the tragedies of her life did not compute. He would have been furious. He would have cursed every god and demanded an explanation. Yet this woman viewed her god as blessing her, even though, to Zenas, all she had received was misery. "You confound me. You are obviously not telling me the whole story. Please fill me in so that I can make sense of a woman I truly admire. What is behind your strength: your lack of fear and resentment in the face of such tragedy, and your assuredness of the future?"

Mary sighed. "It's such a long story. I hope I can tell it in a way that will make sense to you. It started with the message of my son Jesus. He lived and taught that the kingdom of God was upon us and that we have to live by its truth: that God is love. We Jews see God as the Creator of all that is, and above all other gods. He is contained in all existence and experience, but he is really beyond our full comprehension. We only know God by his nature, which is love. Love is the state when existence and experience are in complete harmony, when creation is fully in step with God's intention. Jesus's message and life demonstrated that only humility can reveal this love of God. So, our homage to God is expressed through a humble faith."

"By Jupiter!" exclaimed Zenas. "Move over, Seneca, make room for truth! I'm not mocking you. I have never expected anything so profound. Well, maybe I did. While this all is new to me, it fits easily into my understanding. Only the last part confuses me. Why do you say homage can only be demonstrated through humility? Isn't an honest quest for righteousness a clearer way to exhibit faith and pay homage?"

"I think most well-meaning persons believe that. To be sure, the pursuit of righteousness pays homage and reveals faith." Mary paused and took a long time before continuing, obviously swallowing some tears. "Jesus tragically showed me the folly of that way." Mary's eyes seemed to look far away, but they sparkled so that Zenas could not look away. "His life and teachings, and his horrendous death, clearly demonstrated to me the difference between faith as humility and faith as beliefs demanding a passionate zeal for righteousness."

"Say more." Zenas had no idea where this was going, but he wanted nothing more than to find out. "Who was this Jesus? What did he teach, and how did he die?"

"He was a wonderful rabbi," Mary began. "You would have liked him. He was so popular a teacher that crowds gathered to hear him teach. He could heal the sick, and demons ran from him. The heart of his message was that the kingdom of God was here now, that God was right now establishing his kingdom of righteousness, and we were all called to be active agents of this kingdom. I am so proud of him; it is a message not only for Jews but for everyone!"

"What did he mean by the kingdom of God? Was it an ethereal or spiritual thing? If not, wasn't it a terribly dangerous position to take?" Zenas couldn't imagine someone spreading such teachings if they were supposed to apply to all of life, especially Roman life.

"No, it is not spiritual or ethereal; it is the real thing," Mary continued. "Jesus taught that the kingdom of God meant that God, as love, is the only supreme ruler and that we, his subjects, are directly accountable to God. Repentance for unrighteous behavior and a complete dedication to righteousness are required. You are right; it is a dangerous message. In fact, it got him killed!"

These words were spoken so softly and sorrowfully that Zenas could barely hear them. He felt bad about bringing up such painful memories to this lovely woman. "I'm sorry for leading you to such a sad place. Please forgive me."

"How could you know that your interest would bring me such pain? I am grateful for your consideration." Something deep inside told her that his questions came from a good place, and she wanted to tell him more. "Jesus's message and popularity aroused the people, who were looking for a liberator from Roman domination. They began to look at him as the one who could reestablish the kingdom of David and bring on the final judgment of God and the rule of righteousness. This was not his message, but many of the more radical claimed him their Messiah, the one who would bring about this revolution.

"He was drawing huge crowds in and around Jerusalem, and both the religious and the Roman leaders were well aware of his popularity. One day, he went into the temple and condemned the profane activities being conducted there. This act so aroused the people that they wanted to make him king. The religious leaders had enough. They arrested him, and in a little more than a day, he was crucified."

"Crucified?" asked Zenas incredulously. "Was he judged by Roman law to be worthy of crucifixion? They must have seen his movement as a serious insurrection."

"His trials were a joke," Mary responded. "The high priest tried to convict him through the Jewish courts and could not. They tried to get the Roman governor, Pontius Pilate, to condemn him. Looking for a way out, he sent Jesus to King Herod. Herod, afraid to decide because he feared the people, shuttled him directly back to Pontius Pilate. That tyrant, sop that he was, consulted his wife rather than holding a proper trial. I don't know if placating the Jewish leaders, fear of the crowds, or just his normal appetite for cruelty led him to decide, but he authorized Jesus's crucifixion. It was a total miscarriage of justice. My son was brutally murdered for doing nothing but preach love, which threatened the tyrannical hypocrisy of religious and political egotists. They killed the best man who ever lived. He lived within God's kingdom of love and made it real for others."

Mary's voice softened to a whisper, her eyes wet with tears, hands clenched tightly in her lap. Zenas felt terrible for bringing her such agony. His guilt blocked him from causing her any more pain or arousing memories of afflictions she had never fully shed. He stood up to indicate the conversation was over. Her story certainly confirmed all he had heard about Pontius Pilate, and why he had been unceremoniously returned to Rome in disgrace. Such shoddy dealings were a horrible example of Roman justice. But Zenas hadn't heard enough to tell him why Jesus's life, message, and death made Mary so sure that humility was the true expression of faith. Hopefully, he could pursue that question some other time, in a way that did not bring her such pain.

Salome, who had been sitting back in the corner, listening and thoroughly enjoying watching this man and listening to him speak, now said, "Mama, Miriam will start asking questions if she sees light over here much longer. We never stay up this late."

"Yes," agreed Mary. "We should figure out sleeping arrangements."

"I'll just sleep on the floor. … No, I'll leave now." Zenas was beginning to realize how difficult a problem he was making for these two kind women. He just wanted to get out and remove this sword of danger from over their heads.

"We won't hear of it," Mary quickly replied. "God brought you here for a reason, and we will find out soon enough why you have been brought into our lives. But you were partly right. The only place we have for you to sleep is on the floor … somewhere. I guess the back room is best. Salome, make a bed for him on the floor."

Lying awake, staring at the ceiling, Salome finally had enough.

She sat up, and before she could say anything, Mary said, "You can't find sleep either?"

"No! Your conversation with Zenas earlier keeps going around in my head." Salome was puzzled but strangely comforted by what she had heard.

"Oh! I have been trying to figure out what to do about Zenas. He's in a great deal of trouble, and we are certainly not able to help in any meaningful way. He can't stay here long." Mary then thought about what Salome had said. "What about our conversation has you agitated?"

"I don't know that it is any one thing; really it's more the way you were talking. Most of the radicals see Jesus as the Messiah King who will come back and throw off the Romans and reestablish David's kingdom here in Jerusalem. That talk has always scared me. It has to mean much violence and suffering. It has never made any sense to me. But, tonight, as you were telling Zenas about Jesus and who he was and what happened to him, it sounded so different. As you were talking, I began to think of the messiah not as a person, but as something else, an event or situation. That's such a soothing thought. When Jesus announced the presence of the kingdom of God, did he mean that was the messiah? Am I talking crazy now?"

"Maybe you were just listening differently. Maybe the presence of Zenas, who has no idea of our history, beliefs, or religion, allowed you to listen from a different position." Mary wasn't sure she wanted to go on. She knew she was feeling differently. The three violent deaths of her sons were like sledgehammer blows to her faith. Her faith in God would not be broken, but these events and the terrible unrest within all of Judaism had her thoughts and beliefs in a burlap bag that was having the devil shaken out of it. Salome knew her too well not to notice.

Mary decided to go on. "Now, with James gone, Simon is the only one of Jesus's brothers left. I've always felt that none of the other disciples fully understood Jesus. They all seemed to have their own ideas about who he was and what he should do. They were always arguing and pushing him this way and that. His brothers were the only ones who really seemed to be at ease with Jesus. Maybe this is just a mother speaking. Did you ever get that feeling?"

Salome thought for a moment. "I was pretty young. I was more infatuated with most of them, so my attention was divided. But, surely, the Iscariot had strong feelings about who Jesus should be. And, Peter, the Big Bear, seemed never really quite in step. You're not including Mary when you say that, are you?"

"Certainly not," Mary agreed. "She and Jesus had such a special beautiful relationship. If anyone knew what he was thinking, it was she. Mercy, I miss her so!" There was a long pause, followed by a soft sob. "Her disappearance still troubles me greatly. I'm sure someone wanted her gone; but, who, why?"

There was another long pause before Mary continued. "Oh, do I miss her! She was so good at remembering what Jesus said. She, not the men, was the one able to go inside and see what Jesus's teachings meant. We desperately need her counsel now! I'm so worried! At first, we all seemed to know what Jesus's reappearance meant: that God had ushered in messiah, that we were to be renewed from the inside out, spread this news and prepare the temple for Jesus's return. But then, some started to get ideas about what God was doing, started arguing that Jesus said this and didn't say that. Now we have some going away into the desert, awaiting Jesus's return, while others carry blades under their clothing to rid the temple of impious priests. We even have preachers like Paul. When he was in Jerusalem, I didn't recognize the Jesus he was preaching about. It is obvious he never met him, heard him preach, or listened to him teach. All this troubles me so. Sometimes I wish I could just get it all out of my mind." She yawned and said, "I want to stop talking about it now and try to get some sleep. We have a lot to take care of tomorrow."

Zenas, too, struggled to find sleep. Finally, he got up and

climbed the steps to the upper level. He silently walked past the room the women were sleeping in and continued on up to the roof. The cool night air filled his lungs, somewhat softening the tension gripping him since his escape. He looked up at the imposing wall of the temple. What an impressive structure! His eyes continued up into the night sky, the myriad of stars making him feel very small. He sighed as he thought of the situation he was in. His thoughts went to Rome and to a happier time when he was a boy just turning into a young man. He thought of Marieanne and his first kiss. He remembered how he thought the world had stopped. Then, she ran away, giggling, and that world fell apart. There were a number of Marieanne kisses after that, none ever matching the first. He always knew the day would come when she would run away again. But, ultimately, he ran away, to become a soldier. He looked at the stars and wondered if he would ever see Rome again, or experience another kiss.

A soft noise on the stairs wakened him from his reverie. Salome's head appeared out of the stairwell. As she reached the top of the stairwell, she saw Zenas. She gasped and immediately grabbed the shawl covering her shoulders, took it over her head, and wrapped it across her face, leaving only her eyes exposed.

Zenas smiled. "You are leaving exposed that which has haunted me since I first laid eyes on you. Cover whatever you feel necessary, but never your enchanting eyes."

Salome was obviously surprised to see Zenas. "I did not expect to find you here. Please forgive me for intruding on your privacy."

"A more pleasurable interruption I can't imagine. Assuming your presence is an intrusion mocks the feelings I have upon seeing you." Zenas felt awkward. He didn't want to say anything that would chase her away. "Why did you come up here in the middle of the night?"

"I was wondering the same of you." Salome, surprised by how comfortable she felt with this stranger, found it easy to talk to him, a feeling she seldom felt in the presence of men, especially men she didn't know. She slipped the shawl from her head and let it fall to her shoulders.

"I asked you first." Zenas leaned against the parapet wall and motioned for Salome to come sit on a bench nearby.

"I often come up here when I can't sleep. Here, under the sky, I feel closer to God, and many of my anxieties shrink to mere problems." Salome walked over near the bench.

Zenas smiled at her turn of words. "And what anxieties might you have that brought you here this night?"

"You, for one. I dread to think of what your future holds. I don't know anything about you, but I really like you and don't want anything bad to happen to you."

Zenas was touched by her concern. He also could not stop looking at her eyes. They seemed to reflect the starlight tenfold. "I am truly sorry for bringing my problems and laying them on your doorstep. I see now how grave an error that was. You and your mother have more grief than you can handle right now, and I selfishly placed you in grave danger. You don't know how close I came to walking out of this house tonight instead of coming up here. I'm still not sure why I didn't leave"

"Why *did* you come up here instead?" Salome sat on the bench.

"Maybe it was because of your eyes." Zenas moved over and sat on the bench beside Salome.

Salome jumped up and moved away a few steps. Seeing the look on Zenas's face, she was sorry she had reacted so emphatically. It was obvious that he did not intend to frighten her. She took one step back to him. "You were not thinking of my eyes when I came up here. Your thoughts were legions away from here."

"Yes, you saw me thinking of home, a place that seems farther away now than it ever did."

"Do you miss it, or wish you were back there?"

"I'm not sure I can answer yes to either of those questions." Zenas paused, with a sad expression on his face. "Rome has changed. ... Or, have I changed? As a boy growing up, Rome appeared to be the solution to all the world's problems. But, the older I get and the more I become familiar with the forces of power, the less I like what Rome is."

Zenas stopped. Looking into Salome's eyes, he could tell she listened only halfheartedly. "You really don't care what I think about Rome, do you?"

"Escaping prison and running away from your garrison tells me all I need to know of your thoughts of Rome. You have obviously chosen to take a new pathway." Salome came back to the bench and sat next to Zenas. "Do you know how precarious your situation is? You can't hide anywhere in Jerusalem. With your size, you'll stick out like a camel in a herd of donkeys. I'm worried sick about you."

Once again, guilt swept over Zenas. "See, me being here has brought you nothing but grief and danger."

Salome put her hand on Zenas's arm. "Please stop saying that. I was shocked when my mother said you should stay with us and reacted in a way that surely said to you that I didn't want you here. I was wrong; my mother was right. I'm glad you came back to us. I'm glad you're here."

The sparkle in Zenas's eyes made Salome wonder if she had been too open. Zenas placed his hand on hers. "I can't remember the last time I received the kind of compassion you and your mother have showered on me. I will spend the rest of my life seeking ways to repay you."

Salome looked up into Zenas's face and, with tears forming in her eyes, said, "You speak as if you have a long life ahead of you. Do you really think you can get away from the Romans? What kind of a life will you have if they catch you?"

"I fully intend to escape, but if they catch me, I will be lucky if I spend the rest of my days a galley oarsman. More likely, I will be crucified as an example of the fate of deserters."

Salome shuddered at this last comment. Zenas, recognizing her reaction, knew immediately the hurt exposed by his thoughtless choice of words. He walked to the parapet wall and, with his back to Salome, said, "I do nothing but hurt you kind people. The sooner I am away from you, the better."

Salome hurried over to him and, placing one hand on the small of his back, said, "You cannot get away from this place too soon, but it pains me to think of not being able to get to know you better."

Zenas turned around and placed his hands on Salome's shoulders. She looked up at him, and her expression softened as she realized she did not have the impulse to pull away. Her raven eyes sparkled, and his heart began pound.

"There is nothing in this world I would like more than learning all about you." Zenas's voice was so low, he was almost whispering. "Something deep within me says that the secret to life lies in knowing you. If not for the danger I bring to this house, you and your mother together would not be strong enough to cast me out."

While the twinkle in his eye assured Salome of the lightheartedness of this comment, the warm and tender grasp of his hands on her shoulders suggested there might be more truth than humor in his last statement. Her hands now on his upper arms, she said, "It would be lovely if conditions allowed us to get to know each other better."

He pulled her close and wrapped his arms around her. Salome tensed, sensing that her words might have suggested something beyond her intentions. Other sensations were fighting for recognition. Unable to remember the last time she was in a man's arms, she realized she felt safe. Perhaps the tension was not from anxiety but excitement. The tension began to subside, and she found herself aware of the beating of not only her own heart but also his. She turned her head slightly and allowed it to rest on his shoulder. More muscles relaxed, and her hands slipped around his back in a soft embrace.

Zenas wasn't sure what made him pull her close, but he embraced her strongly. He could sense her tension and wondered if he had done the wrong thing. Slowly she seemed to relax and respond to his embrace. He planted a kiss on the top of her head.

Salome felt the kiss, which went tingling down her spine and rested in a warm spot in the pit of her stomach. She felt her heart racing and wondered if Zenas could feel it too.

His heart was racing, and he could feel his body coming alive. He tried to hide that from her and realized she was also trying to avoid it; yet she did not pull away from him. It was this that spurred him to speak. Pushing her away but keeping his hands tenderly on her shoulders, he said, "Our hearts resist where are bodies wish to go. My respect for you far outshines any erogenous urges. Your embrace has been a moment in paradise, and I will cherish it forever."

With tears of joy, Salome responded, "I have never felt more loved; and I believe I felt paradise too."

They embraced again, and this time, shared a lingering kiss.

Salome pulled away. "Now I know I can sleep."

"Pleasant dreams; mine have already started." Zenas followed her down the stairs and then proceeded on down to the first floor, where he fell into a deep sleep.

Mary awoke when Salome came back into the room, but did not let on that she was awake. She was amazed at how quickly Salome was asleep. She couldn't help but notice how calmly and serenely she breathed.

In the morning, Mary found Zenas already up and sitting in the back room. "You are up early."

"Yes. But I had a glorious sleep." Zenas kept his voice to almost a whisper. The houses were so close together, and he didn't want anyone to know he was there. "For a few hours, I slept like a baby. I know I was dreaming because I could feel myself smiling, but I can't remember anything about the dreams. One thing I know, in those precious hours, my problems flew away. What a blessing!"

"You don't know how good that makes me feel. I'm so worried about you, and I can't think of how to get you safely out of here.

I feel like a mother hen with a fox just outside the door." Mary immediately saw the pained look on Zenas's face and realized she should not have said that.

Speaking louder than he should, Zenas said, "What a scoundrel I am to bring such worry to a woman already burdened with unimaginable sadness." He walked over to the doorway to the rear of the house.

Mary, afraid that he would walk away, rushed over to him. Grabbing his hand and putting one finger to her lips, she said, "Please. God brought us together; nothing could be clearer to me. We will find a way to get you away from here."

Just then, Salome walked into the room wondering what was going on: her mother was holding Zenas's hand, and the two of them stood by the rear door. "Am I interrupting something?" she said with a smile.

A warm smile came over Zenas's face. "Your mother just stopped me from leaving and lifting this heavy yoke of danger off you kind women." Zenas returned to talking in a whisper.

"You don't know her, but I can tell you she has always known what's best. Please let us help you get out of Jerusalem; it's what we want to do."

Mary couldn't help but notice how Salome's attitude had changed from the past evening. "Let's get something to eat and then figure out a plan."

Zenas was amazed at how quickly and effortlessly the two women had a fire going and some thin cakes heated, which they ate along with some olives and cheese. They drank some tea laced with sage.

A plan apparently formed in Mary's mind, because, as soon as they finished eating, Mary said, "Zenas, you must stay up on the second floor while Salome and I seek help. I don't want one of the nosy neighbors coming in here and finding you. Salome, you go to Sarah to see what she can suggest. I'm going to the Sheep Market to see a trusted friend."

Zenas sat on the floor in a corner of one of the upper rooms. How awkward for this healthy young man to sit waiting for two women to sort out his fate! Rather than a tremendous blow to his manhood, he was grateful for their help. He couldn't get to the bottom of his admiration of Mary—her openness, her fearlessness, and her compassion. Where did she get the strength to shoulder the burdens she was enduring? No one he'd ever met, not even Caesar, had such inner strength. Furthermore, the injustices life showered on her would make even the strongest-willed person bitter and hateful. Yet she seemed to love and spread goodness in the face of the most horrible tragedies. Was she an angel?

And Salome—what a gift she had given to him. Her concern and tenderness opened up in him a whole new vista of his manhood. Women had always excited his sensuality, but, last night—and he was not sure how or why—she had helped him realize that sensuality without the heart was as wrong as the mind without the heart. What a blessing she had been to him! He longed to be alone with her again to explore this new world, which could only be called love.

The women were gone a long time. Zenas slept on and off, and waited impatiently, wondering what they were doing. The sun was well past its zenith when the women returned. They brought with them some common clothes and a hairpiece.

Mary explained, "I think we have made good arrangements for you to get out of the city. My nephew is leaving for Palmyra later today. He and a friend signed on as laborers with a caravan. He told the leader of the caravan they had a friend who had to go with them, who was weak-minded and so needed to be with them at all times; he assured the man that he was big and strong and would do anything they asked him to do. The caravan driver accepted when he realized he could pay only two for the work of three. You are that friend. The caravan is forming outside the Lion's Gate, and we have to get you there as soon as possible. I wish we could wait until after dark, but that will not be possible."

Salome came up to Zenas, with a wig and fake beard. "Your Roman cut will not do. We are going to make you into an opposition priest so that we can get you out of here."

Their eyes met, and both knew they wanted to talk. This was not the time.

Zenas put on a white priest's robe, noticeably short and not nearly as loosely fitting as was conventional, but, with his hairpiece and beard, he no longer looked like a Roman. He really looked rather comical, and Salome remarked, "You certainly look the part of a dullard. Do you think you have what it takes to act like one?"

All three had a good laugh, a welcome relief to the tension of the moment. They left out the back door and went down through the Dung Gate into Poor Town.

They hurried to the head of the Kidron Valley, began following the northern wall of the Temple Mount, heading toward the Lion's Gate. Just as they were leaving Poor Town, another priest joined them, and he and Zenas walked well ahead of Mary and Salome. Zenas wondered when he would get a chance to talk to Salome. He had so much he wanted to say to her.

The women followed the two priests, keeping them within sight. Salome believed she was watching Zenas walk out of her life. Her feelings were tumbling over one another: respect and admiration, sadness, lost opportunity, emptiness over what might have been. She found herself fighting back tears. Most of all, she regretted not being able to tell him how much she respected him, and not having the chance to thank him for one of the most precious moments of her life.

The caravan driver was getting nervous. "We must leave now if we are to get to Jericho before dark. Jacob, you said your friend would be here; I counted on his help. Where is he?"

Jacob saw the two priests coming. "He's here now. That's him there, the tall one." Jacob pointed to the two priests approaching.

The driver shouted, "What? A priest? You said he was a laborer. What kind of game are you playing?"

Jacob turned to the driver and said in a whisper, "Please, don't scare him. When he got to Jerusalem, he saw all the priests and wanted to be a priest. Believe me, when we get away from Jerusalem, he will be all I promised, and more."

"All right, he's your responsibility. Get to your positions; we have to leave immediately."

Mary and Salome had just come up to Jacob and Zenas. "Grandmother, we have to leave immediately. We will take care of him," Jacob said, pointing to Zenas.

Mary went over to Zenas and gave him a big hug. "God bless you and keep you safe."

Jacob was motioning for Zenas, who said to Mary, "I'll never forget what you did for me, but, more importantly, I'll never forget you. God has blessed me by letting me meet you."

Salome ran up and embraced Zenas, whispering into his ear, "Thank you!"

"No—thank *you!*" Their eyes met, and, immediately, they each knew the source and depth of the other's gratitude.

Jacob grabbed Zenas's arm and roughly pulled him toward the rear of the caravan. Zenas stumbled after him, assuming his role.

CHAPTER 6

THE RULERS

The new governor, Albinus, paced back and forth across the room, slapping the side of his sword blade against his upper thigh. Compounding the horrendous mess caused by the high priest, Ananus, the disappearance of Zenas could be a huge problem for him. Albinus was well aware of Zenas's connections back in Rome. The thought that this was not just a simple escape, but, rather, a move by someone higher up, fed his paranoia. He couldn't imagine how anyone in Rome could have already heard of Zenas's imprisonment, but anything was possible when it came to Rome. He had to be careful about how he handled this. He let all his anger out on Gaius, his second in command. "Don't let any stone go unturned. I want this traitor captured immediately."

Albinus's frustration almost consumed him. He had to get control of the situation quickly, or his term as governor would be the shortest on record. He knew nothing about this city or its strange people. Never before had he seen a whole city just stop everything for an entire day every week. Not even the strange people in the mountains of Hispania or on the isles of Britannia were this crazy. He really didn't like this city; in fact, to say he hated it was probably more accurate. Emperor Nero had assured him that King Herod Agrippa II would be cooperative in his efforts. Albinus had to get in touch with the king right away. He would welcome the king's cooperation, but Rome was now in total control. A frustrated angry eagle had landed, ready to crush these hapless insurgents.

Albinus's wrath continued to rain down on Gaius. "These rats are about to feel Rome's power! This pitiful collection of religious radicals is about to be introduced to what it takes to maintain an ordered society. The time for playing patty-cake is over. I want this Simon, the brother of James, arrested immediately. My report says he may be a key to unlock this mess. Also, round up all the ringleaders of the radical groups that go by the names of Zealots and Essenes. We have to get to the source of this madness."

Gaius shrugged his shoulders. "You give me the names of the leaders, and I'll have them standing before you by noon." He knew Albinus had no better idea who was behind this violence than he did. He attempted to summarize the situation for Albinus. "The trouble seems to come out of the very stones in the streets and walls of this strange city. Nobody appears to be in charge. I swear, everyone claims to be a priest, and every priest seems to have a different leader. All of a sudden, a priest sticks a knife in the side of some other priest or a temple guard. They are getting bolder. The last three murders happened in broad daylight. Boisterous arguments erupt out of many conversations, and some groups do not hesitate to react to authority by throwing rocks. I think a place called Poor Town is where most of the insurgents hide out. It appears that our most-reliable allies are a group called the Pharisees. They appear to be the most rational, truly concerned about the unrest and most willing to cooperate in putting it down."

Albinus did not hesitate. "Contact these Pharisees immediately. Get names from them of who might be the leaders or instigators. Cast a broad net, and get anyone closely related with those persons out of this city. Split the groups up, not along family lines, and send some to Caesarea, some to Jaffa, and even to Alexandria if necessary. We have to stop this immediately."

As Gaius was leaving, Albinus called him back. "I want to see

King Herod Agrippa. Make sure the Herodian princess named Bernice comes along with him. I hear she is his sister, or wife. I have been told that she can be very helpful in navigating the stormy political waters that swirl around the various Jewish factions." Albinus's cursory briefing on the nature of the Jewish establishment, and the sharp divisions between those who claimed to be the political leaders of the Jews and the religious factions who looked with disdain on the leaders, suggested that Bernice had connections with both sides.

Albinus knew he had entered a hornet's nest, but he had no idea of the religious motivations that were behind the various groups and factions. He would soon learn that the unrest he faced had many heads, each of which was suspicious of the other, so he could trust none of the information he received. Furthermore, the apocalyptic atmosphere threatened insurrection and chaos at every moment. He could not rid himself of the feeling that the massive power of Rome and the order it symbolized was going to be challenged right here in Jerusalem, in a significant way, in the near future.

Ananus sat silent, a broken man. His efforts to gain control of the temple had failed miserably, greatly increasing the influence of the opposition priests. These radicals then ratcheted up their efforts to purify the temple, encouraged by their increased support from the masses. Doing away with the popular priest James had not stopped the insurgency; rather, it only escalated it. What a gross miscalculation! Isolated at Herod's desert retreat now, with only a few loyal priests, he was powerless to influence anything that was going on in Jerusalem.

In Jerusalem, a few leaders of the Sanhedrin were meeting with the remaining members of the high priest's staff.

Judah was furious. "We are being slaughtered! We have no protection. The radicals have begun labeling us as Herodians because of our silence on the king's incestuous behavior. They are trying to keep us from entering the temple. We are the targets of their ridicule and their knives. The people look on us as fools. The lesser priests have all the respect. We look like hypocrites. We are being killed, and for what?"

The establishment priest's anger reflected their precarious predicament. Ananus would certainly be replaced as high priest. Not even his close friendship with King Herod Agrippa II, built over a number of years they'd spent together in Rome, would allow the king to let such a blunder go unaddressed. He had to show Rome that he would not allow such reckless behavior. Ananus was out, for sure. Now leaderless, they awaited the appointment of a new high priest, an appointment by a king whose actions mocked the very essence of their calling. They felt their influence over the people slipping away. The people were moving toward a promised new day, one that severely threatened all the sources of the establishment priests' sustenance.

Simultaneously, in the home of an influential Pharisee in the northwest section of the city, other members of the Sanhedrin were meeting with establishment priests. Ever since the death of the popular priest James, this group lived in fear. The situation in Jerusalem was extremely volatile.

"The situation is out of hand," said Rabbi Jacob. "The king and the high priest miscalculated! Cutting off the head has not killed the snake. The messianic fervor is only growing. It appears that the violent method of Sicarii has infected the Essenes and all the Zealots. The radical teachings of the separatist Qumran Sadducees are even gaining a foothold in the city, and, before long, every radical activist will be taking up arms against the Romans. If we don't find a way to stop this, we are doomed to repeat the disasters of Judas the Galilean, or even worse."

"You are so right, Jacob. We could be wiped off the earth by the wrath of Rome if this craziness is not stopped." Rabbi Shamon was one of the most respected men in the room. "Our cherished way of life under Torah is gravely threatened by these radicals. We must do everything we can to stop their foolishness. The power of

Rome has brought stability and safety to our world, and that can give us the peace we seek to freely worship God."

"Our only course of action," interjected Rabbi Johanan, "appears to be to establish contact with the newly arrived governor, Albinus. We must show him that the vast majority of Jews in this city are not hostile to the Romans and want only peace. Severe harm can come to all from the violence these radicals are forcing on us. I think we should try to convince the governor that all these radicals are one dangerous group. Perhaps he can crush the whole despicable bunch at once."

That wasn't the only conversation that day about the religious radicals. King Herod Agrippa II was beside himself with rage at the foolishness of those unruly fanatics. He had just received a summons from the newly arrived governor, Albinus, requesting that he and his sister Bernice come to him immediately. There could be only one reason for such an urgent request that ignored all the protocol of diplomacy. He was moving quickly and decisively to choke off the violence that had gripped the temple and its priests.

"Religion has always been a thorn in my side," he complained to Bernice. "Those religious fools have no understanding of reasonableness. They'll cut off their hands if they think it will reward them with something in a future world that is nothing but a dream. Meanwhile, we have to try to hold together a world they don't even want to be a part of."

"Just a minute, my overworked king," said Bernice with a mocking smirk. "You know as well as I that religion is our best friend. Nothing controls the masses as well as the fear of a wrathful God. Keep them busy with a myriad of tasks aimed at satisfying a distant God, and they can be led around like sheep. You just have to know how to use religion."

"Yeah, like your friend Paul? Remember how we had to smuggle him out of the city because he was so busy with those tasks? No, he wasn't trying to please a distant God; he was busy creating a new one, and his antics almost brought on a riot. We would be better off if there were no religions; then, we could rely on reason and our best judgment."

"Only if women were in control. Men are so obsessed with power that we would be eating each other if it weren't for the fear of God. Now, maybe, if men handed over the reins of power to women, we could have a reasonable society."

"If you are the example of how women would reign, men would quickly get tired of sexual manipulation. Reason is not created in bed; its roots do not reside between the legs."

"Women use sex as power over men because sex is all men look for in women." Bernice was getting annoyed. She knew that her femininity was the vehicle she used to get whatever she wanted from men. Sex was power for her, and she was not the one to argue for the purity of woman's reasonableness over man's obsessive craving for power.

Changing the subject she asked, "What do you think the new governor is going to request of us?"

"Oh, just that we get all our belligerent subjects together and demand that they stop fighting and go home. Maybe I should just send an aide to pick up the memo, so I can get right to work on sending out the invitations," the king said sarcastically. "I don't have the Roman army behind me; I have about as much power or influence over that rabble as I do over the monsters in the sea. I'm sure he is just trying to humiliate me. He is still fuming over the way we usurped his authority in getting rid of the radical priest James. As far as he knows, all this unrest started after that."

"Maybe this is the time to get this rabble out of our city," Bernice suggested. "You know as well as I that those different groups play off each other. The Essenes keep up the talk of a new kingdom being established, and the radical Sadducees start to twirl their daggers. Some of those who call themselves followers of Jesus say a new world is coming where the law will be replaced by something they call faith in 'the Christ'—whatever that means—and the pious Sadducees go crazy. I think we should direct Albinus's attention to getting rid of all these radical groups. Put the reasonable Pharisees in charge of the temple; that's the way to restore order."

During their meeting with the governor, King Herod Agrippa II was well aware that Albinus was giving all his attention to Bernice. His jealousy simmered just below the surface. He knew that Bernice's suggestions were too simplistic and that, if followed, they would only incite more violence. He also knew that her motivation was in part resentful and retaliatory. She would never forgive the way James and his followers condemned her marriage arrangements, calling it fornication, or the way they treated her friend Paul. It was all too obvious to the king that this was payback time for her. He had no sympathy for those radical followers of James and Jesus, but this was not the right way to deal with them. However, he kept silent, because he could tell Albinus only had ears for Bernice.

"You will not believe this," Albinus said in response to what Bernice was saying. "I just excused a group of priests who said exactly the same thing. They said that the problem is rooted in the influence of a renegade priesthood, the members of which defy the teachings of the temple priests, accuse those same priests of robbing the poor instead of caring for them, and spread wild rumors of a new kingdom that demands their full allegiance. If this isn't sedition, nothing is. I will strike fast and hard. I understand that most of this agitation is focused in Poor Town. I will make Poor Town a ghost town. Thank you for your candor. We must meet again on a more pleasant occasion."

"Do you feel better?" the king asked his sister as they left the Roman compound. "You don't really believe that the problem is limited to Poor Town or even primarily concentrated there, do you? I'm sure it feels good to get some revenge for your pal Paul, but you can't be naive enough to believe that the problem will be so easily solved, or that those temple priests are agents of salvation.

That Roman was so taken by you that he would have lapped up anything you said—anything at all."

"Do I detect a hint of jealousy, or are you suffering from an authority complex?" Bernice was well aware that Herod Agrippa had been almost completely ignored during their meeting with Albinus. She liked the feeling of superiority it gave her. "I am not naive about what is going on. One thing I do know is that the most dangerous group of people is the one who holds their allegiance to a power beyond those established by society. When that happens, religion can destroy law and order. God has no place in politics, and when a group of people seek to bring God into our social order, political power is in jeopardy."

It was obvious Bernice thought more like a Roman than even she realized. Power and privilege were her gods.

The men Gaius was ordered to find were no longer in Jerusalem. Simon had slipped out of the city at night and gone south, beyond Jericho, to the Zealot settlement near the Dead Sea. Zenas had also departed and was now part of a caravan slowly making its way to Jericho and, eventually, turning north, up the Jordan Valley to Palmyra.

Chapter 7

Banished to Caesarea

Mary and Salome could not stop thinking about Simon and Zenas. The women had heard nothing about where Simon was, or even if he was safe. While they had seemed to get Zenas out of the city safely, they were extremely apprehensive about his fate. They knew that, wherever he was, he was safer than he would be here in Jerusalem; however, they would feel much better if he got to Palmyra. Sarah, because of her husband's fame in Palmyra, had many friends and connections there, and they should be able to steer Zenas to safety.

In spite of her apprehensions, Salome felt relieved. No longer would she have to fear every knock on the door, or wonder if Miriam had seen something that would arouse her suspicion. She was also sad. She liked Zenas—probably more than liked him—and the two of them had shared a moment of enlightenment they would each carry with them the rest of their lives. Yes, she was relieved for more than one reason. More often than she would care to admit, she had thoughts and sensations that she felt were inappropriate for a woman to have for a man fifteen to twenty years younger than she. Now she would not have to wonder if she was falling for him. Her thoughts and feelings were bittersweet.

Sarah, visiting Mary, said "You really stuck your neck out to help Zenas. He must have really impressed you."

"I will help anyone whom I feel is following God's will, but, yes, I really admire him," Mary confessed. "He has a good heart and an open mind. He was never cut out to be a soldier. He certainly has the bravery, but his sensitivity and respect for humanity argues against the cruelty a soldier is expected to wield. He would always be in trouble. He is a perfect citizen for the kingdom of God. Jacob will find a place for such a good man. He's not going to keep him as a servant, is he?"

"No, certainly not," assured Sarah. "If Zenas truly wants to walk in the way of God, Jacob is the right man for him to be with."

Very early the next morning, Roman soldiers and local recruits were turning parts of Jerusalem upside down and inside out. They went house to house in the Sheep Market area. Every male they could find, and the families of those who were obviously priests, were told to gather only what they could carry. No explanation was given, and those who resisted were beaten into submission. They were herded like sheep toward the western end of the city.

The scene was much more chaotic and violent in Poor Town. Soldiers tore the crude shelters apart, pushing the helpless out of the way. The soldiers were looking for men healthy enough to cause the unrest in the temple. Women who stood up to the soldiers were taken along with the men. The sick and lame were left with no shelter against the brutal sun that would arrive after the soldiers left.

At the entrance to the leper colony, a few unscrupulous soldiers played a wicked game. Informed that those being hunted hid in the leper colony, they forced one of their captives to go into the colony to look for anyone hiding in there. When he returned and reported that he had found no one, the soldiers cried, "Unclean," and stabbed him to death. The victim's body was quickly removed, and another captive, unaware of what was going on, was sent in. The soldiers were getting great amusement from this game. The fifth captive sent in never reappeared. The soldiers made such a racket that the commanding officer came on the scene and halted this savagery.

Poor Town was left in shambles, increased suffering the obvious result of this brutal incursion.

Sarah came to Mary, visibly shaken, and blurted out, "They are destroying Poor Town and scouring the city. The whole place is in a panic. There doesn't appear to be any fighting, but I'm not sure how long that is going to last. It appears the Romans took everyone by surprise."

Before Mary or Salome could respond, there was a group of soldiers at their door. "Get whatever you can carry and come with us!" one of them ordered.

Mary saw that soldiers were herding a group of people, mostly men, but some women and children too, up the street. Some of them carried small sacks. She recognized some of them as opposition priests and Jesus followers. She also recognized that some of the soldiers appeared to be local conscripts.

"Where are we going?" asked Mary. "What do you mean, 'Get what we can carry'?" She could see that the soldier was impatient, so she began to gather a few things.

Salome's anger froze her to inactivity.

"Please don't resist now, dear," Mary said. "I couldn't stand something happening to you now. We need to be brave. God will protect us if we don't lose our nerve or our faith."

Sarah began helping Mary put some essentials in a sack. She had heard that the Romans disrupted entire communities when they wanted to gain control of a situation. She hoped she would be able to keep from Mary and Salome the raging fear that she felt: it was the same fear that had overcome her when Judas Thomas was arrested. She never saw him again. She could hardly breathe now, the pain was so fresh.

Some Roman governors were known for collecting large groups of people and moving them to strange locations in order to disrupt subversive agitation. Sarah was sure this was what was going on. She didn't know how much to say; she didn't want to upset Mary and Salome any further. "I'm sure they are just getting us to a safe place," Sarah offered weakly. "We must be brave. The one thing these soldiers are uncomfortable with is strong women."

Even though it was a mild, brilliantly sunny morning, there was nothing but gloom on the faces of the people being led up the hill, past the fortress, and into the more open area in the northwestern part of the city. They were crowded into the open spaces between the large newer houses that had been built in this area of the city. These houses appeared vacant. None of the occupants wanted to show their faces, for fear of being gathered up along with these unfortunate people led past them, or of being accused of compliance with the cruel Romans. Fear and anger were everywhere. There were hundreds of people, all milling around, some extremely agitated, clearly resenting the instructions of the soldiers. Mary recognized many who were collected there. The soldiers began separating the people, even breaking apart some families, and forming them into groups. Sarah was separated from Mary and Salome, and eventually released.

Mary summoned up the courage to ask a soldier what was going on. A callous sneer was his only reply. No one seemed to be injured, but some were in chains; it was obvious that no one was going anywhere the Romans didn't want anyone to go. Eventually, the crowd began to move and separate. Mary and Salome were part of a group moving toward and through the Damascus Gate; other groups were headed for the Lion's Gate.

Earlier, before they were separated, Sarah finally told them what she thought was happening. This looked all too familiar. Now Mary was sure they were being taken to some far-off city.

Salome's silence concerned Mary. It was not like her to be so quiet. Usually, when frightened, she became just the opposite.

"Where are they taking us, Mama?" Salome finally asked.

Mary was relieved to hear her speak. "I don't know, but my guess is that we will not see Jerusalem for a while. Your guess is as good as mine."

"What will happen to our home and our things? Will any of our friends know what happened to us?" Salome felt alone.

"That must be in God's hands for now. I know the Romans have a very good set of laws and are fiercely protective of them. It just may be that our property is safer than we are."

Salome's sob made Mary realize she should not have said that. She didn't want to upset Salome further. As for Mary herself, she knew that God would protect them and get them through whatever was ahead for them. The future never seemed to present fear to Mary, only possibility.

As they moved away from the city, Mary kept looking back to the town that had played such an important part of her past thirty years. From this distance, the city looked beautiful. Suddenly, the feeling of agony swept over her. Two of her righteous sons were murdered there! This was not a town where God's justice prevailed. No, it was a town ruled by selfish men of power. She also saw the poor: individuals of want and need, but also dreams and desires, locked in a system that appeared to have excessive means at one end and extreme need at the other. Certainly, this was not the intent of a loving Creator. As she gazed upon Jerusalem, tears welled up in her eyes and ran down her cheeks.

Misery was the one thing all these people on the march shared; except for the soldiers, some who appeared to be enjoying this forced suffering. They had plenty of water and food, and taunted the prisoners, who were rationed. As the terrain grew more severe, the grumblings increased. Although old and young, men and women, even some children, suffered the fate of this involuntary trek, the weakest were left behind to fend for themselves among the ruins of what had been Poor Town. (Sadly, these towns always reemerge, almost overnight, out of necessity.) However, as they moved farther away from Jerusalem, the older and the weaker began to show signs of this ordeal.

The scorching sun offered no relief, relentlessly beating on the unwilling travelers. Cresting one arduous hill only presented them with another, even higher and steeper. The sparse brown valley in between was much too short for adequate repose. By the time they entered the third valley, the occasional flowers that dotted the hillsides were losing their radiance. They moved continuously during all daylight hours, stopping only when it was dark. Some began to falter and needed to be helped by others. The pace slowed, and spirits dropped.

Before midday of the second day, they turned to the north. The days were hot; the nights cool. Lacking blankets to cover them at night, they huddled close together to keep warm.

During the afternoon of the third day, Mary thought about the Sabbath and what a strange one this would be. It was impossible to tell when the Sabbath would actually begin because very dark clouds were forming on the western horizon. Surely, they would be spending a very wet night. She hoped the soldiers leading this reluctant group had the foresight to stay out of the deep ravines the rugged terrain suggested. There would be rushing rivers if the rains were heavy. As they progressed, and dusk approached, the soldiers led the group into one of these ravines. Mary and a few others went up to one of the soldiers and informed him of the impending danger. He rode on ahead, supposedly to tell his superior.

With the ominous clouds upon them, Mary and the others who perceived the danger went among the people, warning them to move as quickly as possible up the steep slopes to try to find a place where they could spend the night. There were few level areas, and most ended up huddled together in small groups, clinging to the rocks that littered the sides of the hills.

While they were still scattering up the slopes, the rain started, not just a gentle rain but a torrential downpour. High winds blew the rain horizontally into their faces. In minutes, they were completely soaked. It was now almost completely dark. The rain persisted, and before long, the sides of the hills began to move downward in some places. People scrambled to more stable areas.

It appeared that whole sides of the hills might be washed into the ravine.

Suddenly, a roar came toward them down the ravine, from the direction they had been traveling. In the darkness, they could barely see the wall of water more than two cubits high rushing down the ravine. The people stared in horror at the river rushing past them. Some now worried if they had climbed high enough. Others openly gave thanks to those perceptive folks who had warned them to move up the hillsides.

Mary desperately prayed for the rain to stop. If it kept up much longer, whole hillsides might come down on top of them. She and Salome huddled together, begging God to stop the rain.

It rained well into the night, but then, it stopped almost as quickly as it had started. In an instant, the sky cleared, and a full moon dampened the sparkle of the stars. Everyone was wet and cold. No one could sleep. They clustered together as best they could to keep warm, awaiting daybreak and dreading the next day.

It dawned clear and bright. The only evidence of the river that had flowed below them during the night were some puddles in the low spots. No sleep and damp clothing made moving out seem unbearable. The warm sun dried out their clothing, but nothing could abate their fatigue. Mary was aware that this was the Sabbath. She knew that the Lord understood her walking, but she resented the loss of this day of reflection and prayer. She wondered if she would be able to continue. Her feet were sore and blistered. Salome seemed to be faring physically better than she. This was the fourth day they had been walking.

"Where do you think we are going, Mama?" Salome inquired. "It feels to me that it is getting a little cooler, and the difference between the days and nights are not as extreme."

"Yes, we are headed north, probably to Caesarea," Mary surmised. "If that is the case, we must still have a way to go."

Sometime during the afternoon of the fourth day, a group of soldiers came up to Mary and Salome, carrying a young soldier on a litter. "We understand you are a miracle woman," said one of the soldiers to Mary, his tone laced with arrogance and abasement. "This unfortunate man was bitten by a scorpion and seems close to death. Work your magic on him."

Salome looked at the soldiers and thought of Zenas. Her heart burned, and her stomach ached. That bittersweet feeling once again overtook her. She would never forget that moment or that man.

Mary asked for a large jar of water and a knife. One of the soldiers was ordered to give her his knife.

"Is it safe to put a knife in her hands?" he asked, hesitating.

"What? Is an old woman going to overpower all of us? Do as I say!"

The soldier reluctantly handed the knife to Mary.

"Where is the bite?" she asked.

"Here, just below the knee," the spokesperson said.

Mary took off her head scarf and tied it tightly around the man's leg, above the bite. She took the knife and cut an X over the bite, to make it bleed anew. Then, she began sucking on the cut.

Salome gasped and looked away, shocked at what her mother had just done. Was she actually going to suck out the man's blood? Didn't she realize what she was doing?

Mary sucked a bit, spat out the blood, took a drink of water to clean out her mouth, and sucked again. She repeated this process for several minutes. Her movements were so gentle, even reverent. She washed the area, then took some white powder from her sack and poured a little of it on the red and swollen spot.

As the other soldiers watched, the transmissible power of compassion showed as the hostility drained from their eyes and faces. Watching Mary tenderly work on their comrade, the tension in their bodies seemed to rise into the air as a mist rises off a lake on a cool fall morning.

Mary wrapped the leg with a piece of cloth she had cut from her head scarf. "That's all I can do for him, except to ask God to heal him," Mary said. "If it has not been too long since he got the bite, what I did might save him. If it has been some time, only God can save him." Mary had her hand on the neck of the young man as she said this. She felt the heart beating weakly. She knew that they brought him to her much too late. She closed her eyes and whispered, "God of love, please bless this young man with your healing powers."

The other soldiers were visibly moved by the obvious concern of this old woman. She offered kindness in the face of insult, and the soldiers were humbled. Feeling unsure of what to do, the leader, shifting from leg to leg, awkwardly expressed gratitude. They gathered up the semiconscious soldier and left as quickly as they could.

"Do you think he is going to live, Mama?" Salome asked after the soldiers had left.

"It would be a miracle," replied Mary, "but, with God, anything is possible. This certainly would not be the greatest miracle God has performed in my life."

Salome felt awkward in asking, "Mama, you took that soldiers blood into your mouth! How could you do that? You know what Torah says about drinking blood."

"Salome, my love, Torah also says not to associate with the unclean, or to work on the Sabbath, but should I have sent him away?"

Salome didn't know what to say.

"The whole basis of the Torah is love. Love would not allow me to do anything other than what I tried to do for that unfortunate young man. Love is not a list of laws but a vibrant force that defines itself in every encounter between individuals."

Salome was still speechless, but now out of awesome respect for her mother.

With a twinkle in her eyes, Mary said to Salome, "I'm sure that young man with the scorpion bite was a Samaritan. Don't you think so?"

"Now that you mention it, I'm sure you are right," Salome replied and then added, "I've heard that the Romans conscript men from the areas they conquer. They will do anything to assure control."

Mary was just glad for the break. She wasn't sure how much farther she could walk. The blisters on her feet had all been rubbed into raw sores that were bleeding most of the time. She had to rip strips from the bottom of her dress to wrap her feet. She wondered where she was going to get more cloth to wrap her feet the next day; she was running low. She did not want to use her head scarf. She needed that for protection from the sun.

The next morning, Mary had to wrap her feet with the ripped cloths she had used the day before. She knew they would not last the day. She wasn't sure what would happen to her if she couldn't go on. Would she be left to die in this wilderness? How could she bear another day of pain? Looking at the other unwilling sojourners, she saw many suffering more than she, which drew her like a magnet to their needs. Before she realized it, the sun was beginning to fall in the west.

This day, they stopped well before sundown, for some unknown reason. The people spread out in a narrow valley, looking to find some protected spot. They heard the bleating of sheep off in the distance. During the day, they had passed near enough to recognize some villages off in the distance. It was apparent that throughout this brutal trek they had not taken the easiest route. Mary had just assumed that the soldiers wanted to avoid towns and villages. Today was the first they had encountered any signs of habitation.

Salome, well aware of her mother's discomfort, said, "I'm going to try to sneak away to see if I can find someone who can provide us with something for our feet." In fact, her feet were beginning to blister and bleed too.

"No, you can't go out there alone. It isn't safe. What if you get lost? It may get dark before you can get back." Mary was just beginning with her list of reasons to stop Salome.

JOSEPH C. NYCE

"Nothing you say is going to stop me. I'm sure there are some people just over that hill," Salome said, pointing to the east. "I'm going to get something for your feet."

Salome left in spite of Mary's objections.

If the soldiers saw Salome walking up and over the hill, no one moved to stop her. Perhaps they figured if one woman was stupid enough to walk off into unknown danger, that would be one less person to look after.

Upon reaching the top of the hill, Salome saw a small valley, surrounded by hills about the size of the one she was on. In the middle of this valley was a smaller hill with a number of small houses built on its sun side. A great flock of sheep grazed in the valley. Salome moved toward the houses. While she was still a good way off from the houses, a young shepherd suddenly emerged from out of a deep ravine. "Are you lost?" he asked, stating the obvious.

Salome went right up to the lad and fell on her knees. "Please help me. My mother and I are part of a large group of persons who have been forced to march all the way from Jerusalem under the heavy guard of soldiers. We are suffering terribly. My mother and I desperately need something for our feet; they are raw and bleeding."

"We saw your group approaching, and when we saw the large numbers of soldiers, we assumed you were prisoners," the shepherd said.

"No, we are innocent people whom the Romans are displacing in their attempt to get control of violence in Jerusalem," Salome explained. "We are not prisoners, just poor victims of bizarre Roman cruelty." Salome surprised herself with her forthrightness.

"I hate the Romans." The lad spat on the ground. "Come with me."

The young shepherd led Salome to the small hamlet of stone houses. A group of nearly thirty women and children surrounded Salome and the lad. Salome quickly found out that they were just east of Caesarea, with only a range of low mountains between them. They would reach Caesarea tomorrow. The women wanted to feed Salome and find out all about her harrowing experience. Salome, concerned about getting back to Mary, told them as much as she could, as quickly as she could. The women wanted to give Salome all sorts of supplies, but Salome only took some cloth to wrap their feet, some cheese and dried mutton, and two skins of water. She thanked them profusely and left them with God's blessing.

The sun had gone down, but a rising moon made it easy for Salome to find her way back to Mary.

Mary rushed up to her and embraced her as if she had been gone for years. "I was so worried!"

"Mama, we are less than a day away from Caesarea! Look at what I brought!" Salome was so excited. If she stopped to think, she was pretty proud of what she had done. "Mama, I'm really glad I didn't let you stop me."

"I am too, Salome, and not just for what you brought back." Mary was aware of how good Salome felt just then. She thought, *What a bright spot in such a dismal journey!*

Before dawn the next morning, someone sneaking by Mary awoke her. She was too afraid to move, and just lay there listening. She heard whispering from someone near. Soon the phantom moved on. Mary mustered the courage to approach the person near her, who was whispering excitedly to someone else. "Am I seeing things, or did someone just sneak by here?"

A middle-aged woman jumped up and grabbed Mary's hands. "You'll never believe this, but someone just tapped me on the shoulder and left this skin of milk and some cheese. All they said was 'I hope this helps a bit.' Then, whoever it was just moved on."

Mary could see in the predawn light that others were standing and talking to one another. Apparently, they, too, had received something from these strange spirits.

Suddenly, there were shouts from the far end of the valley.

Some soldiers were yelling at a group of women, men, and children running up over the hill Salome had gone over the evening before. Obviously, those kind people had courageously entered the camp and distributed what they had in order to try to make the prisoners more comfortable. Impressed by this kindness, Mary immediately thought of Jesus's words that the kingdom of God is among us.

The task of wrapping their feet, so less arduous than the day before, went quickly. Not only did they have nice soft material from their friends over the hill, they knew they would not be walking a full day. The word had gotten around quickly, and spirits soared. The weakest appeared better able to rise and walk, and grumbling or arguing appeared to vanish. While they had no idea what they faced in Caesarea, it had to be better than what they had experienced the past number of days. Some even commented that the range of rolling mountains to the west, which they had to cross, did not appear nearly as high or as steep as the ones they had already traversed. Mary was aware that this attitude prevailed because Salome had gone looking for some cloth to wrap their feet. Her fearless act brought many blessings to this tired group.

Mary also wondered at the purpose of this cruel move on the part of the Romans. There were quite a few women and older men in this group. Very few so-called leaders were present. There were a few rabbis, but the majority seemed harmless, certainly not the real rebel agitators. They had probably escaped before the Romans could organize this pathetic exercise. It seemed to Mary that the whole purpose of this torturous march was to depress spirits. If that was the case, Salome's news of their proximity to Caesarea revealed how much spirit still remained in these abused folk.

The mountain's slopes were not as severe as those previously encountered, and as they reached the summit, a marvelous view lay before them. Rolling green hills sloped to a long sand strip that seemed to go on forever, as did the sea beyond, which reached to the horizon. It was a view that took their breath away. Nestled up next to the shoreline was a city that looked brand-new. Sparkling white buildings spread out along the waterline. Numerous ships lay at anchor in a harbor that looked man-made. From this distance, it looked like a perfect city. The midday sun sparkled off everything: the water, the sand, and the beautiful buildings.

While the view felt like open arms, Mary knew that would certainly not be the case. No city waits with open arms for a group of strangers dumped on them. Roman behaviors were rarely benevolent, and the common folk looked with grave mistrust on all their machinations.

The air here was different. Mary could smell the salt in the air. A cool breeze came off the water, like a soothing salve on her sun-parched skin.

"I've never seen anything like it," Salome said as she gazed out over the sea. "I've never seen a body of water so big you couldn't see the other side. I thought the Sea of Galilee was big! And, is that Caesarea? It's beautiful!"

"Yes, it is beautiful," agreed Mary. "But, remember, Jerusalem is beautiful too, from this far away. Cities are more than buildings. I hope this city is safer than Jerusalem is just now."

The mass of people, more than two hundred, surrounded by almost half that number of soldiers, moved slowly down out of the hills. First, they passed isolated shepherds with their flocks and vineyards scattered over the hills. They approached small farms, with stone houses surrounded by low stone walls. Small fields of vegetables and orchards surrounded these farms. Lazy burros could be seen near most houses, some with their snouts in windows looking for food. The children playing around the houses shrieked at the sight of the soldiers. They rushed to get closer looks, but stayed well out of the soldiers' way, intimidated as the soldiers rode by.

As they got closer to the city, the level ground was covered by gardens of vegetables, vineyards, and groves of fruit and nut trees, all partitioned off by low stone walls. There were no houses here in these larger fields and groves. The workers obviously came from the town. Those working in these gardens and groves stopped what they were doing to watch the strange procession going by. The presence of the soldiers kept them from approaching the prisoners, who looked anything but dangerous.

Arrival at the outskirts of the city erased the dazzling glitter they had seen from the hills. The large buildings in the center of the city were still visible, but somehow looked less spectacular. The houses on the outskirts were small and the streets narrow. The procession narrowed to just a few persons wide, with a soldier in each row. They moved slowly through the streets as curious residents stood in doorways and at windows. An eerie silence accompanied the marchers.

Mary wondered what these people staring at her were thinking. What did those tight lips and furrowed brows reveal? Was that pity in their eyes? Mary didn't want to be pitied, but she sure could use some empathy. Did these people support the Romans, or did they understand their cruel domination?

"This is the most frightened I've been since this whole painful journey started," Salome shared. "I wish I could read these people's thoughts. I feel like a slave walking to the trading block."

"Yes, it is certainly a strange feeling," agreed Mary. "Some of the faces are unreadable, but in others I see real concern. I'm sure we will find some open hearts here."

In the northern section of town, a large structure separated the larger buildings from the houses. This was the Hippodrome, a massive structure built for chariot races. It was a huge oval with gates at one flattened end. The oval end and the sides had tiers of seats for the spectators. Down the center was a long wall that didn't reach either end, which divided the oval in half. Each side was wide enough for five chariots abreast. Crude tents had been set up in the track area. This was where the weary travelers were settled. Mary and Salome moved into one of these tents, wondering what was to befall them next.

CHAPTER 8

OLD AND NEW FRIENDS

Late in the afternoon, one individual came to the small tent Mary and Salome occupied, and asked them if they knew anyone in Caesarea. When they said no, he left. Mary and Salome had not had anything to eat since arriving in this place. Their hunger prompted them to begin looking around for food. They did not seem to be under any control by the soldiers. People were able to come and go as they pleased, and there were no soldiers to be seen. It appeared that they had been left to fend for themselves. Mary and Salome began looking for someplace to get food. At the perimeter of the tent city were persons with small carts, selling food and supplies.

Salome said, "We have no money, Mama. How are we to get food?"

Just then, an unsavory character hearing Salome's question, said, "You don't look too old to be of service. Come with me, and I'll make sure you don't go hungry."

Salome stepped back from the man and looked away. "Let's get out of here, Mama," she said.

"Oh!" shouted the man, "your hunger is not severe enough yet to crush your rudeness. Maybe we will meet again tomorrow."

Mary and Salome huddled together, all too aware of their vulnerability.

"What are we to do?" Salome sighed. "We are at the mercy of anyone and everyone."

Just then, there was a commotion in the middle of the tents. Some were screaming! Women went running toward the sound of the trouble. Outside one of the tents, sailors were obviously taking advantage of a few young women who were half undressed and sobbing. The screams had brought many witnesses to this brutal attack. Women rushed at the sailors, swinging whatever they could get their hands on. There were so many women that the sailors quickly left, laughing at the futility of the female attack.

As the sailors were rounding a large tent, they ran headlong into a group of soldiers who had come to see what the commotion was about. The laughing abruptly stopped. The sailors turned away and began to run.

"Stop them!" the crowd shouted to the soldiers. "They just attacked some of us."

The soldiers immediately gave chase. Mary noticed that one of the soldiers could not run with the others and had a severe limp. She saw that he had a wrap around his leg, just below the knee. The sailors exited through one of the arched entrances to the Hippodrome, with the soldiers in hot pursuit.

By the next day, the sack they had brought with them was just about empty. They had bartered nearly everything away for food. That awful man had come back twice, trying to entice Salome to go with him. The last time, he left with a threat that made them both uneasy. What were they to do?

Occasionally, a Jewish priest would walk through the tent community, apparently looking for someone. This morning, Mary thought she recognized a tall man with a heavy gray beard. As he got closer, she knew who it was. She ran to him, an old friend from out of the past.

"Barnabas! Is that you?" she exclaimed.

The man was taken aback. He couldn't believe his eyes. "Mary. I can't believe it's you! Have you been here all this time? I've been here a number of times since yesterday, looking to help people. How did I miss you? Is that Salome? I had no idea you and Salome were here. Are you alone?" The sight of the two women shocked and sickened Barnabas. They were disheveled, dirty, and obviously uncomfortable. He smothered them in his embrace.

"What a sight for sore eyes!" Salome said. "We are about at our wit's end. We have traded away all our belongings for food, and we don't know where to go or what to do."

"You will come with me," said Barnabas. "There is a strong community of followers of Jesus who will be overwhelmed to see you. What a blessing your misfortune will be for this fellowship. We heard about the terrible events in Jerusalem and have been trying to find places for everyone we can. We had no idea you two were part of this cruel operation."

Mary responded, "The new governor is trying to rein in a streak of violence by punishing old folks, women, and children. That's about all we know. You probably know more than we do."

"No, we don't know much about what is going on. It apparently has not erupted into something bigger so far, but I hear nerves are on edge," relayed Barnabas. "Come, we can talk once you get cleaned up and comfortable."

As they were walking, Barnabas pointed out the home where the fellowship of Jesus followers had its meetings. "There is an active group here eagerly spreading the news of the kingdom and living the love of our Master. We have found places for some of the people who were forced here with you. I feel awful that we found you so late."

When they arrived at what the women thought was Barnabas's house, they were greeted by a man and a woman. "Welcome to our humble home. I am Joseph, and this is my wife Hanna. Whom do I have the pleasure to meet?"

"You'd better sit down, Joseph," Barnabas said. "You are in for a shock! I want you to meet an old friend, Mary, and her daughter

Salome. This Mary is none other than the mother of our Lord Jesus."

Hanna and Joseph could not believe what they were just told. They were speechless. Eventually, Hanna found her voice. "We are so honored to meet you and welcome you into our home."

Mary was becoming something of a legend within some of the communities of the followers of Jesus. Obviously, she was considered specially blessed by God, but some were even saying she was more than human. Now she was standing here in their doorway with her daughter. Joseph and Hanna were visibly shaken. This old woman, dirty and showing the effects of six grueling days, was anything but what they would have pictured the Lord's mother to be.

Nervously, they invited Mary and Salome into their home, a small home in the poorer section of the city. As most homes in this section, it had two floors, with two rooms on the upper level and two on the lower. A small kitchen protruded out the back, with a small vegetable garden immediately beyond the back door. It was sparsely furnished but very clean. The front room was a sitting room, and the rear one had a low table with floor cushions around it. A crude stone stairway led to the two rooms above, separated by a heavy, hanging rug-like tapestry. Joseph and Hanna appeared to be middle-aged. Their children, if they had any, apparently were not living in the house.

Their shock rendered them speechless, and the five people stood in silence. Joseph and Hanna felt unsure how to address their new guests.

Mary, perceiving their discomfort, said, "We are so grateful for your kindness. We do not wish to impose or to cause you any trouble. We are only desirous of a little time to get ourselves situated. We insist on being more help than burden, so please tell us how we can make our imposition as unsettling as possible."

Mary's comments completely disarmed Hanna. She was taken by her graciousness and her willingness to help. She did not at all sound like someone who was looking to be served. Hanna relaxed, went to Mary, took her by the hands, and said, "Our home is yours as long as you need it. It is our honor to have you here, and we ask that God bless a long friendship between us."

Hanna looked at their feet and exclaimed, "Gracious, your feet need attention. Joseph, please quickly heat some water, and get soft cloths and some salve. Please sit and let me get those soiled wraps off."

After Mary and Salome sat, Hanna carefully unwrapped their feet. "Oh! They must be so sore!" She slowly stroked the tops of their feet as she waited for Joseph. When he returned, she carefully washed their feet with water that had some green leaves floating in it. She rubbed a clear ointment on their sores but did not wrap their feet. "You must keep the wraps off as much as possible for those sores to heal. We can wrap them when you need to go out."

Hanna looked to Salome, whom she imagined to be about her age, and said, "You've had a harrowing experience. I'm sure you are exhausted! Please try to make yourself comfortable. Joseph will draw some water so you and your mother can wash, and I will get you both something to eat. You must be famished!"

Salome replied, "We were able to trade some of our things for food, so we are not starving, but it would be wonderful to be able to wash. Thank you so much for your kindness."

Hanna looked to Barnabas and said, "Please go next door and ask Debra for two changes of clothes for Mary and Salome. She has been collecting clothing since she heard all these people were being brought here."

Once Mary and Salome had washed and changed into clean clothing, Hanna could not hold back. "I'm so full of questions. Aren't you sore from the long journey? It couldn't have been easy for you. Were you mistreated by the soldiers? What did you leave behind in Jerusalem? I've heard that the tent city in the Hippodrome was overrun with thieves and thugs. Weren't you scared?"

"To answer the last question first," Mary replied, "yes, one scary man kept coming after Salome. Thankfully, Barnabas found us before he came back again. We don't know when we will be able to go back to Jerusalem, or what we will find when we do. I fear for what is going to happen in Jerusalem. There are so many hotheads involved there now, and the new governor has something to prove. The temple disputes between the high priests and the Zealots are getting violent, and there are so many different factions vying for power, or for the favor of the Romans, that it could erupt into utter chaos. I shudder when I think of Jerusalem."

"But, you, at your age, how did you possibly make such a long trek? I'm sure you didn't have the best of accommodations," suggested Hanna.

"No! It certainly wasn't a pleasure trip," admitted Mary. "We were plenty uncomfortable, but we kept each other's spirits up. We knew God was not about to desert us."

The questions and answers went on through a quickly put-together meal and into the evening. After making sleeping arrangements, Hanna and Joseph excused themselves and went to bed.

Once alone, and free to share their thoughts and feelings, Hanna was the first to talk. "I'm certainly glad we have partially kept a kosher home. The followers of Jesus in Jerusalem are Torah observant."

"Yes, we tend to forget what an issue that was for a while in our fellowship." Joseph thought back to the disputes and angry exchanges that took place as the fellowship tried to deal with the free-spirit Gentiles who accepted Christ, but then had difficulty adapting to the Jewish way of life. The fellowship's solution of "both/and" drove people away on both sides. "That was a painful time in the history of the fellowship. There are still scars, some sores lying just below the surface. I hope Mary's presence will help us mend fences and build bridges."

"Mary was certainly a surprise to me," said Hanna. "I'm not

sure what I expected, but she seems so natural, so comfortable. I would have been a wreck if I had gone through what she experienced the past few weeks. She does not veil her feelings, but she does not throw them at you either. I don't know ... I guess I expected the mother of Jesus to exhibit more self-importance."

"I know what you mean. She does not make you feel uncomfortable to be around her. In fact, it's just the opposite. I felt like I used to feel when I was around my grandmother." Joseph always referred to his grandmother's house as home because it was the most comfortable place in the world for him. "Do you think they will feel at home here?"

"I hope they will. They have had such a harrowing experience. They have lost their home, on top of all their other losses. It's hard to imagine what they must be thinking and feeling." Hanna gave a deep sigh. "We certainly have quite a job ahead of us. So much depends on how comfortable we can make them feel."

"You make it sound like a daunting task. I don't know why, but I feel that Mary and Salome will make it easier than we imagine."

After Hanna, Joseph, and Salome went to bed, Mary and Barnabas found themselves alone. "You are not staying here?" Mary asked.

"No, I am staying with Tobias a few streets over. I just got into town this week. When I heard of James's death, I was on Cyprus. I wanted to go to Jerusalem to see you. I felt so bad for you, and for the fact that we had not been in touch for so many years, that I just had to come to you. Then, I heard that the Romans were displacing a bunch of Jerusalem residents here to Caesarea, so I decided to stay here and help settle those folks. It's amazing how God brought us together."

"It does my heart good to know that you wanted to come to see me," said Mary. "When you left with Paul so many years ago, I feared we might not ever see each other again. That visit caused a whole lot of agitation among the followers of Jesus. Did you know that James was lame for months after that confrontation with Paul in the temple?"

"No, I didn't know that. Paul was a hothead, and he went completely out of control that day. Inside the temple, he claimed that since the good news of Jesus was not only for the Jews but also the Gentiles, the Torah couldn't possibly apply to the Gentiles. His brashness shocked everyone, but Paul seemed not to care at all about the affront he made. James, Peter, and Simon tried to question him and wished to discuss their differences. Paul would have none of it, and he became so irate that he pushed James, who fell backwards down the steps. I didn't know the fall made James lame. The people were so upset with Paul that we had to leave the city in a hurry."

Barnabas, silent for a while, seemed to go over some old memories. He shook his head. Obviously changing the subject, he asked, "How is Simon? Why isn't he here with you?"

"Simon had to flee Jerusalem the day before we were rounded up," Mary responded. "Albinus, the new governor, wanted to arrest him because he thought Simon was behind the murders of the high priest's guards."

"That's ridiculous!" said Barnabas. "Simon would never be involved with violence."

"Of course not!" Mary paused for a moment. "I guess when they couldn't find Simon, they decided to disrupt the whole community. The next day, a whole bunch of people from Poor Town, and some of us who were connected with Simon, were collected and shipped out of the city."

"The Romans certainly have unique ways of social control," remarked Barnabas. "They don't seem to have a heart when it comes to people. They are very concerned about making sure their laws are logical, but they don't seem to give a hoot about how they impact the people."

Mary, aware that Barnabas had changed the subject, asked,

"You certainly moved off the subject of Paul quickly enough. Are you uncomfortable talking about him with me?"

Barnabas thought for a moment. "Uncomfortable, no; embarrassed, yes."

"Why are you embarrassed with me, Barnabas?" Mary asked. "We certainly have been through enough together that nothing should embarrass us at this point."

"Do you remember when Paul and I were in Jerusalem, and you asked me why I was so taken with Paul?" Barnabas began slowly. "I *was* taken with him, especially his intelligence and his ability to speak. His encounter with Jesus shattered his world and gave him a completely new view of God's plan for humanity. It made so much sense, especially when considering our belief that Jesus's good news was for everyone, not just the Jews. We all sensed that, and he had a very compelling plan for spreading that news. He felt specially selected as an apostle for that mission. I believed so too. But I also remember you cautioning me then about him and telling me you did not have good feelings about him and his motivation. I brushed you off then, thinking you were being a protective mother, upset because Paul had differences with your son James. I'm embarrassed now because I did not consider what you were trying to tell me. What did you perceive then that you were trying to relate to me?"

Mary thought for a while. "I'm not sure what I thought then, but the one thing that struck me listening to Paul talk about Jesus was that he didn't know Jesus at all. What he said had nothing to do with what Jesus taught or said. Listening to Paul, I got the impression that Jesus just dropped down out of heaven to be put on the cross—as if he had been nothing more than some heavenly gift to free us from the guilt of our sins. The baby I suckled, the young boy I spanked, the man I admired, all apparently meant nothing to Paul. Rather, he fixated on, and even seemed to glorify, the brutal way Jesus died. Do you have any idea what that does to a mother's heart?"

JOSEPH C. NYCE

Mary paused, desperately trying to choke back tears. "But that is not why I tried to caution you. What appeared strange to me was that I really didn't see any real change in Paul, even though he said his encounter with Jesus completely turned his world upside down. Paul, the follower of Jesus, seemed eerily similar to the Pharisee who, not many years before, had persecuted the followers of Jesus. He appeared the same arrogant person, so sure of himself. I wondered how his encounter with Jesus changed him inside. You know as well as anyone that, once you met Jesus, you were never the same inside. Jesus doesn't appear to change the world outside of us; he moves us inside so that we see ourselves differently in the world. Paul struck me as just another zealot reducing God to a rational package designed to satisfy man's desire to figure out God and life. I think that was what made me want to talk to you."

Barnabas was stricken. He didn't know where to start. "Paul and I parted ways a number of years ago, in Antioch. Did you know that? It's a long story, but the straw that broke the camel's back, for me, was the realization that every place we went, we caused unrest and disruption. Certainly, when we walked with Jesus, there were disputes and arguments. Generally, though, not with the common people but with the authorities, those who saw themselves as having power and who were threatened by Jesus's popularity and success. With Paul, it was different. We upset the common people in the synagogues, and, often, Paul's connections with the powerful protected us. Something just didn't seem right. Furthermore, we were always on the outs with those who walked with Jesus. The basis of these disputes never seemed to get back to what Jesus said and did; they were always about who Paul claimed Jesus was.

"That is the strange part for me. My recollection is that Jesus virtually said nothing about who he was, but always talked about the presence of God's kingdom. With Paul, the focus has certainly shifted, but I'm not so sure why."

Mary was moved. "Say more! I like what I am hearing."

132

"It's just that Paul had this grand salvation scheme, the center of which was his own experience. Jesus, on the other hand, never talked about himself but about the presence of God's kingdom. Jesus talked about living; Paul preaches about being. Jesus's message was an earthy one, pointing us to the poor and the needy. Paul's message is a spiritual one that seems to separate the redeemed from those who should hear the good news. The longer I was with Paul, the farther away Jesus's teachings became, and the more important Jesus and his death became. As hard as it is for us Jews to fathom, Paul believed Jesus was more than just the Messiah. He believes Jesus is God."

Barnabas saw in Mary's eyes that this last comment had a profound impact on her. He wasn't sure how to continue, and he tried his best to curtail the conversation. "Anyway, the bottom line is that I grew more and more uncomfortable with the confrontations, particularly with the way Paul reacted to them. We were building walls, not bridges. I felt it best we part ways."

Mary sensed Barnabas's discomfort. "We've had a long and eventful day; one I will always treasure because it has brought us together again. We will have lots of time to continue this conversation." She took his hands in hers and said, "We have so much to catch up on, so much to share. I can't wait to hear more; but now I need some sleep."

CHAPTER 9

OLD TROUBLES REVISITED

Barnabas could not sleep. He couldn't get the picture of Mary's face out of his mind: the pain he saw in her eyes as she talked about how Paul ignored Jesus the man and celebrated his death, and the look she got when he said Paul claimed Jesus was God. As Barnabas tried to get to the bottom of his feelings, he was struck by images of what he considered one of the worst days of his life.

It was as if it had happened yesterday, but the event had occurred more than ten years ago.

He and Paul were on the steps leading into the temple, talking with James, Peter, and Simon. The incident started innocently enough. Everyone was in agreement that the gospel was meant for more than just the Jews. Paul adamantly proclaimed his calling as an apostle to the Gentiles. No one disputed that. There was no question in Paul's mind as to what that meant.

Paul stated, "If we are to get anywhere with the Gentiles, we are going to have to stop insisting that followers of Jesus become Jews first. The good news is not that they can become Jews, but that they can be redeemed from their sins. Torah compliance and circumcision are real stumbling blocks."

Somewhat puzzled, James said, "The heart of Jesus's message was not personal redemption. According to Jesus, simple repentance seemed to take care of that. It seems to me he taught the presence of the kingdom of God."

"Are you questioning my experience of the risen Lord?" Paul was noticeably irritated.

Taken aback by Paul's defensiveness, James responded, "This is not about you, Paul. It's about the good news Jesus preached and the promise it offers."

"The risen Christ appeared to me and clearly spelled out the purpose of God's plan for redemption," Paul said matter-of-factly.

"I find it somewhat curious that Jesus was not clearer about that in his teachings to us. I don't remember him ever saying anything specific about God's plan; he always referred to God's presence." James tried to tread lightly. He felt uncomfortable with the tone in Paul's voice and his combativeness.

"If you're questioning the presence of the Holy Spirit, I can give you a list of signs and miracles to match those of any of the esteemed apostles."

"Your success in winning followers of Jesus is not at all in question." James was somewhat surprised at Paul's increasing combativeness. "At issue here are the implications of that success. We have gotten word that your teachings about the Christ are creating rather severe divisions between the Jews who follow Jesus and the Gentiles you are instructing."

"That's precisely the point. Torah and circumcision are as strange to Gentiles in Galatia and Corinth as are antlers on a rooster." Paul felt they were finally getting to the point.

"You are a Jew. Have you discarded the understanding of the significance of circumcision and the Torah?" James asked incredulously.

"Yes, I am a son of Abraham, an Israelite, and indeed a Hebrew. I respect and fully honor the importance of circumcision and the Torah," Paul responded proudly. "But, as one especially called out from my mother's womb to personally receive the gospel from Christ Jesus, God has revealed to me that we live in a new age brought about by the suffering of Christ on the cross and his resurrection. The Gentiles do not need to become Jews to receive redemption from their sins. There are believers all over Arabia, Galatia, and Achaia to prove this."

"Jesus taught the messiah. What about the reign of righteousness and the judgment of evil?" James knew that Paul, as a Pharisee, also held these beliefs.

"We are living in the end times. God's judgment is very near. Only those who believe that the sacrifice of Jesus Christ has washed away their sins will be resurrected with him in glory." Paul knew this message well.

"You talk as if this is all a spiritual thing, as if God cares nothing about the whole of creation and is only interested in spiritual beings." James was a Jew, not a Greek.

"God is a spirit, and those who worship him must worship him in spirit and in truth. The body is passing away; all things are new." Paul seemed almost incredulous that James was making so much of this.

"We Jews can never reduce God to a spirit. Our history, our experience of God's presence, tells us that God cares deeply for all of creation, and will never be satisfied until all of creation fully worships God through righteousness and love." James felt that Paul did not understand the essence of his concern. The animosity building between the Jews and those who were beginning to be called Christians belied the love Jesus taught as the presence of God's kingdom.

James would make one more attempt. "Jesus's message was a message of love. I am deeply concerned about the division that is forming within the followers of Jesus. I'm not about to concede that between Jews and Gentiles, both honestly pursuing righteousness, one must be right and the other wrong. Isn't it possible that circumcision, Torah, and the good news are all parts of the pathway to righteousness and all keys to love?"

Paul, frustrated with James's unwillingness to let go of the past, said, "If the Jews want to hang on to traditions whose purpose has been superseded, that's their burden. I cannot impose those archaic practices that give no advantage to the new life in Christ."

At this point, Simon suggested, "Is there room for a compromise? I understand how honoring the whole Torah seems foreign to those who have no connection with Jewish history. What if we ask only that the Gentile believers abstain from that which has been polluted by idols, avoid fornication, and not eat blood or anything strangled?" (In fact, these were the accepted requirements asked of God-fearers who attended synagogue.)

"Now we're getting somewhere!" Paul was delighted. Once there was a crack in the jar, it would not be long before it fell to pieces. "Circumcision is an anathema to Gentiles, a crude and primitive practice that has no meaning to the spirit of Christ."

James looked at Simon. "Did you mean to eliminate circumcision, or were you just speaking of Torah? I certainly cannot discount circumcision. That is the sign of the fundamental covenant between God and Abraham, the father of us all. That covenant, established from the very beginning, symbolizes our agreement to serve the God of love."

"What!" exclaimed Paul. Now he was shouting. "The Jews can cut the ends off their units until the sun turns to cheese, for all I care; it will not bring redemption. Man cannot work off his sinfulness. Only God's love, recognized solely through the loving sacrifice of his son, can bring redemption."

"Jesus never appeared nearly as concerned with redemption from sin as you seem to be," commented James. "He had a pretty simple answer to sin: repentance. He was much more concerned that we get over ourselves so that we can recognize the presence of God in our midst."

"Do I detect insinuation in that comment?" asked Paul.

"Not at all," replied James. "I am speaking of all of us. Jesus never seemed to be satisfied with the level of our selflessness. Only his Mary appeared to really understand him at times."

"You are too locked in the past," observed Paul. "Don't you see that everything has changed since Jesus was resurrected? Why did the risen Christ appear to me if not to indicate that this is a new world?"

"Possibly because you were persecuting his friends and those he entrusted to carry on his message," suggested Simon.

Paul was visibly offended by this comment. He tried to cover his irritation. "My past sins are greater than anyone's. There is no surer demonstration of God's love and grace than his acceptance of me. In spite of my sins, he has visited me with his Spirit and given me visions of his saving grace."

"No one is questioning your experience," exclaimed James. "Our primary concern is what you preach to the Gentiles. If we are spreading the same good news, it should be in such a way as to not denigrate and render worthless the traditions and beliefs of Jesus's own people. We fear that the tension that already exists between the followers of Jesus and those Jews who do not accept Jesus as the Messiah will be matched on the other side by those followers of Jesus who look down on the observance of Torah. If the message of Jesus is good news for everyone, it should not be a message that divides; it should be one that unites. If God is love, why should God among us have us at each other's throats?"

"I am not saying that Jews should not observe Torah, only that Torah has no significance for Gentiles," explained Paul.

"But isn't that saying too much?" asked James.

"What do you mean, 'saying too much'?" Paul's tone indicated he was having enough of this conversation.

Calmly, James continued. "Possibly, Torah means something different for the Gentile than it does for the Jew, but to pass it off as meaningless or obsolete can only create a barrier between the Jew and the Gentile that defies brotherhood."

Paul had enough. "If you think the gospel is some sort of mechanism for congeniality, I'll leave you to your games. Jesus Christ has ushered in a whole new world. God's love has provided the only way for mankind to be redeemed from their sins. The church must proclaim the newness of this event as the only road to salvation. It will mean a break with the past, because the past has been the way of sin and death."

Paul turned and started to leave the temple. The rest of them hesitantly followed. Paul turned around and asked Barnabas if he was coming with him. Barnabas did not know what to say. There did not seem to be anything really wrong with what Paul said, but he also did not appear to be interested in understanding what James was trying to get at.

Then, James, hurrying up to Paul, laid his hand on his arm and said, "I am impressed with your zeal and your assuredness. What troubles me is that you seem to be more convinced of why Jesus died than of who Jesus himself was. Jesus did not have as many answers as you do, or if he did, he did not share them with us. He was more comfortable with questions. The question that was always on his lips was, 'How will God's presence make itself known in this situation?' He was unshakably sure of one thing: that we were living within the kingdom of God, and that made everything new and open. But that seemed to be a different kind of newness than you are talking about. I would like to understand that before another wedge is driven between God's people that will make them forever enemies."

"Wallow in the past if you must," Paul said angrily. "God's plan for redemption demands a new world, and the old forms of Judaism must be thrown off like old worn-out clothing." He pushed James away from him. James, standing on the edge of a step, lost his balance and fell to the bottom of the stairs. Paul turned and hurried away.

The others rushed to James, who lay motionless at the bottom of the stone steps. He was alive, but he seemed badly injured. Barnabas ran for help. When he got back to James, he was conscious and sitting up. Assuming him not badly hurt, Barnabas left to find Paul, whose behavior embarrassed him, to say the least.

The followers of Jesus in Jerusalem reacted severely to Paul's attack on James. Mobs formed, seeking to find Paul and stone him. It was obvious that Paul's life was in danger. Paul, through his connections in the Sanhedrin, made arrangements to sneak out of Jerusalem, accompanied by Barnabas.

Barnabas could not imagine a worse nightmare. He was soaked in sweat! He hadn't heard that James was seriously hurt, and realizing that he had not been concerned enough to stay with James all those years ago, mortified him now. Barnabas had been a loyal accomplice, yet Paul's behavior toward James in the temple that day embarrassed him. Barnabas cringed at the thought that he had let his allegiance to Paul override his compassion for James.

Barnabas, realizing further sleep impossible, got up, dressed, and went walking into the darkness. The deserted streets left him alone with his thoughts. He walked to the sand beach and turned north. Following the massive stone aqueduct, he walked far out of the city. He had left Paul, not because he thought there was something wrong with Paul's message, but because he felt Paul's disposition was getting in the way of the message of the good news of Jesus Christ. Mary's painful expression yesterday, and now his own nightmarish reliving of the temple scene, raised new questions for him. Those questions James had asked in the temple were just now opening a Pandora's box of uncertainty. Obviously, Paul's interpretation of Jesus as the Christ, especially its implications for Judaism, generated serious problems with the recollections of those who knew Jesus and were close to him. They had difficulty connecting Paul's Christ with the Jesus they knew and the message he had preached and lived.

One of James's statements stuck out so clearly now; it was what James had said to Paul just before he was pushed down the steps: "Jesus did not have as many answers as you do, or if he did, he did not share them with us. He was more comfortable with questions." This truth James expressed had never hit Barnabas until now, when he mentally revisited that long-ago event.

Paul certainly did not live with questions. He was a man of answers. He defended his apostleship on the basis of what the Spirit of Christ told him. God's answers to man's dilemma came to Paul through the Spirit of Jesus Christ, who first arrested him on his way to Damascus. God had chosen Paul to speak God's new truth of human redemption. Just as he had done years before by selecting prophets to reveal his truth, God chose Paul to unveil his plan for human salvation. Many Gentiles believed Paul and his powerful message of justification through faith in Jesus Christ. Of course, the Jews who believed Jesus was the Messiah had a more difficult time with Paul's message, because it seemed to strip the heart out of their whole life. Nevertheless, those Jews who could see the spiritual importance of Paul's message found peace in it.

Barnabas looked out over the sea that he and Paul had sailed together so many times, and wondered why this message had come only to Paul. Obviously, from the exchange in the temple, James, Peter, and Simon did not understand Jesus's message the same way Paul did. It is odd that those who traveled with Jesus for more than three years never got this message Paul was proclaiming. Thinking back, Barnabas could not remember Jesus ever saying anything like Paul's gospel in his hearing. Wherever he and Paul went, Paul claimed that he was chosen especially to proclaim this message. Barnabas just now realized how blinded he had been to such an arrogant claim. A cold shiver shook his body. He drew his cloak tightly around him. Only now, almost twenty years after the fact, Barnabas saw the true nature of his discomfort that day in the temple. It was not Paul's attitude or behavior, but the fact that Paul was actually trying to force his message down the throats of Jesus's closest friends and followers; and it wasn't taking. Even when he left Paul a number of years later, this clarity was still missing. The waves crashing onto the beach seemed gentle to Barnabas compared to the turmoil in his head and gut. He walked into the surf. Was he seeking a new wave of understanding?

As the dawn broke, the questions going through Barnabas's

mind brought anything but comfort. Halfway through this mental excursion into the past, Barnabas had turned around. For the past hour, he had been walking back toward Caesarea. Now, back in the streets of the city and passing by Joseph and Hanna's house, he heard singing:

> "I lift my eyes to the hills-
> from where will my help come?
> My help comes from the Lord,
> who made heaven and earth."

Hanna was preparing cakes and singing a tune Barnabas remembered from his childhood. He went around to the back of the house and found Hanna removing the cakes from the oven by the back door.

"Barnabas, do come in," Hanna said. "You are up awfully early this morning."

"Yes, I couldn't sleep," Barnabas explained. "I feel as if I have walked the dawn into existence. I have been walking for almost three hours."

"My Lord, what could possibly be troubling you so much that you walked half the night away?" asked Hanna.

Just then, Salome walked in. She was surprised to see Barnabas. "Barnabas, what are you doing here this time of the morning?"

"Good morning, Salome," Hanna said, "He's been walking half the night and obviously stopped because he's famished," she added jokingly.

"To be sure, those cakes do smell very good, but I stopped because I heard Hanna singing a song I remembered from my childhood," replied Barnabas. "It appears that I am doing a lot of remembering this morning."

"My mother and I heard her singing too," said Salome. "I guess we all remember that song with fond memories. What else have you been remembering that has troubled you so this morning, Barnabas?"

"Is it so obvious that I am troubled?" asked Barnabas.

"Walking half the night away has not erased the anguish from your face," observed Hanna.

"Your eyes tell me you are struggling greatly with something," suggested Salome.

"Is it that obvious?" Barnabas asked again. "It started with Mary's painful expression when she was talking to me about Paul yesterday. Paul really seems to trouble her. To compound this, I had a terrible nightmare. That awful event in the temple years ago with Paul and James, Peter, and Simon came back to me in a nightmare; it was so real that I lived it all again. I woke in a tremendous sweat and couldn't go back to sleep. I decided to go for a walk. Paul's message about Jesus as the Christ apparently upset many who knew Jesus best. Why does a message of hope churn up such trouble?"

"Finally, someone who matters is asking the questions I have been asking forever!" exclaimed Salome. "You walked with Jesus, you heard him preach, you sat at his feet when he taught, and now you are asking the same question that has troubled me for years. Why do men fight over who Jesus was? It's almost as if they never knew him or heard what he said."

"You have been asking that questions for years?" asked Barnabas.

"I was so young, and mostly concerned with whether any of Jesus's followers were interested in me; but even I could tell that what Jesus taught had little to do with what his followers were questioning and arguing about," admitted Salome. "He was so comfortable with the miraculous events touching his life, and never questioned where they came from or what they were about. To him, it was always a simple 'the kingdom of God is at hand.'"

"Your young eyes and ears appear to have been much more perceptive than those of us constantly trying to figure out how and why Jesus did what he did and said what he said," confessed Barnabas. "We were so concerned with putting him into our preconceived notions that we couldn't celebrate what was happening. And then, after his death, we were so dejected by his absence, yet elated by the power of his continued presence, that we were utterly confused. Paul was the first one to really put it all together in a way that made some sense to me."

Just then, Mary came into the room. "I thought you were going to come right back to the room with a few—" Mary began before stopping herself and saying, "Barnabas, what are you doing here?"

"Learning from your daughter," commented Barnabas. "She is exposing some things to me about our years with Jesus; things that are revealing and very unsettling. Did you also see us disciples as confused over what Jesus was trying to teach?"

"Can't we start out with something a little less serious?" Mary asked. "Can't we have a cake before we try to make sense of our troubled past? Why are you here so early in the morning? You did go to Tobias's last night, didn't you?"

"Yes, I went there last night, but I couldn't sleep, and so I ended up walking halfway to Tyre before stopping in here this morning," replied Barnabas.

"Is it safe to walk these city streets at night?" asked Mary.

"No one is going to rob a poor rabbi. You can't get blood from a stone. Furthermore, no one is going to interrupt a rabbi deep in thought, for fear a lecture that has no end might be the result," jested Barnabas. "Actually, I did most of my walking along the beach north of here."

They each got a cake and some tea, and went into the small courtyard at the rear of the house. The four-cubit-high walls covered with vines provided privacy. Low stone walls separated gardens of spices, herbs, vegetables, and flowers. Joseph and Hanna had taken advantage of every space available. The garden was beautiful and inviting. They each found a seat on one of the low walls.

Mary was now ready to hear about Barnabas's nighttime walk. "So, Salome and Hanna were getting an ear full of your night's cogitations?"

"Yes, and more! Salome actually uncovered some notions I have been avoiding for quite some time," Barnabas confessed.

Joseph quietly entered the garden and sat on a wall by the door. He was in awe of Mary. How comfortable she seemed, regardless of her situation. She was a stranger in a stranger's house, yet he felt she belonged here, and she acted as if she did too. He said to himself, *I can't believe this really is the mother of our Lord! The rest of our church will be so thrilled to meet her.*

Mary continued. "So, Salome did some digging around in your comfort zone. That explains the troubled look you are wearing this morning."

"Well, that settles it. I obviously am not hiding my distress. All three of you now have confirmed that I look troubled. Actually, I was doing the digging, and Salome was helping me put the pieces back in order," Barnabas explained. "I had a horrible nightmare last evening; well, it was more like a flashback that robbed me of any possibility of sleep. I found myself back in the temple in Jerusalem with James, Peter, Simon, and Paul on that awful day. I relived the experience as if it were just happening."

Mary's look of horror reflected the look on Barnabas's face. "I can hardly imagine how awful that must have been," she said.

"Some of the things said that day impacted me very differently this morning, especially after our conversation last evening," continued Barnabas. "James, Peter, and Simon were really trying to understand why what Paul preached seemed so difficult to square with what Jesus taught and preached. Last night, you also said you were troubled by how little Paul seemed to care about Jesus and what he taught. Salome was relieved to hear me question why we had to argue over who Jesus was or is. She has been asking that question for a long time. In fact, she claims that it was obvious to her that we disciples often were not reading from the same scroll as Jesus."

"Well," Mary responded, "there were many times when Jesus got frustrated with your questions and squabbles. He often came back to Mary Magdalene just to talk to someone who understood."

"This morning, for the first time," confessed Barnabas, "I got this awful sensation that Jesus may not recognize the message we are spreading today in his name; if he did, he probably would not be very comfortable with it. When he comes back, will he recognize the good news?"

"That's a question I have had on my mind for a long time," admitted Mary. "The constant fighting within the Jewish community over whether Jesus is or isn't the Messiah has been so destructive. Not only has it led to violence, it's also completely distorted Jesus's message. Why is it so hard to understand that the message is the messiah?"

"I haven't heard it put quite that way before," commented Barnabas. "In Paul's circles, the message seemed always to be so clear. Constantly at issue was what to do with the demands of the Torah. That has led to its share of fighting and violence. But, this morning, I had to wonder if we are thinking the same things when we talk about the message. Somehow, Paul's message of salvation does not seem to fully capture the impact of Jesus on those who knew him best."

"If you ask me," Salome volunteered, "the problem is that there are too many persons who claim to know that they have the answers; however, none of their answers are the same."

"You don't know how close to the truth you might be," commented Mary. "My recollection is that Jesus said the same thing about all the different answers of the scribes, Pharisees, and Sadducees."

"That's exactly the thought that has stuck in my mind since my nightmare," said Barnabas. "James told Paul that the big difference between him and Jesus was that Paul had all the answers, whereas Jesus was more comfortable with questions."

Joseph was very uncomfortable. He was one of the first Jews in Caesarea to accept Paul's message. "Barnabas, have you forgotten just how powerful the presence of the Holy Spirit was when you and Paul preached the gospel here in Caesarea? Everyone, both Jew and Gentile, was excited about the assurance of eternal life. Remember the miracles, the speaking in tongues?"

"Of course I remember; no one could forget that. We were caught up in the moment." Barnabas was suddenly aware that his questions were not only causing him pause; they were troubling Joseph. He didn't want to hurt this old friend. He tried to walk this back a few paces. "Nobody can take that ecstasy away from us, nor diminish its significance. The question is, Are we making something out of Jesus that has nothing to do with his life and message, and if so, have we really understood his good news?"

"You haven't been to our fellowship for a long time. You have to bring Mary and Salome. You'll be surprised at how the Holy Spirit moves among us and encourages us to worship and take on the Spirit of Christ." Joseph didn't like hearing Barnabas questioning what he had accepted so fully. He wanted Barnabas to see how alive in Christ his early converts still were.

Barnabas responded, "I would love nothing better. We will definitely go to service with you."

CHAPTER 10

NEW TROUBLES

Before the eighth hour, an excited Rhoda, sister of Hanna, stood at their door, asking to meet Mary.

"My, but the word gets around fast," commented Hanna. "How did you know Mary was here?"

"Everyone knows," exclaimed Rhoda, "and everyone wants to meet her! Just think, to actually see and talk to the mother of our blessed Lord! Oh, the questions that must be asked! Is she here? Can I talk to her?"

"Come in, and I'll get you some tea. I'll see if Mary is rested enough from her ordeal to take on your ravenous questions," said Hanna.

While Hanna was getting tea, Mary walked into the room. The two women looked at each other, neither saying anything. Hanna hurried into the room.

"This is my sister, Rhoda," Hanna said to Mary. "She is anxious to meet you."

"God's blessing on you and your house," Mary said to Rhoda. "I am so pleased to meet a sister of this kind woman who opened up her home to us. You are blessed to have such a generous woman as a sister."

Rhoda was speechless. She seemed to be caught off guard, as

if expecting someone different. She looked as if she might bow down in front of Mary.

Hanna jumped into the silence. "Mary and her daughter were with the group brought here from Jerusalem. They had a harrowing trip and a frightening experience in the camp."

Hanna wasn't sure what had stopped Rhoda's tongue, but it certainly wasn't like her to be at a loss for words. Hanna left to get the tea.

Mary walked up to Rhoda, put her hand on her arm, and said, "It was kind of you to come to see us. Hanna and Joseph have made us feel very much at home, and your coming so soon is evidence that such kindness runs in the family."

Rhoda finally found her voice. "What an honor! I can't believe I am meeting the mother of our Lord! What a joy you must feel to know that your son is the savior of all mankind."

"All of my children are joyous blessings of God," replied Mary, a little taken aback by Rhoda's enthusiasm. "They have been living proof of the love of God."

"Yes, but Jesus was different," went on Rhoda excitedly. "He must have been so different from the rest."

"No two of them were alike," responded Mary. "Jesus was my first child, so everything about him was new and different."

"What was it like? I mean, could you tell he was someone special?" Rhoda asked.

Mary came back with a question: "Do you have children, Rhoda?"

"Yes, three."

"Then you know that each one is someone special." answered Mary. "Jesus was a typical baby. Then James, Joseph, and the twins Judas Thomas and Marta came along, so I had five children, four of them boys, in six years. That was a handful! They were all different and all special. Jesus certainly was the leader. He and James were only thirteen months apart, so they were almost like twins. The other three followed these two around. Being the oldest, Jesus always experienced everything first, and the others wanted to be a part of whatever he was doing."

It was obvious that Rhoda wasn't interested in hearing normal childhood stories. "But you had to know at some point that Jesus was not just a normal boy. I heard that he was arguing with the rabbis when he was barely of age."

"Yes, he was exceptional when it came to studying the Torah. He learned extremely fast and had a very deep understanding of life at a very young age. But then, so did my other sons. How amazing to hear them discuss and argue! They could hold their own with the rabbis. Our house probably experienced as many deep discussions as did the best rabbinical schools." Mary knew she was bragging, but it felt good. "They all were exceptional boys and men. They had deep reverence for God, and their humility was unique."

"The great crowds, and the miracles!" Rhoda pushed on. "You must have been so proud! How did it feel to see your son so popular and healing all those people?"

"The crowds scared me," Mary confessed. "Jesus taught that the kingdom of God was at hand. Anyone who had a new message was looked upon as a possible liberator, and the crowds always seemed to be on the verge of rebellion. Jesus's ability to heal only fed into this fervor. It was scary! The Messiah was on everyone's mind, and some thought Jesus and his message of the kingdom of God meant that he was going to reestablish the kingdom of David."

"They didn't realize he was talking about a spiritual kingdom," Rhoda said. "I can't imagine how exciting it must have been to hear him preach. Paul is a powerful preacher, but Jesus must have been something else. When did you first realize that Jesus was more than just a man?"

"More than just a man?" Mary was puzzled. "I'm not sure I understand."

"You know, that he is God's son, divine," Rhoda clarified.

Mary hesitated. She had heard this before. Every time she heard it, strange sensations went down her spine and settled in the pit of her stomach. She knew that when some called Jesus God's son, they meant more than the usual phrase "the Son of Man." "Only God is divine," she said. "God is one! No man can replace God or place himself alongside God. That is utter sacrilege! My son was a holy man; he was more in tune with the presence of God than anyone I have ever known. He was very aware of God's power and presence. But he never spoke as God; he spoke as a man."

From the way Rhoda was grabbing her dress in her hands, Mary knew that what she was saying was bothering Rhoda. Hanna, too, and Joseph, who had come into the room, looked puzzled. Yet Mary had to say more. "To make a man God makes him no longer a man. What does that make of the baby I bore, raised, and nourished? What does that make of the man Jesus, his life and his teachings? Are we used by God? Was Jesus just an angel walking around in a man's body? Are we God's playthings?" Mary knew she had said too much, and the passion in her voice was upsetting the others.

"I'm confused! That's not at all what I expected to hear." Rhoda was perplexed. "You certainly seem to have a different understanding of Christ Jesus than we do. We believe he came to earth to save mankind, and will soon come again to establish forever the kingdom you say he talked so much about. Isn't that what you believe?"

Mary didn't want to upset these new acquaintances. "I'm not talking about beliefs; only what I have experienced and observed. Jesus taught that the kingdom of God is already here. He taught that if we repent of our sins and sincerely live Torah, we can walk with him in that kingdom. I'm confused when you say he will return to establish the kingdom in the future."

Rhoda was not sure what to say. She looked first at Hanna, and then at Joseph. Both were at a loss for words. Finally, Rhoda reached out to Mary and took her hands. "I'd love to hear you say more about what Jesus did and taught." She liked this woman, in spite of the shock at what she was hearing. She was no longer looking at Mary as if she worshipped her, but as if she wanted to know all about her and be her friend. "Won't you join us at our fellowship? I know the others are very eager to meet you."

Mary hesitated. "I would like that very much, as long as I don't upset them as much as I did you this morning."

"It was really my pleasure to meet you; I so look forward to hearing more from you about Jesus. Good day." Rhoda left as quickly as she had come.

An awkward silence followed Rhoda's exit. Mary saw the anxiety on the faces of Hanna and Joseph, and realized that the conversation had troubled them. "It's obvious that my comments about Jesus are upsetting you, just as my statements about Paul tormented Barnabas. I'm sorry to upset you. We obviously see Jesus differently. The one thing I'm sure of is that Jesus cannot be a barrier to our awareness of the presence of the kingdom of God. His whole life and message sought to erase those barriers. We need to pause when we see them emerge among us."

Mary walked over to Hanna and took her hands. "Our differences confuse and bother us, but they need not separate us. God's love will always reveal the limits of the human mind, if we open our hearts. We have so much to learn about each other." She then went to Joseph and said, "I can't wait to visit your fellowship; that will be a great way to help us know each other better."

The next Sabbath, Joseph, Hanna, Salome, and Mary met Barnabas outside the home where the services were held.

Joseph asked them to wait outside. "I need to prepare the group for the thrill of a lifetime," he said.

Mary thought he was making much too much of this. "Joseph, please don't exaggerate their expectations."

Joseph just gave her a smile. After a few minutes, Joseph came back out and invited Mary and Salome to enter. The door opened into a large room crowded with people. Well more than forty persons were packed into the room, all straining to get a look at Mary. She was surprised to see that the women and men were all intermingled. (Traditionally, men and women sat separately during Jewish worship services.) Mary couldn't discern the expressions of the room's occupants.

Her eyes then fell on a small table in the middle of the room. On the table, next to the Torah, was a crude wooden cross. Mary's heart jumped into her throat. She swallowed a sob. She felt herself getting sick, covered her mouth, and pushed her way out the door. She couldn't control her stomach and vomited onto the ground at the side of the door. She began sobbing and couldn't stop. In an instant, she had been transported back to that dreadful day. Only then, she had time to prepare herself. This had come on her like a bolt of lightning. Her mother's heart was split in two, and her grief poured out, encompassing her whole being.

She was not aware of Salome, tears running down her cheeks, standing beside her and softly stroking her hair. She could not feel Barnabas's strong arms around her shoulders, holding her erect. She did not see the frightened faces of Hanna, Joseph, Rhoda, and many others, who crowded in the doorway, looking on in shocked bewilderment.

"What happened? What is wrong?" they whispered among themselves. "Is she going to be all right?"

No one could imagine what might have brought this on.

Barnabas looked at Joseph and Hanna, and then he said, "We'd better get her back to your place." To the others he said, "Please, excuse us. We will get her comfortable, and I'll be back to let you know how she is. Please go back inside and pray for her."

Barnabas, looking down on a still-sobbing Mary, asked, "Can you walk or should I get a litter?"

Mary closed her eyes and tried to control her sobbing, but it would not cease. Between sobs she said, "I can walk. I'm so sorry for my behavior. Those people wanted to be so nice to me, and I've insulted them. I'm so ashamed!"

Barnabas asked, "What happened?"

Salome knew. She had seen her mother's face go white, and followed her eyes to the figure on the table. "That revolting symbol on the table brought back the most horrible day of her life. Not a day goes by that she does not grieve over that horror, and that figure hit her when she least expected it. What a horrendous thing to have as a center of worship!"

Barnabas was shocked at Salome's outburst. He was about to say something to Salome when Mary put her hand on his arm and shook her head. She looked at him, and he immediately knew that Salome was not far from the mark. Confusion overtook him. The symbol that was the centerpiece of his faith was revolting to the mother of his Lord! Of course, no mother could easily accept the brutal death of her son, but, surely, she understood the whole picture. Or did she? Or did he? Oh, how the questions kept building, and the answers falling by the wayside!

By the time they got back to the house, Mary seemed to be feeling better. She said to Barnabas, "I feel so badly for you, Joseph, and Hanna, and for all the others. I should have been able to control myself and not cause such a scene. Barnabas, please go back to them and apologize for me. Tell them I was rude to let my emotions overtake me, and tell them I seek their forgiveness."

"I can't go back yet," Barnabas said. "I don't know what to tell them. They will not accept an apology for something they don't understand. Frankly, I'm not sure I understand."

"What don't you understand?" asked Mary. "Do you think I should get used to something that celebrates the brutal, unjust murder of my firstborn? You can devise all the elaborate notions you like as to God's design, but nothing will ever convince a mother that a God of love would use her son to prove that love. What a mockery of God's love! My sons' *lives* are the proof of God's love, not their deaths. Three of my sons were killed by men whose selfish beliefs mock God's love."

The faces of Barnabas, Joseph, and Hanna were ashen. They didn't know what to say.

Finally, Joseph sheepishly asked, "Then, you don't believe?"

Mary could see that what she had said had severely shaken all three of them. She didn't want to hurt them, but she also knew she couldn't tell them something different from what her body's physical reactions had already told them. "If I must believe that the God who is above all Gods, this God of love, needed to use my son to prove that love by having him killed, then you must count me among the unbelievers."

Joseph, Hanna, and Barnabas could not believe what they were hearing.

Hanna blurted out, "But isn't that what made Jesus the Christ?"

"I'm not sure what you mean by that. Some have called Jesus the Messiah, as if the messiah were a person. I'm not sure Jesus ever understood the messiah in that way," answered Mary.

"But Jesus's sacrifice was the greatest example of selfless love!" countered Barnabas. "Doesn't that show God's love, in that he was willing to sacrifice his only son to save us from our sins?"

"In order for me to believe that," answered Mary, "I must see love as something totally foreign to everything love means. Self-sacrifice is one thing; the sacrifice of one's offspring is murder. Where is the love in that? Does our selfish desperation for redemption from sin mean we have to distort our understanding of love? Remember, God would not allow Abraham to sacrifice Isaac."

"But man can't save himself," inserted Barnabas, "only faith in God can save him."

"What is salvation?" asked Mary. "Are we so desperate that we must ascribe to God something we would detest in ourselves and then call it love so that we can acclaim ourselves redeemed in the eyes of God?"

"But Jesus also appeared to Paul," asserted Barnabas. "He claims that God's Spirit appeared to him time and again to reveal this very plan of salvation. He says that the Spirit of Christ Jesus revealed to him this truth, which is the only way to eternal peace."

Mary thought for a moment, and then she said, "I know what I am saying is very upsetting to you. But, deep in my heart, I feel that such a distortion of love is just the opposite of faith in a God of love."

Barnabas's head was spinning. Or was it the whole room, even the whole universe, that was spinning out of control? Ever since Mary arrived in Caesarea, one thing after the other was being called into question. Now the very foundations of his faith were shaken. What was he to make of all of this? He finally got up enough nerve to address Mary. "Mary, what you are saying is extremely troubling to us, especially to those who never knew Jesus and have accepted him on the basis of his redeeming sacrifice. Do you not believe that your son Jesus was more than just a man?"

"I know Jesus was fully a man. I felt his kicks in my womb. He suckled from my breasts. I wrapped his scraped knee; I held him as he cried uncontrollably when his favorite lamb died." Mary was again speaking through tears. "I watched him grow, nursed him through all those childhood illnesses. I listened to him mature in wisdom until he baffled the rabbis. I saw crowds of people hail him as the Messiah and saw his disappointed look at such a notion. I saw the crowds turn on him and demand his death for posing as their Messiah." She swallowed a sob that almost choked her. "I saw him die as cruel a death as any man can experience. I heard him cry out to God, whom he felt had abandoned him and his faithfulness. I saw him laid into a tomb, and I saw the empty tomb." The tears were running down her cheeks. "He came to me from out of the tomb, embraced me, and called me 'Mama.' He said to me, 'The good news is God's love; forget yourself, and follow me.'" There was a long pause. "Was he more than just a man? To say that is to say something I cannot know. But I do know that he was such a man that God's presence and love were real when he was around."

Barnabas was visibly moved. He, too, remembered Jesus and knew the truth Mary was saying. He remembered the healings, the persons set free from their troubled minds. He recalled Jesus's uncanny ability to release his followers from their enslaving beliefs that consistently created barriers between people. The stories he told were about how we should act in the presence of God. And, yes, he taught selflessness and constantly encouraged us to walk that path with him. He also knew Mary was right in saying that we cannot know that Jesus was more than just a man. But why not accept that on faith?

After a long silence, he said, "Our belief that Jesus was more than a man only emphasizes his life and message. ..."

"And separates you from all those who cannot believe that," interrupted Mary, with more passion in her voice than she wished. "When beliefs about who God is and what God is doing become our faith, we create barriers between people. These barriers form the foundations of violence. What is behind the violence in our own community? What has the opposition and temple priests at each other's throats? What had your own people chasing you and Paul out of city after city? What killed three of my sons?"

Barnabas's tongue was tied, his head was spinning, and his heart was in knots.

They now all sat down in silence. No one knew what to say.

After a long uncomfortable silence, Salome, who had been quiet through this whole incident, said softly to Mary, "Mama, you have endured more than most mothers. I don't think any of us can fully appreciate what those losses mean to you. I'm with you; that statue on the table turned my stomach too."

Mary gave Salome a look of deep gratitude. "I'm embarrassed by my reaction," said Mary. "Those people don't understand it at all. We have to get back to them and apologize."

Suddenly, Barnabas found his voice. "I'm not ready to go back yet. I have no idea what to say to them."

"I am not ready either," agreed Salome. "All the murders

of my brothers were senseless. All of them slaughtered by men who were threatened by them, and yet they were peaceful, loving individuals. That cross cannot be a symbol of love!"

Mary looked at Salome, and an appreciative smile formed in her eyes. Her lips quivered as she said, "You have suffered with me through it all. I wanted so much more for you than to be my comfort through life's tragedies. You deserve to know love in its fullest."

"I have known love at its finest: you, Papa, Jesus, James, Simon, Joseph, Judas Thomas, and Marta," said Salome. She didn't mention Zenas but thought of him as well.

Mary knew Salome was comfortable with her life. She, James, and Simon had always been totally content with their celibate lives; yet she wished Salome could have experienced the unmatched joys of motherhood.

Suddenly aware of the others in the room, Mary said, "Barnabas, you should go back to the fellowship and let them know that I am fine. I'm sure they are anxious to hear from you. Please take my sincerest apology. An apology is all that is needed right now; explanations can come later."

Barnabas was reluctant to go. He really was baffled as to what to tell the others about what had happened to Mary. He knew they would want to know what had happened, and why. How in the world would they understand? He didn't fully understand. Well, maybe he was beginning to understand, but he didn't want to consider the consequences.

As he left the room, his mind was racing. Jesus on the cross was an anathema to Mary and Salome, probably two of the three persons alive in the world who knew Jesus best. Jesus on the cross was the answer to life for all those in the fellowship. Jesus on the cross was the worst possible symbol of God's love to some, and the most glorious example to others. Jesus taught a life of selflessness and love. His sacrificial death was the ultimate act of selflessness. If Jesus Christ was truly God, then his death was the ultimate expression of God's love. Yet wasn't salvation, the yearning for eternal life, really a selfish demand? Who was man to seek justification? Jesus taught us to repent so we could walk in God's kingdom. Jesus never really said anything about justification. Paul certainly made a big thing about it, but Jesus didn't. When that young Jewish ruler asked him what he had to do to gain eternal life, Jesus said, "Do Torah, forget self and follow me."

By the time Barnabas got to their gathering place, he was beginning to realize how differently the followers of Jesus saw Jesus. The followers of Jesus who called themselves Christians understood Jesus as the Christ, whereas the followers of Jesus who considered themselves Jews did not view Jesus that way. Barnabas was beginning to sense that there was even a difference among the Jewish followers of Jesus: some saw Jesus as the Messiah, and some, including even Mary and her children, saw Jesus as a man proclaiming the era of the messiah, or the kingdom of God. Paul seemed to have had this all figured out. Why was it so clear when traveling with Paul, and so fuzzy and complicated now?

As he entered the fellowship, Barnabas was still wondering what he was going to say. As he looked over his friends of many years, he saw, possibly for the first time, how diverse they were. They were dressed in many different garbs, from the traditional Jewish to the very Roman. All eyes were fixed on him. "Brothers and sisters, first, let me tell you that Mary is fine. She asked me to apologize to all of you for the anxiety she caused. She is very upset for disrupting our meeting."

He paused. *That was the easy part,* he thought. "You saw what I saw, and the explanation is not very comforting. Mary had a visceral reaction to this cross on the table. It took her back to that dreadful day, a day that haunts her daily. That, I'm sure, you can readily understand. She was there and witnessed the whole brutal scene. I can't imagine the mother who would not have a similar reaction when something like this"—he pointed to the cross on the table—"brings back such a memory, especially when she is not expecting it."

He paused as if uncertain how to continue. Swallowed, as if covering a sob, and in a voice tinged with reluctance he said, "She can only mourn his death, as well as the murders of her other two sons, as the horrendous acts of sinful men. She can't entertain such violence as remotely connected with God's love."

The room grew very tense. No one said anything, but the constant shifting of positions revealed extreme discomfort. Desperately searching for words, Barnabas continued. "We have known each other for many years, and shared many Lord's Suppers. We have prayed and suffered together. You have been especially kind to me, respecting me for my experiences while walking with Jesus. Those were the best few months of my life. I would give anything to live them over. I have tried to faithfully recount those experiences to you and relate them to our faith.

"As you know, I only knew Jesus for his last few tumultuous months. I did not benefit from his teaching ministry; I only experienced him when the crowds were trying to make him king and his disciples were constantly arguing over what he should do. Once he was gone from us, we were confused as to what we should do next. A messianic spirit filled all of us. We fully expected Jesus to come back at any time, and we preached that message. Jews, and even God-fearers, began to accept our message. The good news spread to other cities far and wide. At the same time, many Jews, especially those in authority, saw us as blasphemers. 'How could someone hung on the cross be the Messiah?' they asked. As our message became more popular, their opposition became more severe."

"We know the story. Does your telling us stories we already know reveal your discomfort, or are you trying to backtrack what you taught us?" Silvanus was not sure where this was going.

Barnabas, taken aback by the interruption, responded. "The background is very important for us to understand just what happened here. Paul, our father in the faith, instructed us, according to a revelation he received from the risen Jesus. A few days ago, someone came to our city who knew Jesus better than anyone else. Who could know someone better than his own mother? In just a few days, Mary has shaken me and my memory in such ways that I'm not sure what I believe. Just a little while ago, the mother of Jesus told some of us that she will never accept Jesus's brutal crucifixion as an expression of God's love." Barnabas paused as an audible gasp filled the room, and then he added, "You can ask Joseph and Hanna; they heard it too."

The people in the room became very restless and began whispering to one another.

Barnabas knew he could not stop here if he wished to be honest and true to himself. At the risk of upsetting his friends even more, he continued. "To add to my discomfort, some of Mary's comments over the past few days have shaken my memory. She commented on how obvious it was to her that Paul never knew Jesus, and how Paul's message completely ignored Jesus's life and preaching. On top of this, I had a terrible nightmare that brought back in vivid memory that awful incident between Paul, James, Simon, and Peter in the temple a number of years ago. The disciples were questioning Paul about his message, expressing concern about how it seemed to be causing a split among the followers of Jesus. They felt that his position on the Torah was creating a wedge between the Jewish and Gentile believers. I'm sure many of you can relate to that, considering the struggles you have had in the past. Paul was adamant that Christ had ushered in a new era, making the Torah a thing of the past. The dispute hinged on Paul's emphasis on redemption and the disciples' recollection that Jesus preached awareness of the presence of the kingdom and said little about redemption. These events have got me thinking."

Suddenly, someone started shouting from the back of the room. "Whatever happened to faith? It seems to me, there is too

much thinking going on!" Caspius, a Greek merchant and one of
the early Gentile believers baptized by Paul and Barnabas, was not
known for his tact.

A few amens followed his outburst.

Jacob, one of the Jewish Christians in the fellowship, said,
"Perhaps we should be thinking less and praying more."

Barnabas was extremely uncomfortable. These people where
close to him. Many of them had become Christians through
his teaching. He and Paul had baptized the first few believers
a number of years ago. On a number of subsequent visits from
Cyprus, he had baptized many more. Their faith was grounded
on his preaching, and he felt like a traitor. He should have kept his
doubts and questions to himself.

"Just what are you trying to tell us?" asked Caspius. "It seems
you are questioning the very faith that binds this fellowship
together."

"I'm not sure what I am trying to tell you," answered Barnabas
honestly.

Caspius was having nothing of this. "Before we embrace this
weak-kneed man of faith, remember that very recently we had
a real man of faith, Paul, here with us for more than two years.
Even though Felix had him under arrest, we were able to visit
him often, and we received his wisdom. He encouraged our faith
and expanded it. He enlightened us to the limitations of Torah
and helped us find new freedom in the Spirit. Is this faith so
easily shattered by some twenty-year-old recollections and an old
woman with a weak stomach?"

The room erupted. A few applauded, but most gasped in
horror at Caspius's brashness.

Jacob, a recognized leader in the fellowship, stood. "Let's give
Barnabas a chance to explain himself. We will get nowhere with
acrimony or vitriol."

The room slowly quieted, and Barnabas began to speak, now
in a tone revealing uncertainty. "I'm not sure what I am trying to

tell you," repeated Barnabas. "I am simply opening up my heart and troubled mind to you, and asking you to accept me with love, as a brother, along with all my confusion."

"We can easily do that, Barnabas." Tobias was Barnabas's best friend in Caesarea. "You have been like a shepherd to us. You have nurtured us and built up our faith. It is obvious that you are troubled. We have been shaken as well by Mary's reaction. We need to embrace each other right now and seek God's will. If God is love, we need to go forward in love."

No words could have been more soothing to Barnabas at that moment. He sensed more than friendship in Tobias's comment. He felt real compassion for this special group of people. His heart warmed to the moment. "I have no doubt that we have all we need to get us past the uncertainty we are feeling right now. I have never felt the presence of God more strongly than I do at this moment. Let's pray in silence and wait for the Lord to speak to us."

There was a long silence, every so often interrupted with sighs and groans. After a while, there was some shuffling near the back of the room, and some whispering could be heard.

Caspius stood up and said, "The Jewish followers of Jesus have never wanted anything more than to make us all Jews. Now you, Barnabas, are being sucked into their scheme. I, for one, will not be burdened with their superstitions or their law. Jesus Christ has revealed God's love to me, one who never knew the law, and offered me salvation as if I had been the most ardent follower of the law. There is no turning back." He turned and walked out. Four others followed.

CHAPTER 11

THE CHALLENGE OF THE SPIRIT

Barnabas arrived back at Tobias's house, greatly shaken and dejected because of the way he had handled the situation. The two men talked well into the night. Eventually realizing nothing he could say would make any impact on Barnabas's mood, Tobias excused himself and went to bed. Barnabas sat up the remainder of the night.

Very early in the morning, before daybreak, there was a loud knock on the door. The visitor was shocked that the door was opened so quickly.

Opening the door, Barnabas stepped back, seeing Caspius standing just outside. His angry face and aggressive posture gave Barnabas pause. Trying to mask his concern, Barnabas said, "Caspius, good morning. Please come in."

Caspius quickly pulled back the hood of his robe, exposing his head. Brushing past Barnabas and striding into the center of the room, he turned to look at Barnabas. His eyes revealed lack of sleep, and his hands awkwardly stroked his beard. In a very loud voice he said, "Are you aware of what you have done?"

Barnabas, not knowing what to say, raised his hands and said, "Please, not so loud; there is no reason to wake Tobias."

"The whole town should know of your affront and dastardly defection." The sound of someone moving about on the second level indicated that Barnabas's concern was to no avail. "Have you no compunction over ripping the heart out of the gospel of Jesus Christ?"

Just then, Tobias walked into the room and moved in between Caspius and Barnabas. "Caspius, please calm down. I'm sure the whole town does not wish to be awakened by your shouting."

The two men knew each other well and respected one another.

Caspius said, "Forgive me! My temper is my worst characteristic."

Tobias's presence calmed Caspius noticeably.

"We both are aware of how troubled you are, and knowing Barnabas as I do, no one feels worse about upsetting you than he."

Barnabas grabbed Tobias's arm and pulled him aside. "Let me speak for myself. Caspius, I spoke last night before I thought of the consequences of what I was saying. I am truly sorry for upsetting you."

The fire came back into Caspius's eyes. "I didn't come here seeking an apology for hurt feelings. Last night, your very lips suggested doubt about the bedrock of the gospel of Jesus Christ. Is Jesus the Christ God's sacrifice of love as redemption for our sins, or are you now saying we have been sold a bill of goods?" It appeared as if his whole body was asking the question.

Barnabas, rattled by Caspius's intensity, took a step back. "Believe me, Caspius, I fully understand your dilemma. I have never been more troubled in my life than during the past few days. Ever since Mary and Salome arrived, the world seems upside down. I'm sure all the questions you have right now are the same ones that have been ravaging my brain for the past few days."

"What has happened to you? When you and Paul first came to us, you were so filled with the Holy Spirit. Your message was so clear and powerful. We heard none of this second-guessing. Have you lost touch with the Holy Spirit?"

"I'm not sure how to answer that. When we came to you, we were filled with the Spirit of Christ, something we knew as the spirit of Jesus among us. That is how Paul described his experience of the risen Jesus. Paul claimed this same Spirit of Christ revealed to him God's loving act of redemption." Barnabas paused, not sure how to continue. At the moment, he felt no comfortable connection between the faith based on beliefs about Jesus that he and Paul had taught Caspius and the agonizing questions rolling around in his head. "The gospel we taught you claimed that God's gracious act of love made the cross a turning point in history, ushering in the reign of the Holy Spirit. Nothing would remain as it was; all things would be new."

Caspius calmed noticeably. "Yes, we were ushered into the world of the Holy Spirit by you, and freed from the sins of the body. Now you sound yourself again." The anger on Caspius's face was replaced with a look of ecstasy.

"My problem with all this is that Mary, the mother of Jesus and possibly the first to see our risen Lord, appears to know nothing about any of this, and she awakened in me the realization that Jesus never really said anything about this during his ministry—at least not in the few months I was with him."

"Well, why would he? The change didn't come until after he was crucified."

Barnabas looked at Caspius with great compassion and understanding. "My mind, too, has tried to make this all understandable. The real dilemma for me is that Mary does not seem at all receptive to the gospel Paul is preaching. I recall that James and Peter and the others in Jerusalem also had serious problems with Paul's message."

Caspius shook his head. "That stands to reason. All Jews are going to have a difficult time shedding their privileged status with God and accepting all Gentiles as equals."

"I wish it were that easy. Up until now, I passed off this difference as just a struggle for power and influence among leaders of the movement. But what appears to be happening is that everything the Jews hold dear must be relinquished in order to participate in the new world of the Spirit. Thinking back, nothing Jesus ever said or did points to that. It seems Mary is not inclined at all to the things of the Spirit that Paul preached. She is so down-to-earth, so comfortable with herself, and yet so open to others. Nothing she says or does implies that she must deny who she is. She is not focused on herself but on those around her. Sin does not seem to factor into her thinking or associations. We taught that the gospel of Jesus Christ changes you; that you must cast off the body of sin and adorn the body of Christ, a spiritual body. I expected a reuniting with Mary after all these years would bring a clarity and elation to all this. Our beliefs appear to be getting in the way of how we feel toward one another. To say that it is an uncomfortable feeling is a gross understatement."

"Isn't it the Holy Spirit that binds us together?"

"If you believe that, why did you react so angrily to my comments last night? Why did your anger come along with you this morning?"

"What you are saying threatens to undercut everything we—" Caspius stopped himself, not sure how to continue.

"Believe me, Caspius, I know the threat you are feeling. I imagine Mary's comments impacted me just as severely when she said them as they did you when I repeated them to you. You didn't finish your statement because you realized that it wasn't really you who was threatened, but, rather, what you believed. Something stronger than what we believe holds us together. Is it the Holy Spirit? At the very least, we must admit that it is a power stronger than what we believe. I think Mary has something to teach us, regardless of how painful the lesson."

Caspius was uncomfortable. "I'm not sure I like her being here. Maybe she is having a difficult time adjusting to being used by God. I'm sure it was an awful experience for her. It seems to me you are getting caught up in her attempts to rationalize her situation."

"Don't be unkind, Caspius. You were there; you saw her reaction. It was visceral, not at all calculated."

"Oh, come now, Barnabas, do you really think that was the first time she encountered a cross? I don't believe that for a minute. I don't trust her." Caspius's anger was rising again. "One thing is for sure: you keep up what you've started, and you are going to hurt a whole lot of people here in Caesarea."

Caspius couldn't stand still. He paced back and forth across the room. "This is a new world, Barnabas. You preached that to us. You're letting that woman drag you back into your past and saddle you once again with tradition and religious ritual. Jesus broke open the prison called Judaism. We are free to worship God as men and women of the future. The Holy Spirit has replaced the Torah and all its shackles."

Barnabas moved to stand in front of Caspius. "Why don't you give the Holy Spirit a chance? Why don't you give Mary the benefit of the doubt? Open up your mind and heart to her and try to understand her. What can it hurt?"

Caspius's eyes grew big, and his face flushed. He threw out his arms and said, "What can it *hurt*? The gospel of Jesus Christ has freed my soul. I am free from sin's shackles and can glorify God without the drudgery of religious laws and rituals. What can it hurt? I can lose my freedom!"

"And that freedom allows you to cast aside the mother of our savior?" Barnabas knew his words would hit Caspius hard, so he moved toward him in a gesture of compassion.

Caspius pushed him away. "She represents the past, and will only drag us back into the game of religious tomfoolery. Besides, the Jews have always made religion nothing more than a display of arrogance. They hold themselves away from the rest of us, as if they are something special. How can that ever bring us together?" These last words came out with more venom than Caspius wanted, revealing to him, and the other two men, a latent resentment buried somewhere deep.

Tobias, a Jew and a respected friend of Caspius, moved toward him and said, "Please don't confuse arrogance with gratitude. We Jews do not consider ourselves special because of who we are but because of what God did for us. We are no different than anyone else, but we can never forget that God looked on us with favor and freed us from slavery. Our behaviors are never anything more than humble expressions of gratitude for God's love. And we will never forget."

Caspius knew his words hurt Tobias, and he felt bad. He looked at Tobias and then at Barnabas. He felt like something was trying to pull him apart from the inside. His mind and anger were pulling him one way, and his heart and love another. He shook his head, turned his back on the two men, pulled the hood up over his head, and walked out of the house.

CHAPTER 12

A MEETING IN THE WILDERNESS

It pained Simon deeply to leave Jerusalem; he felt he should be there. His heart told him to stay, but his brain argued that he would be of no service to the fellowship if he were in prison. He decided to travel to the seedbeds of violence to do what he could to persuade them to abandon their disastrous course. He planned to travel first to the conclave beyond Jericho, and then head onward to Galilee. By the time he had visited both places, maybe he could safely return to Jerusalem.

Well after midnight, Simon left Jerusalem. Clouds mostly blotted out the moonlight. He felt fairly safe traveling the road to Jericho at night, and the continual downgrade made the walk comfortable. Very early in the morning, he moved off the roadway and into the fields and hills, because many already headed to Jerusalem, bringing their produce and wares to sell at the market. Before reaching Jericho, he turned south and went up into the rugged hills overlooking the Dead Sea. He walked into the settlement of Qumran late in the afternoon.

The community there welcomed him warmly. However, once they realized his purpose in visiting, the reception turned cold. These people were convinced the end times were here. Searching the scriptures for prophecies, they tied the events in Jerusalem over the past few years to the dire prophecies of Daniel. After the last conflict between Paul and James, they fully believed God's judgment was imminent. The temple had to be purified by the righteous. Their failure delayed God's judgment. They were adamant! They had shed the cloak of peace and strapped on the armor of conflict. No amount of argument from Simon could weaken their resolve.

Simon left the settlement, gravely disappointed. His hopes of having any better a response from those in Galilee were very low. The Galileans had been pressing for movement against the Romans for years. Galilee had been a breeding ground for insurrection for as long as Simon could remember. Nevertheless, he felt he had no choice but to try.

Simon traveled only at night and avoided all towns. He made slow progress. He did not look forward to the difficult journey over the rough Judean and Samaritan hills. He reached the rough hills above Jerusalem, exhausted, and spent more than a day resting in a cave.

Zenas left Jerusalem with Sarah's son Jacob and two of his friends, disguised as a slave with a slow mind and unable to take care of himself, but able and willing to do whatever Jacob requested. They, too, took the road to Jericho, but then turned north up the Jordan Valley. Their route was to go north to Scythopolis, cross the Jordan to Pella, and then travel on from there, heading eastward to Palmyra. They had signed on as helpers of a small caravan going to Pella. Each of the three was assigned to a camel. Less than two hours out of Jericho, a group of Roman soldiers approached the caravan, from the north. Realizing the danger this meant for Zenas, the other three secured their camels and began to fight among themselves to such a degree that it drew the soldiers' attention. The three became so belligerent that the soldiers felt they needed to intercede. The commotion gave Zenas a chance to escape. He climbed down a steep bank and hid among the rocks at the bottom.

The merchant who was directing the caravan became furious. He thought the soldiers had attacked his helpers and began yelling at the soldiers. Everyone was pushing and shoving. The soldiers finally drew their swords, and the disturbance subsided. When the merchant informed the soldiers that he was a Roman citizen, things were quickly resolved, and the caravan was allowed to proceed. Jacob and his friends hid Zenas's absence from the caravan captain, who was anxious to make up for this unwelcome delay.

During all the confusion, Zenas buried himself under loose debris in the ditch. He didn't move until well after dark. A nearly full moon made it possible for him to survey his situation. The rugged hills to the west were his best place to hide. He moved toward the hills, which were more rugged than they had appeared from a distance. He kept moving well into the hills before he looked for a place to rest. He came across a cave entrance that looked like it might be large enough to provide some safe shelter and comfort. He crawled just inside the opening and waited for his eyes to adjust to the darkness. Soon he began to pick out shapes within the cave, which was larger than he expected. The hair on the back of his neck stood up as he realized the shape of another man sitting against the far wall. He moved just a short way into the cave and sat down slowly, keeping his eyes on the other man.

The two men sitting in the cave had at least one thing in common: they were both fugitives. Both were hunted by the Romans: one for insurrection, and the other for desertion. Possibly, that was all they had in common. One was an old Nazirite Jew; the other a young Roman citizen. More than thirty years separated them in age. Here, in the desolate hill country somewhere north of Jerusalem, they both wondered how safe they were from their pursuers—and each other.

For many hours, neither man said a word. The approaching

dawn allowed a bit of light to creep into the cave. Each man sized up the other without saying a word.

Finally, Simon asked in Greek, "Have I invaded your humble abode?"

Zenas couldn't help but chuckle. "No. I was hoping you could spare me a room in your inn."

The tension somewhat relieved, both men immediately realized that at least they could communicate; it was a favorable beginning.

Simon was uncomfortable with the way this big man looked at him. More than a stare, it felt like a deep penetration into his inner being.

At last, the younger man asked, "Do you live in Jerusalem?"

"What a strange way to start a conversation," Simon said. "Yes, I do, but why do you ask that? Aren't you more concerned as to whether I'm armed with a dagger?"

"No. I could easily disarm you. For some strange reason, I have no fear of you. I asked that question because the other day, in Jerusalem, I met an older woman who has to be your mother. Or, is it true, as they say, that all Jews look alike"

Simon had to laugh. "You think all Jews look like me?"

"Well, some take better care of their hair than you do. But your eyes remind me of a woman I can't forget."

Simon liked this young man. He had a sense of humor and was not afraid to speak his mind. "You say it was an older woman, so I assume your fascination with her had to do with a civil encounter."

"First, before I answer, let's speak Aramaic. I need the practice. My name is Zenas. I am a Roman soldier who has just escaped from the fortress in Jerusalem. A few days ago, I was sent with a group of soldiers to a home, in search of a leader of the priests involved with the killings in the temple. I met this woman whose eyes remind me of yours. That is why I asked."

Now it was Simon's turn to play a joke. He stood up, put out his hands, and said, "I am Simon, the priest you are looking for. You got me; put on the shackles."

Zenas guffawed. "Had I found you a few days ago, my life would certainly be different than this."

"Yes, and, probably, so would mine," said Simon. "What are you doing here, hiding like a stalked stag?"

"That is quite a story," admitted Zenas. "Much of it has to do with your mother and her eyes." He relayed the whole story to Simon. "So, here I am, having no idea where I am or where I should be going. I have little hope that I can evade my pursuers for long."

"Wow!" Simon said, digesting Zenas's story. "Do you think my nephew Jacob is safe? Did the soldiers take him away?"

"No, they did not. The leader of the caravan made such a fuss that the soldiers let them all go. As soon as he said he was a Roman citizen, the whole atmosphere changed."

"Good!" Simon was relieved. "By the way, your Aramaic is excellent. Where did you learn it?"

"Many years before I was born, the three sons of Herod were wining and dining in Rome, each hoping to be appointed the successor to Herod the Great. One of them gave my uncle a Palestinian slave who became a servant in my parents' home. As a very young boy, I begged her daughter, Leah, to teach me their language."

"She was an excellent teacher."

"Yes, and she was probably no more than twelve years old."

Simon shook his head in amazement. "Your situation is much more precarious than mine. Maybe I can be of some help. At least I know the area and can probably keep you away from the Romans, who will likely stick to the main roads. I'm curious, however; you said that you escaped, not so much to get away from your imprisonment but because of my mother's eyes."

"Well, yes and no. It was not just her eyes. By the way, you have those same eyes. It was everything about her: her openness, her fearlessness, and her compassion."

Simon smiled. "You speak of my mother, for sure. She is such a holy person."

Zenas nodded. "That's a good way to describe her. I have never felt like I did when I was listening to her. It was as if a huge fountain was placed before me, and I could drink from it and ask all the questions I wanted. I have studied under the most prestigious philosophers in Rome, and I never felt such openness, such freedom. Before the encounter with your mother, I probably could have had almost any position I wanted in Rome. I've thrown all that away. Something inside me has to uncover what your mother's secret is. Nothing else matters!"

Simon had never been a father, but the only thing he could think of to describe the feelings he had for this young man was a father's love. It took such fearlessness to throw off power and privilege, in search of truth! Or, if not fearlessness, was it youthful exuberance?

Zenas stood, walked to the mouth of the cave, and looked out over the rocky hills. He turned to Simon and said, "I've told you why I am here. I know you are wanted by the authorities, but why are you running away? Wouldn't you be safer surrendering to the Romans?" As soon as he asked the question, Zenas saw how foolish it was. "I'm sorry! I still get trapped in ideology and lose sight of reality."

"Believe me, if I thought surrendering to the Romans would keep me in Jerusalem, I would have done it. My place is in the temple, but there is so much violence swirling around that place right now that not even the power of Rome can make it safe. I am on my way to try to convince some of the most-radical revolutionaries to cease their violent methods."

Simon walked over to Zenas and said, "Your situation is much more precarious than mine right now. We have to find a way to get you as far away from Jerusalem as possible. The east is the only direction that offers you any real hope of escape."

The hills surrounding them were virtually deserted, strewn with rocks and very steep. Very little vegetation grew on the hillsides. There were no real valleys, as one hill grew right out of the feet of the next. Simon knew that to continue on northward would eventually get them into more populated areas, which would be dangerous for Zenas. He was convinced that they had to cross the Jordan and get into the mountains on the eastern side. From there, they could work their way north, toward the caravan routes that headed for the great river and Babylon.

"Your only way to safety is to the east," Simon explained to Zenas.

"Isn't that away from your mother?" Zenas asked.

"I left my mother and sister in Jerusalem. Neither of us can go back there."

Mention of Simon's sister reminded Zenas of Salome. Not a night went by that he did not think of her and the beautiful, enlightening incident they had shared on the house roof in Jerusalem. He had become a complete man that night. The thought of Salome, and Mary, being harassed by the Romans raised hackles of anger up his spine and neck.

Looking toward the east, Simon said, "I'm not sure how far we are from the river, but we may be able to reach the mountains on the other side in one night's walk. We certainly can't cross the valley in daylight."

"That means we must spend the day here in this cave. Perhaps I can find us some food and water."

"Not an easy task in this stark place," said Simon with a good deal of skepticism.

"We certainly won't find any if we don't try." Zenas seemed confident. "Do you have any containers for water? I only have this small pouch. I did not have time to collect anything when I left the caravan."

"Yes, I have two. Do you want them both? On second thought, sometimes there is water back in these caves; leave one with me, and I will investigate." Simon remembered how, as boys, he and his brothers would explore the caves around Nazareth and often find water in them.

"Are you sure it's safe to explore this cave alone?" Zenas asked.

"I know some tricks from my childhood. I'll be careful."

After Zenas left, Simon took the other water sack and began to feel his way toward the back of the cave. The darkness was almost total. Looking back, Simon could see just a hint of the light from the cave opening. Rounding a corner, the darkness became complete, compressing the blackness into an eerie oneness. Simon lifted his hand to stroke his beard, smiling at this impulsive reaction to total darkness. It took a few moments for his eyes to accept the total absence of light. At this point, the cave had narrowed to where Simon could touch both sides and had to stoop so as not to bump his head on the roof. The way ahead sloped gradually downward, and, after a dozen or so more steps, his right hand fell into an opening that was about waist-high and about the width of his shoulders. He could feel a draft coming out of the opening. He knew there was another opening to the outside somewhere beyond. He dropped to his hands and knees and began to crawl into the opening. It continued at a slight downgrade and narrowed a bit before it started to widen. In about two body lengths, he came to a large space in which he heard water running. Here, he could stand again. He left a sandal at the opening he had just exited, and, following the wall on his right, he progressed toward the sound of the water. It was close, making a constant trickle as water fell over rocks into a pool. Never taking his right hand off the wall, he progressed until his foot indicated that the floor had stopped. The water was somewhere right here; but where? He backed up, got down on his knees and felt for the lip of the opening in the floor. He reached down into the hole in front of him, and there was the water, cool to his touch. He took out the sack, lowered it into the water and filled it. After drawing the string tight, he turned around, and, staying on his knees with his left hand on the wall, slowly made his way back until he felt his sandal. He crawled back up through the tunnel, and, with his left hand over the opening he just came through, he followed the cave until he could see light. He couldn't remember when he had felt such elation. He was a boy again!

Simon waited a number of hours for Zenas to return. When he did, his face showed disappointment. He had a sack full of roots, some lizards, and two small snakes. "This should keep us from starving, but I could find no water." His voice mirrored the disappointment on his face.

"Water is my department," said Simon, holding up the full sack of water.

"Where did you get that?" Zenas said, astonished.

"We have running water here in our cave. Bring your water sack," Simon said with the enthusiasm of youth. "I will show you to our well."

They worked their way back into the darkness of the cave. When they got to the point where they could not stand up straight, Simon stopped. "I will stay here and instruct you how to go. In a little way, you will feel an opening on your right, about waist-high. Crawl into that opening, about two man lengths, and you will come to a big opening. Turn to the right and follow the right wall. Go slow, feeling for a hole in the floor. That will be the waterhole."

"How did you find this on your own?" Zenas was amazed. "You could have gotten lost in the belly of this mountain."

"My brothers and I used to play in caves around our home. I learned some safety tricks."

The total blackness covered Zenas like a heavy wet blanket, forcing him to consciously recognize his being. Crawling into the blackness, he marveled at the thought of Simon doing this on his own with no one directing him where to go.

After a time, he returned to Simon with his sack full of water.

"This and the other one you got should hold us for a few days. I still can't get over you finding that spring."

"These hills and mountains hold more water than you would think; they are just very stingy in giving it up."

The two men walked out to the mouth of the cave.

Looking over the rugged hills, Zenas commented, "I'm surprised to see such barrenness this close to the river."

"One of the reasons I think we need to cross the river tonight is that the hills north of here open up somewhat, and we will run the risk of being seen. There are scarcely any humans or animals right around here, but this barren area is not very large." Simon's constant fear since meeting Zenas was of him being seen. A man of his size was unusual; he would stick out wherever he went. "We have a few hours before it is dark enough for us to travel. We might as well make ourselves comfortable."

The two men seemed relaxed sitting in the shade of the mouth of the cave.

Zenas was the first to speak. "Forgive me for asking a question I'm sure you hear often and are probably very tired of. Please don't give me your sarcastic answer. I ask it out of curiosity, of course, but also out of respect. I do not understand why the Jewish people, who seem very intelligent and successful in the modern world, retain the barbaric practice of circumcision. Why hasn't that archaic custom been left in antiquity?"

Simon liked this man he hardly knew. Was he trying to start an argument or put him down? He didn't think so. Simon didn't know why, but he was finding it easy to trust this stranger. "I take your word that you ask out of respect. The answer gets to the very heart of who we are as a people."

Simon paused and then continued to explain. "Circumcision is the sacred symbol, ordered by God, of an ancient covenant God made with our forefather, Abraham. That covenant said that if Abraham and his descendants would deny all other gods and worship only the one Creator—God—then God would bless

Abraham and his descendants. They would multiply to match the stars of the sky and the sands under the sea, and would be so blessed that other peoples would pray to be blessed as they are.

"Circumcision is the perfect symbol of humility. It signifies perpetual homage to God. It is a sign of humility written on the one part of the male that can portray his aggressiveness. Humility, the essence of man's relationship with God, stands at the doorway of human propagation. As the man approaches the woman, both know and honor the mark of humility. The seed of Abraham is forever reminded of the covenant with God. What you call an archaic custom signifies the essence of what it means to be a Jew, and how a Jew must always relate to God."

Zenas was silent for a time. He wasn't sure what he expected, but he didn't expect such a clear and profound response. "I've only ever looked at circumcision as a gruesome procedure that brought unnecessary pain to an infant, and couldn't even imagine it being done to an adult. Your explanation takes it to a whole other level."

"Concern for human pain is noble and caring. However, we all accept, even welcome, pain, depending on the cause or purpose." Simon was comfortable now with Zenas's interest. He had no reluctance to say more. "Symbolism is often the only way to pass on the most-profound aspects of life. Humility is not easy to teach or propagate. Selfishness so easily gets in the way. Yet humility is our only doorway to love."

Zenas stood up. "How long will it take us to get to safety in the east? I'm not sure we will have enough time for you to unravel all you just said."

"Forgive me! I am a teacher. Sometimes I get carried away."

"There is nothing to ask forgiveness for. There are just a whole lot of gaps in what I have been hearing recently. I like what I'm hearing, but I need to be able to fill in those gaps. I really was impressed with your mother, and I like you. Both of you talk a lot about humility. That is something I just never paid attention to; and no one I ever studied under did, either. That's a whole new mountain for me to climb. From the looks of it, we may be climbing quite a few mountains as I attempt to reach that summit."

Simon was really beginning to be impressed by Zenas. His intelligence was obvious, but his curiosity and openness were even more appealing. He wanted to know much more about Zenas. "I know nothing about you. You referred to people you studied under. Who were they, and where did you study?"

"I got all my schooling in Rome, from some of the most renowned teachers. I was born into a very noble family tightly connected to the powerful in Rome. I grew up playing in the halls of the Senate. My parents and my uncle could have gotten me anything I wanted through their connections. I was uncomfortable with that and wanted to win a reputation on my own merits. I chose to work my way up through the ranks as a soldier. You can see how well that worked for me!"

"This does look like more than just a bump in the road."

There was a long silence. Zenas seemed to be deep in thought. "I've left that road ... by choice. Meeting your mother turned my life upside down, but not in a bad sense. I feel freer now than I can ever remember. I am finally free to understand the true purpose of living. And I love the feeling!" Zenas wished he could share with Simon Salome's contribution to his understanding of life, but fear of misunderstanding and lack of clarity kept him silent.

Such optimism was hard for Simon to understand, given the perilous situation Zenas was in. The older man recognized that this was much more than just the enthusiasm of youth.

CHAPTER 13

A WILDERNESS CLASSROOM

As dusk approached, they prepared to leave the cave. In the last hour of daylight, they traversed the rugged hills on the way to the Jordan Valley. Once they approached the valley, they remained hidden until after dark. Crossing the valley, they passed many groves of fig, almond, and olive trees. There were also fields of vegetables. Around the perimeter of these groves and fields were trees and plants that were not harvested, obviously set aside for the poor and needy. They filled every container they had, as well as all their pockets. Some dogs announced their presence, but nobody seemed to be listening. They crossed the Jordan, walking in water barely up to their ankles, and continued into flat fields of fruits and vegetables as plentiful as on the other side. Long before daybreak, they were well into the hills that rose over the Jordan Valley to the east.

They talked as they walked through the night. The strange story Mary had told Zenas about her son being crucified by the Romans troubled him. Something was strange about that story; even knowing Pilate's brutal reputation, there was more to this story than Zenas knew. "Tell me about your brother. I think his name was Jesus."

The question surprised Simon. "How do you know about Jesus? Has his message reached Rome?"

"That I am not sure about," Zenas admitted. "Your mother told me he was crucified by the Romans, and I found that hard to believe, considering the rest of the story she told. Crucifixion is usually only used to punish treason or rebellion. Was he fostering insurrection?"

"That depends on who you ask," Simon responded. "He proclaimed the presence of the kingdom of God. To some, that meant the overthrow of the Romans. I'm sure Pilate sensed that threat rising up among the people. The same thing's going on today, only, back then, a few incidents convinced a large vocal group of people that my brother was going to lead a revolution. I'm sure Pilate was aware of that movement. It was not difficult for him to locate rebellious evidence, even if it had nothing to do with what Jesus taught."

Zenas continued to probe. "Your mother said that the religious authorities turned Jesus over to Pilate. If that was the case, couldn't Pilate have passed this off as a religious dispute and washed his hands of it?"

Simon, aware that Zenas was searching to make sense of this bizarre situation, asked, "Are you looking for reason and justice when power is threatened? Jesus's message threatened the power of both the religious and political leaders. The presence of the kingdom of God offered an opening of liberty that threatened the established power structures. Whenever power is threatened, reason and justice fall by the wayside. Both Pilate and the Jewish authorities had reason to be rid of my brother."

Zenas felt the first inklings of the implications of his newly acquired freedom. It came with opportunity and responsibility, but also danger.

As dawn approached, the hills they were in were not as rugged as the ones they had left the day before. In fact, Simon was beginning to be concerned about finding a hiding place for the daylight hours. "This area may not be as deserted as we would like. We'll have to be careful. Finding a hiding place may not be the simplest task either." The hills were fairly barren, with little sign of life. "Maybe we should keep on going. There seems to be nothing here, and we might get into an area that provides better cover."

"Are you up to it?" Zenas asked. "How much longer can you go? I'm much younger than you, and I feel the wear of this past night's journey."

"I could certainly use some rest." Simon didn't want to be the cause of their actions putting Zenas in danger. "It certainly does look deserted enough here for us to rest a while."

They found a spot where a hill would provide some shade from the sun, and minutes after they were on the ground, Simon was asleep.

Zenas realized that Simon had concealed his exhaustion. He would have to be more alert to how their ordeal affected this much-older man. He found it difficult to sleep with so much going on in his mind! The strange situation of encountering Simon, the uncanny connection with his mother, and the obvious affinity between them was nothing short of amazing. Both Simon and his mother impressed Zenas immensely. He wanted to know much more about them. He felt that something terribly important lay in his understanding them better. He drifted off to sleep.

Zenas awoke in a great sweat. His oar had just been snapped in two, and the head of a giant shark was coming through the side of the galley, right at him. *Omens of things to come?* he wondered as he woke up to reality. *Fine, as long as it remains a dream.* He must have slept for some time, because the sun would soon be shining on their lair. He decided to look for something to eat. He found a few sparse sage plants and some tubers he knew to be edible. When he returned, Simon was awake.

They decided to push on. Throughout the late afternoon and into the evening, they encountered little difference in the terrain. There were no signs of life, even animal life. This land appeared not to encourage life but devour it.

The same could not be said about the conversation between the two men as they walked into and through the night.

Zenas continued his quest. "Nothing has been the same for me since I met your mother. Everything I yearned for in life now seems worthless. I'm not sure what's come over me! Yet I am not afraid or hopeless. I feel very much alive and free. I want to know more about your mother, you, and a way of life that seems somehow connected to truth and freedom."

"You are on the run. I am on the run. What makes you think there is anything more advantageous in my way of life than yours?"

Zenas did not hesitate. "We are running from outward forces that threaten us. You and your mother have an inner peace that makes these outward threats nothing more than a nuisance. That is real freedom, a kind of freedom Roman power knows nothing about. Every nerve in my body wants to experience such freedom."

Simon was warming to the conversation. "I'm glad you said that your nerves want to experience rather than that your mind wants to know. You have just avoided the greatest barrier man can construct between himself and God. Man is much more than just a mind, yet man wants the mind to control truth. Truth is God's presence, and the Spirit of God speaks through the whole body, indeed through all creation. Our mind is merely a tool to help us understand what our nerves—or, really, our hearts—are seeking."

"What is it with you people? Is such philosophy in the blood? First, your mother, and now you, have started to blow my mind open with your simple yet profound view of life." Zenas was astounded. "Where does such insight come from?"

"We are a simple folk with a long heritage of humble deference to God," Simon explained. "Our history has shown time and again that the God who is above all gods is with us, if we remember that humility I spoke of earlier. God gave us a law to follow—we call it Torah—the sole purpose of which is to remind us of that humility. Many times, we have tried to make it more than that, to make it our blueprint to righteousness, only to have our arrogance shattered. Many times, we have demanded more of God than Torah. By confusing domination with blessing, we demanded a king so that we could rule the world and demonstrate our righteousness to all humanity. In our arrogance, we even want assurance of eternal life. Our insatiable need to know and control our destiny has consistently led us to make demands on God. Invariably, God's presence has brought us to our knees in humble recognition that God's will is not the same as our selfish desires. The one sure thing our history has told us is that faith in God is expressed through humility."

"There's that word again, and it keeps haunting me!" exclaimed Zenas. "You and your mother use it as if I know what you are talking about. What do you mean by humility?"

Simon stopped and sat down on a large boulder. He shook off his sandal and traced a line in the sand with his toes. He stroked his beard and thought for a long time. "Let me tell you a story that might explain humility."

"A prince, through position and power, accumulated great wealth. He had many servants, one of whom drew his attention. He was an old servant who had performed his duties perfectly his whole life. No one had a bad word to say about him. He never cheated anyone. In every task given him, he always went beyond what was required. The prince came to him one day and said, 'You have served well, always being righteous and giving more than required. I have built you a beautiful house where you and your wife and children and your children's children can live in peace forever. Please go and rest with the Lord's blessing.'

"The old servant answered, 'Oh, gracious Lord, your kindness is overwhelming! Please, allow me first to make sure your whole herd is healthy and properly fed. Then I will go.'

"'I can wait,' said the master.

"It was two weeks before the old man returned to the prince. 'Kind master, please allow me a few more days. My neighbor broke his leg, and his wife and children need food. I will go as soon as he is well enough to work again.'

"This went on for more than two years. Each time, the old servant had someone's need as a reason for not leaving. Each time, the prince waited patiently, until, one evening, the old servant died.

"The prince sold all his possessions and distributed the proceeds to the poor and needy of his kingdom, and came to care for the old man's wife and children.

Zenas sat in silence. Reverently he inquired, "Is humility compassion?"

"The closest I can come to defining humility is to say that it is the open recognition of something and someone greater than the self, and the courage to move forward into the uncertainty that such recognition entails. Humility is the only way to approach love." Simon was uncomfortable with definitions; they were too limiting. But Zenas deserved his best attempt. "It is humility that turns our focus outward, the necessary first step to love. Selfishness is so appealing, so comforting, but very destructive. It diminishes everything else, including God. We Jews have Torah. Its purpose is to foster humility. Humility is the sole purpose of what you Romans call religion."

Zenas did not respond immediately. He walked to a nearby scrub bush and peeled some leaves off a branch. He picked up a rock, noticing that there were no signs of life under it. Finally, he returned to Simon, squatted on his haunches in front of him, and said, "Everything you say seems to require a new way of seeing. It seems we grow up seeing ourselves as the center of what is happening, but, as I listen to you, I feel like I am not the center, but, rather, just a part of what is going on around me. This radical shift of focus is really a different feeling."

As he moved through this wilderness of death, so far away from the lures of wealth and power, the only sign of life a strange old man, Zenas felt the first real sensations that freedom was the gateway to compassion. This stark wasteland offered the freedom to look on this strange man differently than he had ever perceived anyone else. Everything was beginning to look different to him. For the first time, he had the sensation that the two of them were partners in the process of living, that his oneness was incomplete without the other.

The two men walked a long way in silence, consumed with the exertion of climbing over the crest of a hill considerably higher than the ones they had been crossing. A different vista spread out before them. Rather than continuous rows of hills, a narrow valley lying west to east crossed in front of them. There was an obvious road or trail running along the center of the valley. The hills on the other side of the valley, which looked like a continuation of the ones they had been traversing, appeared to be considerably higher. They could see no one on the roadway, but it looked well used. They sat down to contemplate this unexpected development. It was well before dawn, so they decided to cross the valley and get as far as possible to the next hills before daylight.

As they walked through the next night, they discovered that the hills differed from the ones they had been in. These were steeper, but they appeared greener and had more life forms. Before dawn, they came upon a small canyon that looked like a good place to spend the day. Since it was overcast, they could not tell how exposed they were. The possibility of game seemed good, and Zenas suggested that they stop and he go look for some food. He had hopes of getting some game that would give them some meat. He suggested that once it was light enough, Simon scout the area to make sure there was no sign of humans. He went off into the predawn darkness.

It was hours after daybreak when Zenas returned. Simon's exploration had proved that they were indeed in a remote area, and they could safely get a good rest here.

"We seem alone in this wilderness," Simon reported. "I see little danger in our being discovered here."

"I agree. This is certainly a very desolate place. Here, have some tubers. It's all I could find. There is not much animal life in this area." Zenas's disappointment was obvious.

"Our conversation is all the nourishment I need," Simon confessed. "Who would have imagined such stimulating conversation in these circumstances?"

"My thoughts exactly," answered Zenas. "And who could have designed a more perfect classroom to learn the truths of existence?" He pointed to the steep canyon walls.

"Are we ever to learn the truths of existence, or can we just experience the presence of truth?"

"There you go again, getting philosophical on me." Zenas was so comfortable with this man. He really respected him and longed to be enriched by his wisdom. He couldn't wait to resume the discussion they were having earlier. "You were saying earlier that the history of your people showed that humility is the only true expression of faith. What did you mean by that?"

Simon thought a while before he answered. "The history of the Jewish people reveals a rocky pathway, indeed. It is probably best described by saying that whenever the people began to believe they knew better than God, and began demanding or expecting existence to produce their desired results, disastrous things happened to them. It was as if they were being chastised by God—put back in their place.

"It was my brother Jesus who made me see things differently. You would have liked him. He was so compassionate, open and free, the characteristics you seem to respect most. He was also fearless, and his message was extremely popular, especially among the common folk. He said that the kingdom of God was here, and we could live according to the will of God by repenting of our selfishness and live Torah, by which he meant live according to the laws of God the Creator."

"And for this he was crucified?" Zenas asked incredulously.

"Yes. It's hard to imagine," said Simon. "The crucial thing for me was what happened after he was crucified. He appeared to a number of us."

"What, as an apparition, a spirit?" This was the last thing Zenas expected.

"I'll let God answer that for you as God has for me. What I can't ever forget is Jesus's overwhelming embrace and his words to me. He said, 'God is love, Simon. Forget yourself, and live for others. Come, follow me.'" Simon's face was radiant, and his eyes shone like the brightest stars in the sky.

Simon continued. "Jesus always taught that God is love, not that God did acts of love, but that God's presence *is* love. Love just is; it pervades everything. Love is not something we do, but, rather, something that happens when we get ourselves out of the way.

"Many years of struggling to condense his message have left me with this: Jesus taught that God is love and the kingdom of God is among us. My mother always says, 'Love is like a river flowing over the whole of human existence. Only by shedding our self-protective fears can we swim in that river.' Freedom is the opportunity to live beyond the self, and humility is the vulnerability to move beyond the self. Freedom and humility allow us to stay afloat in this river of love. Selfishness, in all its forms, pulls us down, and then we drown in our self-indulgence. Freedom and humility are the buoyancy of life."

Zenas didn't know what to say. He sat in awed silence.

Simon leaned forward toward Zenas, and with eyes that sparkled like diamonds, said, "Jesus opened my eyes to see things differently than ever before. But, more than that, it seems to have given eyes to my heart. I have never been the same."

Zenas knew that Simon had just shared with him the most important moment of his life, and he knew that *respect* didn't even begin to describe his feelings for this man he had known for only a few days. Was this love? "I can't find words to convey my thoughts or feelings. What you say is surreal, almost ethereal. Yet it is obviously totally real to you."

"You are so right!" Simon couldn't be more unequivocal. "It has completely transformed my understanding of life and living. It has opened a whole new world for me. Not only has it liberated me from anxiety, it has also finally allowed me to ask the right question: since God is love, what are the pathways of love?"

Zenas felt the sensation of shades being lifted from his eyes. "Yesterday, in defining humility, you said it is the gateway to love. Is that what you meant? We can discover love only if we are free to experience the presence of God?"

In all his years of teaching, Simon had never found a more perceptive student. This got his juices flowing, for he knew that this young man's questions would be avenues of Simon's own new understandings. "Jesus always said that all the laws of God were found in just two commandments: love the Lord your God with all your heart, and love your neighbor as yourself. Living is all about love."

Zenas didn't know what to say. This seemed so profound, yet so simple. Could this be the secret of life? Could the secret of life be so simple? Love the Lord with all your heart and love your neighbor as yourself. But, according to Simon, Jesus hadn't said living was about loving, but, rather, about love. Zenas's face revealed his conundrum.

Sensing Zenas seemed in the depths of this mystery, Simon thought it best to let Zenas have some space to sort these things out on his own. "We need to get some rest. These hills are looking more and more like mountains, and I am not the young chicken I used to be. While these conversations may be nourishment, they certainly do nothing for fatigue." Simon was also aware that the end of sunlight today meant the beginning of the Sabbath. How would he handle that?

Both men were soon asleep.

When Simon awoke, there was no sun. Had he slept well into the night? The sky in the east was still bright, but dark heavy clouds were forming in the west. There was going to be heavy rain soon, unless the weather stayed west of the Jordan, as it often did. If not, they would have a very wet night; walking would be very dangerous.

Many questions flooded his mind about observing Sabbath. Obviously, walking any distance was out of the question. Did Zenas's precarious situation vacate the intention of this prohibition? The lack of imminent danger would suggest not. Question after question came into his head, each one persistently followed by a similar rejoinder. Zenas's appearance interrupted his mental perusal.

"Well, are we ready to move out?" Zenas seemed to be well rested and ready for a vigorous night's march.

"This day must be a day of rest and prayer for me."

"What?!" Zenas was sure he had misheard Simon.

"Sundown initiates the Sabbath," explained Simon. "Torah instructs us to rest on the seventh day, just as God the Creator did in creating the world. Walking any great distance is considered work."

"I am aware of that custom among the Jews, but aren't there extenuating circumstances that would override such requirements?"

Simon wasn't sure if irritation prompted Zenas's question. "I do not regard Torah as dictates but as directions for openness to the presence of God. We are certainly safe here, and a day's rest could bring us blessings we are unaware of. Besides, the weather seems to be turning ugly. Those dark clouds in the west are ominous. We could be caught in a ravine at just the wrong time. We are safe and sheltered here, and I think the prudent thing is to tarry here another day."

Zenas found no will to dissent. In fact, he eagerly looked forward to a full night and day of conversation with this man who was quickly becoming a sage in his mind. He struggled to integrate what he was hearing from Simon with what he had learned as a young man growing up in Rome. This would provide a whole night and day to help him sort this out.

They laid out the last figs and berries they had picked in the Jordan Valley, and then lay down to make themselves comfortable. It appeared the storm to the west would pass them to the southwest.

Zenas couldn't wait to start the conversation. "I've been thinking that the notion of a people who understand their entire existence as a real relationship to the Creator of the universe is appealing. But how is that different from the position of Rome, which considers its very presence as the essence of the universe?"

"No different, if you fail to see faith as humility," answered Simon. "That's precisely the point. Faith is not knowing. The mind demands to know, but God is that which is beyond knowing."

"Man cannot ignore the curiosity of the mind," exclaimed Zenas. "The mind's goal is to know truth."

Simon liked the way Zenas pushed the issue. "Yes, but truth about God is an unobtainable goal. Man cannot know God as the mind wishes to know. Man can only experience God through the senses. God can only be known by the heart. The roots of all evil lay in human arrogance that there is no God, and the beliefs that man's mind can know God. All violence and debasement grow from these binary roots. That is why faith must be understood as humility, as a question; otherwise, there is no check on human arrogance." Simon paused. "Why are you smiling?"

"It's not what you are saying that is making me smile. It is the irony of you speaking such wisdom, with berry juice running down your chin." Zenas pointed to Simon and laughed.

Simon laughed heartily too. "I guess that does deflate the gravity of my utterances."

The humor did not deflect Zenas from his quest. "Social order cannot be maintained through questions alone. Those whose answers are the closest to the truth must rule those whose uncertainty would disrupt society. That is the beauty of Rome."

"Yet you are hiding from such beauty," said Simon.

"I hide not from Rome, but from those who abuse justice and blemish the glory of Rome," responded Zenas stoically.

"Why, then, are you running away? Why not put yourself at the mercy of the rulers of Rome? Why not make yourself a symbol of Rome's glorious justice?" asked Simon.

Zenas hesitated at this rebuke. "Perhaps I do run from Rome not because the ideals of Rome are faulty, but because the men responsible for managing those ideals do not measure up to the task," admitted Zenas. "However, I do not feel I am running away from Rome as much as I am running toward something that offers greater freedom."

Simon smiled. "You are making my point. Real freedom only exists in humble obeisance before God. Freedom is grounded in the creative love of God. All efforts of authoritarian rule, which aim to control others, go against freedom."

Zenas was amazed. What a simple philosophy! This man, whose eyes radiated truth and openness, was making too much sense. He needed to know what was really behind this man. He and his mother were so assured of themselves, yet so open. They were not at all like most other religious folk. He was not sure where or what he was running to, but he knew this man was a source of critical nourishment along the way. He continued to want to know more about him and his people.

"You are a Jew," Zenas said. "Tell me about the Jews, and why a man like you should have anything to fear. Why are you running away?"

Simon gave a big sigh. Sadness invaded his whole person. After a long pause, he said, "Yes, I am a Jew. Your request to tell you about the Jews fills me with great grief. To be a Jew at this time is to live with tremendous sadness. Jews battle with one another over what it means to be a Jew. Jews kill other Jews over these battles. Too often it appears that we are no different than the Romans or any other group who has decided that one particular interpretation represents truth. Instead of living open to the presence of God, we latch on to a set of beliefs we hold as God's truth. Our sacred scriptures, Torah, get reduced to laws and duties instead of lessons for humility and faith. What was intended to open us up to God's presence becomes chains around necks. We have lost our way.

"Because we follow the mind instead of the heart, Torah now divides us. We are many different groups, squabbling over such unanswerable questions as to whether our bodies will be resurrected after death or they will not. We divide ourselves over whether this man or that is the Messiah. If we agree on who the Messiah is, we then separate over whether we need to observe Torah. We not only divide, we also kill one another."

Simon realized his agitation. After a calming pause, he continued. "We have allowed our faith to become a system of beliefs to be defended. We have forgotten that our minds can never get us to God, only our hearts can. We have forgotten that faith is humility, and humility is the gateway to love."

Zenas was confused. "But aren't you fleeing the Romans, not your own people? How are the Romans involved in what sounds like a family dispute?"

"It is both the Romans and the Jews who make Jerusalem unsafe. The Jewish religious leaders and the Jewish and Roman political leaders all depend on power. Authoritarian power is the result of dependence on the mind. The mind separates and differentiates and then becomes the arbitrator. The enemy becomes all those who think differently than you do. Power struggles and violence are the result when faith becomes the expression of beliefs instead of the exhibition of humility."

"Wow!" Zenas exclaimed. "You make it sound as if everyone who doesn't think like you is your enemy."

"Yes, when functioning on the basis of faith understood as the expression of beliefs." Simon continued. "That is why faith must be understood as humility and openness to the presence of God."

"By Jupiter!" Zenas stood and rubbed his hands through his

hair. "I have to think this through." He walked away, his mind going in many different directions. He climbed one of the canyon walls and sat on a ledge near the top. The view was breathtaking. It appeared almost devoid of all forms of life, yet pregnant with promise and possibility. This wonder and beauty of nature blended with the sensations his body was feeling. He luxuriated in the sensation of his mind being an open receptacle. Was Simon helping him shed the dogmatic tendencies of the mind?

When Zenas returned, Simon was asleep. He realized he needed some rest if they were to travel through the night. When both men awoke, it was dark. They set off again, to the north, under a bright moon. They talked as they walked. Zenas loved to hear Simon talk about the history of the Jewish people. It fascinated him to hear history described as if it had intention and purpose. Heard this way, history was not a series of static pictures but a process that was going somewhere. God had a purpose for creation, and the Jews saw themselves as participants toward that goal. This way of looking at existence appealed to Zenas. Throughout the night, he peppered Simon with questions. The two men found real pleasure in each other's company.

Their night's journey brought them into a different environment. While there were still continuous hills and narrow valleys, they found more vegetation and wildlife. Before dawn, they stopped to camp.

Zenas said, "I'm going to look for something to eat before we lie down. I need to eat some real meat."

A few hours later, Simon was wakened by an excited Zenas. "Look what I found at the market. The proprietor was gone, so I just took it," Zenas joked. He was holding a wolf by its two hind legs.

Simon was more than surprised. He tried to cover it with a question. "How in the world did you kill that?"

Zenas's pride was obvious in his answer. "I was in a special unit where we were trained to protect ourselves from wild animals. I never thought I would put it to this use. I was concerned that you might need some meat, that just roots and vegetation might not be the best diet for you."

Simon's shocked look meant something quite different to Zenas than it did to Simon. "Your concern is really greatly appreciated, but I can't eat that."

"I fully mean to cook it," explained Zenas.

"No, it isn't that," Simon explained. "My vow prohibits me from eating any meat."

Now it was Zenas's turn to look shocked. "You expect me to eat all this myself?" He was not quite sure how to proceed, and joking was a way to veil his discomfort.

"Please don't take it as an affront," said Simon. "I have vowed, as a special form of self-discipline, to conform to a very particular diet. Your pleasure in providing food for us is well founded. I take it as a generous act of sharing, and I am truly grateful. It will be simplest for us if I just take care of my own food needs."

Zenas looked at Simon with wonderment. This man had many layers, yet none of them seemed to decrease Zenas's affinity for him. Everything he learned about this man only increased his desire to know more.

Simon left to find some food.

After skinning the wolf, Zenas started a fire and cooked a piece of meat. He couldn't get his mind off the unique man who was out there in the wilderness, foraging for food. He seemed to be so free, yet he burdened himself with the strictest eating habits. Did this Torah that he referred to so often require such obedience, or was he exercising the kind of self-discipline Zenas was quite familiar with in his training to be a soldier? This man was an enigma, but a pleasant one.

When Simon came back, Zenas resumed his questioning. "You talk about freedom and humility, and Torah; how does your vow to not eat meat fit into that?"

Simon thought for a while, then began to explain. "So far, this is where my questions and experiences have led me. We humans do many things out of necessity. Our existence depends upon how we eat, sleep, propagate, and interrelate. Torah's purpose is to help us do all of that in a way that is in step with the God who created us. There is an aspect of existence that integrates the mind with the senses. Some call it spirit. I call it the presence of God. Torah prepares us for the presence of God. Torah's primary purpose is to help us get beyond ourselves. The function of the human mind is to serve the self. Only by moving ourselves beyond the limits of the mind can we experience God's presence. If we eat, sleep, propagate, and interrelate solely out of instinct, our mind controls what we do, and self-preservation degenerates into selfishness. Torah joggles the mind into a place of uncertainty where we are open to what is outside of us.

"Torah has been mislabeled as law. The only law in Torah is 'Love the Lord your God with all your heart and your neighbor as yourself.' All the rest of Torah is commentary. My vow to not eat meat is not in obedience to law, but, rather, in an effort to joggle my mind to see beyond myself and recognize God (love) in my neighbor."

Zenas could not get enough of this man. He was so deep and so authentic. Yet he was also so common and down-to-earth. Zenas wanted to learn all this man could teach him. "Where are you headed? I want to go with you. I want to learn from you. ..."

Zenas paused and ceased speaking. He was suddenly very aware that he increased Simon's danger tenfold by accompanying him. "I'm sorry to have said that. The Romans may be interested in finding you, but they are obsessed with finding me. It is selfish of me to even think of staying with you. I must go my own way and be thankful for all I have learned from you in our short encounter. You have blessed my life immeasurably, and I am eternally grateful. But I must separate myself from you as soon as possible."

Simon stood, reached up, and put both his hands on Zenas's

shoulders. Looking up into Zenas's eyes, he said, "You are *more* than welcome to travel with me; you are desperately *needed*. We are meant to be together. It is not your presence I fear but your absence."

There were tears in Zenas's eyes. The truth in Simon's words could not be doubted. The two men embraced, truly like father and son.

Simon and Zenas traveled cautiously through this more hospitable wilderness. Simon was sure that if they kept on a northerly track, they would eventually intersect the main east-west routes to Palmyra and Mesopotamia. His gut told him that Zenas would not be safe anywhere this side of the great river. They were careful to avoid any contact with others, for fear of being discovered. He felt he needed to accompany Zenas at least as far as Palmyra. It would be a long journey, made bearable by their conversations, which never stopped. A special bond formed between these two, who were totally at ease with each other. Nothing about their upbringing or cultural experience brought them together; something much stronger formed the bond between them. One saw it as a humble awareness of the presence of God; the other as a life-consuming passion for the truth of the meaning of life.

They talked much, and Zenas became more and more convinced that Simon was the man from whom he wished to learn. There was such an authenticity to him, an honesty and fearlessness that evidenced the very best in a man. The most appealing characteristic Zenas saw in Simon, however, was the way his heart controlled his head. He had one of the most agile minds Zenas had ever encountered, yet nothing Simon's mind contemplated directed his speech or actions without the transforming nature of his compassion. Love seemed to dominate his being. The deepest, most profound thought was always subjected to his awareness of the other with him, the world around him, and that indescribable something that pulled him into the future. Here was a man whose heart truly controlled his passions. The more intimately Zenas got to know Simon, the more his thoughts turned to love. Simon said, "God is love"; he claimed humility as the way to experience God, and the gateway to love. He also described love as forgetting yourself and living for the other. Was that which Simon called love actually the answer to life? Now Zenas began to more fully realize the gift Salome and he had given each other just a few short days ago.

Zenas rolled this notion of love over and over in his mind. He thought about his life, his childhood, and his experiences. Was his past dominated by love? No; power, position, and privilege were what had dominated his past. Thinking back, the two times in his life when he had felt free to forget himself were when he decided to become a soldier and when he escaped from prison. Was the first step toward love shedding the fears that keep one focused on self? Just as important, the freedom to choose was essential. Perhaps that was why the God above all else, the Creator of everything, must be recognized. Where else could this freedom be grounded? *So,* he mused, *it is God who gives us the freedom to forget ourselves and live for the other. And it is power that stands in the way of love: the power of fear and the power to control the actions of another.*

Zenas grabbed Simon's arm. "Power is the absence of love!"

"What?" Simon was surprised at the intensity of Zenas's paroxysm.

"Power—the power of Rome, the power of your religious authorities, the power of parental and societal pressures, the power of our own fears and desires—it is power that stands in the way of love. Power is what prevents us from forgetting ourselves and living for the other. If something or someone can control us, we are not free to love." Zenas wasn't sure where he was going with this, but he was enthused.

"I have never thought of it in quite that way before. Love can be powerful, so I don't know if power is the absence of love."

Simon was aware that these conversations with Zenas were ideal classrooms where learner and teacher constantly changed places.

"Maybe that is not the right way to express it." Zenas was well aware that he was speaking way above his own understanding, perhaps actually trying to speak from his heart. "My entire life up until I chose to become a soldier was dominated by my parents' decisions, my decisions to either please them or to allay subconscious fears, or my selfish desires. Both the choice to become a soldier and the choice to escape prison were made free of the fear of concern for myself. They were experiences of real freedom. When I consider what I am now free from, it is my own selfishness, but it is also all external powers over me. In both cases, I was face-to-face with my very existence. You helped me to see this as being open to the presence of God. Maybe I should have said that love is the absence of power over another."

"I can certainly agree when considering most expressions of power these days." Simon was grateful to Zenas for relating love and power. He hadn't thought of it in that way before. "Certainly, the position of authority can easily foster the sense of doing something for others that they cannot or will not do for themselves. When it functions without love, power can easily be a deterrent to freedom. Sadly, most authoritarian structures grow away from love."

"Rome has become much worse than that. It has become a culture of abusive power serving only the selfish, lascivious, licentious lusts of the privileged. The whole world now slaves to satisfy these needs. I'm convinced that the greatest gift reason can give humanity is to limit power over another."

"Your picture of Rome is not a whole lot different from the way the Jewish religious and political leaders see the common folk as serving their needs. Love is a foreign word to such power." Simon paused, and then he was silent for a time. "Sadly, too many seek to use the avenue of violence to overcome this injustice. Violence knows nothing of love, and will only bring on more violence and abusive power."

As if these revelations were coming to him one at a time, Zenas hesitantly said, "The only legitimate expression of power is in the service of freedom, and freedom's only positive weapon is love."

Simon could only say, "Bless you, my son."

As they walked along in a prolonged silence, Zenas reflected on this man walking beside him, a man he could only describe as holy. Where was he grounded? What gave him the strength to battle adversity with such a gentle demeanor? It appeared as if love always surfaced first in him, regardless of what he encountered. One thing Zenas knew for sure: he loved this man, whom he had only known for a few days, more deeply than anyone he had ever loved. Zenas felt himself growing inside, a result of the privilege of meeting Simon.

Zenas attempted to wrap his mind around that growth. One thing had become very clear: The freedom he now experienced was grounded in something beyond anything he had ever experienced or understood. Simon's God above all gods offered a comfortable grounding for freedom. Certainly, the degenerate integration of deity and emperor that the Romans claimed offered no freedom. It denied the existence of God and condemned humanity to violence and the misuse of power. He longed to know Simon's God as Simon did, and was quickly becoming aware that this meant understanding love.

He turned to look at Simon, and became keenly aware of the strain this arduous flight was having on him. He walked more bent over than when they left the cave above Jerusalem. Beads of sweat formed on his shoulders and ran down his back. His first concern from now on would be to lessen the burden of their plight on this wonderful man.

Zenas was overcome with the desire to try to tell Simon how much he had blessed his life. He sought out a sheltered place where they could rest and he could express the depth of his gratitude. He suggested they cease their night's trek on the northern slope of a hill overlooking an extensive valley, where they would be out of the burning sun. After arranging a spot where they were both comfortable, Zenas said, "It's impossible for me to covey to you all you have done for me in these few days we have been together. You have changed my world. While I studied in Rome, the intellectuals and philosophers constantly mocked the religious, claiming their beliefs only masked ignorance. Religion was passed off as a crutch of the weak and unlearned, something devised by humans to explain the unexplainable. Your talk of faith as humility has stood that mockery on its head. Yes, religion is a creation of mankind in an attempt to deify that which is beyond comprehension, obeisance to the Creator of all that is. Religion should not be mocked, but venerated. It is essential if humans are to realize their true place in creation. But, it is also dangerous because it can mask arrogance, not ignorance. In attempting to recognize God, it consistently slips into the position of knowing God, and then assumes the place of representing, instead of worshiping, God. That's why you and your mother constantly see faith as humility. Humility is the only thing that can preserve freedom and ward off arrogance. Your description of God as love is what allows us to shed selfishness and create room for the other."

There were tears in Simon's eyes as he looked on Zenas with joyous amazement. He couldn't imagine a better description of an example of Jesus's command to "follow me."

CHAPTER 14

DROMEDARY ASSISTANCE

Simon's concern for Zenas's safety increased daily, their slow progress toward Palmyra the cause of his worry. "Palmyra is a long journey on foot from here. Until we are there and you have safe plans to get farther east, I will be uncomfortable. We will probably have to attach to some caravan in order to get there. I'm just not sure how to do that."

"I'm going to go out and try to find some more food for us, since we are in well-vegetated hills right now. When I come back, we can try to come up with a plan." Zenas left the secluded spot they had chosen for a camp. Simon decided to climb the hill in front of them to see what lay ahead for the next night's walk. His spirits were lifted as he stooped and picked the small wildflowers that covered the ground. The scrub bushes held birds, whose singing brought music into his life for the first time in days. It felt good to be in a place where life was an evident presence instead of an interloper. When he reached the crest, there were hills as far as he could see. However, the color of the hills appeared to change. The hills in the distance were higher than the ones they were presently in, but they looked very brown. Simon surmised that they would soon be traveling under-less-than favorable conditions once again.

Zenas's delayed return troubled Simon. He walked a number

of times to the edge of the hill Zenas had disappeared over to see if he was returning. Well after the sun had crossed the center of the heavens, Simon saw Zenas approaching, struggling with a great heap of something that Simon could not identify. He hurried toward him. "Let me give you a hand. What in the world is this?" As he asked the question, he realized that it was a large pile of hides. "Where did you get these?" he asked incredulously.

With a pained expression, Zenas looked at Simon. "It's a very sad story. I ran across a man on the ground next to this pile of hides. He looked quite elderly and wasn't moving. I quickly determined that he was dead. I crossed both the hills in front of me and behind, but, as far as I could see, there was no sign of life or habitation. I could think of nothing else but to bury the man and bring the hides with me. If I had to guess, I imagine he was heading to where he hoped to sell his hides. It appeared he was heading in the same direction we are. I would not be surprised if we were to encounter a caravan route or a town somewhere up ahead."

Simon helped Zenas drag the hides back to their camp.

Zenas had an idea. "I'm sure I'm beginning to look like a wild hunter. Let's take these hides with us and see if we can sell them or use them to barter a ride. It will be slow going, but if that old man thought he would be able to get them wherever he was going, the two of us should be able to do it."

Simon was skeptical. He didn't like the idea of Zenas exposing himself that much. "It sounds like a precarious plan that will put you way too much at risk."

"We can leave the hides here and continue on as we have been, but you were saying that we probably will have to join up with someone else, and the hides may be a way to do that without arousing suspicion."

"You have a point. Maybe we can use these hides to our advantage." Simon, though uncomfortable with the plan, could not come up with a better idea.

"I'm going to make a sled so we can move these hides more easily."

Zenas left to get some materials. He came back with long flexible roots, some short branches, and strong vines. Before long, he had made a sled large enough to carry all the hides. It had two long handles that looped over the shoulders so that one could pull the sled.

Simon was impressed with the younger man's ingenuity.

They rested before beginning the night's travel.

After a day and a half's journey, they came across a southwest-to-northeast route that appeared to be well traveled. They camped over a hill out of sight of the route and waited for someone to pass by. They decided it would be safer to intercept a southbound caravan, the likelihood being higher that they would not have any knowledge of the troubles in Jerusalem or the fact that certain individuals were being hunted.

Shortly before dusk, they saw a cloud of dust off to the northeast, suggesting an approaching caravan. However, long before it arrived at the hill they were camped behind, the dust cloud settled, suggesting the caravan had stopped.

"It appears that the caravan has stopped for the night. Do you think there is a town nearby?" Zenas asked.

"I certainly hope not," said Simon. "That would mean there could be quite a bit of activity there. I didn't see any signs of anyone approaching from the southwest, so I believe that caravan just decided to rest for the night. Possibly, there is a place over there as comfortable as the camp we found a few days ago."

"Before it gets too dark, why don't we get a little closer and try to see what is in store for us?" suggested Zenas.

"We have to be careful; we may not have as good a hiding place as this when we get there," Simon cautioned. "We could walk right into trouble."

"Good advice," admitted Zenas. "We should probably wait here where we can surprise them when we stop them."

They settled in for the night. Before dawn, they were awakened by the noise of a small herd of oxen driven by three men on donkeys going northeast. They appeared in a hurry, and had no idea they were being watched.

About one hour after dawn, the dust cloud arose again, to the northeast, and began moving slowly toward them. It was almost an hour before the caravan causing the dust cloud came into view. Large, with upwards of a dozen camels, all heavily loaded, the approach revealed that this was just the kind of caravan the two men hoped for. They rose and began to move toward the route, where they could stop it.

Zenas moved to the center of the pathway and put up his hand to halt the lead camel. The procession stopped and Zenas greeted the man on the camel, in Greek. "We humbly beg your forgiveness for delaying your progress, but we have some very special hides we are trying to get to Palmyra. Could you be so kind as to direct us there?"

To Zenas's relief, the man spoke Greek. "Now I have seen everything: a nomadic hunter who speaks Greek!"

"My tribe would have disappeared generations ago if we could not sell to the Greeks," answered Zenas.

Simon guessed the man to be Phoenician. He was very interested in the hides but looked suspiciously at Zenas. "Palmyra is a journey of more than five days," he said, "and in that direction." He pointed to the way they had just come. "Perhaps you would consider selling those hides to me. We are on our way to Caesarea, a market much more desirous of those hides than Palmyra."

"What would you have that would be of interest to my tribe?" asked Zenas.

"We have mostly fine silks," answered the camel driver, who had dismounted and now came closer to Zenas.

"My good sir," responded Zenas, "we have little use for fine silks."

The man gestured to one of his friends to dismount. The two

men both started looking through the skins with a good degree of scrutiny. They walked a distance away and conferred with each other in a language Zenas could not understand. Finally, the Phoenician came over to Zenas and said, "We are willing to make quite an offer for your skins. Even though it will jeopardize the remainder of our journey, we offer you one of our camels for your skins, if you will include the sled. We will need that so we can pull it with one of our remaining camels."

"What good is a camel to me?" asked Zenas. "I am a hunter! A camel will only be a burden to me."

The man looked shocked at Zenas's response. "I've never before met a man who would refuse a camel. If you feel the offer is unfair, we might sweeten it with some silver. I believe forty pieces would be more than fair."

Zenas knew nothing of the value of a camel. "I have no use for a camel, but if I could swap it for something, what would it be worth?"

"I have never paid less than five hundred pieces of silver for a camel. My beasts are bred from the finest stock. You could easily double that from the right buyer."

Simon had moved close enough to hear the conversation. He stood stooped over and shook his head slowly from side to side. Zenas knew he was trying to help him in the negotiations. "My elder seems to be telling me I am making a mistake," he said, gesturing toward Simon. "Please excuse me while I find out what he is concerned about."

Zenas went over to Simon, and the two men walked off out of earshot.

Simon said, "The camel could greatly shorten our journey; we could sell it once we get close to Palmyra."

"I'm aware of that, but we have no idea whether we will encounter a buyer; nor do we know the actual condition of the camel they are offering—unless you know more about camels than I do. I want to get as much real money as possible to get us to Palmyra," explained Zenas.

"I have full confidence in your negotiating skills," said Simon. "I really wanted to get you over to suggest that you try to get the route to Palmyra out of them as you are talking to them."

"Good idea," said Zenas. "I'll see what I can do."

Zenas slowly walked back to the two strangers. "My elder thinks we would be better off following our original plan of getting these hides to Palmyra. We know of someone there who will give us a fair deal. Will this route take us to Palmyra?"

"Yes, this route goes directly to Palmyra," said the man. "But, as I told you before, it's a journey of more than five days, even more than that if the two of you have to pull that sled. You will not get a better offer for your hides in Palmyra than I am offering you. I am willing to double my offer to eighty pieces of silver, but that is my final offer. We have to be on our way immediately."

Zenas stroked his chin and said, "Let me see the camel you are offering."

The men led Zenas to a camel near the end of the caravan. It was somewhat smaller and loaded only half as heavily as the other camels. "This is a female in the prime of her life; she will foal in the spring. That is a bonus when you go to sell her."

"Why is this camel loaded more lightly than the others?" asked Zenas.

"She is a fertilized female. We are always careful not to overload a beast in such a condition. She is the only female in this line. A female will be easier for you to handle if you are not familiar with these beasts." The man was trying hard to seal the deal.

"Is there a popular oasis along this route, and is it probable we could sell this camel there?" asked Zenas. "That way we could return to our tribe." Zenas pointed to the southeast.

"In less than half a day's journey, where this route intersects the Pella-to-Bozra route, there is a very large settlement. We stopped there yesterday," answered the man. "You will find much interest in this beast there." The man was so interested in the hides that he ignored the feeling he had that there was something about this hunter that didn't seem right. He just wanted to be on his way, especially glad to be rid of this camel, which he feared would not complete the trip.

Zenas looked at the man and said, "We would need some food for this beast, at least enough for four days, in case we have some trouble selling her."

"Of course," said the man. "If we have a deal, I will get started transferring her load to the other camels. We will leave four days food for her. You will not need water, as there is plenty at the settlement. Do you want us to rig her with two seats so that you two can ride?"

"Yes. We have a deal, and it would be nice to not have to walk for a time," answered Zenas.

The man called the others to dismount and begin transferring the load. He went back to his camel and from a side bag took out a sack from which he counted out eighty pieces of silver. He handed them to Zenas and said, "Your hard work has been rewarded. A man with a camel is rich indeed, and you have silver besides. May your gods bless you with much happiness."

"It will be a blessing to me to know that those hides have added to your prosperity," responded Zenas. He took the silver and returned to Simon.

Simon and Zenas watched the men transfer the load and rig up two seats on top of the food sacks they loaded onto the camel. When they were finished, the man came to them and said, "The camel is ready for you. I suggest you move a distance away while we leave, because the camel will want to follow us if she sees us depart."

The man kicked the camel to get up. He handed the reins to Zenas and said, "God be with you."

"And also with you." Zenas pulled on the reins, and, reluctantly, the camel began to follow.

Simon and Zenas led the camel over a hill, out of sight of the rest of the caravan.

Simon, with a twinkle in his eye, said, "A man with a camel is rich indeed. How do you propose to get this beast to recognize your wealth and authority?"

"I will be satisfied if she only recognizes my authority," confessed Zenas. "I have no idea how to get this beast to do anything. All I know at this point is that you kick it to get it to stand up. I hope she doesn't have anything in her mind but to please me."

A rising cloud of dust indicated the caravan had begun to move away. Once the cloud had moved a great distance away, Zenas and Simon decided to head toward the settlement. They hoped to get there by nightfall. As they approached the route where the transaction had taken place, the camel turned to follow the path the rest of the caravan had taken. It took Zenas and Simon, both pulling as hard as they could on the reins, to restrain the camel. They tried their best to pull the camel in the other direction, but there was no moving the beast. Eventually, the camel sank down on its knees. Evidently, they were not going anywhere anytime soon.

Zenas went to look for some food, and Simon stayed with the camel. After about an hour, Simon recognized a cloud of dust slowly moving from west to east along what was probably the Pella-to-Bozra route. As the cloud got closer, the camel apparently got wind of it because it shifted and looked as if it might get up. Simon knew he could not restrain this large animal if it wanted to take off. He decided to see if some food would be of more interest to the camel than the scent of some far-off dromedary. That seemed to do the trick. Once Simon got out some food, the camel's interest focused solely on Simon.

Zenas finally returned, with a hen for himself and some roots for Simon, and started a fire.

They decided that if they could get the camel to move, they

would head immediately toward the settlement, even though it was getting dark.

After they had eaten, Zenas kicked the camel to get it up. It arose and stood there with its nose in the air, pointing toward the dust cloud, which was now near the spot where they had first spotted the caravan yesterday.

"It must be approaching the settlement," said Zenas. "Let's see if we can get this beast to move in that direction."

With almost no effort, the camel began moving up the path. Both men tried to walk beside the camel, but the strides of the beast were so great that the men had to run to keep up.

Zenas ran up in front of the animal and pulled so hard on the reins that he brought the beast to its knees. The camel sat the rest of the way down.

"Maybe we should ride in the seats," said Simon. "At least, that way, we can keep up with the beast."

"Yeah," said Zenas, "but, once we are both sitting in the seats, who is going to kick the animal to get it up?"

"So, camel husbandry was not part of your military training?" asked Simon jokingly.

"No, and I don't speak camel, or even the native tongue of her former owners," confessed Zenas. "We may be at this animal's mercy. Perhaps we should sell it as soon as possible."

Once they were both sitting on the back of the camel, Zenas gave the reins a sharp jolt, and, surprisingly, the beast stood up. It began at a quick walk in the direction of what Simon and Zenas assumed was the settlement. The ride was not as smooth as Simon had hoped. The camel's gait, which might have been beneficial for the camel, was brutal for the men in the seats, which, for Zenas, were at least two sizes too small. They held on, so as not to be thrown to the ground. The seats they were in responded to the movement of the beast's front foot in a way radically different from the movement of the hind; the result was a jarring front-to-back motion for the riders. If a camel's walk had a rhythm, it did not translate into the seats containing the men. They were being jolted toward Palmyra. Speaking was difficult, and thinking almost as laborious. Both men yearned for the serenity of walking.

At dusk, a sliver of a nearly full moon breasted the horizon. As they crested a hill, they saw in the valley below some structures surrounded by a fairly large stand of trees. This seemed to be a small village or hamlet. There was a fairly dense stand of trees surrounding most of the settlement.

"Do you know how to stop this beast?" asked Simon. "Or is it going to just carry us up and deliver us to whoever is there? We are fugitives, remember."

Zenas jumped down and pulled hard on the reins to stop the camel. It slowed down and stopped reluctantly. He led the beast to a gully out of sight of the settlement. "I'm going to secure this animal so it can't get away, and then I will go to see what is awaiting us up ahead," said Zenas.

After tying the reins around a large rock, Zenas took off toward the settlement. As he approached, he could see a large number of camels tied up in a crude corral, suggesting that a fairly large caravan had stopped at the settlement. He stayed in the cover of the trees and went around the town to see what was on the other side. He stopped abruptly. A little more than a stone's throw away was a Roman sentry. Behind him, there were about a dozen tents, and two horses tethered to a pole. He immediately recognized this as a foot patrol, and the camp looked as if they would not be staying long at this location. He hurried back to Simon.

"We cannot stay here, even for a moment," he said. "There is a Roman foot patrol camped out just beyond the town. They look to be only staying here for the night. We must put as much distance between us and them before daybreak. I wish I knew which way they were heading."

"It makes no sense to go back," said Simon. "We are safest if we can get to Palmyra. Why don't we try to parallel the route? We can check a few times a day to make sure we are on track."

"That means we have to travel by daylight. At night, we would never be able to see the route. We also have to get some water for the camel," continued Zenas. "I'm sure the camels got water when the caravan stopped here yesterday, but I don't know how far it will be until we can get water again. From the looks of those trees, there should be a stream running down in that valley. We should try in get to it after we get out of sight of the town."

Making a large loop around the town, they came up to the route where it crossed a narrow stream with just a trickle of brownish water flowing in it. The camel did not have any interest in the water. The men filled their water sacks, and they moved on, away from the small town. After traveling on the pathway for about an hour, they decided to stop and wait out the rest of the night. They moved off the pathway for a distance, and there they slept until just before dawn.

Before they left this campsite, Zenas saw that the camel had relieved herself and that the dung was liquid. Perhaps this explained why the camel was expendable to the caravan.

Keeping hills between themselves and the road, they moved on throughout the next day. It was slow going because the camel was not as sure-footed on the rough ground as on a beaten path. The men walked much of the time, talking as two old friends. When they were riding, conversation was more difficult because each man's seat was on opposite sides of the hump, so they could not see each other as they talked.

The camel had become fairly docile, and it took little effort from the men to get it to do what they wanted.

During one of the times they were riding, Simon found himself deep in thought. What was he doing moving farther and farther away from his beloved Jerusalem, with a man he hardly knew? His responsibility was in Jerusalem, in the temple; if ever his people had needed his counsel, it was now. Yet he felt such a strong bond with this man that here he was, on his way to Palmyra to do heaven knew what. Was he out of his mind? Had he lost all sense of judgment? And, really, who was this man? Was he leading him to safety or to his doom? He wondered if there could be any upside to this dangerous flight.

On the other side of the beast, Zenas was also pondering their situation. Was it fair of him to assume that an older man could endure the hardships they would face on the grueling trip ahead? Why had he allowed Simon to talk him into accompanying him? Simon was on a mission that was very important to him, a mission he just abandoned to travel with Zenas. What had he done to deserve such impressive company? That was the thing! He, Zenas, could not get enough of this man. The desire to know all about him and take in just some of the wisdom he exuded was so strong it overran concern for the danger he was bringing on him. He felt guilty, but also tremendously responsible for Simon's safety. He would not let anything happen to this man.

Another small group of structures loomed ahead. Should they avoid it, or seek out information that might help them get to Palmyra? Both men entertained this same thought. The camel had become such a manageable beast that neither of them thought about selling it.

Simon said, "I believe I ought to make my way into that town to find out just what we are facing. It would be good to know how great a risk we are taking by thinking this camel can get us to Palmyra. I should not be recognized here, and it should be fairly easy for me to get helpful information. I wish I could find a place to clean up and change. It would be a lot easier for me to pose as a traveling priest than a nomadic hunter. I don't know when I'll be back."

With a great deal of apprehension, Zenas watched Simon take off on foot. Simon would not listen to any of Zenas's objections about him going alone. Zenas felt helpless, a feeling not well received by a man of action. The rest of the day went by very slowly for Zenas, and, as evening came and darkness fell, he began to worry. He couldn't sleep! All night, he paced and looked into

JOSEPH C. NYCE

the darkness, waiting for Simon to return. Dawn came with no sign of Simon, and, as the sun rose to its zenith, he could hardly contain his urge to head off to the town to find Simon. Only the greatest determination kept him from striking out immediately. His better judgment told him that the cover of darkness might be advantageous for him, and he decided he would wait until the sun went down before entering the town.

When only half the sun was still visible over the hills to the west, Zenas spotted Simon coming over a hill, not from the direction of the town but from the northwest. He ran to meet him. "I was beside myself with worry!" he exclaimed. "What in the world took you so long, and what were you doing over there?" Zenas pointed to the northwest.

Simon explained, "The short version is this: "I went directly to the synagogue and found one of my own, a Nazirite, who immediately took me to a small village about an hour's walk from the town. Those people would not allow me to leave until they had bestowed what seemed like a year's pent-up hospitality. I got the information we need and much news I didn't need. It appears that knowledge of the unrest in Jerusalem has reached here. Neither of our disappearances are a secret. Apparently, Albinus is as upset with my escape as he is with your desertion. What folly to concentrate on two insignificant individuals when the whole city is ready to go up in smoke! Anyway, we have our work cut out for us. We have four to five days of travel to Palmyra, depending on how often we can stay on the road. There is a fairly big mountain range we must cross and at least one day of desert. However, I do not think we have much choice. If word of us has already reached here, I'm convinced our safest place will be in Palmyra, where my nephews can help us."

Simon, always uncomfortable with running away from problems, felt something deep inside telling him of the importance in helping this young man. The one thing his faith had taught him:

216

listen to the urgings of the heart; they are more surely grounded than the machinations of the mind.

They set off early the next morning, stopping by the village Simon had visited yesterday to get provisions. They were on their way by midmorning. They decided to use the roadway as much as possible.

During the day, the men got to know each other so well that they truly were like father and son. The evening was something else. Under starry heavens, and with the soft chewing of the camel's cud, Zenas was at school. He continued to learn about Judaism, about Torah, and about the fascinating story of Jesus. He continued to learn about a people whose entire existence rested on a special relationship with God.

Simon was a special teacher, his Judaism fundamentally rooted in a strong affinity for the priestly tradition. However, his experience with his brother Jesus had unequivocally altered his life. No longer were his beliefs of highest concern. God, the object of beliefs, regained dominance. Jesus's teachings on the presence of the kingdom of God brought God and Judaism back into proper perspective. No longer could the dictates or dogmas of the synagogue come before the presence of God's love. Time and again, Jesus pointed out the hypocrisy produced when beliefs take control instead of being catalysts to opening us up to God's presence. Jesus showed that Torah was a vehicle for freedom rather than a set of laws to be obeyed. His life gave evidence to Simon that God was not to be feared, but, rather, a presence to be approached with humble openness. Simon's Judaism—no longer dependent on definitive statements about God and man and the steps necessary to retain or regain a proper relationship between the two—offered a way of living and being that freed one from selfishness and opened the doors to God's love.

Zenas sensed this freedom and openness in both Simon and his mother. It had such an appeal that it became his life's goal. He cared about nothing else, for it seemed to him that this promised the fulfillment of his manhood. He was a perfect student. Every insight brought on a new bevy of questions. Nothing was complete until it had satisfied his senses. His mind, never left on its own, was constantly challenged by his feelings. Comfortable in his own skin, he nonetheless always possessed a feeling of incompleteness, which could not be satisfied by the self alone. Open by nature, he yearned for freedom. Both men reveled in their conversations. The strenuous efforts of the journey were completely washed away in the delight of their conversations.

The camel had become weaker as they moved on. The men spent more and more time walking, the pace of the camel now an easy one for the men to match. They knew that they were not going to reach Palmyra in a total of four or five days. It might be twice that. Each night, they were more exhausted and spent from the day's walk, but that didn't shorten their discussions, because of the joy of their exchanges. And, of course, the classroom continued through the daytime walks as well.

Sometime before noon on their third day of travel, Zenas became concerned about Simon. He did not have as good a color as usual. He was perspiring more and seemed to be laboring to keep up.

"You don't look so good," Zenas said to Simon. "Why don't you ride for a while?"

Zenas was even more worried when Simon did not resist.

They stopped the camel, and Simon climbed up into the seat.

"I'll walk alongside," said Zenas. "No use putting any extra stress on the beast."

Their progress was even slower than usual once Simon was riding on the camel, and, by late in the afternoon, the camel was walking quite slowly.

Zenas decided they would stop at the first convenient spot. He did not like the way the camel looked.

They went nearly an hour before they found a place that Zenas thought satisfactory for them to spend the night. He pitched a rough tent between some bushes to get Simon out of the sun, and put some water and food out for the camel. The animal did not offer at either.

"I don't like the way that animal looks," Zenas told Simon. "She seems quite weak and won't eat any food."

"It's quite a bit earlier than we usually stop," said Simon. "Perhaps she is such a creature of habit that she is waiting for dinnertime." When Zenas only smiled at his humor, Simon knew the depth of the younger man's concern for the camel.

There was not much conversation that evening. Simon fell asleep almost immediately after they had eaten.

Zenas went out of the tent to see how the camel was doing. The beast was lying on its side, not with its feet under itself as it usually did. It was breathing heavily and intermittently. Zenas did not like what he saw. He went back into the tent and tried to sleep. Again, thoughts of Salome filled his head, and his heart quickened. Even these lovely thoughts would not bring sleep. He found himself straining to listen for the camel's breathing. When he couldn't hear anything, he went back out to the camel. He felt a wave of anxiety as he realized the camel was dead.

CHAPTER 15

GOING HOME

Zenas knew he had changed. He was not the same man who'd first encountered Simon in the wilderness north of Jerusalem. This strangely religious man had radically transformed him. This pious Jew, with all his odd eating habits and quirky practices, had given him a new set of eyes and opened his heart. Now, he was overcome with concern for Simon, who was not well. Their situation was dire, and he feared for Simon's life. He guessed they were still a number of days away from their destination. Now they were without any means of transportation. Zenas knew that Simon was not strong enough to reach Palmyra on foot. They had to look to someone to help them. He knew how risky that would be, but now that no longer mattered. He would do anything to get Simon to Palmyra, where he said he had friends.

Zenas could not sleep. Listening to the labored breathing of his friend, he tried to understand how this old man had been able to affect him so radically. After every conversation, Zenas would feel the world changing around him.

How different this experience was from his past life! He'd had the best education the Roman Empire had to offer. His teachers always praised him as the best of their students, and it was no secret that everyone who knew him saw him as eventually reaching the highest seats of power. Once he had served his military duty, he would quickly be inserted into the Senate. The sky was the limit for him.

Yet he had never experienced anything like what he experienced with Simon. Zenas's prior teachers expected him to learn what they already knew and master what they were teaching. The future was already established, awaiting his maturity. With Simon it was different. Zenas never felt that Simon had the answers to his questions, but, rather, that his questions were as open ended to Simon as they were to him. In fact, it always felt as if the questions were more important than the answers. What a feeling of freedom that offered!

These thoughts reminded Zenas of an exchange he and Simon had a number of nights ago, a conversation that he had not been able to stop thinking about. Zenas began to reminisce.

Zenas had said, "You are a pious man; it is evident in everything you do. I am a man of the world, nothing I do could be identified as religious. Yet, here we are, like father and son. What connects us? Something much more than the fact that we are both fugitives holds us together so closely."

After a long pause, Simon had replied, "It is not fear that binds us but love. Our connection with each other is through the heart. God is love, and it is this life force that connects us. We share a common goal: we yearn to be free to realize the purpose for our existence. Freedom rests on one thing and one thing alone: the unbreakable and incomprehensible bond between the self and the Creator. Life, the manifestation of the self, is a gift from God understood through the heart.

"Our minds are what create separations. The mind quantifies and qualifies, and it constantly forms distinctions. The only critical separation is between the Creator and the created. The mind ignores this separation by assuming an affinity with the Creator, which sanctifies all subsequent separations.

"My brother Jesus always reminded us of the incident through which he learned this valuable lesson. We were trying to get away from the crowds when a Gentile woman, I believe she was from Syria, came up to us and begged that Jesus drive a demonic spirit from her daughter. Jesus implied that his mission was to the Jews by saying to the woman, 'Let the children be satisfied first, it is not fair to take the children's bread and give it to the dogs.' She answered him by saying, 'Even the dogs under the table eat the children's scraps.' Jesus, recognizing the offense in his arrogant response, told the woman to go home, that her daughter was healed. I can't count the number of times Jesus reminded us of this lesson of humility, how our beliefs stand in the way of the presence of God.

"So, you see, Zenas, we are running away from all those structures that restrain us from realizing the true meaning of our existence. We have been betrayed often enough by our mind to realize that only through the freedom of the heart can we realize our goal. That is what ties us together: not the logic of our minds but the commingled beating of our hearts—where we are free to experience the power of our Creator. Together, we stand in the gateway, with only a humble faith in God."

While reminiscing, once again, Zenas faced the phrase "faith as humility." Now it was beginning to make sense to him. This was the change that was coming over him—a subtle change, but one that seemed to have earth-shattering consequences. He saw it as nothing more than a shift in internal grounding. Rather than relying on the brain for guidance, seek the counsel of the heart. Rather than a passion for righteousness supported by beliefs and logical social structures, we should open up to the freedom of the heart through which the love of the Creator flows. The activities of the brain create divisions among us that always keep the self as center, whereas the heart fosters connections by making space for the other. Was it just that simple? This explained for Zenas the compassionate personas of Mary and Simon. They were so open and accepting, so comfortable with their situation, and seemed to lack any apprehension about their future.

In spite of this insight, Zenas couldn't get over these people. Their lives were so full of tragedy! Mary had lost three sons, and if they were anything like her and Simon, it was impossible to see how anyone could have wished them ill, let alone harm them. Both Mary and Simon were being harassed by the occupying Roman army, even though they appeared to have no political ambitions. What was wrong with this picture? What was Zenas missing? Could faith as humility be that dangerous?

Simon was awakening. Zenas dreaded telling him the bad news about the camel.

"How do you feel this morning?" Zenas asked.

"It's amazing how much a night's sleep can do for you," answered Simon. "I feel worlds better than I did last night. We should be able to get a good deal closer to Palmyra today."

Zenas was not sure how to break the news. "We have one big obstacle to overcome in that regard. The camel died during the night."

"Oh, that poor beast!" lamented Simon. "I feel the cause of her demise. I was just too much for her to bear."

"No," Zenas said. "I'm convinced that there was something wrong with that camel from the beginning. No one would give up a pregnant camel as easily as we obtained her if there had not been something wrong with her. We were probably lucky to get as far as we did with her. We should bury the beast, but, it is much too big for us to move. I'm glad we camped away from the main highway. The buzzards will have a feast.

"Before we start out, let me try to get some food. We will have more days in this wilderness now that our progress will be slower." Zenas left to search for some food.

Simon wondered how much of his strength had really returned. He certainly felt better than yesterday, but now that he would have to make the rest of the journey on foot, he began to worry about his stamina. On this trade route, he was sure that Zenas was in much more danger than he. The farther away they moved from Jerusalem, the less he would be sought. However, there were probably patrols of Roman soldiers on this route, and every one of them would obviously be on the lookout for this deserter. He was sure that their progress would be slower because of his weakened condition, which would only heighten the danger for Zenas.

When Zenas returned, Simon said, "I think we should go our separate ways. My slow progress is going to greatly increase the danger of you being captured. Nobody is concerned about me this far away from Jerusalem, and I can take my time and join up with the first caravan that comes along."

"Get all those crazy notions out of your head," Zenas snapped back at him. "I am part of you, and you are part of me. We go wherever we go together. Adopt me as your son if you must, but you are not going to proceed alone."

The tone of Zenas's rebuke showed Simon the uselessness of arguing. They were a team, whether he wanted that or not. Each man, totally consumed with the safety of the other, made separation no longer an option.

After eating, they started out. Their track began to bend toward the northwest, and, by midafternoon, it terminated onto a much more heavily traveled route going from southwest toward the northeast. They proceeded to the northeast, and, toward evening, it appeared that they were approaching an area where there were a few hamlets and little villages. They felt they should try to avoid these as much as possible, so they stayed off the main route. This made their progress much slower and certainly more difficult.

The next morning, they set out again, keeping off the main road. During the first few hours, they made some progress. But, as the sun got higher in the sky, Simon began to slow his pace and needed to stop more often. As the day wore on, they spent more time resting than they did moving.

Simon became aware that he would never be able to get to Palmyra on foot. "One thing I'm sure of: I will not be able to complete this journey on foot. I will need assistance, and that will put you in grave danger."

"That leaves us with few options," Zenas replied.

"Why don't we find a safe place and rest the whole day and night?" Simon suggested. "The rest will do me good."

Zenas refrained from reminding Simon that they had just done that for his Sabbath two days ago.

Much to Simon's surprise, Zenas agreed. "Tomorrow, however, we begin to search for someone to help us get to Palmyra. We can't continue to fool ourselves that you can complete this journey on foot. If you don't agree, I'll insist on carrying you the rest of the way."

Simon reluctantly nodded in agreement.

It was not long after they had settled in a safe place that Zenas resumed the conversation. This time it was not a question. "I've been putting some things together in my head."

"Whoa! Isn't that dangerous territory?" Simon said with a smile in his voice.

"Always. But sometimes you just have to give the horse its reins. You never know—you might just end up in a new exciting place."

"Yes, but make sure you're on a horse you trust."

"That's why I want you along for the ride."

"I'll hang on with both hands. Where are we going?"

Zenas thought a bit before he replied. "I have not known many Jews in my life, nor have I ever placed much importance on religion. But, since meeting your mother, and you, something has completely overwhelmed me to the core of my being." He thought of Salome, but didn't mention her. "You have ignited a burning desire within me to understand why I exist. It's not ambition or a desire for fame, but a yearning to sense that every breath I take, word I speak, and deed I do is fully in harmony with the movement of creation. I want to be like you. Do I want to be a Jew? I don't know. Do I want to be a priest? I don't know. I just know that there is something out there that is calling for me, awakened by the three of you. (Zenas was aware of the slip of the tongue in saying *three,* but decided to go on.) And, for the second time in my life, I sense the freedom to realize my purpose in living. Yet there is so much uncertainty. You have helped me to see things differently, but clarity is wanting. There are so many questions!"

The fatigue overlying Simon's countenance receded as he warmed to Zenas's zeal. "My life has been richly blessed since you walked into that cave back near Jerusalem. God's will needs no greater an ambassador than your passion. Ardently and openly pursue your questions; they will not lead you astray if you seek love."

"I don't want my questions to weary you. Your concern for my well-being has brought you to the edge of exhaustion, and I don't wish to compound this arduous journey for you by giving you any mental exertion."

"Your interest has been my sustenance. Please do not delay."

Simon's sincerity was obvious, and it encouraged Zenas to continue. "I'm trying to put together what I am learning into a package of guidelines for living. First, since the mind can't fully comprehend that which created it, humility is the proper attitude toward that which can't be understood—call it God. So, I understand why you describe faith as humility. Second, if God is love, and God is the Creator of everything, then love is the motivating force of existence, making it the measuring stick of human behavior, placing your neighbor's need on a par with your own. If, on top of this, we see our existence as a real expression of the purpose of creation, human behavior becomes significant to the course of history, and the role of religion becomes essential. I'm beginning to understand all of this."

Simon sat silent, stroking his beard.

Zenas continued. "We non-Jews call the rationale for the way we live religion, and I now see it is an essential part of who we each are. Our thoughts and behaviors do not make sense without it. But

I'm guessing you prefer to call it faith, because to recast it as beliefs and behaviors robs it of its openness to the unknown. This is why faith is humility, because it is always open to the mystery of God. As you can see, I'm trying to make sense of what has drawn me like a moth to a candle."

"I'm astounded by your ability to see below the surface, to the essence of who we are," said Simon, with real admiration.

"Authenticity needs no publicity. Your openness is like a magnet to a curious mind."

Lines formed on Zenas's forehead as he continued. "Your comments about love, freedom, and power have helped me realize what has been happening to me. I am running from Rome. Its use of power is completely unchecked by love. Roman freedom is completely regulated by those in power, who answer to nothing but their own lusts. What has happened to me is that I see freedom in a completely new way, thanks to your love and humility. I am running from Rome, but I no longer wish to hide. I want to discover how my new freedom can make the world a better place. I want to make a difference, not through power but through love."

Simon beamed. "I have never heard a more beautiful expression of the good news. The kingdom of God is surely among us."

"Yet one thing puzzles me greatly, "Zenas remarked. "I was impressed by your comments about the heart, through love, uniting, and the mind, through its activity, separating. However, don't the strange practices of the Jewish people separate them from the rest of society? If this separation is essential, doesn't it work against love?"

Simon loved this man. He seemed to get right to the heart of an issue. "We do what we do as a direct response to God. Our living is worship. We seek only to find our place in God's plan for creation. Our behaviors and practices demonstrate our devotion to God. There is no intention to separate."

"What about your practice of not associating with the Gentile, and the whole practice of keeping kosher?" Zenas had never understood that.

"Those very issues consistently got my brother Jesus in hot water with the religious authorities. But he never allowed those issues to get in the way of love. We do hold to the pure holiness of God, and we believe that the presence of the kingdom of God requires the pursuit of holiness and righteousness. However, our humility reminds us that we are imperfect and can only strive to be holy. Whenever those efforts preclude love, they are misguided. We must always let openness to love be our guide."

"That certainly describes what I have experienced from you, your mother, and your sister."

Simon had never heard Zenas speak of Salome before and wanted to pursue that, but it would have to wait for later. Zenas's question deserved an immediate, and deeper, response. "You, however, bring up a crucial point, one that consistently troubled Jesus's disciples and continues to disturb all who seek to follow him. How do these practices not stand in the way of love? I'm sorry to admit that, many times, they do. Love, by its very nature, is communal, and thus only recognized by its impact on the other. Torah stands squarely on the battle line between physical survival and the will of creation. Torah requires discipline and sometimes self-sacrifice, which yearns for the comfort of company. As that company grows, the focus blindly shifts from the other back to the self, but it is now a collective self. Without plan or intent, selfishness becomes ingrained within the collective, in the form of tradition, and love can be an outsider looking in. This subtle transition, if not guarded against, ultimately results in a hypocritical situation in which the leaders defend the tradition by robbing its members of the freedom to recognize love. So, yes, while we are collective beings and will always be determined by our behaviors toward one another, if love is not our constant goal, we will separate and close off the pathways of love. No one understood this danger better than my brother Jesus. He was constantly at odds with the leadership over just this very thing. It's what drove them to the point of wanting him eliminated."

"Oh, how I wish I could have met him and learned from him as you have." Zenas could not imagine anyone more loving than the three members of his family whom he had already met.

As the day went on, they talked, then napped, then talked, and then slept some more. Time went by quickly. Before dusk, they thought they saw the smoke from a campfire off to the northeast. That night, they agreed that their chances of encountering someone were quite high.

The following morning, they set out at a slow pace. It wasn't long before they became reasonably sure that someone was approaching on the same pathway they were traveling. A cloud of dust continued to approach them directly.

Soon the approaching caravan was in sight. It was small and moving quickly to the southwest. It had three camels, each with two burros tethered behind, all heavily loaded. The burros suggested that this was a local caravan rather than a long-distance one. Sensing little threat, Zenas decided to approach the caravan. He hailed the lead camel driver and motioned for him to stop.

The man and Zenas were having trouble communicating. Zenas had difficulty understanding the man's accent.

Simon, hearing the conversation from a distance, realized that the man was a Galilean. He walked up to the man and recognized him immediately. "Judas, you don't know what a relief it is to see a familiar face!"

"Can that be you, Simon? What in the name of the Lord are you doing here, and who in the world is your giant bodyguard?"

"This is Zenas, a Roman soldier who escaped from the garrison in Jerusalem, and I am trying to get him to some friends in Palmyra who may be able to hide him," Simon answered. Turning to Zenas, he said, "Meet Judas, a friend from my hometown of Nazareth. He was just a young man when my brother was teaching around Galilee, but we have kept in touch over the years."

Judas grabbed Simon by the arm and said, "Don't even think about going to Palmyra. I have never seen so many soldiers between here and Damascus. They are stopping every group of travelers going north, looking for someone. Now I guess I know who they are looking for. How did you get mixed up in this?"

"That's a long story, but the truth is, they are looking for me too. It seems that the king or the leaders have convinced the new governor that I am behind all the killings that have been happening in the temple."

Judas spat on the ground. "That pompous traitor! He will do anything to get on the good side of the new governor. Anyone with half a brain knows that you are not behind any killings."

After a pause, Judas said, "Why don't you come with me? I can hide you as my two camel drivers until we figure out what to do. At the next town, I will give my two drivers off and pick them up on my next trip through here. No one pays much attention to my small outfit, especially now that I'm traveling south."

Simon and Zenas, looking at each other, had no need to say a word to realize both felt that being with friends would certainly not hurt.

"But you are heading south. Isn't that the wrong direction for us to be going?" Simon asked.

"It appears that you are not safe, at least as far as Damascus," Judas said, "so I think your safety, if there is such a thing, is better off in the hands of friends. I am on my way back to Caesarea, and we will go right by Nazareth. I'm sure our friends there will do whatever is necessary to provide for your safety."

Simon raised his eyebrows at the serendipity of actually ending up at his original destination. "Well, I started out for Galilee, but I had no idea I would get there this way. Those back in Jerusalem knew I was heading for Galilee. I don't want to walk Zenas into a trap."

"I'm sure they have scoured that place fully already if anyone still connects you with Nazareth," Judas assured him. "Your family has been away from Nazareth for a good many years."

"You may be right. I'm most concerned about Zenas. I'm not sure where he is safe or where he can go to get away from the Roman pursuers."

"We have some time to try to figure that out on the way," said Judas. "We have better than two days' travel before we reach Nazareth."

As they made their way southeast, Simon noticed the changes around him. The hills were not so desolate, and, here and there, small crude dwellings suggested the difficulty of scraping out a living. As they came over a rise, one whole hillside was covered with the small yellow flowers of wild arugula. Simon got the warm feeling of coming home.

That evening, they made camp outside a town. Judas paid his two camel drivers and made arrangements to reconnect with them on his way back. The men were all too glad to have some time off with money in their pockets.

After tending to the animals and eating the evening meal, Zenas, Simon, and Judas sat around the campfire.

Judas was full of questions for Simon. "When is Jesus going to return? Many are losing faith. What do you make of the long delay? So many of my friends are talking of armed insurrection and a violent overthrow of the Romans in Jerusalem! I know you never believed that was the way the kingdom of God was going to come about. But, if this is the time of the messiah, why are the followers of Jesus so divided over what we should be doing? Many are saying that the meaning of Jesus's life, and, particularly his death, is that Torah is no longer necessary. I know you have never taught that, but those who do are growing greatly in numbers— especially when you get farther and farther from Jerusalem. For these, who call themselves Christians, the temple has no meaning anymore. Those of us Jews who have been forever changed by the life and teachings of Jesus feel like the world is slipping out from under us. What are we to believe? Simon, what do you believe?"

Simon was silent for a long time. Looking into the eyes of Judas, Simon recognized his agony. Softly he began to speak. "Judas, you are asking the same questions we all are asking. In fact, these are the same kind of questions that used to excite vigorous discussions when we were traveling with Jesus. I can't tell you why, but the questions never seemed to bother Jesus. Some of us, especially Peter, used to get so upset because the questions used to go on and on, and we never seemed to arrive at definitive conclusions. To Jesus, the questions were always more important than the answers. He used to respond to these questions with stories, many of which could be taken in different ways. Often, his followers would go away shaking their heads and arguing with each other. You asked what you are to believe, and what I believe. I guess I'm not comfortable starting there."

Judas was anxious. "I'm not starting there; uncertainty is where I'm ending up. Nothing is making sense."

"I know what you are saying. Our minds want to put things in order, to understand the reason or purpose for being. I guess what I am trying to say is, that may not be the best way to approach uncertainty. Jesus always seemed to push us toward asking more questions instead of finding answers. His message seemed to be that it was often our answers that blinded us to the presence of the kingdom of God."

Zenas thrust himself into the conversation like a schoolboy who had the right answer. "You mean, like you were saying yesterday: our heads build beliefs that blind us to the messages of the heart."

"Precisely, Zenas. Say more."

"No, I'm just the novice here. I know nothing about what Judas is asking. You are the—what do you call it—rabbi?"

Simon ran his fingers through his white hair and leaned back, looking at the stars. After a bit, he spoke. "Let me see. It is God who causes the wind to blow, the seeds to sprout, and the heart to beat. Because God is God and we are human, the only avenue to God is through the heart. God gave us Torah as a way to open our hearts to God. We have devised many ways to try to administrate Torah—all exercises of the mind claiming knowledge of God's will. We demanded kings so that, through power, we could demonstrate God's justice. The Greeks have helped us divide ourselves into body and spirit so that we could explain the inconsistencies of life. Then along comes someone who points out the hypocrisy of our dependence on the mind and the beliefs it creates, and we don't know how to react to him. Some want to destroy him, and others want to make him God. I have this sinking feeling that we can't get our beliefs out of the way long enough to hear what Jesus had to say, or to see the way he lived."

Judas was puzzled. "But I thought the center of Jesus's message was that the kingdom of God had arrived and that he would soon return as the Messiah, to claim his throne and bring justice and peace to the world."

Simon stood and walked off, about ten paces. He stared off into the night sky. He turned slowly and returned to sit beside Judas. "Many of us thought that, even believed it. What Jesus taught and did was seen through many different lenses. All of us who were close to him tried to make sense of his brutal murder and his reappearance to us. However, trying to fit him and his message into preconceived beliefs about the Messiah, or trying to discover the truth of his life and message within prophecies from the scriptures, have always felt like shackles on my heart. It is like my faith in the presence of the kingdom of God has to be somehow contained within what I know. Never a day went by when we were traveling with Jesus that our beliefs weren't shattered by the awesome power of the presence of God. I have continued to experience that wherever I encounter love. God's kingdom is among us."

"Then, you don't expect Jesus to return?" Wonder mixed with incredulity was in Judas's question.

"Jesus has returned to me. He told me that God is love and the kingdom of God is among us. He told me to live love; he told me to forget myself and to live for the other. That is the good news, and that is what I seek to live."

Judas still wasn't through. "Aren't you bothered by the disputes that are growing very ugly between the Gentile followers of Jesus and the Jews who follow Jesus? Now that James is gone, our only hope is for Jesus to come back and clear up all this confusion."

"Yes, that dissention bothers me greatly. My comfort lies in the fact that God always has a way of bringing us up short and forcing us to change the way we think about things. Maybe Jesus's return will be as much a surprise as was the presence of the kingdom of God. Maybe Jesus is already among us, and we need the faith and humility to see him and listen to him.

"Those who follow Paul and the Zealots in Galilee are grounding their faith in beliefs rather than humility. That is so much easier! Faith is not knowing, a bold uncertainty that resides in the love of God. Certainty binds the hands of God. Faith in God is not for babies or cowards. On the other hand, faith in God is not telling God who he is and what he is about. Faith in God is being open to the love of God, and being willing to follow the leadings of that love. Faith in God is courageous because it is completely open to the future; but it is also dangerous, because it threatens all those who have decided who God is and what God wants. It also threatens those who believe there is no God. But the irony of it all is that faith as humility is the only way to be open to God and to each other. Faith as beliefs ties the hands of God and builds walls between us."

Judas wasn't convinced. He just shook his head in uncertainty.

Zenas, however, was smiling. Everything Simon said confirmed what he had experienced in both Simon and his mother: openness, confidence, fearlessness, and compassion that made you feel at home. Simon was describing humble faith by differentiating it from righteous knowing. Zenas knew he was in the right place, learning at the feet of Simon.

Simon yawned. "That's enough of this! I need some sleep. I'm ashamed that I get to ride my camel while you two walk most of the time. But there is more to driving a camel than I had ever imagined. In reality, the camel is driving me, but it still tires me out. I'm just glad my camel is so infatuated with you, Judas, that it wants to follow you everywhere."

Zenas laughed. "Yes, my camel seems to have the same infatuation with Judas. Let's get some sleep."

The second day's travel was through some pretty rough and barren country. As the afternoon was slipping by, Simon began recognizing the terrain as more familiar. They stopped and made camp before he could identify any place in particular.

This evening, it was Zenas who opened the conversation around the fire. He looked directly into Simon's eyes. "We are headed straight for the heart of all the forces who wish us captured. There is no telling what is going to happen to us. Before we get separated forever, I want you to know just how much you have given me. You have changed my life forever and given me the greatest gift anyone can receive. You have given me life, indeed eternal life, because you have uncovered for me the meaning of life. I almost said you have given me freedom, but freedom cannot be given; it must be taken. Yet you, and your mother and sister, have shown me that only freedom to honor the Creator can unlock the mysteries of life.

"You have taught me that Jesus said God is love. Love is the human understanding of the force behind all that is. Love, the humble immersion of the self in the lives and needs of those around us, is the human key to the mysteries of life. It's as simple as forgetting self and living for the other. Yet it's as difficult as denying selfishness.

"But you have taught me so much more. I am a Roman brought

up to be proud of our laws and our government, through which we rule the world. However, your way of living revealed to me that law and government begin when love has failed. Love needs no laws or government. They are the management of hate and selfishness. Law and government can never bring righteousness or goodness; they deal only with hatred. The road to righteousness and goodness is lined with people who have humble faith in the God of love and who seek to realize God's kingdom, here and now. Our laws and government must be seen as necessities because of evil, not as tollgates on the road to righteousness. Rome, and all it stands for, must see its limits, and thereby recognize that only love has the faculties to assure freedom and unlock the mysteries of life."

Tears lined Simon's cheeks. Unable to speak, he realized, once again, the blessings of humility: the privilege of learning from his student. What a joy this man has brought to his life. He rose, walked behind Zenas, and put his hand on his head. Finally, he regained the ability to speak. "You're a blessing beyond expression. What a joy to learn from a young man who speaks wisdom well beyond his years. I thank and praise God for the many years this world will be blessed with your message of the good news of the gospel of Jesus."

The crackling of the fire revealed the solemn air encompassing the three men. No one spoke as they rose and began rolling out their bedrolls.

Judas banked the fire and walked off, looking up into the star-laden night sky. He struggled to identify his feelings, overshadowed by the thought that he wished his friends in the Jesus fellowship in Nazareth could have heard Zenas.

As they traveled to the southeast, the feeling of coming home overwhelmed Simon. The hills became more and more familiar. The terraced gardens on every slope reminded him of the home of his childhood. They passed through towns he recognized as places where he had worked as a mason and carpenter, along with his father and brothers. They passed so close to the sea the locals called Gennasaret that he could smell it. It brought back so many memories. The crowds, the debates in the synagogues, the elated people dancing away, freed from controlling demons. They went through towns like Chorazin and Cana, where Jesus and his mother had argued over the wine. Because Judas was concerned about the possibility of Roman soldiers in the town of Sepphoris, they took a detour around that town. Simon would have loved to see the many buildings he had helped construct. He wished he was close enough to talk to Zenas. He could have told him so many interesting stories.

By midafternoon, they were approaching Nazareth from the north. As they crested a hill, the town spread out in front of them, cascading down the southern face of the steep hill. The town looked smaller to Simon than he remembered, but then, places seen later in life always look small compared to childhood recollections. The caves he and his brothers explored were just around the hill to the right. Ironically, they were just a stone's throw away from the sheep pen Simon would never forget. The four boys thought it would be fun to open the pen door one night. Their father did not share their idea of fun, and his discipline made a lasting impression. The small caravan had to pass through the town, since Judas's small place was south of the town. It wasn't long before the whole town was aware that Judas had different camel drivers.

Immediately on arrival, Judas quickly tied up the animals, and then took Simon and Zenas to a remote cave a short distance from the village. "Stay here while I make sure that the town is safe and see what is going on in town. I'll be back in a while."

It was approaching dusk before he returned. "One of the busybodies asked why I had different drivers and wanted to know what had happened. My answer will not shorten her nose for long. Everyone else I feel comfortable with. Simon, it will not be possible to keep your identity a secret, but I don't think that will be a problem. Everyone here respects you greatly and will do whatever they can to protect you. I'm not sure we should tell them who you are, Zenas. It is probably best if we just say you are a disciple of Simon."

"There is nothing more truthful," answered Zenas.

"Good," said Judas. "Please, both of you, come to my home. My wife has a meal prepared for you."

The three of them went to Judas's house. A neighbor, self-designated watchman of the village, saw that Judas's drivers were going to have dinner in Judas's house instead of out back with the animals, as they usually did. This was something that needed further investigation.

It was not long after the morning prayers that the whole town knew that Simon, the brother of Jesus, was at Judas's house. Everyone wanted to see him and talk to him. There was great curiosity over his sudden appearance, but genuine respect as well.

Esther was one person Simon wanted to see, if she was still alive. As soon as he found out she was still living, he walked up near the top of the town to see her. Simon wasn't sure how old Esther was, because he had thought she was an old woman when he left Nazareth. She was always a favorite of the children of Nazareth because she gave them dates dipped in honey. Simon's mouth watered when he thought of these dates. But he most remembered Esther for her stories. She always had a story for the children, who sat at her feet in rapt attention. Much of what Simon knew of the history of the Jews came from Esther. As he approached her house, he recognized the low wall he used to sit on while listening to her stories. He called out her name. Almost at once, a stooped old woman stood in the doorway.

"Who is calling my name?" she said, as if she were looking right through Simon.

It was apparent to Simon that she was blind.

"You probably don't remember me. I am Simon, the son of Joseph and Mary."

Esther rushed up to Simon and threw her arms around his waist. Her head barely reached his chest. "I heard you were in town. I was so hoping to see you. Now you are here at my humble house. Sit, sit; we must talk."

"Not unless you give me a date soaked in honey."

Esther laughed. "That was a long time ago, when my husband had the stand in town. We always had plenty of dates and honey. I'm sorry to disappoint you. I haven't given out one of them since Levi died almost thirty years ago. I remember your family so well. We were so sad when you moved away to Jerusalem. All you boys have become so famous. I'll never forget the time when the twin Judas Thomas was lost for more than a day. I often tell that story."

"Yes, that really scared all of us." Simon hadn't thought about that in years. He recalled it now. "Judas Thomas had gone off alone, and he got trapped in a cave. No one knew he had gone off, so when we realized he was missing, we were at a loss to know where to look. He must have been about six or seven years old. After we found him—thanks to Jesus—Judas Thomas said he screamed and screamed for us, but we never heard him. Somehow, Jesus had this feeling to look in an area we seldom went to, and there he found him. It was the talk of the town for a long time.

"You mentioned your stories, and that is the real reason I wanted to come see you, Esther. I wanted to thank you for those stories. You had a way of telling about real events in our ordinary lives that made them seem almost miraculous. You could turn a mule kick into a lesson of looking out for another. You made stealing an orange seem like spitting in the face of God, and pulling the legs off a chameleon like killing your grandmother. More than anyone else in my life, you helped me realize how important my behaviors were, and how much they impacted others. I love you, and I loved your stories."

It was now Simon who hugged Esther.

CHAPTER 16

NO GREATER LOVE

Zenas stayed in the background while they were in Nazareth, concerning himself mostly with the animals. A small group of boys formed and gawked at this mountain of a man who looked like he could pick up one of those donkeys and throw it at them. Zenas noticed the boys and went over to them. They shied back, but did not run away. Zenas quickly disarmed their fears and, before long, was in a friendly conversation with them. Within hours, all the boys of the village were playing games with Zenas and engaging in contests of throwing, lifting, racing, and many other feats of strength. The boys were in awe of Zenas; they followed him around seeking his attention.

The day after they arrived in Nazareth, Amos, a cousin of Nathaniel, who lived on the edge of town, stopped to visit. He was from Tiberias on the Sea of Galilee. Hearing about Simon's presence enraged him. Simon and his brother James, alone, had blocked the efforts of the radical Zealots to drive the Romans out of Jerusalem. These two pious Nazirites, and their silly notions that the temple had to be purified before God would bring about the liberation of the Jews, had frustrated revolutionary efforts for too long. Amos cut his visit short to return to Tiberias. He was sure he had heard that the Romans were offering a reward for information about Simon. What a break! Not only could he get rid of a big problem for the movement, he could also fill his sack with some Roman coins.

Amos went directly to the Roman garrison in Tiberias. He gave them information as to Simon's location. With forty pieces of silver in his sack, Amos went to tell his friends. He would be a hero.

The next day, at the crack of dawn, there were twenty-four Roman soldiers outside Judas's house, demanding that Simon come out. Zenas, working in the animal shelter, heard the commotion and immediately went up to the Romans and asked why they were there. The commander demanded that Simon surrender.

Zenas, now very worried, said, "What could you possibly want with that old rabbi? That mild man could not possibly be of any interest to you."

"We have our orders," replied the captain.

"Let me offer you a deal," Zenas shot back.

"Who are you to have anything to offer that we would possibly be interested in?"

At this point, Simon saw from the doorway that Zenas was talking to the soldiers, and rushed to his side. "What are you doing?" Simon turned to the captain and said, "Don't listen to this man; he makes up strange things in his mind."

Zenas pushed Simon behind him and said to the captain, "Hear me out! I'm sure you have heard of Zenas, that high-ranking officer who deserted from Jerusalem. If you will let this man go, I can tell you where that scoundrel is, and it is not far from here."

This got the captain's attention. "How do you know about that? Where did you hear that?"

"Everyone around here knows about that. In fact, he passed through this very town. Do we have a deal?"

Simon tried to get in front of Zenas. "No! No!" Simon cried, but Zenas would not let him get to the captain.

The captain hesitated. He knew that if this man was bluffing, and he agreed to the deal, he could kiss his career goodbye. However, if this man could actually lead him to Zenas, he would be a hero, and there was no telling how much that would elevate him up the chain. "I have to have more than just your promise that you can deliver that deserter to me. What else can you tell me?"

"If I tell you something more, do we have a deal?" Zenas asked. "I will give you unquestionable proof, if you will assure me that you will let this man go free."

Simon grabbed Zenas around the waist and began to sob. "Please, oh, please, don't do this."

The captain came up close to Zenas and said in his most threatening voice, "If you can lead me to this man, the old rabbi will go free; you have my word." The captain and Zenas bumped forearms as a symbol of agreement. "Now, what is your proof?"

"I am Zenas, who was third in command of the garrison at Jerusalem," Zenas admitted. "I escaped from detention twenty-five days ago."

Simon fell to his knees in agony, sobbing. "No, God! Please don't let this happen."

The captain was shocked. He stepped back and raised his lance. This man in front of him certainly had the physique of a mighty Roman soldier; yet this was too good to be true. Was this just some deranged mind in a gladiator's body?

Zenas could see the indecision on the captain's face. "I'll prove it to you. No camel driver from Galilee would know how to fight with a lance. Give me your lance, and I will beat your best two soldiers here at one time."

"Do you take me for a fool? No one would put a lance in the hands of his prisoner," the captain retorted.

"I'm offering you proof that I am who I say I am. Are you so insecure of yourself and your men that you think I could take on all of you and kill you all?"

By this time, there was a crowd of people looking on. They all heard Zenas's challenge and looked to see how the captain would respond.

"Get these people out of here," the captain demanded, "and I will let you prove who you are. If you can defeat two of my best men, I will know that you are one of the elite among the soldiers of Rome."

Zenas was not sure the people would listen to him, so he asked Judas, who had come out to get Simon, to ask the people to get away. Simon had collapsed and was in need of assistance.

Judas begged the people to go back to their homes. The number of soldiers was enough to convince them to cooperate. They moved back, but stayed close enough to watch what was going to happen. Judas then helped Simon into the house.

The captain had the soldiers make a large circle around him and Zenas. He then chose two of his soldiers to step forward, gave Zenas his lance, and stepped back into the circle.

The three men started to circle around. One of the soldiers took a swing at Zenas, who ducked under the circling lance and swiftly brought his own lance up, catching the soldier across the left ear and knocking him to the ground. The other soldier, now behind Zenas, swung his lance overhand to come down directly onto Zenas's back. But Zenas used the momentum of his swing to move him just enough to escape the blow, which glanced off his shoulder. In one continuous movement, Zenas, using the centrifugal force of his lance, swung around and caught the second soldier on the back of his head, just below the scull. The man went down with a thud, unconscious. The other soldier regained his feet and assumed a defensive stance. There was blood flowing down his cheek and fear in his eyes. With three classic moves, Zenas had the man on the ground, disarmed. The fight was over! The soldiers stood in awe. Surely, this man was a champion with the lance—a match no one looked to engage.

"Do you need any more proof?" Zenas asked, his breathing hardly accelerated. "Can such a demonstration come from any but one who has reached the highest levels of Roman military training? Take me, and honor your word and leave the poor old rabbi alone."

The captain would not go back on his word. "Bind this man, and let us be gone!" he ordered.

The soldiers bound Zenas's hands behind his back and shackled his feet so that he could only take the shortest of steps. Two soldiers lifted the semiconscious soldier and draped his arms over their shoulders. The whole contingent then moved slowly away from the village.

Simon, who had regained some composure, stood in the doorway, with tears streaming down his face. He could not believe what had just happened. Zenas, a vibrant, extremely gifted young man had just sacrificed himself to save an old washed-up rabbi whom he had known only a few weeks. In the throes of deepest sorrow, he heard Jesus's last words to him: "I will return; where I am, there you can be." Simon shuddered at the thought.

When the soldiers returned to Tiberias, the captain could not wait to report the good news. The commander of the garrison knew Zenas immediately when he saw him. The captain was relieved and elated. They had gone out to catch a little fish and came back with a whale. He was on top of the world.

The commander immediately sent a dispatch to Jerusalem to get orders as to what to do with Zenas. The messenger was as puffed up as the captain. What laurels would soon pour down on this little garrison in hostile Galilee!

The soldier carrying the message to Albinus couldn't wait to deliver the good news to the new governor. He was proud as a peacock to have been chosen to deliver such news. Albinus, obviously pleased with the news, immediately asked whether the Jewish priest whom they had been ordered to arrest was also in custody. When the soldier proudly informed the governor about the bargain the captain had struck to be able to get Zenas, Albinus flew into a rage. "What earth-crawling snake has the right to defy my orders and make deals without my approval? The first thing a soldier learns is to follow orders! I want that captain brought here to me in chains immediately! Lock this man up for bragging about disobeying orders. What has happened to the great army of Rome?"

The soldier was flabbergasted. He stood shaking before the governor. Albinus immediately issued orders for the arrest of the captain and for the replacement of the commander in Tiberias. He also ordered that all the soldiers who were part of this mission be sent to Jerusalem to be disciplined, and that other soldiers be sent to Tiberias to replace them. As soon as this was accomplished, he wanted Simon arrested.

Back in Nazareth, Simon was beside himself. He couldn't eat or sleep. His mind was full of nightmarish thoughts of what Zenas was going through. Zenas had become like a son to Simon, and now he felt responsible for what had happened. Adding to his consternation, Simon had just found out that his mother and sister were in Caesarea. He knew little about how they had gotten there or what their situation now was. He was told they were safe with some Jesus followers, and that an old friend, Barnabas, was looking after them. He was desperate to see his mother and sister, and to assure himself of their safety and comfort. A definite bonus would be to see Barnabas, a fellow disciple of Jesus, and catch up on all that he had experienced since their last encounter in Jerusalem, now a number of years ago. Simon begged Judas to take him to Caesarea.

Judas thought that might be good for Simon. He also needed to deliver his goods to Caesarea and set up a new delivery to Damascus. He made arrangements for two drivers. Two days later, they set off for Caesarea. Simon rode on one of the camels.

About midafternoon of the day Judas and Simon left Nazareth, a group of Roman soldiers came for Simon. They could get no information from anyone in the town about Simon's whereabouts. Since Nazareth was on the western boundary of their jurisdiction, they searched all the neighboring towns to the north, east, and south, and asked questions of everyone they saw, trying to get some idea of where Simon was or where he had gone. They could get no helpful leads from anyone. They returned to Tiberias, fearful of how Albinus would react.

CHAPTER 17

THE POWER OF LOVE

Mary was deeply troubled. She had heard of the rift at the meeting and felt fully responsible for it. She could feel the tension with Joseph and Hanna. She felt terrible about hurting these kind people who had been so gracious to her. What could she do to reconnect with them? She knew that God's love was what bound people together, not what separated them; and yet, she also knew that Joseph and Hanna were not feeling anything like God's love right now.

Salome shared her mother's misery and felt her mother's pain as if it were her own. Yet she, too, had no idea what to do. "Mama, we have to do something. We can't be the cause of such pain. Maybe we should leave."

"No," Mary replied, "running away is no solution. That will only solidify the barriers that we have created. We have to talk to Barnabas and try to understand what he said that was so troubling to them; maybe that will help us figure out what to do."

Barnabas's dejection was obvious. He sat and stared at the walls for hours, brooding. His mind was running him around in circles. He knew he had said too much. He shouldn't have shared with others questions he was uncomfortable with himself. Did he expect those kind folks to solve his problems? The longer he sat, the more he punished himself. Oh, if only he had just relayed

Mary's apology and left it at that! How could he have been such a fool? Not only that, but he had passed on to them things Mary had said to him that she would never have said to them. Mary hadn't asked him to tell them what she'd said, just to apologize for what she'd done. What a lesson in openness! He wasn't being open with his feelings; he was insisting that they share his uncertainty. The more he ruminated, the deeper he sank into despondency.

A knock on the door startled him. When he opened the door to Mary and Salome, they both rushed into his arms. He held them tightly; he didn't want them to see his face. Mary pulled away slowly, but Salome kept her face buried in his shoulder.

Mary spoke first. "Oh, Barnabas, you're really troubled."

Barnabas couldn't answer. His lips quivered, and his eyes filled with tears.

Mary put her hand on his arm and said, "I can see your heart is broken. We came to you because we are terribly distraught, but, obviously, we are not suffering as much as you are. Why don't you share your burdens with us?"

Silently, he led the two women to a small room in the back of the house. Sitting uncomfortably on the edge of a low couch, he said, "Mary, I have done something awful. Instead of just going and relaying your apology, I tried to explain why you did what you did. I told them things you had said that you only intended for me to know. And, on top of that, I started to share all the questions and doubts that have been swirling around in my head since you arrived here the other day. In only a few minutes, I destroyed everything I helped them build over many years. I never remember being such a fool."

"Don't be quite so hard on yourself, Barnabas," Mary said. "I'm sure my upheaval had a lot to do with everything that happened." Mary's attempt at humor did nothing to lift his spirits. "From what I heard, there were only a few who are still really angry; the rest are mostly concerned for you and what you are going through."

Salome added, "Barnabas, these people really respect you and look up to you; a small indiscretion is not the end of the world."

"It was more than a small indiscretion, I'm afraid. I blew their faith apart!" Barnabas moaned. "Mary, I told them you said that if you had to believe that God had your son crucified in order to save us from our sins, you could not call yourself a Christian. The very thing that Paul and I came into this town preaching is the same thing that I just told them Jesus's own mother cannot accept. These people believe they are redeemed and assured of eternal life because Jesus died on the cross, and I just told them you consider that an anathema."

Mary got up and put her hand on Barnabas's shoulder. "Slow down a minute. You certainly caused a ruckus, but if you truly believe that faith is rooted not in beliefs but in humility, then you may have caused them some consternation in regard to their beliefs, but in no way did you destroy their faith—unless their faith is solely based on what they believe. Remember, what really matters is not what we believe, but how we treat each other. Jesus made that point over and over again."

For the first time since this terrible event, Barnabas found himself able to take a deep breath. "Mary, you are God's blessing! What you just said offers a ray of hope I have not felt since I shot off my mouth."

"What matters now," Mary said, "is not what you said that upset them, but how we react to the chasm that has been created between us. Is the love that binds us together in God's kingdom stronger than the different beliefs we have? Now is the time to demonstrate that we are more truly connected through our hearts than our minds."

Barnabas's spirit was rising. "What a simple yet lovely way to put it! A few minutes ago, I was terrified of meeting those people again. Now I can't wait to embrace them and show them how much I love them."

"Yes," Mary said, "let's go directly to Joseph and Hanna. They have been so kind to us. We must clear the air; and then we can go to the rest of the fellowship."

Hanna and Joseph were surprised to see Barnabas coming back with Mary and Salome. The tension between them was palpable.

Barnabas was the first to speak. "I wish to offer my sincerest apologies for upsetting you so badly. They are offered with no provisions or excuses. I upset you, and I want you to know that I am truly sorry for that."

Joseph and Hanna both sensed the regret in Barnabas's voice and were warmed by his sincerity.

Joseph responded, "Your apology is fully accepted. We love you and know that your intentions toward us are always the best."

Barnabas was quick to add, "I want to be able to give the same apology to the fellowship, just as soon as possible. The sooner we affirm how strong the love is between us, the better."

Hanna was relieved. "I'm sure we all want to put this whole incident behind us. Joseph and I will try to get everyone together this evening. I'm not sure Caspius and a few of the others will come, but we will try to get them here."

That evening, the largest room in Joseph and Hanna's house was full. Some were standing outside the windows so that they could hear what was going on inside. Caspius did not show up, but one of the men who had originally walked out with him was standing near the doorway. Mary, Salome, and Barnabas were in the center of the room. Instead of the normal clamor that preceded the fellowship meetings, a pregnant silence pervaded the room.

Barnabas spoke first. "The purpose of our meeting this evening is for me to sincerely apologize for my insensitive comments the other evening. I said things that I should not have said, most likely misrepresented someone we greatly respect, and imposed personal concerns on you before I had any idea about what I truly thought or felt about them—or about what impact they might have on you. Please accept my sincerest apology for causing you such anxiety.

"Walking over here this evening I was reminded of a strange little story Jesus often told; a story that has profound new meaning for me in light of all that has transpired. Jesus used to describe the final judgment this way:

"It is like a shepherd who separates his sheep from the goats. The king will place some at his right hand and others on his left. To those on his right, he will say, 'You have my blessing; come and enjoy the fruits of the kingdom. When I was hungry, you gave me food; thirsty, you gave me drink; alone, you took me into your home. When I was sick, you visited me; naked, you clothed me; in prison, you visited me.' Those on his right will ask, 'When did we see you hungry or thirsty, alone or sick, naked or in prison?' Then the king will say, 'Each time you did this to the least among you, you did it to me.' But, to those on his left, he will say, 'The joys of the kingdom cannot reach to you because when I was hungry, you gave me no food; when I was thirsty, you kept your cup from me; and when I was alone, your door was closed. I was sick, and you came not to me; naked, and you gave me no clothes; in prison, and you did not visit me.' Then those on his left will ask, 'When did we see you hungry or thirsty, alone or sick, naked or in prison?' The king will answer, 'Every time you refused to do this to the needy among you, you refused to do it to me.'

"It's obvious to me now why Jesus told this story so often. The blessings of the kingdom of God are not based on what we believe or our pious devotion to God, but, rather, on how we love one another. What happened the other night was that fears, incited by threats to what we believe, dominated and overshadowed the presence of love. Those fears immediately erected barriers among us and snuffed out the love that should always infuse our interactions. I was the greatest offender."

At this point, Mary stood up to speak. "I have only spoken to a few of you, but my actions have already had a monstrous impact on you. For that I am terribly sorry. I regret and apologize for the fact that I could not control my reactions when I entered your meeting the other evening. Your kindness to me deserved so much better a response. My response was visceral, and I hope you understand that. It was not a commentary on what you believe. I am aware of the many divergent beliefs that have developed around my son Jesus. My reaction to that is this: it matters little to me what we believe, as long as those beliefs help us to realize the reality of the life and message of Jesus. His life demonstrated God's presence and the accessibility of God's love. I encourage anything that demonstrates God's love and offers opportunities to participate in it. On the other hand, anything that denies or inhibits it, I have no time for. What I've experienced through the outpouring of your kindness to us since we arrived overwhelms me. I wish only to return such kindness tenfold."

Mary sat down. A hushed silence prevailed.

Then Aaron stood and said, "We are the grateful ones, for you coming to us." He then quoted Psalm 85 from memory:

> "Lord, thou hast been gracious to thy land
> and turned the tide of Jacob's fortunes.
> Thou hast forgiven the guilt of thy people
> and put away all their sins.
> Thou hast taken back all thy anger
> and turned from thy bitter wrath.
>
> Turn back to us, O God our savior,
> and cancel thy displeasure.
> Wilt thou be angry with us for ever?
> Must thy wrath last for all generations?
> Wilt thou not give us new life
> that thy people may rejoice in thee?
> O Lord, show us thy true love
> And grant us thy deliverance.

Let me hear the words of the Lord:
Are they not words of peace,
 peace to his people and his loyal servants
 and to all who turn and trust in him?
Deliverance is near to those who worship him,
 So that glory may dwell in our land.
Love and fidelity have come together;
justice and peace join hands.
Fidelity springs up from the earth
and justice looks down from heaven.
The Lord will add prosperity,
and our land shall yield its harvest.
Justice shall go in front of him
 and the path before his feet shall be peace."

Next, he began to sing the song from Exodus chapter 15:

"The Lord is my refuge and my defence,
He has shown himself my deliverer.
He is my God, and I will glorify him;
He is my father's God and I will exalt him."

Soon everyone was singing, joining hands, and linking arms. The room filled with joyous music that spilled out of the room, over the threshold, and into the street. By the time the singing stopped, a dry eye could not be found. Everyone wanted to hug Mary, Salome, and Barnabas. However different their beliefs, they were not barriers of separation now. Those in the fellowship all were one.

Chapter 18

Faith and Uncertainty

Over the next few days, many of the persons who had attended the meeting at Joseph and Hanna's house came to talk with Mary and Salome. The whole community fell in love with them. Mary's openness, empathy, and compassion drew them like a magnet. The information she gave and the stories she told gave them a vastly expanded picture of the person they now worshipped as their savior.

However, as the number of questions about Jesus mounted, Mary's responses began to foster an uncomfortable sensation among the questioners. While they wanted to hear about Jesus and his godlike behaviors, Mary always seemed to want to take them beyond Jesus and focus on what was happening around him. It was as if Jesus was the focus of their questions, but not the focus of Mary's responses.

Rebecca, a quiet but very astute young Jewish follower of Jesus, finally addressed this phenomenon directly when sitting alone with Mary. "You seem reluctant to brag about your son Jesus, and I guess that is understandable. But no one could ever have been like him. Your responses to our questions almost seem to downplay his importance."

"It's impossible for me to downplay Jesus's importance," Mary replied. "His life and message are eternally crucial for all

253

of humanity. He preached and demonstrated that the kingdom of God is among us, and called us to live that reality in everything we do."

"But, when you talk about him, I never get the sense that you think he was more than just a man."

"You're not the first one to say that since I have been here. I'm not sure how to answer you. Where did you get that idea?"

Rebecca was a bit uncomfortable. She thought that was the bedrock of her faith. "From Paul! He was here in Caesarea for the past two years, in custody for I'm not sure what. Our fellowship was able to meet with him a number of times. He is such a powerful preacher. He said Jesus is actually God's son, and God sacrificed him to redeem us from our sins. That is the only way we can have eternal life. He said our only path to salvation is to believe this and have faith in God's act of love."

Mary looked with great compassion at Rebecca. She had heard this before, and, each time, it mystified and troubled her. How did such a selfish, even arrogant, demand for eternal life become the essence of Jesus's message? Where was that promise grounded? The gift of life was the opportunity to participate in God's grand plan. And, certainly, the afterlife—whatever that might be—would reflect our contribution. But, to say what that plan was, seemed to be saying more than we could know. Faith was the acknowledgment of uncertainty. Beliefs were our answers to uncertainty. Paul, it seemed to Mary, was trying to combine the two. Mary knew the futility of confronting this head-on. "Has Paul's message been helpful to you?"

"Oh yes!" Rebecca said with great satisfaction. "It has freed me from feeling so guilty for all my failures, and allowed me to be more open and caring with my friends."

"That sounds wonderful! So, you are experiencing God's presence."

"Well, with some of my friends, the ones in the fellowship. That is really why I wanted to talk to you." Rebecca hesitated, apparently unsure of how to continue. Since Mary did not respond, she continued. "One thing has really troubled me ever since I joined up with the fellowship. The beliefs at the heart of our faith seem to be driving a wedge between me and some of my closest friends. They see that our fellowship is placing less and less importance on Torah; but, more importantly, they can't understand how Jesus's brutal death on the cross has somehow miraculously redeemed them and why they have to accept that to be one of us. They describe it as having to buy into a mystery religion, and they can't see how that brings them any closer to God or righteousness. We are spending less and less time together, and I miss them. I find it hard to accept that our faith should drive us apart."

"Not your faith, your beliefs. Faith lives in uncertainty, which gives little reason to break the ties between us. Beliefs ride on the wings of conviction, and possess the power to destroy." Mary's face grew very sad. She closed her eyes and took a few deep breaths.

Rebecca waited for her to continue, feeling uneasy in the silence, but not knowing what to say.

Finally, Mary spoke in a soft voice loaded with grief. "Jesus's tragic death has overshadowed his amazing life and message. Crowds flocked to hear him. However, he never pointed to himself as the focus of the presence of the kingdom; rather, he taught that we should focus on what God was doing around us. The sick were being made well, the blind could see, the lame got up and walked, and the confused or possessed were made whole. Jesus believed the messiah was among us. He was so open to the presence of God's love that everyone around him was affected. I'm convinced that he believed that God has initiated the time when God's love would rule over all mankind.

"However, even his *beliefs* were shattered." Mary struggled to continue as tears fell from her eyes. Almost in a whisper she said, "I'll never forget those agonizing words he uttered from the cross:

JOSEPH C. NYCE

'My God, my God, why have you forsaken me?'" Sobbing, she said, "I don't remember a time when my heart sank lower."

Mary struggled to regain her composure. She got a strange look on her face, and her eyes seemed to be looking far away. "I'm sorry for the emotion. I don't know if you heard, but he came to me from out of the tomb. He said the work had just begun, and we had to spread to one and all the good news of the presence of the kingdom of God and the reign of love. He will be with us always.

"Making Jesus the focus of the good news is to do precisely what he refused to do. He was aware that the presence of the kingdom of God meant that the age of love had arrived. In order for love to reign, we must move beyond the self. In order for love to reign, he had to live by faith as humility and mercy. That is what he did, and that is why humanity will never be able to forget him. But the crucial thing is not who he was or what he did, or even what he believed, but whether we can live by such a humble faith that the mercy of God's love can flow among us. That is why I answer you the way I do. He personally asked me to continue to preach the good news."

Rebecca sighed. "Oh, how I wish my friends could hear this! What you just said has nothing in it that would push us apart. It offers lots of places where my friends and I can work together instead of arguing over bizarre beliefs that separate us."

"That's just the point," responded Mary. "Jesus was always being challenged by the religious rulers, who completely ignored the good that was happening. They always wanted to argue over Torah, completely forgetting that Torah's sole purpose is to foster humility, to shift the focus from self to the other. They couldn't see beyond the rules for living that their beliefs had constructed, missing entirely what God's love was accomplishing.

"As near as I can tell, the true measure of humble faith displaying God's loving mercy is selfless compassion for one's neighbor, especially the less fortunate. All of our history, and Torah, point to that. Life is service: living the truth of God's love."

Rebecca jumped up and threw her arms around Mary. "Please … can I bring my friends to talk with you? I know they will just love it."

"It would be an honor to meet your friends," Mary said sincerely. "I also want to continue to go to your fellowship. I really am impressed with those people."

Rebecca left smiling. You could tell by her steps that she really felt like skipping.

The elation Barnabas felt from the meeting at Hanna and Joseph's counterbalanced his despondency over the rift with Caspius. Word quickly got back to him that Caspius openly mocked his weakening faith. Tempering the great bond of trust generated from the meeting, the questions swirling around in his head offered no solace for the scorn aimed at him from this troubled believer. The fact that he shared many of Caspius's questions only compounded his discomfort.

Nevertheless, Barnabas could not deny the strange evolution going on inside him, unquestionably the result of his reunion with Mary. He had paid little attention to her when he was with Jesus. He knew Jesus respected her greatly; and she and Mary Magdalene were very close. But Barnabas had never thought of Jesus's mother as a central figure in the movement. The few encounters these past number of days had made it abundantly clear to him that Mary, possibly more than anyone else, embodied the message of Jesus. Now, with James gone, no one on earth knew Jesus better than Mary; furthermore, it was now quite evident to Barnabas that no one had a better understanding of Jesus's message than Mary. But it was even more than that. Mary was living Jesus's message, and bringing about a radical change in Barnabas.

Barnabas struggled with getting a handle on the importance of the changes coming over him. He knew he could never address Caspius's challenge until he did so. He desperately wanted to understand the significance of what Mary was teaching him.

He couldn't get over the way this current crisis resolved so

JOSEPH C. NYCE

easily; this was so radically different from how things resolved when he was traveling with Paul. The two of them went from town to town, intoxicated with the success of their message. Many more than they ever expected eagerly received their message and changed their lives by accepting the good news of Jesus Christ. But, time after time, their elation turned to panic as they fled the ire of many in these towns. As much as their message fed the souls of some, it induced bitter hatred in others. The message of God's love so divisive when he was with Paul, and yet, here, the same potential seeds of bitterness yielded a blessed togetherness. Why was that so?

The message he and Paul presented was not about what Jesus said and did, but who he was. Paul's message rested on beliefs about who Jesus was and why he died. The faith they proclaimed was in Christ crucified, which had to be accepted on faith. But what was this faith? Blind acceptance of specific beliefs! There was no uncertainty about God or the future, only a bold assertion of knowledge of God's grand plan. Yet Barnabas knew that faith was the home of uncertainty, and faith was also grounded in humility.

Barnabas kept reflecting. Paul's message was one of salvation. He didn't remember Jesus ever speaking about that. He certainly said a lot about repentance. When Paul preached about salvation, he always described what God was doing and why. Was he saying more than humans could ever really know? Weren't he and Paul proclaiming things about God and then telling folks they had to accept these beliefs by faith? Wasn't the need to have assurance of eternal life the very opposite of faith, and, possibly, the ultimate expression of selfishness?

Jesus, on the other hand, preached repentance, regret for all acts of selfishness. Repentance recognized the error of placing oneself ahead of God and the other. Repentance was an expression of humility before God. Seeking salvation was actually making a demand on God, whereas repentance was making oneself

258

vulnerable to God's love. The two really did reveal a radical difference in focus.

Paul also made a big thing about being a changed man. He talked about how he had cast off the old man and put on the new, that the spirit of Christ was in him, and we should be like him. But Jesus was constantly telling us to forget self and be concerned for the other. What a radical difference in focus! Jesus never seemed to think that he was the cause of the miraculous things that were happening; it was all because God was present. He really did forget himself.

Barnabas continued to ruminate. Was seeking salvation merely another form of selfishness? What was selfishness, anyway? Certainly, lust and greed were the repressive forms of selfishness, but did it have a more outward or aggressive form? Perhaps, insisting that someone think and be like you was a form of selfishness, as was insisting that person change in order to remain connected with you. He thought again about his mission activity with Paul. The objective there wasn't putting the self aside and making space for the other but changing one's beliefs. Barnabas began to wonder if spreading the good news meant changing beliefs or living love. A cold sweat began to form on the back of his neck.

Barnabas's mind continued to jump over itself. It was all because of Mary! That lovely old woman had come back into his life and upset his whole world. He thought again of the tremendous sense of peace he'd felt coming away from the meeting at Joseph and Hanna's.

Just then, there was a soft knock on his door. He was pleasantly surprised to see that it was Salome. "Come in, come in," he said with more excitement than he wished to admit. "What brings you to me?"

Salome entered a bit reticent, but hearing the warmth in Barnabas's voice confirmed her trust in coming to talk to him. "I've been doing a lot of thinking, as I guess all of us have. I want to talk to you about what just happened between us and the fellowship."

"Come in and sit. Let me get some tea. I have just been ruminating over that very thing." Barnabas hurried to get some cups and heat some water. It struck him that he was terribly anxious to hear what Salome had to say. When he returned, he gave her a steaming cup of tea and said, "I can't wait to hear what you have been thinking."

Barnabas's obvious interest helped Salome to relax. "I need to talk to someone, to get some of these feelings out in the open. I have a sense that the events of the past few days may be breaking some things open for me. I have always been extremely uncomfortable with the arguing, bickering, and downright hostility that have been a part of our community, especially since it is always around the importance of Jesus and who he was. It has always felt to me that our ideas are more important than our feelings for one another. Over the last number of years, it feels like the followers of Jesus are being driven apart. Those who wish to remain faithful to Torah are ridiculed by those who feel they have been liberated from it. And those who defend Torah are growing more and more hostile toward those who no longer follow it. But, in the past few days, I have experienced something that I have not seen before. People from both of these positions have actually met together and received each other in fellowship. This is just beautiful. I'm not sure what is happening, but I thought you might be able to explain it to me. Do you see the same thing, and do you feel the same hope I feel?"

Barnabas was encouraged by Salome's observation. He, too, recognized the uniqueness of the past few days. He was sure it was somehow the result of Mary's presence. "I have noticed the same change you have. But you may be in a better position to explain it to me than I can to you. I'm sure whatever is going on has to do with your and Mary's arrival into our community. Your presence—particularly, Mary's dramatic introduction to the fellowship—has provided a different way for us to see each other and ourselves. So, maybe you should tell me what it is that you have brought to us."

"I have no idea. We were dumped on you by fate."

"Maybe," Barnabas suggested, "it was the hand of God."

"I know the Lord's hand was present when he led you to us, because you rescued us from a terrible situation." Salome felt like hugging Barnabas. "All I know is that right now we seem to be most interested in the things that bind us rather than the ideas or beliefs that separate us."

"That is obvious to me as well," said Barnabas, shaking his head. "Maybe that is the answer."

"What do you mean?"

"Maybe all we need to do is open up to the leading of our hearts, instead of trying to justify the machinations of our minds. Maybe that is what Jesus was trying to tell us when he repeatedly told us to forget ourselves and follow him."

Salome jumped up. "You have to make that your next lesson for the fellowship!"

Barnabas nodded, but he was not really thinking of what Salome had said. This was possibly the first time since she and Mary had arrived that he actually saw Salome as someone distinct from Mary. He was disgusted with himself for such a slight. He could be so unobservant sometimes. His eyes softened, and a frown formed on his face.

Salome noticed the change and wondered how what she had said brought about such a reaction. "Are you thinking about what I said?"

Embarrassed that she recognized his excursus, he said, "I heard what you said, but I must admit I was admiring you instead of thinking about what to say to the fellowship. I have to apologize to you for my cursory treatment of you since you have been here. Your mother has upset my wagon, and I am struggling to get all my thoughts back in place. You coming here alone and speaking your concerns has opened my eyes to realize what I have been missing. I really like your deep compassion. I like you and want to know more of your thoughts and feelings. I think you may be able to help me right my wagon."

Salome felt awkward hearing these comments from someone she looked up to, and she felt at a loss for words. She began to self-consciously rub the material of her skirt between her fingers. "Thank you for your kind words. I have always looked up to you and respected you. The suggestion that I can help you takes me to an unfamiliar place. But I like you too, and I would love to share thoughts and feelings with you." For the second time in as many weeks, Salome found herself talking to a man in a way unfamiliar to her.

"I'm glad to hear that." Barnabas was as unfamiliar with this kind of exchange as Salome. He struggled to find the best words. "You are out from behind your mother's apron, and no one is happier about that than me."

"My mother is a wonderful woman, strong and courageous. Sometimes I feel that she must be an angel. I understand how others get lost in her presence. I'm glad you were so open with me; it makes me even more comfortable with you. I must go now. Thank you for helping me, and bringing something bright into the future."

"No, I should be thanking you."

Salome left feeling much better than she had when she came. She felt a comfortable connection with Barnabas, so at ease in his presence.

Barnabas liked this woman. She was so soft-spoken, but there was obviously a lot going on under that demureness. He was aware that her visit incited feelings he hadn't experienced for years. He watched her walk away and realized she had always been the woman in the shadows—the shadow of her mother and of her popular brothers. Yet, every time he saw her, she was doing something for someone else. She never asked to be noticed, but she was always an important part of what was going on. Possibly more than anyone else he knew, Salome lived for the other. Was she his metaphor for love? At that moment, he realized that he wanted her to be the most important part of the rest of his life. He would make all the room necessary for her in his life. As he watched her walk away, he shuddered, seeing two Roman soldiers emerge from a doorway across the street and follow her.

Upon arriving back at the home of Joseph and Hanna, Salome was surprised to hear Mary talking to a stranger in the rear garden. "Who is Mama talking to?" she asked Hanna.

Hanna shrugged her shoulders. "A young soldier came alone, asking for her. Mary obviously knew who he was when she saw him. The young man asked to speak to her in private, so they went to the rear garden."

Salome went to see if she could see who it was. She recognized the young man immediately as the soldier Mary had saved from death. She came back to Hanna. "I know who that is." Salome could hardly contain her excitement. She proceeded to tell Hanna about the incident that happened on their long march from Jerusalem.

Hanna just shook her head in amazement when she heard the story. "I just can't get over your mother. What a wonderful woman she is!"

Salome wanted to go out back to see what the young man and her mother were talking about. If he had come to thank her, why would he have asked to see her alone? Curiosity was an awesome force, against which Salome needed all her powers of restraint.

Hanna smiled inwardly at Salome's obvious struggle.

In a space of time that seemed like forever to Salome, Mary and the young man came into the back room. Mary was relieved and grateful that he had survived. It was obvious he did not recognize Salome. Mary introduced him to Hanna and Salome, and they moved on toward the front entrance. After a cordial farewell, she came back into the kitchen.

Before Mary was completely in the room, Salome spoke. "Tell

me what that was all about. I could hardly restrain myself from coming out there to hear what you were talking about."

Turning to Salome, Mary said, "I'm sure you recognized him. Doesn't he look great?"

Salome nodded. "Yes, he does, but what was that all about? If he just came to thank you, why did he want to meet with you alone?"

"Your deductive powers are working well." Mary paused, apparently trying to put the story together. "Do you remember Rebecca, the young woman who came to see me the other day?" Both Hanna and Salome nodded. "He met Rebecca a while back, when he was still recovering from the scorpion bite. Apparently, she changed his dressing or something. The two have been seeing each other. He told her about the incident in the wilderness and expressed to her that it changed his goal in life. He no longer wants to be a soldier and can't wait to get out. He became interested in the fellowship Rebecca attends and wanted to know more about it. Rebecca suggested he come to me and hear what I thought about the fellowship."

Mary paused and then continued. "He seems to be a wonderful young man. His mind appears to be as open as his heart. By the way, we were right, Salome: he is a Samaritan. He was forced to enlist and has four more months on his conscription. He is serious about Rebecca."

"What did he say about you treating him on the journey here?" Salome asked.

"I guess he didn't know it was me, and I didn't tell him."

"What? Why not?"

"That's not why he came to talk to me, and I didn't want that to influence what I said about the fellowship. If he attends the fellowship in the future, I'm sure we will get a chance to celebrate that miracle."

Not all the discussions that day centered on the harmony within the fellowship. Outside Jacob's stall at the market, some shoppers had stopped because of a man speaking in a raised voice. The man was pursuing Jacob, who was obviously trying to avoid him.

Caspius's face was bright red above his ocher beard. "Jacob, are you going to just stand aside and say nothing? You've got to realize how damaging Barnabas's comments were, especially to those who just joined the fellowship. He's going to crush their faith before it has a chance to grow roots."

Jacob turned and put his hands up to keep Caspius at arm's length. "Caspius, quiet down. I'm willing to talk to you, but I won't be harassed."

"I'm sorry. I really am upset. I know that is no reason to jump all over you. But you do see my point, don't you?"

"Yes, I do see your point. I also see a lot of other things. I see an old trusted friend, Barnabas, about as troubled as a man can get. I see two Jewish women come into our community with a totally different experience of the person who has been presented to us as the Christ. I see the ship of faith being buffeted by the storms of life. I see the need for calm reflection."

"You may be a wiser man than I, Jacob, but I see a battle between the old and the new, between the antiquated ways of tribal religions and a faith open to the challenges of the future. The modern world has moved well beyond Judaism, and faith cannot get sucked back into its suffocating embrace. Jesus as the Christ moves us beyond the earthbound world of Torah and into the world of the spirit—and there is no going back."

"Come back to earth for just a moment, Caspius. If you look into the eyes of Barnabas, Mary, and Salome, what do you think you will see?"

"Why do you ask that? How do I know what I will see?"

"That's just the point. You have made judgments about what they have said and what they are doing, and those judgments are based on nothing except how they impacted you. Perhaps you should try to see more before you pronounce judgment."

"I know I am impulsive, but my gut is pretty reliable. I have been pretty successful following its impulses."

"Success has many levels; not all of them exemplify righteousness."

"What? Are you assaulting my integrity? I didn't expect that from you, Jacob."

"Not at all. I'm just suggesting the prudence of harnessing impulses.

"Look, Caspius, you do not know Barnabas very well, and you know nothing of Mary and Salome. I know Barnabas very well. If he is deeply troubled about something, you can be assured it is serious. He is genuine, down to the soles of his feet.

"What is happening among us right now is most important. What matters is not what we believe but the way we relate to each other. You and I are businessmen. We exist on the exchange of things. But we both know the really important part of being a businessman is realizing you have done something or provided something that has bettered the life of someone else. There is no satisfaction in cheating someone. It may add to your success, but not to your sense of well-being. How we treat one another is all-important."

Caspius looked Jacob in the eyes. "I respect you, Jacob. You've spoken strong words to me that give me pause. I will treat your wisdom with respect, and I will seriously consider the counsel you suggest." He warmly embraced Jacob and turned to leave.

Jacob reached out and grabbed his arm. "Thank you, Caspius. We are more than just what we think. God bless you."

"God has blessed me to know you. May God bless you, my brother."

"Mama, what is love?" Mary and Salome were alone in the room on the second floor of Joseph and Hanna's home.

"Why, out of the blue, do you ask the question everyone has asked countless times during their life? What has raised your curiosity?"

Salome, never one to veil what was on her mind, responded. "Many things, all raising the same question. What just happened among us and the members of the fellowship, for one. Also, I went to see Barnabas this morning, and things were said that incited feelings I have seldom ever felt. (She thought of Zenas, but sensed a difference in what she felt today.) Love seems to mean a lot of things. We are taught to love God and neighbor. Is love something you do, or is it something that just happens?"

"Now my curiosity is aroused. What went on between you and Barnabas?"

"Nothing but some kind and generous words that made me feel special. They also opened my eyes to see him in a completely different light. I've always seen him as one of Jesus's disciples, somehow separated out as different and set apart. Today, we talked for a bit as real friends, as if nothing separated us. It was such a warm feeling. I can't get it out of my mind."

"What a joy it is for me to hear you say that! My prayer is that you can say that every day. I'm convinced that our purpose in life is to make sure those we meet can always repeat those words. They do make you think of love, don't they?"

"Yes. That's why I asked the question."

Mary paused to think. "Jesus said that God is love. Yet God has always been unfathomable, beyond our comprehension. Does that make love unknowable? Probably it does, to the mind—but not to the heart. I know you have often heard me say that love is a river that overflows all of creation. Its potential is everywhere. We are its shroud: our thoughts, feelings, demands, and prejudices. We know love when we experience it, even though we can't explain it, because it comes from beyond ourselves. We have to make room for it by getting off dead center. You would never have felt like you did today with Barnabas as long as you saw him as Jesus's disciple. That is your shroud to love. The greatest struggle in life is for the self to get off dead center."

CHAPTER 19

REUNION WITH SIMON

Judas needed to get to Caesarea early enough to unload his cargo and take care of his animals before Sabbath. He wanted to get Simon to his mother but was not sure where she was. He knew that Jacob, a Jewish merchant in the market where he delivered his goods, and a Jesus follower, would know. While his two drivers began unloading the cargo, Judas took Simon to Jacob. Jacob made a big fuss over Simon and assured Judas that he would get him to Joseph and Hanna's house.

Jacob instructed his helper to put the merchandise away early and close up the shop. He then took Simon to the home of Joseph and Hanna.

Mary and Salome's jubilation at seeing Simon was quickly doused by the look on his face. He was deeply troubled.

Mary thought he might be concerned for their safety, since the Romans were hunting him. "Simon, what's wrong?" Mary asked. "I see fear in your eyes. Do you fear that you are putting us in danger?"

"Sadly, no, Mother," Simon lamented. "I have been ransomed! That is the source of my heartache. It's a long story to tell, an effort I'm not sure I can accomplish without my heart breaking."

Slowly, and with much effort and pain, he told them about Zenas. He told them how they had met and of their growing

268

affection for each other with each passing conversation. As the story unfolded, Mary and Salome dreaded its conclusion. They knew, from Simon's demeanor, his sorrow stemmed from something dreadful happening to Zenas.

Salome, yielding to the fear of her expectations, left the room.

Mary's heart grew heavier with each dreadful turn of the story. As Simon described the tragic conclusion, Mary felt a sharp stab of recognition deep in her abdomen. It was almost as if her womb turned upside down. She broke down, sobbing. Not since James's tragic death had she experienced such sorrow. All she could think of was what torture and abject misery Zenas must be experiencing—if he was still alive.

Simon could offer no comfort to her. He shared her pain, but those feelings lay buried under mountains of guilt. He felt as helpless and hopeless as he had those dreadful hours after Jesus had been hung on that horrid cross. Once again, the world was falling apart. Where was this kingdom of God that had come? Life was nothing more than a bad dream where the powerful got their exercise trampling the poor and lowly under their feet. The good and gifted were swallowed up by the evil and greedy. Where was the love of God? Over and over again, humble faith got mocked by ruthless power.

Salome could not stay away. Simon's inward ranting was interrupted by Salome's cold hand on his arm. She didn't need to hear the horrid details of Zenas's fate, but she was concerned for Simon. Her only remaining brother now in deepest pain, she wanted only to console him. "Simon, something more than just sorrow is weighing upon you. What has killed your spirit? You have always been the calm one, the one we leaned on in our lowest moments."

Simon slowly found his voice, though it was hardly more than a whisper. "You didn't hear the end of my story. My heart is encased in guilt. We were in Nazareth, the home of our childhood. The Romans came for me, and Zenas sacrificed himself to save me. He was warming to the good news of Jesus's life and message, and would have been a messenger like no other. Yet he laid his life in front of the Romans to save my wrinkled neck. I'm on my way to the grave, while he had his whole life ahead of him. What's wrong with this picture? Is God asleep?"

Salome felt a horrid stab of grief at the thought of Zenas in the hands of the Romans. At the same time, she felt as if he had offered life's greatest gift. "What a courageous and compassionate thing to do! He's an angel!"

"But a dead one!"

"Simon, Simon, please, you don't sound yourself." Speaking about not sounding like yourself, instead of the news about Zenas tearing her apart, Salome saw his action as one of ultimate love. "You know, Jesus always told us to forget about ourselves and live for the other. Is *that* what he meant? Isn't that what Zenas did? My Lord! Are we to go that far?" Salome couldn't believe she was saying this; she almost felt like she was outside herself.

For the first time in many hours, Simon's eyes cleared, and he looked at Salome. "You know, as I was watching the soldiers drag Zenas away, I clearly heard Jesus saying, 'I will return. Where I am, there you can be.' Could it be, Salome, could it be?"

They looked at each other in utter amazement. Neither could speak. Tears were falling down their cheeks. Their anxiety over Zenas clashed with the frightening thought of what God's love really meant. They couldn't move, each overcome by the feeling of how vulnerable life was in the face of God's love, but also how central love was in revealing the meaning of life. The lesson of love wasn't lost on them.

Once they regained composure, they still were at a loss for words. Nothing seemed to sound right. Their hearts told them that they had just received a visitation from God, an event their minds could not find words to express.

All Simon could say was "Oh, Zenas, Zenas, Zenas!"

That evening was extremely strange. In the first place, ever since Mary and Salome's arrival at Hanna and Joseph's home, their hosts tried to make them as comfortable as possible. For Hanna and Joseph, this meant that they had to reinstall some of the Torah requirements they had let slip since attending the fellowship with the Gentiles. The meal this evening was a completely kosher meal. This reversion did not go unnoticed by Mary and Salome, who received it as just another kindness these good people had showered on them. Secondly, Simon was so quiet and preoccupied throughout that Mary was really worried about him, but she could read in his silence that she should not press him.

Word that Simon, Jesus's brother, was in Caesarea spread quickly from Jacob's stand in the market at the heart of the community. In the market, you found out everything going on in the community. Every stand and stall had a few chairs where people could sit, sip flavored tea, and share the news of the day. It didn't take long for every Jesus follower in town to know of Simon's presence. They all wanted to meet him.

The home where the fellowship met was crowded the next morning. Simon had agreed to attend. He didn't know what to expect. He knew that the farther away from Jerusalem you were, the more the meetings in many of the synagogues changed. On arrival, it surprised him to see that the men and women were not separated, but he was comforted to notice that the Torah was in a prominent position. His throat constricted when he saw a small cross in an alcove on the far side of the room. Simon recalled the days years ago, in Jerusalem, when Paul was so adamant in proclaiming the importance of Jesus's death on the cross. Simon could never get his mind to convince his heart that this vile symbol of human violence was the ultimate expression of God's love. Even today, more than twenty-five years later, the image of his brother on the cross broke his heart; its only message being a horribly cruel expression of human power completely contrary to the presence of God. Simon tried to eradicate the caustic thoughts that were rushing into his mind. He pushed himself to be in a spirit of prayer and expectation.

Everyone wanted to greet Simon, and he was showered with questions. After much persuading, the people settled down.

As a silence fell over all, a young man rose and began reading from Psalm 23:

> "The Lord is my shepherd; I shall want nothing.
>> He makes me to lie down in green pastures,
> and leads me beside waters of peace;
>> he renews life within me,
> and for his name's sake guides me in the right path.
>> Even though I walk through a valley dark as death
>> I fear no evil, for thou art with me,
>> thy staff and thy crook are my comfort.
>>> Thou spreadest a table for me in the sight
>>> of my enemies;
>>> thou hast richly bathed my head with oil,
> and my cup runs over.
> Goodness and love unfailing, these will follow me
>> all the days of my life,
>> and I shall dwell in the house of the Lord
>> my whole life long."

After a prolonged silence Azariah, the oldest member of the fellowship and one who was greatly respected by all, stood to speak. "There is no question in my mind that we have received a special blessing from God. Not only have the mother and sister of Jesus come to be with us, but now his brother, one of his blessed disciples, has come to us too. We have among us the three persons in the world who knew Jesus the best. Except his return, which we all eagerly await, nothing could bring us closer to our master. They shared his childhood, they saw him heal, they heard him preach, they saw him die, and they embraced him beyond the tomb. We are truly blessed to have them among us. Who better to explain to us the good news he preached?"

Just then, Barnabas came into the room. He had spent the past eighteen hours with Noah and Ruth, whose seven-year-old son had been trampled by a Roman soldier's horse. Though, obviously exhausted, he brightened when he saw the crowd.

Simon recognized Barnabas immediately and hurried to him. They embraced. The two disciples of Jesus shook with emotion.

"I heard you were here, and wanted so badly to come immediately to you, but an emergency kept me away," Barnabas explained.

Simon clasped Barnabas's shoulder with one hand and shook his hand with the other. "What a joy to see you! I never thought we would meet again. The last I heard of you, you and Paul were converting both Jews and Gentiles to be followers of Jesus."

Barnabas shook his head. "We have so much to catch up on, but it must wait; we are interrupting the meeting." He then turned and spoke to the gathering. "You all must hear from this holy man. He and his brother James spent many years in Jerusalem proclaiming the good news Jesus taught." He motioned to Simon to stand and address the people.

Simon stood and looked over the whole room before he began to speak, his face full of sorrow, his eyes brimming with tears. "I stand before you now only because a brave Roman soldier clearly understood the true meaning of the good news Jesus taught. Let me tell you a story from when we were traveling with Jesus: 'A young man of great authority and wealth came to Jesus and asked what he must do to inherit eternal life. Jesus answered that he must live righteously and follow Torah. The man said he had faithfully done that but that didn't seem like enough. Then Jesus told the man to go and sell all his possessions, give the money to the poor, and come follow him. The man went away in great sorrow.'"

In a voice choked with emotion, Simon continued. "I start

with that story because it is the story of Zenas, the Roman soldier I just mentioned, but with a different ending. I met Zenas in the wilderness. We were both being hunted by the Romans. Zenas asked the same question the man in the story asked, only he embraced Jesus's answer instead of rejecting it. He sacrificed himself to save this old man standing before you." Simon struggled to get the words out. After a pause, he continued. "The Romans found out where I was and came to arrest me. Zenas offered himself in exchange for me. Now I stand here before you, while he lies chained in some dungeon, awaiting certain death. He actually may already be dead. He gave himself in an act of ultimate love." This last was said through sobs of anguish. Simon could not continue.

Mary walked over to her son. Her face was distorted in anguish. She embraced Simon for a long time. The silence was unsettling. Everyone in the room was anxious; no one knew what to do.

Mary finally began to speak. "I know so little about Zenas. In Jerusalem, he came to our house to arrest Simon and was there for no more than fifteen minutes. When Salome and I were arrested, we talked with him one night from our cell; he was in a neighboring cell, placed there because he showed respect to us instead of arresting us. He escaped from prison and came to us, and in less than a day, we helped him get away from Jerusalem. Yet that short encounter told me he was a special person. Extremely uncomfortable in his role as an arresting officer, he treated Salome and me with dignity and respect. He was kind to us from his cell, and refused to divulge our private conversations to his superior when asked. These two acts revealed him to be a man of principle and integrity. During the few hours he was with us in our house as we planned to help him escape Jerusalem, he was so open, curious, and concerned about making trouble for us. I really, really liked him."

Simon, having regained control of his emotions, stood to

speak. "Mother, you are so right. Everyone here must know Zenas, because to know him is to understand the good news of Jesus's life and message. Zenas is a beautiful man in every sense of the word. He's an exceptional young man—warm, open, and accepting. He is highly intelligent, handsome, big, and strong as an ox. As far as opportunity goes, he had the world in the palm of his hands. The son of a Roman senator, he had the best education Rome could provide. He was being groomed for great things. Anyone who knows him, or is with him for just a short while, knows that he will rise to the top of anything he does. When we met in a cave in the hills north of Jerusalem, he had just thrown all this away because of an encounter he had with you, Mother. What he saw in you made him loathe his life and what he was doing. He told me he deserted the Roman army to discover the truth you personified."

Mary interrupted. "I'm sure that is an exaggeration. He was obviously disillusioned with his situation before he met me."

"That might be, Mother, but you were definitely his motivation. He said that, instead of being frightened by his situation, he felt elated by the freedom, which reminded him of the openness and fearlessness he saw in you. Once he found out who I was, he wanted to know everything about you. We spent days together in the wilderness, talking every moment we were awake. We formed a very special bond. Those conversations changed both of us. Initially, his curiosity focused on our Judaism, what he called our quaint habits and behaviors. Before long, however, he wanted to understand the secret behind our freedom to act and our lack of anxiety toward the future. He told me that you had made such an impression on him that he would spend the rest of his life searching for this inner peace.

"Since we couldn't travel by daylight, we spent night after night in deep philosophical discussions of power, authority, religion, and the human condition. Early on, we realized that what bound us together was the yearning to be free to pursue those things that gave ultimate meaning to our lives. We talked about evil, which we associated with the human sins of arrogance and greed. His probing questions helped me realize that the root of all sin is selfishness."

At this moment, a commotion was going on out in the street. People were shouting, and a great crowd began forming around the building. It looked like they were trying to shield or protect the building.

Simon continued. "Zenas was moved by the idea of one creator God, and he was deeply impressed by a people who saw their whole existence in response to that God. He repeatedly asked questions about faith as humility, and, ultimately, he arrived at the conclusion that humility is the only way to respond to God."

The ruckus outside was getting louder, and the mention of soldiers was heard. The people strained to hear Simon.

Simon raised his voice above the noise from outside. "Zenas expressed his faith so clearly: 'God, the Creator of all things, is love, and the human response to God is humility, opening us to God's love.' Hearing Zenas say this so simply confirmed for me once more why Jesus will be with us always. Jesus was able, because of his humble faith, to live in the presence of the kingdom of God. He was able to respond with selflessness to whatever life dealt him, always opening up to God's love. His life and teachings will live forever as the radical symbol of freedom in God's presence, against all forms of human efforts to dominate and control."

At this moment, a Roman soldier burst into the room. Behind him, people were pushing and shoving. There were other soldiers who were being prevented from entering the room by both men and women grabbing them and pushing them away. The lone soldier shouted, "Where is Simon, the renegade priest from Jerusalem? He is under arrest and must come with me."

Immediately the soldier was surrounded by dozens of irate persons, all of them shouting at the soldier. He stepped back, realizing there were no other soldiers behind him.

Jacob went right up to the soldier. "Have you no respect? This is a religious service you are interrupting. Since when does Rome not respect our religious rights?"

The soldier retreated from the house. He saw that some of the other soldiers were using their lances to hold off some who were pushing and shoving. He realized that this could get ugly if he didn't do something quickly. He drew his sword and struck it sharply against the top of a stone wall. The sharp crack made everyone stop for a moment. "Stop immediately!" he ordered. "Otherwise, this will get very bloody. Men, draw your swords!"

This made the crowd move back away from the soldiers, who quickly formed into a large group. There were more than thirty soldiers. The captain ordered some to go and seal off the rear of the house, and then he led the rest back inside.

A number of people had surrounded Simon and were attempting to get him out of the house through the rear exit. As they reached the rear door, they were greeted by a half dozen soldiers. The group retreated back into the main room, and an audible moan filled the room. Women began to cry, and the crowd surrounded Simon. Quickly, a number of soldiers came into the room and roughly pushed the people aside. By this time, it was obvious which one was Simon. They bound Simon's hands behind his back and, using their swords, began pushing the crowd aside.

Mary rushed up to the captain. Grabbing his arm and speaking through tears, she pleaded, "You are arresting an innocent man. This is my son, a holy man who has never harmed anyone. Where is your humanity?"

The captain pushed her so hard she fell backwards. Many arms caught her and held her tightly. Salome and Barnabas rushed to her. She sobbed uncontrollably. The three embraced, drowning in their sorrow.

The soldiers moved quickly out of the house and into the street. The people poured after them, shouting at the soldiers and pleading for Simon's release. Slowly, the people returned to the room. No one knew what to say. Sadness didn't begin to describe the atmosphere in the room. There was abject grief over what lay ahead for Simon. The affront of injustice was there too: an innocent man was carried away by beasts who so willfully profaned worship. It was much more than sadness; there was anger opening the doors of hatred.

As the sobs subsided, Mary looked at Barnabas and said, "I want to say something."

Barnabas couldn't believe the strength of this woman. "Are you sure?"

Salome, too, couldn't believe what she heard. "Mama, please! You're not yourself right now."

Mary looked with appreciation at Salome for her concern, but stood and faced the people. There were tears running down her cheeks, but her voice was strong. "We have to pray for Simon. Now is not the time for despondency, anger, or hatred. We have to remain strong and rely on our faith in God's love. We must pray that Roman justice will recognize Simon's innocence. He has done nothing wrong under their law. They have nothing against Simon."

Mary seemed to be embarrassed at the tears that continued to flow down her cheeks. She continued to wipe them and kept talking. "Just before Simon was arrested, he said that Jesus's message will never die because it stands as a stark contrast to all human efforts to dominate and control. Neither the Romans nor the religious leaders in Jerusalem have anything that can stand up to Zenas's act of love, which Simon described. Simon began his comments with a story. We have usually understood the lesson of that story is that wealth and possessions make it extremely difficult to live as a citizen of the kingdom of God. Jesus often made that very point. But Zenas shows us that the harder path is to follow Jesus. His life and message is about faith as humility: forgetting oneself and living for the other, in the presence of God. Jesus's message is as uncomplicated as that. Live by love."

Mary looked over at Barnabas, as if to say, "Have I said too much?"

The room was deathly silent. No one moved.

Barnabas just nodded, as if to say, "Go on."

Mary continued. "Jesus will live with us forever because he was willing to forget himself and live open to the presence of God's kingdom. It is not a kingdom of kings, laws, priests, beliefs, or dogmas. It is a kingdom of humble faith in God's presence, understood through selfless love: giving oneself over to the needs of the other, loving one's neighbor as much as one loves self. Hearing today of Zenas's selfless act of love made me realize the truth in Jesus's last comment to me: 'I am with you always.'

"We have grossly distorted and complicated the good news. Out of our selfishness, we have attributed to God elaborate schemes of salvation and created specific paths to righteousness. We have made Jesus God, a spirit, creating a spiritual path to God involving only the self. We have complimented ourselves by claiming that God has chosen us to be the heralds of this enlightenment. We have established massive barriers of beliefs and feats of righteousness to separate us from evil, but these barriers only separate us from each other. In our efforts to gain our own salvation we have left no room for humility or love.

"I lament what is happening to the legacy of my son Jesus: his tragic death converted into eternal salvation, a commodity peddled over the world. If that belief makes you feel better, fine; but it has nothing to do with the essence of his life and message, which demonstrates the presence of the kingdom of God, a kingdom that proclaims that love is the driving force of living. We can all be citizens of that kingdom if we get over ourselves and our selfishness, profess God as love, and seek that love waiting for our participation."

At this point, the tears poured down her cheeks, and amid sobs she said, "My greatest sorrow is that Jesus has been used to divide us from ourselves by reducing faith to beliefs, making him more than a man, and distorting the presence of God. Humankind has always found ways to divide us. Jesus as the Christ is just one more. We have too many already. God is love, and life is love. Zenas's life is a clear expression of Jesus's message and proof of his return." These last words were barely audible as Mary collapsed into Barnabas's arms.

Barnabas's ashen face stared down at Mary in his arms. Some of these words cut deep into the pit of his stomach. This grieving mother in his arms knew God's love intimately and suffered tremendously under arrogant human efforts to codify it. This realization went directly to his heart.

The room was as still as death, the silence so complete one could hear the hearts beating. The rustle of Salome's robe as she stood sounded throughout the room. She moved close to Barnabas's side.

Mary opened her eyes and looked up into their two faces. A weak smile formed on her lips. She remained silent.

After a long silence, Jacob walked up to Mary, still in Barnabas's arms, knelt in front of her, and said, "We have been so blessed by you coming to us. You have opened our eyes to the true message of Jesus. We will never be the same."

Mary asked to sit up, and many came and embraced her.

The room then slowly began to empty. Once out in the street, the people began questioning one another as to what they had just witnessed.

Barnabas and Salome helped Mary exit the house. Her sorrow overwhelmed her. She could not stop thinking of Simon in the hands of the Romans, and of Zenas sharing the same fate. With every breath, she prayed for their safety and release.

Chapter 20

The Amphitheater

When word of Simon's capture reached Jerusalem, a sinister smile came across the face of the governor. Rubbing his hands together, Albinus said, "I have the perfect plan to make it clear to these rebellious, ungrateful subjects that the power and authority of Rome is not to be challenged." He then rattled off a list of orders. "Keep Simon, the renegade priest, in Caesarea, under severe guard; I want nothing to happen to him. Make sure no Jews—or, what do they call them? Christians?—get anywhere near him. I want you to continue to keep Zenas in solitary here in Jerusalem; and then take him to Caesarea on the last day of the week. Continue to make sure he is not flogged or harmed in any way. I want him to appear in perfect health and form when he is introduced to the public on the first day of next week. On that day, the people of Caesarea will be treated to the highest form of Roman justice. These two treasonous creatures will be given the opportunity to save themselves from Roman punishment by simply winning a battle with the king of beasts. I want the spectacle to be well publicized. Blanket the city with notices. Oh, and by the way, please invite that beautiful Jewish princess Bernice to be my honored guest. I guess you have to include her boring brother, the king."

Flyers announcing the great spectacle scheduled for the first day of the week were posted everywhere in the city: "Come See the *Deserter* and the *Renegade Priest* Fight for Their Lives against the King of Beasts." The town was all abuzz. There had not been anything like a festival event in Caesarea for many months. A carnival atmosphere filled the city.

Just the opposite environment dominated the community of Jesus followers, who were devastated over Simon's arrest and the subsequent news that he was the renegade priest on all the circulating flyers. Little doubt existed that the deserter on these flyers was Zenas. While nobody but Mary and Salome had ever met Zenas, the concern these two women had for him infected the whole group, who now prayed for both Simon and Zenas. They felt helpless to do anything. Compounding their grief, everywhere they went, they encountered people who were jubilant over the upcoming event in the amphitheater. The thirst for violence and blood revealed the precarious foothold humans have in civilized society. There is more animal in us than we care to admit.

No one suffered more than Salome. "I'm ashamed to call myself a human being. Are we nothing more than animals? How can a man hug his child when he leaves his home in the morning, and then the first thing he says to his friend in the street is that he can't wait to get to the amphitheater to witness this upcoming slaughter? I'm glad that I have not brought a child into this violent, ugly world. Mama, what in the world has Simon done that he is to be thrown to the lions? I hope I do not wake up tomorrow morning. It would be a blessing if the Lord would bring on the final judgment tonight."

Mary's voice was tinged with sorrow. "We are worse than animals! At least animals do not enjoy the violence they inflict on one another. That amphitheater will be full of humans salivating over the brutal destruction of two truly loving men. Evil seems to have completely taken over the minds of men. Mankind has no heart! Simon has never done a thing to warrant his death at the hands of other men. The Romans are advertising this massacre as if it were the ultimate in equitable justice. 'A sporting chance at freedom!' Humbug!" Mary was aware that her anger was overtaking her sorrow. "I don't know how I can endure my last son being killed. What madness! Jesus said we must turn the other cheek, but I don't have four cheeks to turn."

Mary buried her face in her hands and began to weep. Salome could offer no comfort. For both of them, strength had always come from Mary's unshakable faith. There was no evidence of that faith now, just abject sorrow.

Hanna came into the room, announcing that Barnabas had just arrived. Salome's heart jumped, and Mary stopped crying at the news of their dear friend's company. She tried to compose herself and repress the anger that was grinding deep within her.

Barnabas's dejection covered his entire being. His spirits needed lifting as desperately as Mary's and Salome's. The two women rose to embrace him. Words didn't come easily, and tears rose to fill the void. Barnabas finally broke the silence. "I can't stop thinking of what Simon must be going through. Does he know what he is facing? If only I could go and be with him! The Romans aren't allowing anybody to see him. It's hard to imagine how alone he must feel."

Mary gained strength from Barnabas's concern. "We both know he is not alone. The last thing he said to us was that Jesus said he would always be with him. The depth of our sorrow must show how big our hearts can be. We must try to understand what the message of love is in such a horrendous situation." Mary could hardly believe what she was saying. These words came from deep within, completely bypassing her thoughts of anger and pain.

"That sounds so nice, Mama. Did you somehow find the fourth cheek?" Salome wasn't sure she was keeping the anger from her voice.

Barnabas reached out and took Salome's hands. "The one thing we do know is that we cannot engage this murderous brutality with anger and malice. Love guards against us acting out these feelings on others, regardless of how harmful or hateful their behavior is to us."

Mary asked a question that had been haunting her for a long time. "Why is authority so threatened by the presence of the kingdom of God and the love it generates? All four of my sons dedicated their whole beings to love, to serving the less fortunate; yet all four will have been murdered by those in power, two by the Romans and two by the religious authorities. Why is love so threatening to power? Will the way of love be forever shadowed by the violent hand of power? Is the presence of the kingdom of God an enemy to power?" Mary was terrified by these thoughts. Did the message of good news Jesus asked her to proclaim have as its constant nemesis destruction and death by authority and power? "Barnabas, I'm frightened by my thoughts. Are we spreading a gospel that will continually bring suffering and death to those who choose to follow Jesus?"

"Oh, Mary, you have just asked a question that has troubled me deeply for a long time. Paul used to say that the suffering heaped upon us was a badge of honor, a sure sign that we were truly engaged in the ultimate battle with evil. Are we to understand that, until Jesus returns, those who spread the good news will suffer continuously at the hands of those who wield earthly power? Must the ugly cross be our symbol of the presence of the kingdom of God? I agree with you: the cross symbolizes the ultimate in human tyranny and mocks all meaning of love."

"You are so right, Barnabas. Those who claim the cross is the symbol of God's love are saying God is willing to accommodate human tyranny in order to grant eternal life. A mother's heart can never respond to such sophistry. Why would any mother ever choose to bring a child into such a demonic plan?"

Mary paused for a time and then continued. "Barnabas, we are blessed. We two are of a dwindling number who experienced what it was like living completely surrounded by the reality of the presence of the kingdom of God. Didn't Jesus say he would be with us always? Why do we keep waiting for him to return? Is it possible that we are the ones preventing the kingdom of God from being alive among us? I'm convinced we are focused on the wrong thing. The cross is not the symbol of God's love and should not be our focus. I think we are too focused on Jesus and not enough on those around us. After all, Jesus said we are to *follow* him, not *worship* him. Jesus wasn't focused on himself. Why should we be?

"It reminds me of what was happening in Jerusalem when we left. You may have heard that James and Simon were the leaders of our efforts to provide for those in dire need. In fact, our activities were centered in a part of the city labeled Poor Town. Both James and Simon were convinced that while the temple symbolized the presence of God among us, it was our actions of love toward the more unfortunate among us that made that presence real. But, whenever followers of Jesus—who called themselves Christians— would come to Jerusalem, they were more focused on what Jesus had done for them than on what they can do for others. They were all about signs of the presence of the Holy Spirit and speaking in strange tongues. They seemed to be lukewarm to the hard work of caring for the poor. They were always more interested in what we believed about Jesus than they were in our activity among the poor, especially those who were not professed followers of Jesus. Those people were making Jesus God. Once Jesus is God, how is it possible to really follow him?"

Salome was anxious to do something for Simon. "Mama, what does this have to do with Simon's predicament? Shouldn't we be trying to do something for him or get to him?"

Mary was a little taken aback by Salome's question. "You are right; we should be trying to determine how we can get to Simon."

"In case you didn't hear me," Barnabas offered, "the Romans are not letting anyone near him. Perhaps they will be more welcoming to you than they were to me, though I doubt it."

"Shouldn't we at least try?" Salome wasn't ready to give in.

"Of course we should, Salome," Mary agreed. Turning to Barnabas, she asked, "Do you know where they are holding him?"

"No! They gave no indication of where he might be, but they were certainly adamant that no one was going to get to see him. I think we should get the fellowship together to pray."

"I'm sure we all are already praying for him," Mary said, "but it would sure be comforting for all of us to pray together."

The Sabbath before the governor's big event was one of severe agony for the Jesus followers in Caesarea. Everyone prayed for Simon's safety and release. Many secretly begged for signs of the presence of the kingdom of God, reminding God this would be the perfect time for Jesus to return. They sought each other's company, their sorrow mocked by so many in the city eagerly awaiting tomorrow's spectacle.

The morning of the extravaganza in Caesarea found a town divided. Many were only too eager to see wild beasts tear apart some helpless humans. On the other hand, some of the Jews were appalled by the Romans promoting the spectacle as demonstration of Roman justice. Nothing the Romans did was graciously received by those who felt their presence was an abomination to God's promise in the covenant. Some refused to open their shops on this day of vile defilement. The fellowship of Jesus followers chose to meet and pray.

The amphitheater was lavishly decorated. Extra benches had been set up on the side open to the shore, so the whole amphitheater was surrounded with spectators. People had come hours early to get seats or good standing locations. There were even people on the roofs of the buildings behind the amphitheater, choosing the elevation so that they could see over the crowds. Some even occupied the seats in the theater that had a view of the amphitheater's surface.

As the crowd gathered into the amphitheater, two different columns of Roman soldiers approached from opposite directions. Centered within each of these columns was a man shackled hands and feet. One was a young man, standing half a head above the rest of the soldiers. He walked as if the chains were of little trouble, his expression unreadable. He seemed oblivious to the soldiers around him. The other prisoner, also tall but a much older man, struggled under the weight of the chains. The soldiers constantly prodded him to keep up with the procession. In spite of this maltreatment, his expression toward the soldiers was one of forgiving compassion.

As they reached the amphitheater, both prisoners could hear the noise of the crowd. Were they cheering the arrival of the governor and his party, or were they just eager for some blood? Many flowers were being thrown onto the floor of the arena. Included in the governor's party were the beautiful Bernice and her brother, Herod Agrippa II, the king of Israel. The governor asked Bernice to sit by his side. The crowd hushed as a gate at one end of the arena opened and a line of floats, each pulled by eight horses, entered the arena. Elaborately decorated with flowers, each held a statue denoting something of significance about the governor. The last float had a statue of the governor himself. As the floats made a big circle around the arena, the crowd's reaction was curious. Very little ovation came from any of the crowd, other than from the special boxes that surrounded the governor's box.

Once the floats had exited the arena, another gate opened, and a giant lion ran into the arena. The crowd went wild! The lion circled the arena, swishing its plumed tail. It ran up to the wall, and the spectators scurried back, even though the wall was much too high for the lion to jump over. Some of the spectators worried that the temporary wall along the beach would not retain the lion. Every so often, the lion reared on its hind legs and thrashed its forepaws into the air. Each time it did this, the crowd would roar. The lion made a number of circuits of the arena, and then moved toward the center of the arena and stopped. It stood there, swinging its head from side to side.

At the blast of four trumpets, two gates opened at opposite

ends of the arena, and through one strode Zenas, clad only in a loincloth. He came a few steps into the arena and stopped. From the other gate, an old man in a long priest's robe slowly walked into the arena. Zenas immediately recognized Simon, let out a yell, and began running toward him. The lion looked at both men and immediately began moving toward Simon. The lion was soon upon him. With one swipe of its paw, the lion knocked Simon to the ground and opened a gash down the side of his head. Simon did not move, and the lion opened its massive jaws and bit into Simon's shoulder and neck. The lion lifted its head and lifted Simon half off the ground. Simon appeared lifeless.

Zenas was screaming wildly as he rushed up to the lion. He jumped onto the lion's back and wrapped his arms tightly around the lion's throat. Simon fell from the lion's mouth. The lion scratched at Zenas, digging its claws into his arms and legs. The lion's movements became slower and less forceful. Zenas kept his grip on the lion as its legs began to wobble. Soon the lion fell to the ground. Zenas grabbed the lion's upper jaw in one hand and it's lower in the other, and broke the jaw apart. He then placed his knee on the shoulder of the lion and pulled its head back violently, breaking its neck. The lion fell in a heap next to Simon's still body.

Zenas dropped to the ground and grabbed Simon up in his arms. Simon's eyes were dull, and only a faint breath could be felt coming from his mouth. With much effort, Simon softly breathed the words, "God bless you, my son." Then his head fell back, exposing a large hole in his neck where the lion had buried its teeth.

Zenas quickly stood up, with Simon in his arms, and carried him to the wall of the arena. "Please, someone, help!" he yelled. "He is still alive."

Eager hands reached over the wall and took Simon. They rushed him out of the stands and laid him in the shade of a tree. One of them hurried off to get help; another rushed to find Barnabas and Mary.

By this time, the crowd was going wild. They showered the arena with flowers and started shouting "Free him, free him!" Somehow they had found out that his name was Zenas, and the crowd began chanting, "Zenas, Zenas, Zenas! Free him, free him, free him!"

The chant grew louder and louder.

Four soldiers came up to Zenas and escorted him over to the governor's box. The soldiers moved back, and Zenas stood alone before the governor. Zenas's arms and legs were bloody from the lion's claws.

Some members in the governor's box were cheering along with the crowd.

Albinus and his bodyguard, Gaius, both looked at Zenas with extreme hatred.

Bernice stepped forward to place a wreath around Zenas's neck, but the governor grabbed her arm and pulled her back.

The crowd quieted.

Bernice turned and, looking puzzled, said to the governor, "I thought you said this was to be a just fight. This man won and should be freed."

Bernice's infatuation with Zenas showed in her eyes, and this did not escape Albinus's notice. Albinus snapped back, "Justice for the priest, yes; but why for a deserting traitor? This man disgraced all that is Roman, and he has forever cast himself beyond the arms of justice."

"Are you going to go back on your word?"

Bernice's question enraged Albinus, but other feelings had a stronger pull. "Certainly not! However, desertion from the army cannot go unpunished. His feat today gives him the opportunity to redeem himself. He must admit his transgression and declare his ultimate allegiance to the emperor, and then he can accept a lesser punishment of banishment."

Turning to Zenas, Albinus asked, "What do you have to say?"

With a deep bass voice heard by many in the crowd, Zenas

answered, "In the last few weeks, I have experienced a freedom Romans can only dream about. I have met people whose devotion to God the Creator gives them the ability to see with concern and compassion their fellow humans. In these weeks, I have come to realize the purpose of life: to love your neighbor as you love yourself.

"You ask me if I am willing to submit myself to the justice of Rome. First of all, don't these bleeding limbs prove I have just done that? Obviously, that was just a ruse.

"You ask me to pledge my allegiance and put my trust in Rome—a Rome whose emperor's only weapon to deal with dissent is death; a Rome whose lust for power uses greed and privilege to make slaves of most of the rest of the world; a Rome whose armies subjugate rather than liberate. In all that tyranny, greed, and lasciviousness, where does anyone find freedom?

"Governor, you have the power to take my life, but you can no longer take my freedom. I choose to live in the presence of the kingdom of the God of love. Exercise your destructive violence if you must. I pity you that you are not free enough to do otherwise. My freedom has shown me that violence only breeds more violence. My prayer is that all humans will someday know that only love brings peace."

Albinus's anger had now risen above reason and the allure of feminine wiles. "You have denounced and demeaned Rome. You have sealed your fate. Take this man and have him crucified before sundown tomorrow."

The four soldiers behind Zenas were now joined by eight more, and the dozen soldiers bound Zenas and escorted him out of the arena, through the governor's entrance.

The crowd was waiting for Zenas to be released and for him to parade triumphantly around the amphitheater. As word spread that he had been escorted away in chains, the crowd grew incensed. They stormed the arena and began to riot. They poured out of the arena and into the streets, turning over vendors' carts, looting all open stores, and throwing stones at any Roman soldier they saw. The soldiers withdrew quickly because they were greatly outnumbered.

The governor's party was quickly sped to the governor's palace. There, he gave orders for the full contingent of soldiers at the barracks to immediately move into the streets to quell the riots, using whatever force was necessary. He also ordered another full legion of soldiers to be brought from the outlying areas to the city immediately.

By nightfall, the rioting had been suppressed, but not before more than a hundred bodies lay victims of the Roman soldiers.

At the house where the fellowship met, some Jesus followers were disrupted by an out-of-breath man. "Simon is alive! Come quickly! Bring a litter; he needs help."

A group of young men rushed to the amphitheater to get Simon. They carefully placed him on a litter and carried him back to Joseph and Hanna's house. Simon appeared very weak, probably from loss of blood, but it appeared that he would survive.

Mary, Salome, and Barnabas arrived soon after the men had settled Simon onto a bed.

Mary rushed to Simon's side and embraced him. "Oh, my son, my son! Thank God, you are alive! You look badly hurt. Can you speak? Quick, someone get some warm water and some cloths, we have to take care of his wounds."

"Mama, all of that is already here. Let someone who is less upset take care of him." Salome was worried about her mother. How much more could she take?

The two women moved back and let Hanna and her sister dress Simon's wounds. They were amazed at how superficial they were. It appeared that Simon had suffered more from shock than anything else.

Salome thought about Zenas. "What happened to Zenas? Where is he? Is he all right?"

Just then, Josiah, a young man from the fellowship, came

running in, all excited. "You'll never believe what happened. Zenas killed the lion with his bare hands. He ripped the lion's jaw off and broke its neck. I think he saved Simon's life."

"Whoa, slow down. Simon is here. He's going to be all right." Barnabas tried to calm the youth down. "What about Zenas? Have you heard anything about him?"

"No. I sneaked into the crowd on the beach side, and saw it all. The last I saw was Zenas standing in front of the governor. The crowd was going wild and shouting for Zenas's release. They started to storm the amphitheater grounds, and I got out of there."

As the details of what happened to Zenas reached those at Joseph and Hanna's house, so did the rioting. The streets were full of people totally out of control. Joseph shut up the house tight, but not before they heard that Zenas was sentenced to be crucified the next day.

Mary was immediately taken back to that awful day. Back then, two soldiers had to restrain her, preventing her from running up to Jesus. His groans, as they drove those nails through his hands and feet, were more than she could endure. Part of her died with Jesus that day. A dark hole formed at the center of her being on that day, and that hole had never gone away. Now she didn't know how she was going to get through this night and the next day. She knew she had to be there for Zenas, but she wasn't sure what it would do to her. The only thing that kept her in control of herself was her concern about Simon.

Salome was beside herself; she could not be consoled. While Mary fully shared the depth of Salome's grief, she was troubled by the level of anger that had taken hold of her daughter.

"This is madness!" Salome ranted amid sobs. "Three brothers brutally murdered, and now this! What have any of them done to deserve death? Not one of them has ever done a thing to harm another human. Yet they are hunted down like murderers by authorities who are supposed to protect the people and do what is best for them. Humanity is sick to its very core."

Mary knew Salome was right. Grief was painful enough, but, when imposed unfairly, it was unbearable. However, anger, even righteous anger, could be harmful, and Mary would not be able to bear it if Salome's anger brought harm to her. Salome and Simon were all she had left of what was once a glorious family.

"Salome," Mary offered, "we drink from a shared cup of grief. Our tears flow from two hearts so close they beat as one. But don't let your anger overtake your concern for Zenas. We have to remain open to love and pray for him. Anger can so easily enshroud the heart that it blinds out the love Zenas showed us. I'm not sure how many times our hearts can be broken, but we both know that God's love can overcome that which anger can't begin to touch. Let our river of tears be prayers of thanksgiving for Simon and petitions of safety for Zenas."

"Oh, Mama, the hole in my life just gets bigger and bigger. How can I be thankful when goodness is rubbed out by evil and hatred? Does God even care about what happens to us or to Zenas? The powers of evil are making God appear very small." It was obvious that Salome was not looking for consolation.

"God is love, Salome. We cannot expect to find God in acts of violence and hatred. All the horrible events of my sons' deaths have convinced me that God's love is only evident in how we respond."

"Mama, your righteousness is making me feel guilty."

Mary, taken aback by Salome's comment, said, "What is there to feel guilty about?"

"My anger is real, and I think fully justified," Salome responded. "But, when you start talking about how we must show God's love, I feel guilty about my anger."

"There's no need to feel guilty. I just don't want your anger to close off your heart."

Salome could feel the nature of her grief changing. Anger was slowly giving way to a deep sadness and concern for Zenas. This man she knew so little about, but who, during their shared moment, had also given her a gift as precious as life itself, now became the focus of her compassion. She fell into her mother's arms and began to sob.

Mary let Salome's tears, and her own, flow freely. They needed each other, knew that need, and felt its consolation.

Barnabas wasn't sure if he should go into the room where Mary and Salome were alone with Simon. He sat down in the outer room and waited a while. When he heard the women moving around, he decided to go in. Simon was asleep.

Salome was the first to see Barnabas, and she rushed into his open arms.

Mary felt a warm feeling come over her when she saw him.

Still holding Salome in one arm, Barnabas reached for Mary and pulled her close with the other. "My heart breaks for you, Mary. No mother should have to endure what you have endured with your sons. Thank God, Simon is still alive, although this ordeal must have hurt you terribly. Your strength to endure is obviously a special gift from God. Rome—what a disgusting example of human depravity! Simon is as holy a man as there is. Evil and hatred know no bounds!" He shook his head and patted their shoulders. "How can I be of comfort to you?"

"Your kind voice and warm hands are just the comfort we need right now." Mary's gratitude was obvious. "We are struggling to suppress the anger that wants to overtake us. Please help us keep God's love our focus and goal."

Mary couldn't help but notice the calming effect Barnabas had on Salome; it was the way her face relaxed as she rested in his arms. He was good for her.

Barnabas, too, realized a calming feeling holding Salome. Something beyond his awareness drew him to her. She was good for him.

Barnabas said, "My grief today took me back to those times many years ago when we were all with Jesus. The disciples were always making demands on him because they were confused about what his real mission was. Simon—and, of course, Mary Magdalene and James—seemed to always be comfortable and at ease with Jesus and what he was doing. Simon never appeared to try to impose his own ideas on Jesus or his ministry. It was as if he fully felt God's presence, just as Jesus did. I have not been close to Simon for many years, but that image of him comes so clearly to me as I see him sleeping there."

Salome was quick to respond. "He has lived nothing but love his whole life. If there is one needy person in Jerusalem who has not been helped by Simon, I would be surprised. He spends much of his time serving the lepers and making their colony comfortable. The sick are always on his mind, and he will never pass up an opportunity to visit the jail and advocate for the comfort of the prisoners. He is God's angel to the poor and needy. For those brutes to feed him to a lion shows that they have no hearts and no idea who he is. The true beasts sit in the seats of authority!" Salome stopped. She could feel the anger beginning to well up again.

Barnabas nodded his head and thought, *The more I think about it, the more I believe that religious authority and political authority have the same agenda: control of the people and access to their money. The more you can dictate behavior, the more you can control. Religion uses beliefs, and government uses laws. They battle over territory, but in the end, they control the people by dictating behaviors. Freedom is their real enemy.*

Barnabas remarked, "Jesus was such a threat to both the Jewish authorities and the Romans. He revealed the freedom to live in the presence of the kingdom of God. That is why the high priest and the king had to sic the Romans on Simon: he was a threat to their control of the people, and they convinced the new governor that he was just as much a threat to him. Jesus did not die in vain. He displayed the way to live in God's presence. Jesus's message lives today in Simon, you, and many others who follow him."

Mary knew that Barnabas's words were true, but they did

not diminish the hurt. They did, however, reinforce her faith. Life has meaning only when we are free to love, only when we are able to forget ourselves and live for the other. She thought of how the presence of the Romans restricted everything they did; how their presence created such a fear that one was constantly focused on one's actions, so as not to get into trouble. Torah had become such a duty that one was constantly focused on one's own behaviors. None of this freed; none of this allowed for love. She thought about how the beliefs about the expected Messiah so divided those who wished to follow Jesus that it drove them apart. She could easily see how the new beliefs that Jesus was really a God would further divide his followers until it would not only be Jews killing Christians but also Christians killing Jews. Barnabas was right: beliefs and power were instruments of control. They were threatened by freedom—especially the freedom to respond to the presence of the kingdom of God, to the presence of love.

Mary looked at Barnabas. "It really is as simple as faith as humility: the humility to recognize God's presence and to forget oneself and live for the other. As Jesus said, 'Sell all that is keeping you focused on yourself, give to the poor, and follow me.' We each must live a life of love."

Later, the three sat in silence. Salome was sitting, resting her head on Barnabas's shoulder. Barnabas looked deep in thought. Mary had a pained look on her face, as she could not get Zenas out of her mind.

Finally, Mary broke the silence, asking "Do you believe that the Romans will actually crucify Zenas tomorrow?"

"Yes," replied Barnabas. "I have little hope for anything else, especially after the rioting today. The governor will try to make a statement out of this."

Mary and Salome each let out a groan of agony. The thought of this kind man being crucified broke their hearts and turned their stomachs. It was maddening.

"I want to go and plead with the governor to save this man!"

Mary cried. "Maybe the mother of Jesus would be a bigger feather in his cap."

"Don't talk foolishness, Mama!" Salome couldn't ever remember speaking to her mother in such a tone. "He would only laugh at you and make a mockery of your concern."

"We are exhausted from our grieving." Barnabas was feeling as drained as the two women looked. "We must try to get some rest. Tomorrow is going to be a terrible day. We must get the fellowship together and hold a vigil for Zenas. Prayer is the only help we can give him now."

CHAPTER 21

ROMAN JUSTICE: THE CROSS

The next morning, the city felt like a volcano about to erupt. During the night, soldiers had come into the city from all around the area. The city felt like an armed camp. The governor had ordered that every street be patrolled by fully armed soldiers and that no riotous activity be allowed anywhere. There were more soldiers on the way, from as far away as Joppa and Sycaminum. Albinus was not going to let this incident blight his career. These people be damned; this traitor could not go unpunished. The very discipline of the Roman army was at stake. A stark example had to be made of Zenas's act of defiance. This city would witness the full extent of Roman justice, and no one, not even the son of a senator, was above the law.

The people of the city were angry. They had been lied to, the hypocrisy of lauded Roman justice rubbed in their faces. They were furious, but totally disorganized. Any expression of their anger would incite severe reactions from the soldiers patrolling everywhere, with nothing accomplished but more bodies to bury. The town did not open that morning. No one went to work. No shops opened, and no workers went to the docks to work the waterfront. The bakers' ovens were cold, and the marketplace was barren. It was a ghost town, with anger behind every closed door and anxious soldiers patrolling every street.

Merchants coming into town to the market were turned back by the soldiers. The farmers and peasants from the hills set up to sell their wares on the outskirts of town; their only patrons were those who headed to the market and turned back. Apparently, there was going to be only one event in Caesarea this day.

While crucifixions usually occurred early in the morning, so the victims would succumb before nightfall, Albinus postponed this one until late morning, allowing more soldiers to arrive. The inactivity in the city suggested that this was an unnecessary precaution.

Word spread quickly throughout the fellowship that there would be an all-day vigil held for Zenas. The sun hadn't been up two hours, and the house was already overflowing. Barnabas was surprised to see Caspius sitting near the rear of the room. He hadn't been back to the fellowship since Barnabas's hurtful remarks to the worshippers.

Numerous persons offered prayers on Zenas's behalf, even though none of them but Mary and Salome had ever met him. A number of men read from the Torah.

Finally, Barnabas got up to speak. "Today, we will face something some of us faced years ago that has changed our lives forever: the cross. For many of us, this has become a beloved symbol of the love of God, for we believe it is the symbol that signifies that Jesus is the Christ, the Son of God."

Just then, there was a commotion. Everyone in the room turned to see what was going on. Barnabas stopped speaking, and surprise showed on his face. Coming into the room were Mary and Salome, and between them was Simon. Simon had bandages on his neck, shoulder, and face; he had a loose robe thrown over his shoulders. He was walking on his own.

Mary spoke to the crowd. "Simon insisted on coming to speak to you, even though his injuries make it difficult for him to talk. Jesus's brother has something he wants you to hear."

Someone brought a chair for Simon to sit on, but he refused it. In a voice that was hoarse and breathy, Simon began to speak. "I am not badly hurt. My great pain is inside. Once again, Zenas has saved me; he has laid down his life for me. Today, this brave and loving young man is to be brutally murdered by being hung on a cross. Every heart that beats should be torn in two today. Once before in my life, someone who meant the world to me was hung on a cross by the Romans. The cross is a symbol of human brutality designed to instill fear of authority into the hearts of the people. But, in fact, it is a symbol of authority's fear of truth."

Mary was uneasy. She had never heard Simon speak this way. Was he letting his anger get the best of him? Simon was not aware of all that this group had been through over the past several days. She was concerned that he was going to reopen all those wounds. "Simon, I know you are distraught over Zenas, and feeling it is all because of you, but don't let blame allow anger to take over. Anger will never succeed in proclaiming the good news."

"I'm not angry, Mother. I'm deeply concerned that what the cross symbolizes for many of the followers of Jesus is creating a barrier that will forever divide those who seek to live in God's presence. To see the cross as a symbol of God's love is to deny what is happening to Zenas today. Today's butchery flies in the face of God's love. The cross symbolizes the difference between my brother Jesus and Jesus the Christ. It creates an ethereal barrier used to justify humans slaughtering other humans. Now it is Jews slaughtering Christians. Before long, it will be Christians slaughtering Jews. Eventually, other revelations will be used to slaughter both Jews and Christians."

Mary knew that was what he was going to say. She shared his concern. "Sadly, these people already know the effect the symbol of the cross has on me."

Barnabas moved to Simon's side and said, "Today's cross will reopen wounds I thought were healed by God's plan for salvation. Sadly, that is not the case. Today, the cross is as ugly and offensive as it was on that dreadful day many years ago. Jesus's cross, Zenas's cross, and every cross ever erected will always stand for the pathetic attempts at justice exercised by those in power who are fearful of the truth. Perhaps we should focus on something else. Simon, take us back to before Jesus's cross, to the man who proclaimed the presence of the kingdom of God."

"What a great suggestion, Barnabas. I'm convinced that knowing the man Jesus and understanding what he taught is the way forward for all of us." After a moment, Simon began to speak. "Jesus was a man like no other man I have ever known. His message was simple. He taught that the kingdom of God was among us and God's love was at our fingertips. All we had to do was repent of our selfishness, forget about ourselves, and follow him. Forgetting about ourselves and following him meant living concerned for those with us. We experienced and witnessed the power of love many times over. We saw the blind regain sight, the lame walk, and the demon-possessed made whole. That love allowed us to sit at table with tax collectors and others we thought of as sinners. It allowed us to commune with Samaritans and Gentiles. That love opened us up to persons our beliefs had condemned as unrighteous and impure. That love saved us from ourselves and our trifling beliefs of separation."

Barnabas interrupted. "That same love brought this very fellowship back from the brink of separation just a few days ago."

Caspius jumped up at this point and said, "What about pardon for our sins, and the promise of eternal life? Paul taught us—and you were with him, Barnabas—that the only way to obtain eternal life is to accept Jesus as our personal savior, that he was sacrificed by God to save us from our sins. I thought that was the essence of the gospel. Why don't I hear anything about that?"

There was an uneasy murmur in the room.

Barnabas began to answer, but Mary stood, put her hand on Barnabas's arm, and said, "Let me try to answer that. Jesus based all his teachings on the law of love: love God with all your heart and love your neighbor as yourself. I never heard him describe God's love; he always said God *is* love. He taught that we understand that not through our beliefs about God's love but through our being immersed in loving. The cross does not symbolize love. The man they hung on the cross does. Jesus lived a life of love because he ordered his life according to God's law. It ordered his life and governed his behavior. Since God is love, love governed his life. He will always be with us because of the way he lived, not the way he died. That is the gospel."

Barnabas got up and said to Mary, "Please let me talk. I specifically need to answer Caspius. Caspius, I sincerely apologize for misleading you. I came with Paul, preaching Christ crucified, when we should have been preaching the presence of the kingdom of God. Jesus asked us to follow him, not worship him. We convinced you to believe something when we should have asked you to open your eyes to love. We encouraged you to believe something that can separate you from those you are to love.

"I'm sure many of you are asking, What am I to believe? Believe what brings you closest to truth, but be sure that what you believe does not get in the way of caring for your neighbor. I misled you. I thought I was serving you out of love. What I didn't see was that what I was teaching was creating barriers to love. Mary, Salome, and Simon—and, now, Zenas—have shown me that love is living in the presence of God's love. Only one belief matters: that God is love. And love can only be recognized through the act of caring. The act of caring is only possible by suspending one's selfish desires—which, said differently, means repenting for your selfishness—and living for the other.

"The things I taught you that closed off opportunities for love, I sincerely apologize for, and I humbly beg your forgiveness. We don't need to be taught how to love; what we need is encouragement to get over ourselves. Love, the presence of God, is just beyond our selfishness."

The room was deathly silent. No one spoke or even moved.

Finally, Mary spoke. "Barnabas, that was beautiful! It might well have been Jesus speaking. He often spoke in stories that described the presence of the kingdom of God. They always spoke of our obligations to each other. I can't remember him ever expounding on what to believe. And, when the religious leaders would challenge him about beliefs, his answers would always dumbfound them. He lived well beyond beliefs.

"Ever since he has gone away, his followers have been mired in disputes over what we should believe. Each one of these disputes creates another group. They never appear to bring us together; rather, they separate us. I've always thought that Jesus's message of the good news was too simple for the human mind. We resist being humble enough to accept the simple truth of love. The good news can only be recognized by the heart."

Simon now stood to speak. "This has surely been good for all of us. Yet it has done nothing for my sadness. I am having a very hard time loving the Romans today. Zenas is one of them, but he is no longer controlled by their demonic power. He does not deserve to be murdered under their sick system of justice. He was so taken by my mother's example of a humble faith, living open to God's presence, that he sacrificed everything to understand and live that love. He was going to be a tremendous ambassador for the kingdom. Help me find the compassion I need."

"You don't know how often I have been in that exact place." Mary had tears in her eyes. "I'm convinced that God does not direct the hands of man. We create our own evil. All we can pray for is that Zenas lives love through to the end. I have this strong feeling that the only way he can do that is if we hold up our end. He has chosen to be with us, and we must not let him down now."

"Mother, you are right. Today, probably more than most days, our humble faith is being put to the test. Love is being mocked today. Another human life is being sacrificed to human arrogance and tyranny, and that arrogant power is being rubbed in our faces.

"We must try to get close to Zenas today. It is so important that he feel the presence of God. We must do whatever we can to assure he is surrounded by the presence of God's kingdom."

Barnabas suggested that they pray for Zenas.

After many prayers and tears, the whole assembly agreed to try to line the route along which the soldiers would take Zenas to his execution.

The heavens had blanketed the city with dark clouds that hardly seemed to move. No cooling breeze came in off the sea. A stout breeze from the east formed a barrier to the sea's cooling, depositing a heavy humidity seldom felt in Caesarea. Everyone was covered in sweat, not the kind that comes from exertion, but, rather, a sweat that seemed to fall from the dark ominous clouds. Nothing seemed normal on this day.

In spite of the enormous number of Roman soldiers, many people lined the streets that formed the prisoner's last walk. These crowds were restless and pushed against the column of soldiers lining the route. The only places there was not active pressure against the soldiers were the number of spots where members of the fellowship had gathered. They waited in sorrowful silence for the procession to appear.

The crowds were severely harsh in their condemnation of each and every soldier. They mocked them with signs and slogans pointing out their hypocritical justice. A noted upsurge in jeers suggested that the prisoner was on his way. The crowd mocked and jeered at the large column of soldiers who surrounded the prisoner. Zenas stood taller than any of the soldiers. Wearing only a loincloth, the deep scratches from the lion were vividly visible on his shoulders and arms. He walked with strong, definitive steps, which seemed to mock the reluctant gait of the soldiers. He carried his own crossbeam, in an almost casual manner, even though the weight of it would have been a severe burden to most men. Only one crucifixion was on the docket for today, as there were no other prisoners in the procession.

Mary, Simon, Salome, Barnabas, and a number of others had

found a place near the site of the crucifixion. Well behind them stood Caspius, under the shade of an olive tree. His eyes focused on Mary. Ever since his conversation with Jacob, he couldn't get her out of his mind. He really didn't know anything about her; his negative feelings were rooted in fear and ignorance. Jacob had ignited a curiosity Caspius could not suppress.

As the procession approached, Zenas recognized Mary, Simon, and Salome in the crowd. He moved toward them. The soldiers, almost as if Zenas were leading them, reluctantly allowed him to alter his path. Putting down the crossbeam he stopped in front of Simon. He placed his hand on Simon's shoulder and said, "Never will the world know a finer teacher, father, or brother. You have opened God's love to me and freed me to live forever. Nothing I can say will ever fully express my gratitude."

He turned to Mary. Seeing the tears on her cheeks, he said, "Mary, please don't cry for me. Instead, cry for these poor soldiers who are doing the very opposite of what they thought they would do as soldiers. They feel like caged dogs carrying out orders they abhor. They wanted to protect the *people*, not the careers of arrogant, selfish officials." He leaned down, brushed the tears from her cheeks and said, "I am the most fortunate person in the world for having met you. That was the most important day of my life. Thank you for saving me from myself and giving me real life by showing me the way of love. My only regrets are that I will not have the opportunity to follow you as you bring life to others by teaching love."

Mary fought to find the calmness to speak. Softly stroking the open wound on his arm, she said, "You have strengthened my faith. The presence of God's kingdom radiates from your being. You are a blessing to my life. The realms of heaven will be blessed today, and humanity must grieve a great loss. There is no greater feast for the eyes than to look on a man whose heart is bigger than his self. But there is no greater sadness of the heart than to see selfish men reject the love that could save them. Once more, my heart breaks with uncontrollable grief." She broke into sobs.

Zenas took her in his arms and kissed the top of her head, then pushed her away, got down on his knees, and kissed both her hands and her feet. He stood and slowly backed away.

Zenas then looked to Salome, who was standing between Mary and Barnabas. Touching his fingers to his lips, he said in a soft voice, "Thank you."

Salome's face broke into an indiscernible expression. Was it euphoria or disconsolation? With a loud sob, she replied, "No—thank *you*." She fell into Barnabas's arms, still sobbing. Each sob brought another realization: *You saved my brother from the lion; you gave up your life for my brother; you protected my mother and me in prison; and you opened my eyes to selfless love. Truly, you are a son of God.*

The soldiers circled around Zenas, he picked up the crossbeam, and the procession continued.

Salome felt Barnabas soften to her feelings, and her sobs subsided. Her grief for Zenas flowed in waves of compassion over his short walk into the brutality of Roman justice.

Behind them, Caspius's face displayed incredulity. The exchange between Mary and Zenas shattered numerous barriers that his mind created and his beliefs reinforced.

When the procession reached the site for the crucifixion, the reluctance of the soldiers was fully evident. Zenas laid the crossbeam on the ground, and everyone just stood around. The captain took control. He ordered some to dig a hole and others to attach the crossbeam to the upright. When that was finished, he ordered Zenas to lie down on the cross.

Zenas looked at the captain with pity. "Your orders mean nothing to me, but I will do what you ask." He lay down on the cross, and looked up to the captain. "Your bellowing reveals your discomfort. I'm truly sorry for you."

In a fit of anger, the captain grabbed the maul and nails from a soldier standing by and began violently driving the nails into Zenas's wrists and feet. Not a sound came from Zenas as the nails went through his flesh. Still incensed, the captain ordered his men to set up the cross. When the cross was set up, Zenas, in a voice revealing the strain from being hung by the wrists, said to the captain, "I harbor no hatred or anger toward you or your men. You are dutifully following orders, which we all were trained to do. Fortunately, I met some people who allowed me to see that the orders of the heart are the only ones that really matter. What I now know is that you can't love others if you don't love yourself, and you can't love yourself if you don't love what you are doing."

As Zenas was speaking, a young soldier, who had been irritated earlier by what he thought was Zenas's haughty attitude, was visibly moved by his comments. He rushed up to the cross and drove his spear deep into Zenas's chest. Zenas died instantly. Some of the other soldiers grabbed and bound the attacker and dragged him away.

From afar, Salome witnessed it all. She felt as if a huge blanket of dread was slowly pushing her right into the ground. Yet, amid all this anguish and pain, a warm spot formed deep within her chest as she watched the soldier's spear pierce Zenas. She saw love on the tip of that spear. Again, she collapsed into Barnabas's arms, sobbing.

Now there was real fear among the soldiers. Nothing like this was supposed to happen. How would the governor react when he heard that the crucifixion had been botched? They couldn't cover it up; there were too many observers. They huddled together to try to figure out what to do.

Mary, watching from a distance, was shocked by what she saw. Salome was sobbing, and Barnabas was trying to comfort her. After a period of time, it was obvious that Zenas was dead. Mary didn't know what to do. Looking at Simon, who appeared weak, she asked some friends to see him back to Joseph's house. She looked at Barnabas, who was gently stroking Salome, trying to calm her. Mary was startled by the thought that came to her at such a tragic moment. Salome and Barnabas, two people she loved so deeply, should have the joy of experiencing the greatest love of all: creating life out of love. Somehow, at that moment, Mary knew that was going to happen.

Barnabas said to Mary, "I think we should try to get the soldiers to turn over Zenas's body so that we can bury it before the end of the day."

Barnabas and a few of the men with him went up to the captain and asked if they could have Zenas's body. The captain, afraid that the crowds might get out of hand again, consented.

Once the body was removed from the area and taken back to the home where the fellowship met, Caspius, the man who had reacted so angrily to Barnabas a few days ago, came to Barnabas and offered a burial site he owned; they could use it to bury Zenas. The women of the fellowship prepared Zenas's body as if it were one of their own. The men then placed it in Caspius's tomb.

The atmosphere in the room was death-like. They were back in the large room in Joseph and Hanna's house. Hanna was in the back, preparing something for them to eat. Joseph sat in a corner, the picture of dejection. Salome and Barnabas sat on a small sofa, Barnabas with his eyes closed, and Salome with her head resting on his shoulder. Mary sat on a chair by the window, looking out at the approaching dusk. Her eyes appeared to be the only thing alive in the room.

Salome noticed and asked, "Mama, will it ever be any different? Will the powerful and corrupt always win? Is death always going to be the fate of the good, the gentle, and the kind? Will love ever win? Will evil always have the final word?"

Mary, recognizing the utter agony in her daughter's voice, walked over to her, knelt down on the floor in front of her, and took both of Salome's hands in hers. "Today was nothing new for us. We have been through it before. I wonder how often our hearts can be broken before they just explode. Yet something beyond ourselves calls us on.

"Will love ever win? Not if death is our gauge. Love doesn't fear death. Power and authority fear death. Love is a threat to the powerful and all who need to defend or protect something. The vulnerability of love is a threat to all who need to control and dominate. It exposes them to the unimaginable potential of God's creative nature, which threatens the very foundation of their power.

"We know that death is nothing more than a transition in the kingdom of God. We have experienced it, and that truth is reinforced whenever we have been able to forget ourselves and live for another. We have embraced our Jesus, who came to us beyond his death. Death is no longer our gauge. The kingdom of God is much greater than death, which is now merely the pathetic foil of all those who see life only through the eyes of selfishness."

These words stirred something deep within the soul of Barnabas. Now he realized the blessed gift Mary had brought to him and the Jesus followers in Caesarea: a deeper understanding of selfishness and its barrier to love. *Greed and lust are the repressive forms of selfishness. But,* he thought, *there is an aggressive side that insists the other think and be like you, whenever righteous doctrine and self-esteem join hands and see the other as lacking or wanting. The mission of the gospel of the presence of the kingdom of God is not selling what I have, but making space for the other. Love is not something you do but something you allow to happen, by forgetting self and following Jesus. Now we only see the backside of Jesus. Jesus is not the Christ we put on, but the shadow of the Son of Man we follow, a shadow that breaks down the barriers of selfishness and opens up the gates of love.*

Barnabas stood, went over to Mary, and lifted her into his arms. With a face beaming with joy, he said, "Thank you for reintroducing me to the man Jesus and the real presence of the kingdom of God. Faith truly is humility—the humility to see beyond the self."

Mary's heart, drowning in grief, swelled beneath Barnabas's crushing embrace.

CHAPTER 22

BEYOND THE CROSS

First thing each morning, Mary visited the grave of Zenas. She would sit and ponder the meaning of his tragic death. Would she ever understand the interface between love and violence? Three of her sons, all men of peace and nonviolence, had encountered violent deaths. Zenas, a man who started out by fighting violence with violence and who, instead, then chose love over violence, also ended up a victim of violence. It appeared to her that God's presence and its medium of love had little impact on curbing violence. In fact, if she honestly acknowledged her feelings, God's presence and its medium of love appeared to incite violence. She thought the purpose of the good news was to reduce violence and make life better. *Are we placed here on earth only as a test to see if we qualify for eternal life?* Mary wondered, and then, embarrassed by such a thought, she quickly clarified it. *No. God would not use us as pieces of a giant game.*

In the presence of Zenas's grave she remembered the gratitude with which he had addressed her on his way to his crucifixion. He certainly did not see himself as a victim of a playful God. In the face of the imminent end of his life, he spoke as one whose life was full to overflowing. He wasn't obsessed with his own situation, but, rather, concerned about her and the soldiers around him. He was living love, and that seemed to be all he needed. The violence around him and inflicted on him did not seem to matter. Did violence, then, not matter to love?

These were the kind of circular obstacle courses her mind would run through as she sat by his grave. Her heart was broken in grief, but her mind would play games with her emotions. Yet, still, she came to the grave, because many years ago, one empty grave had revealed to her the secret of life. That empty grave, and now, Zenas's life, was all the assurance she needed that God's love could rule our lives if we lived by a faith humble enough to be able to forget oneself and live for the other.

Deep in her heart, Mary knew that the tension between violence and love would always remain. Violence was really just an extreme form of human efforts to control behaviors. It erupted whenever peaceful means of behavioral control failed and desperation set in. It was supported by righteous beliefs that considered order to be more important than life. Violence was simply the ultimate weapon in the arsenal of control. Freedom, although not the opposite of control, was the opportunity to choose what governed behavior. Jesus always spoke of the presence of the kingdom of God as his choice of where to seek governance. He taught that this was the fundamental choice of human existence. He also taught that Torah was a way of articulating that choice.

Never in her life had Mary been surer of the truth that the good news Jesus taught was that we are free to choose the governance of God's kingdom, and its universal principle: love. His living this good news changed the world around him. His three brothers then continued to live this good news of love.

Mary's insatiable grief was rooted in the realization that such a demonstration of the good news consistently elicited a violent reaction from all in authority, both religious and political. So, the real dilemma was between not love and violence, but love and control. The presence of the kingdom of God was a threat to all those seeking to control the behavior of others. It offered a governance of life based on love that severely threatened control based on fear.

In the middle of these thoughts, Mary felt someone's presence. Looking around, she was startled to see Caspius standing a few paces away. "Oh, forgive me; I did not realize you were standing there," she said, walking over to him.

"I am sorry to interrupt your grieving," Caspius cautiously remarked. "I desperately want to speak to you. What Barnabas and you have been saying has severely shaken my faith. My life has been turned around by the blessing of the gospel brought to us by Paul and Barnabas."

Mary's confusion was obvious in the question she then asked him. "What have we said that could possibly shake your faith in God?"

"You do not know me," Caspius replied. "Let me tell you my story. I built up a successful business as a merchant, doing whatever was necessary to make a business succeed. I never shied away from deals that would benefit my business, ignoring legalities and concerns for fairness. Success and gain were always the bottom line. I took pride in the things I had and the influence I could wield. The needs of others were always looked upon as avenues for self-gain. In spite of all this success, there remained an empty feeling within me, the recognition that there must be more, the yearning for self-fulfillment that was never satisfied. Success never seemed to get me closer to the feeling of righteousness. Then, I heard Paul preach the gospel of Jesus Christ, explaining the difference between pursuing the desires of the flesh and seeking the calling of the spirit. Paul exposed to me the wages of sin, and he presented the gracious offer of salvation through faith in God's unfathomable act of love in Jesus Christ. He showed me that my sins, which were always buried under my ambition to succeed, would only lead to death; but he also emphasized that eternal life could be attained by realizing that my sins were washed away by God's sacrifice of his Son, Jesus, on the cross. Just by accepting this loving act of God, my yearning for righteousness fell away, and I no longer had that empty feeling. All I want to do now is praise God for this wonderful gift of love. However, you and Barnabas now appear to imply that none of this is true, that Jesus is not the Son of God and that the cross is not our means to salvation. My faith has been severely shaken! What am I to believe?"

Mary looked with compassion upon this man. He was obviously disturbed. She admired his strength in coming to her and so openly revealing his heart. She could relate very well to the battle raging between his mind and his heart. "You are not alone in wondering what to believe," she said. "The duty of the mind is to protect the self. Death and negation are the greatest threats to the self; so, the mind creates beliefs as ways of confronting these threats. Differentiating sin from righteousness is one method that the mind uses in an attempt to protect the self. If we put our faith in these beliefs, they will dominate us and overtake the role of the heart. The heart beats with the rhythm of creation; it is our sole connection with the Creator and all that is created."

Now it was Caspius who looked confused. "You're getting philosophical! Paul said the gospel is so simple that it is folly to the wise."

Mary paused. She was now keenly aware of what lay at the core of her grieving soul. The gospel, the "good news" Jesus asked them to continue to spread, meant different things to those who had walked with Jesus over the hills of Galilee and those who had been taught by Paul. For the first time, she saw the stark difference between Torah and the spirituality of Paul's gospel. Now she understood why Paul was so adamant that Torah was old news. They were two very different ways of understanding ourselves and our relationship with God. Torah was a humble realization of the incomprehensibility of God, whose nature could only be understood through love, by shifting the focus from self to the other. Paul's gospel gave the self access to God through the spirit. One focused outward; the other, inward. If the self had direct access to God, where was the check on arrogance? Nothing prevented the knower from having power over the ignorant. The mind used its weapons of beliefs, truth, and righteousness to arbitrate power, creating order through restrictions on freedom. Where was love in all of this? Love was then diminished to acts of righteousness instead of openness of oneself for the other. God was thereby reduced to confirmations of human reasoning.

Mary looked at Caspius. She really respected him because of his courage in coming to her. She saw the softness around his eyes and mouth as revealing anxiety, not anger. She desperately hoped Caspius was strong enough to recognize the love behind the harsh words she was about to utter. "Please hear these words with your heart and not your head. The good news Jesus asked us to spread and the gospel Paul preaches are not exactly the same. Paul's gospel is a gospel of salvation; Jesus's good news is that the kingdom of God is among us. The object of Paul's gospel is the individual; the object of Jesus's gospel is our interactions with one another.

"Self-interest is natural. It is necessary for survival. However, all forms of human debauchery abound when self-interest becomes selfishness. Love is the only antidote to this transition from self-interest to selfishness. Love shifts the focus from individuals to relationships. I fear that Paul's gospel creates a byway that can allow the self to ignore love and reconnect with all that separates us and thereby brings about violence. Each individual is unique, but if the self is the focus, it moves us away from integration and love.

"Jesus's message, which I like to call his messiah, is something like this: the kingdom of God is like a river that flows over all creation. It is the intention of the Creator. Its name is love; its doorway is freedom. To be in harmony with the flow is called righteousness. We all swim in this river, and the goal of life is to swim with righteousness. The good news of Jesus is that righteousness is available to everyone, just beyond our selfishness, our sin. Our human perspective is much too narrow to understand the full purpose of love. We can only contribute to its intention by directing our thoughts and actions to affirm love, not negate it.

"You say your faith is shaken, but it really is your beliefs that have been shaken. Your faith is what you depend on. In reality, beliefs are created by your mind. Hasn't your mind demonstrated often enough that it cannot be depended on? The beating of your heart is the only thing you can truly trust, and that beating is your sole connection with God. Faith is dependence on the presence of God, and that is realized through the beating of the heart. Faith is dependence humble enough to be able to get beyond the self and live open to the other, because God is love."

Mary moved close to Caspius and placed her fingertips on his arm. She looked up into his eyes and said, "Paul offered you a plan for redemption that satisfied the guilt of sin. This plan relies on a number of beliefs about who God is and what God has done. It is a plan to solve the divide between sin and righteousness; a divide that the mind has created. If it has helped you to be a better person, less sinful and more righteous, that is of great value. But contrasting sin and righteousness gets us no closer to God. It keeps us focused on ourselves. My son Jesus never talked much about a plan of redemption, but he constantly asked us to repent as a necessary first step to live in the presence of God.

"Plans for redemption play off of fear. Fear is the opposite of faith. Jesus demonstrated how to live by a humble faith in God's kingdom. God's love is the sole law of that kingdom. Jesus called us to follow him, to give all we have to the poor and follow him, to live love.

"The secret to humble faith is a radical shift in focus, from inward to outward. That is the purpose of Torah. It appears the Christians are seeking another way to understand faith. There may be other ways. The proof of each way is answered by a simple question: Does it lead to love? God is love, and love is not found deep within each of us, but, rather, in our connections with one another."

Aware that her words greatly affected Caspius, Mary said, "I have talked so much, your ears must be hurting. I hope my words have not created distance between us. Are you sorry you ever came to me?"

"No, certainly not. ... But—" Caspius stopped, biting his lower lip, his chin quivering. Yet his eyes revealed a deep searching. He looked at Mary, as if trying to untangle what she had said. Twice, he tried to start a statement, managing to only say, "But ... what—" and then stopping. Finally, he dropped his hands and shook his head. "I can't deny you have threatened my beliefs, beliefs we obviously do not share. I have let this separate us, yet you seem to imply it need not. What am I missing? Does what you call a humble faith see through barriers of stone?"

"No. It bypasses the defenses of the mind by simply seeing and hearing with the heart. The mind justifies our thoughts and deeds as expressions of the self, whereas the heart sees them for their impact on others. Humble faith has this freedom because it realizes God as love."

Caspius's expression changed as he realized the difference between his actions and the impact of his actions on others. He looked at Mary in wonderment. "You make it seem so simple. Is the good news nothing more than really making the neighbor as important as the self?"

"That's how I understand love. But, while it may sound simple, it surely isn't easy." Mary's face reflected the deep grief she felt here by Zenas's grave. "As if suppressing selfishness isn't difficult enough, it seems that all human efforts to socialize are opposed to love. All those in authority, both political and religious, have gone out of their way to eliminate the efforts of everyone I know who has chosen to live love. Zenas is just the most recent. They tried to take Simon too."

"Your life has certainly been tragic," Caspius admitted. "I'm amazed at how you stay so strong in the face of such adversity."

"Once you have experienced the power of God's presence, everything else recedes. Love is the essence of living, the gateway to eternity."

Caspius grabbed both of Mary's hands and said, "I started out mistrusting you, maybe even hating you and your presence. Please forgive my ignorance. I can't tell you how happy I am that I came to you. You have blessed me beyond expression. To realize the presence of God without guilt or fear is truly transforming. I could stand here the rest of the day praising God, but now I see that love does not happen until I touch someone else, not for my own gain but for that person's. Thank you, Mary, from the bottom of my heart." He kissed her hands and left.

Mary could not contain her emotions. At times like this, she could feel Jesus as close as he had ever been.

Here, at Zenas's grave, Mary couldn't get over the way in which Caspius had ended their conversation. It was not fear or anxiety that motivated him as he left her, but eager anticipation to live for another. She thought how different this was from what motivated most people. Fear was the great motivator of humanity. The Romans had the whole world cowering in their homes from fear of a life of slavery. The Jewish political leaders ignored Torah in order to form alliances, and religious leaders of all kinds enforced laws that ignored love because they feared loss of influence and power. Paul had driven a wedge through the followers of Jesus, based on fear of eternal damnation. Secularists used fear of the destruction of the world in order to control human behavior. Fear, supported by all kinds of beliefs and reasoning, was used to control people and keep them focused on themselves.

Only love, where two or three gathered together in unselfish concern for the other, could break open these bonds of fear. A feeling of realization and remorse came over her as these thoughts visited her.

She knelt by the grave and cried. Her voice barely more than a whisper, she said, "Oh, Zenas! We too easily allow violence to distort reality. Brutality so easily overshadows compassion. Only now do I realize that love killed you, not abusive power or hatred. That young soldier was so moved by your words from the cross that he saved you from the suffering you were about to endure. Your words of compassion transformed that man's life. He gave up himself to stay your suffering. Even in your death, you have spread the good news."

She got up, walked down the hill to the garden in back of Joseph and Hanna's house, picked a handful of flowers, and returned to the grave. She placed them on Zenas's grave and walked to a nearby olive tree. In the shade of the tree, the cool breeze from the sea reminded her of the hills overlooking the Sea of Galilee. Jesus had often taught there. His lessons were not about revolution and overthrow of the Romans. They were not about the end of the world and God's radical judgment. They were not about obtaining eternal life. They were about how we are to live and treat each other. His focus was always on what we are doing, not on what God is doing. If she had to reduce Jesus's message to one simple statement, it would be: The kingdom of God is upon us. Sin is selfishness. Repent from sin, and live in love.

She thought of Zenas. Jesus must love Zenas, just as she did. Jesus would have been proud to have him as a student. She thought of this fellowship in Caesarea that she had known for such a short time, and of the synagogue back in Jerusalem. A broad smile came across her face as she thought of these groups that were such an important part of her life. She recognized the importance of their interactions with the wider community. Love, the lifeblood of the kingdom of God, was the antidote to human depravity. Torah, and communities committed to living the reality of God's kingdom, are the seedbeds of love. Jesus lived that in every action and teaching. Zenas, by choosing to live love, again exposed its eternal truth.

Mary moved over to the grave and knelt. Placing her forehead onto the ground, she remembered a prayer she had whispered many years ago, when she first realized she was with child:

"Tell out, my soul, the greatness of the Lord,
rejoice, rejoice, my spirit, in God my savior;
so tenderly has he looked upon his servant;
humble as she is.
For from this day forth,
all generations will count me blessed,
so wonderfully has he dealt with me,
The Lord, the Mighty One.

His name is Holy;
his mercy sure from generation to generation
toward those who fear him;
the deeds his own right arm has done
disclose his might:
the arrogant of heart and mind he has put to rout,
he has brought down monarchs from their thrones;
but the humble have been lifted up high.
The hungry he has satisfied with good things,
the rich sent empty away.

He has ranged himself at the side of Israel his servant;
firm in his promise to our forefathers,
he has not forgotten to show mercy to Abraham
and his children's children, for ever."

Tears ran down her cheeks, but her heart was warmed by these words from so long ago. Never once had she doubted the greatness of the first fruit of her womb. Jesus was always exceptional as a

319

baby, a child, and a man. Life flowed from him like water from a spring. It was contagious! His brothers couldn't help but follow him. There was something about him and his message that would forever break open human arrogance and lay bare all efforts to usurp the word of God.

Once again, she thanked God for the blessings bestowed upon her. She was so grateful that Simon was still there to bring this humble faith into the arrogant deliberations of religious leaders. She knew other Zenases would come, time and again, to recognize the ruthless nature of control and choose the governance of God's kingdom. Her belief that God was love and creation was called to reveal that love had been reaffirmed by knowing Zenas. He had reassured her that there would always be those who chose to follow Jesus, those who were willing to forget themselves and live love. Yes, Jesus would come back again and again to those who followed him. Yes, he was the promise of eternal life. Mary thought of Salome and Barnabas. Yes, there would always be those who chose to follow Jesus.

Mary rose and began walking back to Salome and Barnabas. It was time for them to marry and enjoy the ultimate of God's love: the blessing of giving life.

As Mary returned to the house, Salome rushed outside to meet her. "Mama, there's a nervous young man inside who says he is running from the Romans and wants to see you."

Instinctively, Mary knew it was the soldier who speared Zenas on the cross.

When she entered the room, the young man rose and asked, "Are you the woman Zenas stopped to address on the way to his crucifixion? I am the soldier who killed Zenas. I had to meet you. I know I will not be able to evade the authorities for long, but I had to try to find what Zenas found."

"Bless you, my son," Mary said, "You have already found it."

ACKNOWLEDGMENTS

Acknowledging all who contributed to this endeavor is a daunting task as the lengthy list would probably omit more than it included. However, I must recognize those closest to me and the ones who participated directly. In the laboratory of love, God is the chemist, we only particles in the test tube. Those closest to us endure our efforts to live love. My wife Kathryn, son David, daughter Shari, parents, sisters and brothers, granddaughters, and in-laws have all shared my crucible of ambition, realized and unrealized expectations, false positives, and the occasional miracle. They have all been participants in my brush with the love of God. Most of what I know about life and love grows out of their gifts and blessings. Many of the cuts and bruises on their lives are rooted in my slow awareness that one's selfishness is the hardest to recognize and suppress. I struggle for adequate words to express my gratitude for their enduring care and support. They fill my scrapbook of God's love. I must add that it would have been impossible for me to write a book about Mary the mother of Jesus without the example of feminine, compassion, strength and beauty exhibited by my wife Kathryn, and the numerous expressions of love from the other women at the center of my life.

A number of years ago I was contracted to sing tenor at St. Luke's Methodist Church in Bryn Mawr, PA. Hearing about my seminary background, they asked if I would lead an adult Bible study after service on Sunday mornings. Out of the searching, open and honest questions and testimonies of Marilyn Arnott, Rick Hellberg, Anne Kybert, Elaine McDermott, Betsy Monahan, Sally Newport, Nancy Pantano, Lisa Santomen, Roy Schollenberger, Pastor David Tatgenhorst, Kathy Taylor, and Robert Woolston Mary's Lament was born. In those frank discussions we realized that our searching faith brought us together, while our beliefs presented barriers among us. We discovered that one aspect of living in the presence of the kingdom of God is to allow our faith to break down the walls created by our beliefs.

As the novel developed I received encouragement from a couple of friends, Barbra Scianna and Tim Mathews, who confirmed my hunch that many religious folks struggled with the issues we discussed at St. Luke's.

Early encouragement and valuable critique came from professors Karlfried Froehlich and Paul Rorem from Princeton Theological Seminary, Jerremy Adelman and James McPherson from Princeton University, pastors David Tatgenhorst, Richard Lichty, John Potter, the late Brewster Hastings, and Rabbi Gadi.

Invaluable feedback came from two discussion groups, one the participants of the Bible study class at St' Luke's. The other included Chris Bencsik, MaryLee Chittick, David Chittick, Andrew Johnson, Sam Lapp, Carolyn Weidman and Drenning Weidman.

Jacob Alderfer could not attend this meeting, but offered suggestions in person.

Special thanks to my sister, Alyce Peifer for the sketch on the cover of this book. She drew inspiration from a program commemorating our maternal grandmother, which also contained the poem *Mother in Israel*, by a life-long friend.

Rachel Adleman offered suggestions for songs and readings used in the story.

Finally, I wish to express my deep appreciation to Westbow Press for their excellent editorial work and efficient guidance through the publishing process.

ABOUT THE AUTHOR

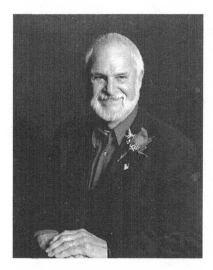

Joseph C. Nyce grew up in a Christian home in Eastern Pennsylvania, and after earning his bachelor's degree in civil engineering from Lafayette College, he settled down in the family business manufacturing concrete and blocks. Yet Joseph felt God's call, uprooted his wife and two young children, and enrolled at the Princeton Theology Seminary, where he would go on to earn his master of divinity and PhD degrees. While there he established a general contracting business in the Princeton area. He also sang and conducted adult Bible studies for St. Luke's Methodist Church in Bryn Mawr, Pennsylvania, where touching and soul-searching discussions inspired him to write *Mary's Lament*.